Brothers' Fury

www.transworldbooks.co.uk

Also by Giles Kristian

Raven: Blood Eye
Sons of Thunder
Odin's Wolves

The Bleeding Land

For more information on Giles Kristian and his books,
see his website at www.gileskristian.com

BROTHERS' FURY

Giles Kristian

BANTAM PRESS

LONDON · TORONTO · SYDNEY · AUCKLAND · JOHANNESBURG

TRANSWORLD PUBLISHERS
61–63 Uxbridge Road, London W5 5SA
A Random House Group Company
www.transworldbooks.co.uk

First published in Great Britain
in 2013 by Bantam Press
an imprint of Transworld Publishers

A CIP catalogue record for this book
is available from the British Library.

ISBNs 9780593066164 (cased)
9780593066171 (tpb)

Addresses for Random House Group Ltd companies outside the UK
can be found at: www.randomhouse.co.uk
The Random House Group Ltd Reg. No. 954009

The Random House Group Limited supports the Forest Stewardship Council (FSC®),
the leading international forest-certification organisation. Our books carrying
the FSC label are printed on FSC®-certified paper. The FSC is the only
forest-certification scheme supported by the leading environmental organisations,
including Greenpeace. Our paper procurement policy can be found at
www.randomhouse.co.uk/environment

Typeset in 11½/14½pt Sabon by
Kestrel Data, Exeter, Devon.
Printed and bound by
CPI Group (UK) Ltd, Croydon, CR0 4YY

2 4 6 8 10 9 7 5 3 1

Brothers' Fury is for Lynne and Andrew,
whose support for the cause means so much.

'Thou wouldest think it strange if I should tell thee there was a time in England when brothers killed brothers, cousins cousins, and friends their friends. Nay, when they conceived it was no offence to commit murder.'

A Royalist's Notebook
Sir John Oglander

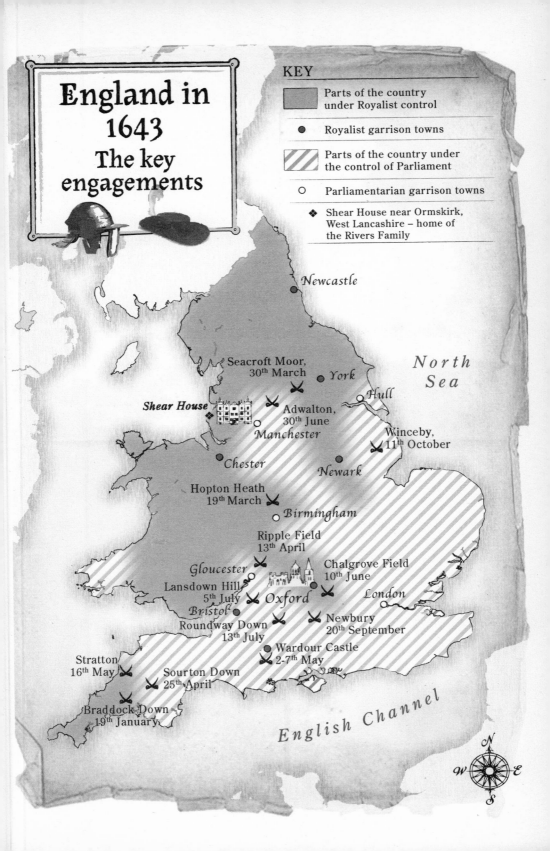

England in 1643
The key engagements

Newcastle

North Sea

Seacroft Moor, 30th March

York

Hull

Shear House

Adwalton, 30th June

Manchester

Winceby, 11th October

Chester

Newark

Hopton Heath 19th March

Birmingham

Ripple Field 13th April

Gloucester

Chalgrove Field 10th June

Lansdown Hill 5th July

Oxford

London

Bristol

Newbury 20th September

Roundway Down 13th July

Wardour Castle 2-7th May

Stratton 16th May

Sourton Down 25th April

Braddock Down 19th January

English Channel

N W E S

CHAPTER ONE

_____

14 January 1643, Lancashire

GOD ALMIGHTY, IT WAS COLD. A LITTLE AFTER MIDDAY, YET THE pallid sun clung to the horizon, throwing the riders' shadows far ahead of them in spindly misshapen caricatures that seemed to gush across the ground like black water. The night's frost still held the land in its frigid grip, whitening tussocks and heather, sheathing leafless branches and making a hoary-haired old man of the peat moor. It was a white, silent, frozen world, and it was empty.

But for the passing of a small troop of horse.

Mun – Sir Edmund Rivers when he was not out on patrol with his men – twisted in the saddle, blinking watery eyes against the biting air. Cocooned in cloaks and hunched into themselves as though protecting some feeble flame that yet flickered within their chests, the men of the column resembled corpses swathed for burial and lashed to saddles. But for a slight sway as their mounts trudged on, they barely seemed to move, all flesh trussed up leaving only the eyes visible, and even these were slitted defensively, so that Mun could not read their thoughts.

Not that Mun needed to see their eyes to know their minds.

He supposed they resented him for leading them across the empty, bitter-cold moorland when all sensible folk were inside by their hearths. Even the great armies of Parliament and King had, for the most part, settled in for the winter, Essex's force at Windsor and Charles's at Oxford, that city having become for all intents and purposes the seat of his court and the Royalist capital. And yet not all had sheathed their blades and let their match burn out, and Lancashire remained a battleground upon which Parliament was seeming to press the advantage.

There were still powerful men waging the King's war here in the north-west, Mun knew. Men such as Richard Lord Molyneux, the wealthy Thomas Tyldesley, and the most powerful of all, James Stanley the Earl of Derby. But the earl had been deprived of his best regiments for service with the King elsewhere and had been forced to abandon his siege of Parliament-held Manchester the previous October. Now his forces had consolidated around Preston and Wigan and had made their headquarters in Warrington, just twenty miles south of Shear House.

Meanwhile the rebels were growing bold. They were recruiting.

And Mun was hunting.

'Winter either bites with its teeth or lashes with its tail, my da used to say,' O'Brien, riding beside him, muffled into the cloak covering the lower part of his face, 'but this whore-hearted bitch has had us with her claws too as she's walked across our backs.' The big Irishman pulled the cloak down and dragged a sleeve beneath his nose, breath pluming in the cutting air. 'No bugger's daft enough to be out in this.'

Mun would have wagered that every trooper in the thirty-six-strong column was thinking the same, but only O'Brien had the nerve to say it.

'*We're* out in it,' he said, watching rooks and jackdaws rise and dip across the heath, foraging amongst the frosted clumps of bilberry and heather, feeding if they could, making the most of the scant daylight hours.

'Aye and what does that make us?' O'Brien muttered to himself.

'Would you rather be a lapdog or a wolf?' Mun asked, the cold air hurting his teeth.

'On a day like this I'd be a bloody cat,' O'Brien said, 'all curled up on some pretty wench's lap by the fire.'

Mun smiled grimly at that image, for O'Brien was a giant of a man, red-haired, red-bearded and in battle as savage as this long winter's claws. Twice as dangerous too. But the Irishman was right about the cold and Mun had not known a harsher winter. He recalled something his own father had once said, that in winter every mile is two, and watching the scavenging birds he decided not to range too many miles more before turning for home. Perhaps an hour had passed since they had skirted the town of Longridge above the Ribble river, eight miles north-east of Preston, and now they were at the fringes of the Forest of Bowland and the fells were no place to be after dark, especially in weather like this. Mun knew the black moor could swallow their whole column, freezing man and beast as solid as the rocky outcrops and gritstone boulders that tore through the wild heath, and no one might ever find them.

We'll turn back at Deerleap crag, he thought, if we have caught no sight of the enemy by then. But the damned traitors were out there somewhere and he hungered to find them, would have that rather than all the warmth and comfort Shear House – his home and the Rivers family seat, Royalist bastion and now headquarters for his own operations – could offer.

'Just a little further,' he called over his shoulder, receiving no answer but for a loud snort from one of the horses that was eloquent testimony as to what they felt about being out on such a day.

'As much as I enjoy giving the rebel turds a good hiding, this should be down to Derby, not us,' O'Brien said, hawking and spitting a thick gobbet into the snow. 'We can't be more than nine, ten miles from Preston. It's those buggers should be out here freezing their balls off instead of sitting around scratching their arses.'

'True enough,' Mun said, 'but the earl and the other commanders are more concerned about the lightness of their purses and the gaps in their ranks than they are about waging proper war. And while they fret, the rebels recruit. They reinforce. Get stronger. Our lads were given a good kicking on Hinfield Moor, booted out of Leigh, and then earned a bloody nose for their troubles when Sir Gilbert Houghton tried to retake Blackburn.'

'Aye, well that was a wet fart of a thing,' O'Brien said. 'I heard Sir Gilbert gave up the siege so that his men could eat their Christmas pies at home by their own hearths.'

Mun could not tell from his tone whether the Irishman thought that was deplorable or admirable. He suspected the latter. 'Whatever the reason, they're not fighting,' he said. 'And if they're not fighting they're not winning. But I promise you this, Clancy, the rebels are not safe. Not even in this God-forsaken weather. Not from us. Not from me.' Gloved fingers instinctively caressed the curved butt of the twenty-six-inch-long firelock pistol holstered on the right of his saddle's cantle. The weapon's twin nestled snug in its leather sheath on the saddle's other side against his left thigh. 'We're going to find them,' Mun said, watery eyes ranging across the frosted land, 'and we're going to kill them.'

'Aye, I suppose that would be agreeable. There's nothing like a bit of a fight to stir some heat into the blood,' O'Brien said. 'And the boys will play the part, won't you, lads?' he called over his shoulder, his helmeted head wreathed in his own fogging breath. A few mumbled ayes rose from the column but most of the swaddled troopers kept their hot breath inside their chests, shoulders hunched, heads pulled in. The column comprised the best riders and most capable men from Shear House's garrison and, though most were relatively inexperienced, they were fit, healthy and strong.

'Men learn quickly in war, my lady,' Major Radcliffe had assured Mun's mother when she had voiced concern at Mun leading them out into winter's savage maw to track and kill rebels. 'Sir Edmund is proof of that.'

'We have all been changed by this war, Major,' Lady Mary had said, and Mun had avoided her eyes then, not wanting to see the sorrow in them.

'They may be miserable as bloody Puritans in a brothel, but they'll sing loud enough when the shooting starts,' O'Brien assured Mun now, snuffling back down into his cloak.

'Like avenging angels,' Mun muttered, remembering the day he and Captain Smith – now Sir John Smith – had brazenly ridden back onto the killing field at Edgehill and wrested the King's colours from a well-armed knot of Roundhead soldiers. A Catholic and not shy to admit it, Smith had announced to a group of dragoons that he and Mun were two of St Michael the Archangel's soldiers come with swords of fire to smite God's enemies.

And smite Mun would, for the rebels had destroyed his family. His father was dead, slain at Edgehill, as was Mun's good friend, his sister Bess's betrothed Emmanuel. Then the traitors had besieged Shear House and killed many of its defenders before Mun could break the siege, the scars carved into the house by their demi-cannon serving as a constant reminder of that desperate episode. Added to all this the feckless enemy had recruited his brother Tom, meaning that Tom and he were now foes, and this had ripped the heart out of their once proud family. It was a wound that would not, could not heal. And for all this the rebels would pay in blood. Which was why Mun had not returned to his regiment despite having given his word to Prince Rupert that he would join him as soon as he and the mercenary Osmyn Hooker had raised the siege of Shear House.

Be sure to return to us with news of the rebels' movements in the north-west. Had those not been the Prince's words? So rather than sit idle in Oxford with the King's army, watching the enemy grow stronger and letting the edge of his sword dull, Mun would hunt. He would kill. Surely a child of war like the Prince would understand his reasons for remaining in Lancashire, would rather Mun remained a thorn in his enemy's side than became a swaggering wineskin like most of the gentlemen Cavaliers in Oxford.

'You don't have much faith in the peace negotiations I take it,' O'Brien said, one bushy red eyebrow hoisted. Tack and armour jangled and clinked and horses snorted; those sounds and the occasional raucous *koww* of a crow the only interruptions to the silence of the frozen fells.

'There's more chance of you taking holy orders and ending up the Bishop of bloody Bath than there is of His Majesty going along with Parliament's demands,' Mun replied.

O'Brien cocked his head thoughtfully, as though the scenario Mun had suggested was not entirely inconceivable. 'The concessions they demand of him are unrealistic,' Mun went on. 'Just think it through.' He doubted the Irishman would. 'The King will not relinquish his sovereign control of the militia. Honour prevents him handing over those whom Parliament would scourge. His religion will not let him put an end to bishops, and only a fool would disband a growing army that shows signs of being useful.'

Mun clapped his hands together and pumped his fists, trying to get some warmth into them. 'No, the negotiations will come to nothing, mark my words, and if I know the Prince he'll be stalking around Oxford like a caged animal.'

Mun thought about the Prince and his seemingly boundless energy for war. 'Actually, I'd wager he is ignoring the sham of peace entirely. He'll be up to the same as us,' he said, patting the pistol's butt, 'trying to further our political advantages by means of steel and shot, for he knows better than anyone that our failure to take London has cost us dear.'

O'Brien sniffed loudly. 'Well let's hope the royal fellow doesn't decide to use his steel and shot on us for not rejoining the regiment.'

'You're free to leave. Bugger off back to Ireland if you want. I won't make you stay,' Mun said, looking straight ahead, feeling a stab of irritation. Or rather disappointment to think the Irishman might want to leave. Yet he knew it was unfair to expect O'Brien to risk punishment for Mun's own dereliction.

'I'll freeze my arse off a while longer if it's all the same to you.' O'Brien looked off across the frost-hardened heath. 'You need me to look after you. Besides, little Francis would miss me something terrible if I buggered off now.'

Mun felt the cold air bite into the cracks in his lips as he smiled, for who would believe that, aside from their friendship, a baby was truthfully the main reason why O'Brien had not turned his mare south and ridden to Oxford. Mun knew the big man had grown fond of little Francis, Bess and Emmanuel's baby who had been born to the demi-cannon's roar during the siege of Shear House. The dear fatherless boy's first taste of life had been bitter with the acrid smoke of muskets, his little ears full of the screams of the stricken and dying, but he had brought a tenderness out of O'Brien that Mun guessed few had ever witnessed. Though how an infant did not wail with terror at the sight of the red-haired giant was a constant surprise to Mun.

'It's all the same to me but Prudence will be happy to hear of it,' Mun said, watching from the corner of his eye for O'Brien's reaction. Which was a great shiver and beard-splitting grimace. The cook did not boast looks that Anthony van Dyck would have got his brushes wet for, but she clearly thought the Irishman did and her ears and cheeks would flush red whenever she saw him.

'The way she leers at me . . .' O'Brien growled, 'as though she'd put me in one of her pies and wolf me down with a wash of ale.'

Mun laughed, his breath blending with Hector's, fogging around his face. Then the stallion neighed, the bit in his mouth jangling against his teeth, and Mun knew Hector well enough to follow the beast's gaze into what little breeze prevailed against them from the east.

And that was when he saw it. A faint stain on a ridge of ground thirty paces off his right shoulder, where the frost had been knocked off the heather.

'Come on, boy,' he said, clicking his tongue and pressing his right knee against Hector's warm flank, 'let's take a look, shall we?'

O'Brien flicked his reins and made to follow. 'Good idea. It won't be so damned cold if we get off the high ground,' he called, thinking that Mun would lead them over the swell and down into one of the many deep river valleys that cut through the moorland. But Mun did not answer, because he did not know yet what he was looking at.

'Could be deer,' O'Brien said, drawing alongside, looking down at the disturbed clump of heather. 'Or a sheep that has wandered off.' Behind them the rest of the column had halted in a cloud of their own fog, some of the men slapping their upper arms for warmth, others sitting their mounts as though they had already frozen to death. 'Mary mother of God!' he said then, seeing what held Mun's eye: a column of infantry down in the valley, trudging towards a copse of skeletal oak, ash and alder. There were several horsemen too, one of whom had evidently scouted up the valley's steep side and left his tracks in the frost: tracks which now led all the way back to the column. 'Do you think he saw us?'

'I'd wager a half crown on it,' Mun said, twisting and gesturing for his troopers to join them. 'That's why they're heading for the trees.'

'So we know the buggers aren't ours then,' O'Brien said, 'else they wouldn't be scarpering like mice back to their little hole.'

'You're assuming that scout knew who *we* were,' Mun said,

sweeping out an arm towards the men and horses that were bunching around them. 'We're not the Prince's Horse now.'

O'Brien frowned, casting an eye over the Shear House men who had become Sir Edmund Rivers's cavalry troop. 'Aye, you'd think us a horde of starving cut-throats,' he said. None of the men disagreed, their liquid eyes fixed on the column of foot below.

'Not cut-throats. Not with these horses,' Mun said, 'yet the sight of us was enough to curdle that scout's blood and put his whole company to flight. All, what, forty of them?'

O'Brien grinned wickedly. 'Horses put the fear of God into infantry.'

'That's part of it,' Mun said, 'but there's another reason they're wetting their breeches.'

The Irishman's gloved fingers raked the thick red bristles on his cheek until the answer struck him. 'They're bloody recruits!' he said. 'Not even proper soldiers, but for those officers sitting nice warm beasts, boots out of the frost.'

Mun nodded. 'Those officers have come north. From Blackburn.' He gestured at the handful of riders who were corralling those on foot towards the trees, which were still four or five hundred yards away by Mun's reckoning. 'They've come looking for wool traders and farm boys to turn into soldiers, those who were not in the villages when the sergeants came banging the drum.'

'To give the traitorous fellows their due it looks as if they've found some,' O'Brien admitted.

That was true enough, Mun thought. The rebels knew Derby was holed up forty miles south in Warrington and they'd guessed correctly that the Preston garrison would be keeping their bones warm. So here they were, out in the freezing cold. Recruiting. Mun felt the blood begin to tremble in his limbs. It was the battle thrill coming on him.

'The brazen bastards,' Trooper Harley said, winding his wheellock. Many of the others were doing likewise, slipping spanners over the square section of their weapons' wheel shafts and filling the still morning with a salvo of clicks before priming the pans with powder and pulling the pan covers shut.

'We're going to tear them to shreds,' Mun said, checking that his own weapons – the two firelocks and his carbine – were secure. His heavy sword was snug in its scabbard on his saddle behind his left hip. He still wore the old back-and-breast he had bought from a trooper in Nehemiah Boone's company whose place he had taken after breaking the man's leg, but beneath it he now wore a fine buff-coat stripped from the dead captain who had led the assault on Shear House. Downing had been the man's name and his leather coat – so fine that it could not have cost the captain less than eleven pounds – fitted Mun perfectly, providing not only protection but much-needed warmth. As for Nehemiah Boone, just the thought of him was enough to sour Mun's belly. They might both fight for the King but there was as much bad blood between Mun and the captain – the first of it spilled by Boone himself the day they had met – as there would soon be amongst the frosted tussocks in the valley below.

'If we let those men live they and others like them will be at the gates of Shear House before spring,' he announced to the troop, taking off his gloves. 'They will threaten our families. They will try to kill us.'

'Whoresons can try,' a hard-looking man with a weathered face said. His name was John Cole and from what Major Radcliffe had told Mun and from what Mun had since seen for himself, Cole was a useful man to have with you in a fight.

'They will spread their sedition and we shall never be rid of this war,' Mun went on, tying his helmet's leather thong beneath his chin then shoving cold hands back into the gloves. 'So we kill them before they get to those trees.'

'Do we offer quarter?' a wide-eyed lad named Godfrey asked, pushing his wheellock back into its saddle holster with a trembling hand.

'You can offer by all means, lad, but kill them first,' O'Brien said, pushing his own helmet down snug over his thick red tresses.

'Kill them,' Mun said, holding Godfrey's eye with enough steel in the gaze to make the young trooper more afraid of him than of the enemy below. And with that he gave Hector a touch of heel and urged him over the frost-stiffened tussocks of the ridge, his eyes riveted on the men below, whose formation had disintegrated now in their panic to get to cover.

Mun knew it was unwise to ride at any sort of speed down such a slope, but he also knew that if they descended at a walk the rebels would gain the trees and he would lose the advantage. So they went at the trot, hooves thudding against the iron-hard ground, armour and tack clinking and jangling. Mun felt the icy wind bite into his face, blurring his vision and dragging tears from the corners of his eyes. The bitterly cold air scorched his throat and lungs but he relished it, his whole body thrumming now with the excitement that always flooded his veins before mortal danger. And now he could hear the men in the gully below shouting, could discern fragments of commands mostly lost amongst the wind gushing past his face and eking into the gaps between helmet-steel and ears.

'For England and King Charles!' he roared, and that's when the first muskets cracked in the valley, etching a grimace between Mun's lips, for this all but confirmed that the troops below were Parliament men and in truth Mun had not been utterly certain before. 'England and King Charles!' he yelled again, and this time several others repeated the war-cry as they followed Mun's lead and gave the spur, breaking into a gallop, a fear of flying lead hunching shoulders and pulling in heads. O'Brien, no great admirer of the King but a sworn devotee of killing men who pointed muskets at him, gave his own cry of 'Ireland', as a stuttering volley of musketry shredded the crisp afternoon. Mun felt a ball whir past his left cheek, and the frantic rhythm his troopers' horses beat against the ground.

They galloped down onto the valley floor, men folding forward and grunting with the impact of coming onto flatter ground, and now Mun could make out the faces of his enemies one hundred feet away, their eyes wide with terror as their freezing hands fumbled at powder flasks, scouring sticks and glowing match-cords. He saw one man drop his musket and another turn and run, but Mun's prey was a buff-coated officer sitting a chestnut mare, who was screaming at his recruits to form a line and for the love of God load and give fire.

Forty feet away.

Taking the reins in his left hand Mun reached behind him with his right and hauled his carbine round on its belt, though he did not fire because the weapon was jolting wildly.

Twenty feet.

The rebel officer must have fired his pistol already for now he drew his sword, but Mun gripped with his knees and brought his left hand up to steady the carbine's barrel and the rebel threw his other arm across his face in vain as Mun squeezed the trigger. The carbine roared and its ball punched a hole through buff leather, skin and breastbone, and through the rebel's heart, spraying gore-flecked bone and slivers of glistening meat out of the ruin of his back, and then Mun was flown past him.

A callow-faced young rebel raised his matchlock and Mun cursed, thinking himself a dead man. But in his fear or inexperience the musketeer had misjudged the length of match clamped in the serpent's jaws and the tip of the burning match missed the priming-pan, or else he had forgotten to open the pan, and Mun spurred Hector forward so that the stallion's chest slammed into the man, catapulting him backwards with the sound of bones snapping. 'King Charles!' Mun clamoured, drawing a pistol and shooting a rebel between the eyes, who collapsed, a dark stain blooming on the crotch of his breeches, his brains spread across the frosted tussocks like spilled porridge.

Mun twisted and saw O'Brien bury his poll-axe in another

mounted officer's shoulder, heard the rebel scream like a vixen before the Irishman leant across and shoved his pistol into the man's belly and gave fire, gobbets of flesh and spine erupting from a void in the officer's back.

Some rebels were still running for the trees and so Mun hauled on the reins and kicked back with the spurs that had once been fastened to the boots of the King of England himself, urging the stallion on, breaking away from the chaos to cut down the fugitives.

'Wait for me, you greedy bastard! Sir!' O'Brien yelled and pulled his own mount round to gallop after Mun. Who was already pulling his heavy sword out of its scabbard and into the raw, death-filled day.

CHAPTER TWO

MUN HAD CUT DOWN TWO MORE REBELS AS THEY FLED FOR THE trees, his heavy sword hacking into the first man's shoulder, all but severing the arm, then lopping off a goodly chunk of the second rebel's skull as Hector bore him past at the gallop. Surprisingly it was the first rebel who had died first, almost instantly, bleeding in rhythmic gouts that melted the frost. The second man, with half his skull gone to expose the glistening brains, had lived long enough to mumble that he had wanted no part in the argument between King and Parliament and wished even then, his brains leaking, to be left alone that he might go home to his ill mother.

'We've all got a part in this but you should have joined the right bloody side, lad,' O'Brien had said not unkindly, though he was cleaning his poll-axe on the dying man's tunic at the time. The young rebel had seemed about to answer this when he was gripped by a sudden convulsing and frothing about the mouth, soon after which he died with eyes full of tears.

'He lasted longer than I would have wagered, what with his skull opened up like a boiled egg,' O'Brien had said, but Mun had not replied because despite his previous order to his men to give no quarter, he was now trying to rein them in and stop the killing.

'Hold, Shear House men!' he yelled at twelve of his mounted men who were corralling nine stunned and bloodied survivors together like a noose around a neck. 'Spare them if they have yielded.'

But his men, who were thirty paces off, were blood-drunk and wanted more.

'You heard Sir Edmund!' a man named Goffe bellowed, urging his mount in amongst the press of mostly younger men. 'Pull that trigger, Bull, I'll knock yer bloody ears off and you'll be picking the frost out of 'em.'

Bull was glaring at a rebel who was on his knees, his peaked montero-cap gripped before his terrified face, but Goffe's threat pierced Bull's rage and, cursing, he lowered his wheellock, keeping his finger on the trigger. Mun walked Hector over to them, grateful to have Goffe with him. A tenant farmer, Goffe had proved a solid soldier, the kind of man who would be made a corporal in the King's real army. The other men respected him as one of their own and listened to him, which was just as well for the surviving rebels. At least for now.

'Take anything worth having,' Mun said, dismounting and leading Hector by his bridle, 'and share out the powder and shot. Lash the muskets together in fours and let the lighter men tie them across their saddles.'

They knew well enough what to do, had done it before, and dismounted to set about their task. Other Shear House men were spread across the site of the carnage, looting the dead, cold hands fumbling at the boxes on slain rebels' bandoliers, emptying the precious black powder into their own flasks. Two of the younger troopers were doubled over and puking, the vomit pattering onto the frosty grass and steaming, and Mun knew it was the shock of seeing men butchered. He felt the thrum in his own limbs intensify now that the fight was over: his body's way of confirming that it still lived, that the heart still thumped in his breast whilst other men's hearts had beaten their last and were growing cold.

It had been a wild but utter victory. They had swept down into the valley in a wave of death and if they had been wolves and the rebels sheep the result would not have been any different, for they had killed thirty and lost not one. Mun dared to wonder if this proved that God was on his side; on the King's side too, yet he pushed such thoughts back into the dark corners of his mind. Because God was merciful and would wish Mun to be merciful now.

But Mun had not stopped the killing out of mercy.

'You command here?' a rebel barked, eyeballing Mun even as John Cole snatched his knapsack off him and began to rifle through the contents.

'I do,' Mun replied, walking over, letting go of Hector's bridle so that he could slide his sword through a scrap of cloth torn from a rebel's shirt.

'You devil! You gave us no opportunity to surrender,' the man protested as Mun tossed the bloody rag aside. He was in his thirties, clean-shaven, clear-eyed and with a strong jaw that Mun guessed had been honed to sharp edges by the yelling of commands. He did not seem afraid, which might have been surprising given that his newly raised troop lay butchered before it had ever served Parliament's cause. Yet good commanders knew that fear spread like fire. Good officers learned to smother it, whether in the presence of their own men or the enemy.

'Would you have allowed us to surrender?' Mun asked, holding the man's eye, and to the rebel's credit he held his tongue rather than lie. 'No you would not,' Mun confirmed, 'and if we had given you warning and thus chance to properly defend yourselves, your men would still be dead now' – he pointed his sword at a rebel whose lifeless face was a blood-sheeted grimace – 'but many of mine would be corpses too.' Mun shrugged, pushing his blade back into its scabbard. 'This is your reward for treason,' he said. 'Death is your payment for taking up arms against your king.'

'You mean to murder us in cold blood?' The man was wide-eyed, the bridle slipping off his fear at last.

Mun shook his head. 'Not me,' he said, glancing up at the wan sky, his breath rising in a cloud. He turned to the rest of his troop who were still plundering the dead. 'Shear House men, mount up! We have done our work here.'

'You're going to leave us out here like this?' the rebel leader asked, ignoring Cole's growled threat to take off his buff-coat or else die with it on. Goffe, Harley and even young Godfrey were working fast, relieving the stunned rebels of food, spare clothing, tinder boxes, flints and steel, bottles, blankets and money; stripping them as thoroughly as a dog paring flesh from a bone. 'We'll freeze to death,' the man declared as his men looked to each other fearfully. 'The nearest village is ten miles east. If we don't find it before dark we'll die.'

'There's a village called Longridge five miles back that way,' Mun said, thumbing south, seeing hope spark in the rebel's eyes. 'But if I see you there I will kill you. Your only hope lies east. Whalley village.'

'Who are you, you devil?' the rebel officer asked as he was shoved this way and that by Cole who was pulling his plain buff-coat off him, leaving him clothed merely in shirt and doublet so that much of his white skin was now at the mercy of the biting cold.

'He's the man that gave you a good hiding,' O'Brien said at Mun's shoulder, pouring powder down the muzzle of his wheellock. Some of the rebels grimaced, disgusted though perhaps not surprised to discover that an Irishman had played some part in their destruction.

'My name is Sir Edmund Rivers,' Mun said, taking hold of his saddle's cantle and hauling himself up onto Hector's back. 'If you do not freeze to death out here you would do well to remember me.'

'Then I shall pray to the Lord, Sir Edmund, that He sees

fit to preserve me that I might meet you again and avenge these men whom you have barbarously slaughtered.' His eight companions lacked their leader's boldness and either gawked pathetically at their enemies or looked at their shoes.

Mun regarded the man for a moment, saw that he was beginning to shiver, the raw air sinking teeth into his bones. Part of him was tempted to give the order to kill the prisoners where they stood and be done with the thing. Then his mind dragged up an image of his father lying plundered and stripped in the bloody mire of Edgehill. It was not a memory, for he had never found Sir Francis or Emmanuel after the battle, yet he knew the image to be true all the same.

Let them freeze, he thought, and with a click of his tongue he turned Hector around and walked him south away from the Forest of Bowland, looking up at the pale, grey-hazed sun and looking forward to getting himself in front of a roaring fire in Longridge village.

Tom Rivers had found more comfort than he would have dared hope for in The Leaping Lord. He had been back in Southwark some seven weeks now, drawn south to London because he knew not where else to go and wanted to be at the least far away from Shear House and the ruins of his former life. London was buzzing, her people still jubilant after their victory at Turnham Green where twenty-four thousand soldiers and townsfolk – men and women – had stood side by side to defend the road into London. Together this huge if unusual army had mustered on Chelsea Fields and marched westwards to deny their king entry to the city.

'What a sight it was. A vision I shall never forget,' Ruth Gell had told Tom the night he had come to the Lord. At first she had not recognized him – later she admitted to assuming him to be a beggar – but then she had looked properly into his eyes and she had gasped in shock, seeing through the unkempt hair and beard – and the scars – to the young man she had known before the war. There had been no available rooms and Tom had shared Ruth's bed as in old times.

Her eyes had shone as she recounted the tale. 'All the proud ensigns of the Trained Bands danced in the wind and we stood there shoulder to shoulder with fighting men,' she had told him, 'men who had stood against the King at Kineton Fight. And hundreds more were scattered amongst the gardens and orchards and waiting in narrow lanes beside the Thames. And we were prepared to fight, too!' she had announced, as though daring him to dispute it.

He had not disputed it. 'We knew that devil Prince Rupert and his cavalry couldn't hurt us in the streets,' she had said, 'and you know what His Majesty's men did? They watched us. They watched us eat and they watched us pray and damn their eyes but they did not know what to do.' The ghost of a smile had lit her eyes. 'It wouldn't look good, would it, the King sending his soldiers against so many ordinary folk? And we knew it. You should have seen it, Tom. It was like a miracle.'

Ruth had shrugged, accepting that he would never know how it had felt to be among them on that glorious day. 'By evening it was all over. His Majesty and all his haughty lot buggered off.' Her plump lips had curled then, like a cat settling into its basket. 'We danced and sang and drank until we fell over. Oh but you should have been there, my handsome man. You should have seen us.'

Tom had listened, barely saying a word, barely even stirring other than an occasional nod to usher her on with the story, and Ruth had obliged, washing the dirt of the road from his skin and tracing callused fingers over scars and the puckered flesh of wounds that had not been there when she had last known his body by candlelight. Only in the early hours of the morning, when Tom had been vaguely aware of his limbs slackening, his body surrendering at last against Ruth and her lumpy bed, had she murmured that she had thought he was dead.

'Some of your friends were here,' she said, her voice barely

29

above a whisper, as though she was compelled to tell him but hoped he would not hear. She pushed his long hair behind his right ear, fingertips brushing his cheekbones and the taut ridge of his brows. 'Matthew Penn and Will Trencher. They've been in a few times. They said you were killed at Kineton Fight.' Tom felt some small lifting of his soul's burden at the mention of his friends. 'They miss you, Tom. Never said as much of course, but I could see it in their faces. You men can't hide things like that. Matthew said you fought like a demon. That you weren't afraid of anything.'

'I was afraid,' Tom heard himself mumble.

'One of the others saw you ride into the King's men, saw you shot from your horse.' There was a short heavy silence. 'I'm sorry if Achilles is gone,' she said, 'you loved that horse better than you love most people.' *Better than you love me*, her eyes said. Tom said nothing and Ruth nestled a kiss amongst his hair and pressed her cheek against his head. 'No one has heard from you since.'

A short while later he heard Ruth say: 'Well you're safe now.'

And then he had slept.

Now it was mid March and freezing still, and Tom had resumed his old duties at the Lord, clearing tables, hefting barrels and doing whatever else Abiezer Grey, in grudging tone, asked him to do. Grey had not been cheered to see Tom again, had visibly chafed when Tom had said that he would work for food and fodder for his mare but not for a room, being as he would share Ruth's bed. But it was more than distaste at the thought of Tom lying with Ruth, more than simple jealousy that Tom had seen in the innkeeper's eyes. If it was not quite fear it was fear's cousin, and it was a look he was coming to recognize in patrons of the Lord and in whores and tradesmen, even in the jakes farmers and rag-and-bone men he dealt with.

For Tom was a killer. People saw it in him and it disquieted them so that if they could they avoided him. If they could not do that, they would equip themselves with dourness, incline towards few words and eye him askance. And for his part Tom did little to assuage their unease, saw no point in trying to be anything other than what he was: a man who had butchered others in the red-hot madness of battle. A man who had lain with the dead, been pecked at by the carrion feeders, and yet had been turned away from Hell itself and brought back to life.

The freezing night he had spent on the plain below Edgehill was a haunting from which he could not unshackle himself. In the daytime, when he was busy earning his food and beer, the memory of that great battle was a thin gossamer web clinging to his soul. But at night, after they had enjoyed each other and Ruth was sleeping soundly beside him, its horror spread like a dark heavy stain that threatened to spill into his mouth and drown him. Somehow the smell of death, of open bowels and the copper stink of blood, would seep from his memory back into his nose. Pain would bloom in the wound in his shoulder – all healed now – where scalding hot lead had ripped through his flesh. He would clench his right hand, the savage stub of the third finger throbbing, reminding him of the indignity of being mutilated by thieves who had flocked to loot the dead.

And he would hear again brave Achilles's scream of pain as the musket ball punched into his noble chest.

And yet he kept it all, its foulness and its shame, its savagery and its . . . thrill to himself. He knew Ruth would gladly hear the whole if he would tell it. She would listen sympathetically and then she would minister to him in her fashion, show him kindness the way a young girl will tend to a lame dog or a bird with a broken wing. No, that was unfair. There would be more to it than that, more than some ingenuous need to mend him. Truth be told he knew the girl was more in love with him than he was with her. Her eyes had betrayed as much when they had coupled the night after his return and Ruth's soul had, for one fleeting moment, lain as bare as her body. Yes Ruth would care for him, and even given the affections of such as her, a serving girl who is every man's friend, it would perhaps prove balm to his soul.

But he said nothing, instead feeling the rank memory of that late October night suppurate and fester like a wound that is bandaged tight and given no air.

Now, The Leaping Lord on Long Southwark, which Abiezer Grey leased off Mark Sayer for an annual rent of fifty pounds and a sugar loaf, was the nearest thing Tom had to a home, and each day he found himself doing the kinds of jobs that once, in a distant life, would be done by servants without him barely so much as noticing.

'Looks like rain,' Ruth said now, looking up to the slate grey sky as she handed two pails of kitchen slops to a small grubby boy named Snout on account of his snub nose.

'I'll not complain if it dampens down some of this damn smoke,' Tom replied, putting a beer barrel down onto the cobbles and straightening to drag an arm across his forehead. The breeze was coming from the west, bringing with it palls of acrid coal smoke from the glassblowers, soapmakers and cloth-makers clustered cheek by jowl along St Saviour's, so that even Tom's sweat was grimy with soot.

'When it comes, Snout, you stand out in it for a while, do you hear?' Ruth said to the boy who nodded contritely. 'Let God's rain wash some of that filth off. I've known rakers that'd look like gentlemen of the King's Chamber if they stood beside you. And tell old Jacob I'll be expecting some bacon from him before long.' The boy shuffled off with the heavy pails and Tom smiled to himself because he suspected it would be some time yet before Ruth saw any bacon in return for the Lord's kitchen slops. He knew that old Jacob Payne kept his pigs up past St Margaret's Hill and Blackman Street in St George's Fields. Yet several times Tom had seen Snout turn right down Long Southwark instead of left. It was a far shorter walk north past St Olave's and to the river than to Payne's farm, and he would put money on the slops more often than not ending up in the Thames mud rather than the pigs' trough.

'He's a little devil that one,' Ruth said, shaking her head as she watched Snout go. The boy, no doubt feeling eyes on him, turned left this time, though that was nothing a detour across the road and through St Saviour's wouldn't fix.

'I should go back to my regiment,' Tom said, turning a palm up and eyeing the grey sky indifferently. A heartbeat later the first fat drop splashed onto his hand and he closed his fist around it.

'You've done your part in this whole mess, Tom,' Ruth said, 'and no one can say otherwise.' She did not have to speak then of the scars on his body for him to know that her mind's eye was completing an inventory of them, and instinctively he closed his good hand around the right one with its ugly stub where the ring finger was gone. 'I dare say the great argument will rage on very well without you, for all your ferocity.' There was almost a smile with that last but not quite. 'Let London's other young hotbloods follow the drum,' she said, 'God knows there are enough of them. Do you good to leave it alone till it blows over.' She turned back to look through the passage at the traffic of carts and horses and folk on foot streaming past. 'I'll bet that little bugger's going to cross over and double back towards the river,' she said suddenly, turning to eye Tom as though he were in league with the imp. Tom said nothing. 'He's a devilish little sod, that boy,' she said, then seeing Ralph Hall, the Lord's cook, who was on the way out, she reminded him to buy more tobacco from Timothy Bowell, but that no matter how much Bowell protested about his starving family, Hall was not to pay more than a shilling a pound for it.

Then, hefting his own barrel from the vendor's cart, which had parked on the street because its new young driver had been too afraid of scraping his master Jonas Reede's wagon against the passage (though there was, all could see, room aplenty), Abiezer Grey swaggered back through the archway into the

Lord's courtyard. Seeing Tom resting, the big innkeeper shot him a disapproving look, though said nothing as he staggered on with his precious cargo of beer. Deliberately Tom waited a long moment, as though daring Grey to challenge him, then Ruth shot him a chastising look, the kind of look with which he imagined Snout was wholly familiar, and so Tom bent his legs and wrapped his arms around the barrel, lifting it into the rain that was beginning to dash against its oak lid.

'I don't know why you have to antagonize him,' Ruth said, shaking her head. 'God knows there aren't many landlords who would have you in their employ and under their roof.'

'Because I fought? Because I was killing men while they were filling cups and keeping their heads down?' Tom asked, puffing with the effort. Normally they would roll the barrels, but the cobbles of Long Southwark had been known to bust a stave and that was a risk Abiezer Grey was not prepared to take with Reede's beer.

'Because you are the worst worker the Lord has seen for ten years!' Ruth said.

'I earn my bread,' he called behind him, then scraped his knuckles on the Lord's doorframe and cursed as he entered the dark, musty-smelling inn.

'Aye, maybe,' Ruth said, suddenly behind him so that with a grimace he straightened, making the load look lighter than it was. 'But you're too proud to make a decent servant and too surly to be good company.'

'Which is why I should be back with the regiment,' he said, as a knot of men and women who were wreathed in their own pipe smoke and talking all at once parted to let him, and more importantly Reede's beer, through.

CHAPTER THREE

―――――――――

IT HAD NOT BEEN EASY SAYING GOODBYE TO RUTH FOR THE SECOND time. Two nights ago, when most of The Leaping Lord's patrons had either staggered off to their lodgings or home to their beds, he and Ruth had shared three pitchers of Reede's strongest beer and a handful of the tobacco which Ralph Hall had, to his credit, bought off Timothy Bowell for tenpence a pound. Tom, who had in his mind loaded and primed the issue of his leaving, in the event found himself reluctant to pull the trigger and inwardly wondered at this cowardice which he had never felt in battle but which now held him to ransom.

In the end, after hours of empty talk, it had been Ruth who gave voice to the thing, exhaling smoke that floated up to the dark-stained roof in a perfect, ethereal circle.

'You're leaving. When? Tomorrow? The day after?' she had said, then taken a long draught of beer as though it meant nothing to her; yet all this outward disregard achieved was to betray the truth. She cared a great deal.

'Tomorrow,' Tom had replied, caught off guard and feeling that one word both inadequate and cruel. 'My wounds are healed.'

'Are they?' Ruth asked, blue eyes glaring, her plump cheeks flushing red.

He had shrugged. 'I have my duty. This war is just beginning and I won't hide from it.'

'You want revenge,' she accused him.

He had not disagreed with that and they had sat in silence for a long moment. Then Ruth had stood, thrusting her cup at him, so that some of the beer sloshed over its lip onto the table.

'If you leave tomorrow then do not come back, Thomas,' she had said, holding his eye, then downing the remaining beer in one go. 'You will not be welcome here again.' And with that she had turned and pushed off through the last of the Lord's drinkers. The next day, an hour before dawn and his head ringing like the bells of St Saviour's church, Tom had put all his worldly belongings into a knapsack and left The Leaping Lord.

He had followed the Thames upriver, riding some eleven miles to Richmond where, he had heard, Sir William Balfour was recruiting. For Robert Devereux, Earl of Essex and commander of Parliament's forces, planned to move west to take Windsor, Henley-on-Thames and Reading, and the bitter winter months were the time to forge an army. A renowned man of principle and a good soldier, Balfour would be integral to Essex's ambitions, Tom knew. The Scotsman had commanded Tom's regiment as lieutenant-general of horse at Kineton Fight and Tom respected him. He was a fighter, a man who had broken several regiments of the King's foot, and Tom believed that his own best chance of re-entering the fray, of exacting vengeance upon his enemies, lay with riding in one of Balfour's troops.

But five months had passed since that bloody day when they had ridden their horses into the storm of musketry and flesh-ripping pikes, and when faithful Achilles though shot through the chest had run on, carrying Tom towards his enemies until at last the stallion had faltered and fallen and bled to death in the mud. And now Tom stood shivering in the gathering dark, waiting for a corporal in Captain Clement's troop to return and tell him whether or not Clement would see him. He had found the army easily enough, its myriad camp fires casting a copper glow on the dusk sky above the royal park, and he had walked his mare past infantry regiments each comprising anything from three to thirteen companies, their tents ranged across the uneven ground like the spume of wind-whipped waves. But from then on, when he came amongst the horse brigades, he had been sent from pillar to post and troop to troop because no one seemed to know which regiment was where. The open land of grass and pollarded oaks upon which the King so loved to hunt his deer was now a seething mass of men and beasts on which an army's sense of order was struggling to impose its will.

'What makes you so special, lad?' the corporal had asked, his shadow-played face hard and scornful, tempered by a harsh winter spent in the field. 'Why would the captain want to waste his time with you?'

'Because I am back from the dead,' Tom had replied, knowing that appearing insane was unlikely to ingratiate him with the surly man, but not caring. 'Tell Captain Clement that Black Tom has come back from the dead to kill Cavaliers.'

The corporal had eyed him suspiciously, scratching his stubbled cheek, then shrugged and turned, walking off into the dark without another word.

Tom realized he was shivering, but rather than from cold it was more akin to the feeling he got after a fight, when his very blood seemed to bubble in his veins and his soul trembled like the ground under a troop of charging horse. He recognized the feeling for what it was: the thrill of being back amongst others like himself, men who had known the savage joy and the animal instinct to survive at all costs. It was not quite a sense of belonging, but it *was* something similar.

He waited for what seemed a long time, letting the atmosphere of the camp – the noise and bustle and men's raillery, the stink of latrine pits, damp wool and wood smoke – wash over him. Men were cold and likely hungry and were surely missing their homes and families, and yet the occasional peal of laughter or good-natured insult threaded officers' bellowed orders and the horses' neighs and the lowing of the artillery train's oxen, so that Tom was reminded of those heady days when they all had thought it would be a simple matter of giving the King's army a bloody nose to prove their resolve. Remove the King's wicked advisors, they had said, and His Majesty would hear his subjects' plight and attend to them. But it had not been as easy as that. Now the country was at war and men on both sides were preparing for the river of blood that must surely flow in the spring if the current peace negotiations failed. In his heart Tom hoped that they would.

The corporal returned, appearing as a silhouette with a fire's glow behind him. 'You're in luck, lad,' he said, knuckling snot from his nose. 'The captain says he knows you. Follow me.'

Leading his mare by the reins Tom followed the man past tents and a troop of between thirty and forty men all clustered around a fire that was raging, cracking and spitting as it devoured three gnarly old oak boughs and other deadfall. Despite the cold and the apparent lack of wine and beer being passed around, the men seemed in good spirits. They were swaddled against the chill, red montero-caps rolled down to protect the backs of their heads and necks, and about half had pipes clamped between teeth. Five or six, Tom noticed, even had women sharing their blankets, had their arms wrapped around them like war booty, and he knew that this was a sure way to make yourself unpopular with those who had all but forgotten the feel of a woman's soft flesh.

Then he passed a horse picket and some of the animals looked up at his mare, tossing their heads and snorting steam into the cold air, and for a heartbeat the loss of Achilles hit him like a thin blade in the gut. But the horse they had let him ride from Shear House was a fine animal too. The bay mare had Arab's blood in her, that much was obvious from her refined, wedge-shaped head, the good arch to her neck, the long, level croup and a high tail carriage. But Tom recognized the Hackney in her too, in the high knee and hock action that gave her a gait that appeared effortless and made her a pleasure to ride, and in her powerful shoulders and large expressive eyes. She had speed, endurance and was strong of bone, and Tom knew he had done the creature a disservice by not yet having given her a new name to get used to. He resolved to remedy this and just then the mare snorted, which sounded like derision, as though she knew her new master's thoughts. Then Tom recognized the man ahead taking his leave of a well-fed, fur-swathed quarter-master: the long face with its great livid stain.

'Here he is, sir, the lad who says he's back from the dead. I'll bet the King's quaking in 'is boots,' the corporal said, a snort escaping his nose as he gave Tom one last look up and down before the officer dismissed him with a curt nod.

Tom rubbed his mare's poll but she was not in the mood and tossed her head and dragged a foot through the grass.

'Sir, my name is Thomas Rivers. I fought with you at Kineton Fight.'

Captain Clement, who all knew was a dour man, spread his lips in what would have been a smile on anyone else.

'I heard tales of spirits walking the plain after that bloody day,' he said, face tight as a good knot, chin jutting. 'They say that ghosts of the slain have contested that fight many times since. I put it down to nothing but the idle prattle of superstitious fools. And yet here you are, Thomas Rivers, an apparition before my eyes.'

The captain wore a simple montero-cap like those of his men and a cheap russet cloak tied at the neck over his buff-coat, so that on first appearances his rank would not be in the slightest bit obvious. But his religion came off him in waves and with it a cold authority that, if not beheld, was certainly felt.

'I was wounded,' Tom said. 'But I am hale enough now.'

'You spent that night on the field?' Clement's eyes were slits.

Tom nodded.

'And looters took your finger for the ring on it.'

Tom was not aware he had even revealed his mutilated hand. 'I was unconscious,' he said, ashamed for what he had let be done to him. Clement's face, half of it stained the deep burgundy of strong wine, was gripped by an almost zealous scrutiny.

'Your friends saw you fall. They said you were shot. Will Trencher said you were beaten to death.'

'I *was* shot, sir.' Tom shrugged. 'But the ball passed through the flesh. Achilles my horse was killed. In the morning they carted me off with the dead bound for a hole full of corpses. But that's when I . . .' he paused, holding Clement's eye for a long cold moment, 'came back.'

'I remember that night well enough, Rivers,' the captain said. 'It was a cruel cold.' He looked up to the smoke-filled night sky. 'Colder than this. You spent the night with the dead. And yet you did not become one of them. I would know how you survived.'

'God didn't want me,' Tom said. 'Neither did the Devil.'

Clement's lip curled at that. 'Where have you been? Kineton Fight was last October.'

'A family from the village took me in. Stitched my wounds and hid me from a troop of the King's horse. Good people,' he said, thinking of Anne Dunne, the pretty daughter of the couple who had hidden him in the priest hole concealed in their roof. But then his mind played a cruel trick, turning Anne's golden hair raven black, her pink cheeks bone white, until this vision of his lost love Martha Green caused him to start.

'You're wild in a fight, Rivers,' Clement said. 'I remember you. I remember ordering you back. You disobeyed me.'

Tom could remember nothing of that. He recalled his friend Nayler being killed, his throat ripped out by a musket ball. He remembered seeing his enemy Lord Denton, a man for whom Tom's hatred burnt as hot as Hell's fire, and trying to get to him. Beyond mortal fear, beyond all senses other than the lust to kill the man whose vile machinations had forced Tom to take up arms against his king and side with Parliament against his own family, he had forged on until . . .

They had beaten him to the ground.

'I don't want men in my troop who can't be controlled. I will have discipline. Order.'

'I am a killer,' Tom said. 'I have a talent for it.'

Clement's brows arched. 'That's as maybe, Thomas Rivers, but I do not want you in my troop.'

'Told you it was him! Tom!'

Tom turned. There, their faces cast in shadow by the fire behind them, stood a knot of hard-faced men all shrouded and trussed against the cold night air.

'I told you it was him, Penn, it's Black Tom back from the dead!' Despite the dark, Tom would have recognized Weasel by his narrow shoulders and quick hands alone.

'As God is my witness,' Matthew Penn said, 'it really is you, Tom.' Tom felt a grin tug at his lips as he took in the incredulous expressions of the men with whom he had ridden and fought. There were seven or eight of them who had left the fire to take a look at him. If they were not all friends, they were brothers-in-arms, drawn from their comfort by the miracle of a man risen from the dead.

Will Trencher's bald head gleamed in the flame-glow, his cap clutched to his chest. His mouth hung open, so that he resembled more the awe-filled Catholic witnessing a statue of the Virgin Mother crying tears of blood than the stout Protestant he was.

'Hello, Will,' Tom said, then nodded to his other friends. 'Matthew. Weasel.'

'Forgive us, sir, we don't mean to interrupt,' Trencher said, pointing the cap towards Tom, 'but we never thought to see this lad again. Reckoned him killed.'

'Reckoned?' Matthew Penn blurted. 'Saw, more like. Saw poor Nayler get his throat shot out, then saw Tom murdered.'

Having gathered his courage, Trencher stepped forward and held out his hand, a smile softening his pugnacious face. Tom gripped the hand firmly as Matthew slapped his shoulder and Weasel and some of the other troopers stood grinning like fiends.

'You can't bloody kill Black Tom, eh, Rivers!' a broad-shouldered, big-bearded man called Robert Dobson said, pressing his thumb against the side of his nose and shooting a wad of snot onto the ground.

'Are you back with us then, Tom?' Matthew asked, the whites of his wide eyes reflecting the fire's glow.

'I'll not have him in my troop,' Captain Clement said, turning his scrutiny on Penn and the others. The troop's camp fire suddenly flared, illuminating the party and lending a savage aspect to Clement's long face with the great red smear across it.

'Come now, sir,' Trencher entreated, 'you don't believe in the walking dead now do you? I've seen this lad cut down Cavaliers like he was scything bloody wheat. He's a good soldier.'

'Being a killer does not make a man a good soldier, Trencher,' Clement said, 'it makes him dangerous to his own side.' He turned and eyeballed Tom again. 'Rivers is a sword that does not fit its scabbard. He'll not ride for me.'

'But sir—' Matthew began before he was cut off by Clement's raised finger.

'Hold your tongue, Penn,' the captain warned, not taking his eyes off Tom's. 'I've been a soldier long enough to know that some men bring a troop bad luck. They perhaps don't mean to but that's the truth of it.'

'Never saw you as a superstitious sort, Captain,' Trencher said. 'Thought we left all that to the papists.'

'Aye, and the old women,' Weasel murmured.

'Where there is slaughter and carrion there are ravens, Trencher,' the captain said. 'If it's true it's not superstition. I know men. And this one is a raven.'

'But what will he do?' Penn asked, looking from Clement to Tom.

'It's all right, Matt,' Tom said, rubbing his mare's cheek and muzzle, 'I'll find another troop.' He felt the twist of a grimace. 'I kill Cavaliers. There'll be a captain hereabouts who'll find that of some use.' He clicked his tongue and the mare started forward.

'Rivers,' Captain Clement said, 'seek out a man by the name of Crafte. Captain James Crafte. He's with the foot, on the earl's staff. Tell him I sent you.'

'I am a harquebusier, not a pikeman or a damned musketeer,' Tom said, 'and I'll outride any man in this regiment, you included, Captain.'

Clement frowned. 'Crafte doesn't lead a troop. Truthfully, I have no idea what the man does besides attend Essex like a damned shadow.' He rubbed a palm against his stained cheek. 'But find him, Thomas Rivers, and you may get your chance to kill Cavaliers.' Then Clement turned and walked off to join a knot of officers who were standing smoking pipes by a pollarded oak, and Tom's friends swarmed in on him again, slapping his back and shoulders and bombarding him with questions.

'This Captain Crafte can wait till tomorrow,' Will Trencher said, taking the mare's reins off Tom and handing them to a young trooper with a curt order to take the horse to the picket. He was grinning savagely, the smile at odds with the carved granite of his face. 'It's not every day a ghost joins our fire.'

'I didn't think you were superstitious, Will.'

'And I thought you were dead, lad, so it looks like we were both wrong,' Trencher said, and together they all walked back towards the flames around which the rest of the troop sat huddled.

'Weasel,' Trencher rumbled, 'we've all of us heard General Balfour bemoaning the theft of his personal stash of brandywine. Now would be a good time to chance upon a drop.'

Weasel grinned and broke away, heading for his tent, and Tom went with the tide, enjoying the fire's heat on his face and the company of men he had presumed he'd never see again.

And in the morning he found Captain James Crafte.

'And this Captain Clement rides with Sir William Balfour's Regiment of Horse?'

'Yes, sir.' Tom glanced over at the three men sitting behind tables, busily scratching away with their quills, only pausing to dip them into ink pots or scatter sand across the paper.

'And yet I barely know the man, have perhaps been in his company twice – if as much as that. Certainly to my knowledge he owes me no favours.'

'Perhaps he intends for you to owe him one,' Tom suggested.

Captain Crafte was frowning, though Tom suspected that was as much down to poor eyesight as to curiosity. 'Thomas, was it?'

'Yes, sir,' Tom said.

Crafte's eyebrows furrowed and then released. 'Whatever the man's motive, I must assume that he does not have need of you,' he tilted his head to one side, 'or indeed want you, in his own troop.' His neat little nose wrinkled. 'Forgive me for saying so but, given that most troops are coming up short on the preferred muster, that does not speak well for you, young man.'

Tom could not argue with that and so he said nothing, at a loss to determine what he was doing in a room with a captain who did not lead men in battle and three secretaries who were so intent on their writing that they had not so much as glanced at him since he arrived.

'Interesting,' the captain said, finger and thumb stroking the tuft of brown hair that jutted from his chin.

Captain Crafte was a small, neat man with a neat man's economy of movement, so that when he walked, as he did now towards the window, he barely disturbed the old straw on the farm kitchen's earthen floor.

'Are you perchance a relation of Sir Francis Rivers, who died at Kineton Fight?'

'He was my father,' Tom said, seeing no reason to lie. Crafte stopped still, staring out of the narrow, stone-mullioned window whose pane afforded a murky light. Candles burnt here and there about the room.

'And may I ask how you came to fight against your father's master the King?'

'You may ask, sir, but you'll get no answer. I have my reasons.'

His back to Tom, Crafte was still as stone, hands clasped behind him. 'You come to me seeking employment and yet your tongue barely stirs to promote your cause.'

'I come seeking nothing. I do not know why I am here,' Tom said, growing irritated by the incessant scratching of quills on paper. 'Captain Clement might not want a killer in his troop, and that makes him a strange officer if you ask me, but I never thought the man a fool. He told me to find you and so here I am.' He shrugged. 'Clearly there has been some mistake, sir. By your leave I will go and find a troop that wants fighters.'

Crafte turned round, his small nose crinkling like a mole's. 'Of course you don't know why you are here,' he said, a smile touching his watery eyes. 'I dare say Captain Clement has only the vaguest notion of what it is I do here. How I labour for the cause and do it all unseen. Imagine, Thomas, if you would, a band of bell-ringers pulling on the ropes. Well, I am the man who tells them which ropes to pull and in what order. The resulting peal, that euphony which carries far on the wind, is my design. And yet I am never seen.' He tugged his tuft of beard, his small eyes boring into Tom's. Tom had the sudden notion that the man might be mad, that perhaps the dour Captain Clement had a sense of humour after all and had sent him to Crafte for his own amusement.

'But I need men to pull the ropes,' Crafte said. 'What would you say are your . . . talents, Thomas Rivers? And I would not include geniality amongst them,' he added with the merest twitch of a smile.

'I can ride,' Tom replied. 'There are few men in England who can handle a stallion as I can.'

'Yet you came here riding a mare,' Crafte said.

'My stallion was killed under me at Kineton Fight,' Tom said. 'He would have galloped through the gates of Hell for me.'

Crafte seemed to consider this for a moment. 'What other abilities do you possess, young man?'

'I can shoot straight and I can use a sword.'

Crafte flapped a hand as though shooing a fly. 'Firelocks and blades. Mere tools,' he said. 'Useless without the intent of the hands wielding them. How many men have you killed for our most righteous cause?'

For the cause? Or for myself? Tom wondered. 'I do not know,' he said honestly. 'Many.'

'That's a good sign,' Crafte acknowledged with a careful nod. 'You are not plagued by foul, dark dreams after taking a man's life?'

Tom shook his head. He had known dark dreams but they were of Martha Green hanging by the neck, swinging gently beneath a stone bridge, and Crafte had no business knowing about them.

'Can you hear that?' Crafte said, cupping a hand to his right ear, his head half turned towards the window.

Tom shrugged. 'Just the sounds of the camp,' he said.

'Precisely,' Crafte said, 'but soon you will hear the peal of bells. They will chime for England and her people. For I have a job for you, Thomas Rivers.'

CHAPTER FOUR

THOUGH HER CHEEKS WERE NUMBING, BESS FELT THE FAINTEST touch of the tear coursing down her cheek. She cuffed it away just as Joseph glanced at her from his saddle, the concern in his eyes not quite daring to find voice and offer words of comfort.

'It is bitter cold,' she said, not meeting his eye, hoping that the young man might take her tears as a symptom of their riding into the wind. The day had begun still and cold when they had set out from Warrington, but now a biting south-westerly was scouring the Cheshire plain, buffeting an array of ravens and jackdaws that came barrelling through the nearby woods to roost, and causing the skeletal hedgerows to shiver incessantly.

'Take my cloak, my lady,' Joseph said, raising raw, gloveless hands from the reins to remove the thick woollen garment.

Bess shook her head. 'Thank you, Joseph, but it is only my face that feels the chill,' she lied, giving him a smile that was meant, if not convincing. 'And remember you must call me Bess, simply Bess. To be safe.'

The lad nodded, pushing two fingers against his mouth as if chastising himself for forgetting their arrangement, and Bess waved a hand as though it were of no matter, at least whilst they two were alone out there. The young man riding with her, a blunderbuss strapped across his back, was as thin as a birch and would likely freeze to death without his cloak, which meant that his kind offer was another blade in Bess's conscience. For she knew Joseph would do anything for her, that freezing to death would be a contentment to him if she would only wear his cloak. Which was, of course (she had no illusions) why she had asked him to ride from Shear House with her, the two of them slipping away through the pre-dawn cold the night before last.

Well, she had not exactly asked him; she had told him of her intentions, perhaps at that time simply confiding in him because there was no one else she felt she could tell. But Joseph had offered to go with her, to guard her, had all but insisted, and perhaps Bess had known that he would. Certainly her protestations that he must remain with the garrison or surely face Major Radcliffe's wrath had felt hollow on her tongue. And had she not admitted that she *would* feel safer on the road with a brave man such as he beside her?

'I can see that your mind is made up to go, my lady,' Joseph had said with a determined nod, 'and I will not have you travel alone.'

She had smiled at him then, a warm, true smile that was for him certainly, but half for herself too and the excitement of the planned journey upon which she had set her mind to embark. Not that she was without fear, for even in times of peace it would be a dangerous enterprise for a woman to set off across the country as Bess had done. To do so in the midst of war, and with Bess being who she was – a woman long on privilege but short on experience – was recklessly foolish and Bess knew it. But she would risk anything . . . everything to bring her family back together, to have her brothers back under the roof of Shear House and spare them the fate of those she had loved and lost. Was she not as brave as they? Was she not a Rivers too?

'You are a good friend, Joe,' she said now, stifling a shiver that ran up the backs of her arms, 'and I'm lucky to have you. Do not think I don't know it.'

His head lifted at that, his boy's eyes giving away too much, the smile on his chapped lips joy tempered by pride.

I owe him that much at least, she thought, and this time she cuffed away the tear whilst it yet welled in her eye. Because if she felt guilty for drawing this young man into her scheme, it was as nothing compared with the shame that sat in her belly like a coiled serpent for leaving her baby.

She had tried to smooth the thing in her mind countless times. Little Francis, her love, her pride, would be fine, she had told herself. Mother will dote on the boy, will see him rarely leave the crook of her arm and all his needs attended. For where else could Lady Mary's heart settle now, with her husband dead, her sons off fighting in the war and Bess gone without so much as a parting word?

And yet she had missed her baby from the moment she had last kissed his soft cheek and inhaled his scent, and it had been a cold writhing in her guts ever since.

'Do you recognize the place, Bess?' Joseph asked, watching a great white owl that was observing them from atop an old post stuck in the marsh that bordered the stream on their left. Ahead, at the end of a well-worn track from which grass and weeds sprouted in tufts, stood a rambling old farmhouse that seemed to Bess to be subsiding into the wild profusion of climbing plants surrounding it.

'I came here once but I was too young to remember it,' she said. Then, on reflection: 'I do recall orchards. I remember challenging Tom and Mun to see which of them could steal the most apples without getting caught.' That faint memory was a blush of warmth on a frigid day. 'My grandfather was a strict man.'

'And who won?' Joseph asked, seeming genuinely keen to know.

'I don't remember,' Bess said, though if pressed she'd have

wagered that Tom would have retrieved the most apples but would also have got himself caught.

The nerves were beginning to announce themselves, her skin suddenly sensitive to her linen's weave and even the coarse wool of the travelling cloak on her shoulders and back, now that she was so close to the old place. To her grandfather. If he is even alive, she thought, for no one in Shear House ever spoke of Lord Heylyn, Earl of Chester, nor had they since his and his daughter Lady Mary's great falling-out more than twenty years ago. It had been a sharp disagreement and barely sheathed, so that everyone within sight of Parbold Hill knew that Lord Heylyn thought his daughter had married beneath herself in Sir Francis Rivers. The earl had threatened Mary with being cut off if she went ahead with the marriage, or so Sir Francis had revealed to Bess and her brothers one Christmastide around the table, when the malmsey had loosened his tongue and the festivities were in full flow.

Bess's mind tortured her now by conjuring the memory, even gilding it with the dancing flames of the parlour hearth, and her family as it once was. Sir Francis with his pipe resting between his lips. Their mother dressed in the old fashion, a ruff at the neck and wrists, copper eyebrows raised indulgently at her husband, perhaps wishing he would not speak of it, but it being too late now to stopper the bottle.

'But your grandfather might as well have tried blowing the wind back the way it came as tried telling your mother what to do,' Sir Francis had said, a mischievous smile cinching the pipe's stem. 'Besides which, your mother was always going to marry beneath her, no matter the man.' This had been meant as a compliment, Bess had realized years later. At the time, though, she (and her brothers, too, perhaps) had reeled in shock at their grandfather's threat and she remembered feeling – unfairly, she knew now of course – more sorry for her father because of the insult than for her mother because of Lord Heylyn's indifference to her heart's desires. But Bess had been a girl and a girl will always pity her father.

The thing had of course unfolded neatly enough so that all knew their place around it. Lady Mary had made good her own ambition, marrying Sir Francis because she loved him and going north with him to Shear House. The earl had proved as stubborn and resolute as his word, having nothing to do with his daughter or her new family other than a handful of solemn requests to see his grandchildren when they were young. And even those requests had dried up, perhaps because those children, the progeny of a mere knight, whenever they came pillaged his beloved orchards.

'Well, someone is here,' Joe observed, nodding towards the grey-black smoke rising silent as the long dead from a shamble of chimney upon the farmhouse roof. The wind was whipping the smoke eastward, up into the bitter, heavy sky. For a long moment Bess watched it rise, reflecting that it was her grandfather's ire itself, still smouldering after all these years, bitter idle fumes that availed an old man nothing in his loneliness.

Strange, she thought, that a man so obdurate regarding the formalities of his class should favour a near derelict farmhouse over his grand estate lying on the River Dee's south bank at Handbridge. Then again, what did Bess know? Lord Heylyn, Earl of Chester, was a stranger to her, for all she now hoped to convince him that that was not so, for all her determination to haul on the halyard of his remorse and raise him to her cause.

They had dismounted and tethered their horses, each to an iron ring beside a mounting block by the front door, and now Bess found herself sheltering from the wind in the oak-timbered porch as Joe grasped another ring, this one forged with a dog's-head knocker, and rapped it against her grandfather's door. Near by, three hens scavenged in the mud, their plumage bristling in the chill.

'He will not know me,' Bess said, watching Joe huff into red raw hands. The poor lad's felt broad-hat had holes in it, she noticed.

'I think he will, Bess,' Joe replied with a frown, knocking again, louder this time.

Bess had braided her hair and pinned the long tresses against her head, covering all with a simple linen coif and then a loose felt hood which she now removed for fear of the thing obscuring her face.

Let him be alive, God, her mind whispered, a shiver running through her flesh as the door opened and a balding servant in her grandfather's blue livery enquired after them.

'I am Elizabeth Rivers, daughter of Sir Francis and Lady Mary Rivers of Parbold in Lancashire. I am here to see my grandfather the earl.'

For a moment the servant's inquisitive eyes scoured her face, then slipped down to take an inventory of her modest dress: the russet cloak and, beneath that, the simple neckcloth pinned around her shoulders to cover her décolletage. Likewise her bodice was deliberately unworthy of remark and her skirts, though full and of multiple layers, were of thick, dull green wool.

Then the man's eyes jumped across to Joe but did not linger on him, the appraisal done in a heartbeat, and returned to Bess, a lift in the brows intimating that perhaps it might be possible that the girl before him was indeed his master's relation.

'Do you doubt me, sirrah?' Bess challenged.

His blue eyes, which were watery from the sudden cold air, widened, and he gave a slight nod, the few strands left on his liver-spotted head floating wispily.

'Cry your pardon, madam,' he said, 'but we do not receive many visitors, fewer still since the troubles. Please.' He swept an arm back into the dark interior. 'Come in from the cold.'

Joe thanked him but Bess held her tongue as they stepped into the house, their eyes adjusting to the dark as the servant closed the door on the day and went to announce their arrival.

They waited for what seemed to Bess an age, as her memories sought form and familiarity that would not come, and she breathed the air that was sweet with wood smoke yet cut by the tang of an old man's urine.

'Lord Heylyn will see you now,' the servant said, beckoning them into the parlour beyond whose threshold came the crack and pop of a roaring fire. 'May I advise you to speak up and with clarity, for my lord cannot abide mumbling.'

'Drink!' The word was drawn out and had the sound of an ancient tree falling, ripping its roots from the earth.

'Yes, my lord,' the servant said, nodding that Bess and Joe should enter the parlour, then hurrying off along the gloomy hall.

'Wait here, Joe,' Bess said, noting what looked like relief in the young man's eyes, then she took a deep, smoky breath, exhaled, and went to meet her grandfather.

That the man was old should not have surprised her, and yet it did. Seeing his face had lit a memory of him which, until that point, had been at best shadowy. Now, though, the past came flooding in on the scent of gently rotting apples stacked on racks amongst countless books behind her, beyond the reach of the fire's warmth.

'You have your mother's face,' the old man said, holding up a candlestick to better see her. His hand trembled though he did not look weak.

'As do you, Grandfather,' Bess said. For it was true. The old man's hair was still thick, hanging unkempt in waves of black and light grey to his shoulders, and his beard, which was almost all grey, was thick and voluminous as camp-fire smoke on a still day. Yet beneath all this the thin flesh on his face was tight over the bones, his cheeks prominent up to the lined skin and soft bulges beneath his eyes. As for the eyes themselves, which seemed now to drink of her, they were narrow and tired-looking, though still deep as wells beneath tufted grey brows.

'It has been a long time, Grandfather,' Bess said, wishing she knew what the man before her was thinking.

Lord Heylyn leant in closer to Bess, so that she smelt his old skin and hair, caught a whiff of garlic and stale tobacco on his breath.

'You've got your father's eyes, I see,' he said, a hint of tooth revealing itself within the bloom of grey bristles. He sees well enough, Bess thought, for it was true that although she resembled her mother in many ways her eyes were her father's, more blue than green.

'May I sit?' Bess pointed to a chair, one of two by the fire. Her grandfather nodded, still staring at her.

'Is she dead?' he said, meaning her mother.

'No. But my father is,' she said, sitting and raising her hands to the flames. Books and apples, most of the fruit withered, littered the room. Here and there a candle flickered. 'He died protecting the King's ensign at Kineton Fight. They never found him.'

The old man followed, easing himself into the other chair, which creaked from long use. 'He was no coward, your father,' he said, at which Bess felt herself nod, relieved that his first words had not insulted her father's memory. 'If he had been, Mary would never have turned her back on me for him.'

'He died for the cause, Grandfather,' Bess said, 'as did the man I was going to marry. Emmanuel.' She said his name for herself, not him, for the old man had never met Emmanuel and his death would mean nothing to him. 'We were handfast and would have wed.'

'Then along came this war,' her grandfather said.

Bess nodded. 'Emmanuel and Edmund rode to the King when His Majesty raised the standard at Nottingham.'

Bess ached whenever she thought of her love, lost for ever, and her heart with him. And yet even the aching was something to which she could cling.

'God's wrath is England's fire,' Lord Heylyn said. 'Drink!'

he yelled again, eyes blazing as he looked towards the door for sign of his servant returning. Then he turned back to Bess, big hands gripping the ends of his chair's arms so that the knuckles were bloodless. 'Then your mother is well?'

'Quite well,' Bess said, aware she had raised her voice for the old man's benefit. 'For all her own efforts towards the war. We were besieged. Before Christmastide. Mother led a sortie and fought the rebels herself.' Her grandfather's eyes widened at that, which was hardly surprising, Bess thought. 'I was delivered of my son whilst we were besieged. Little Francis.' Another name to squeeze her heart, for the loss of her father and the missing of her baby. 'Edmund returned and—'

'Broke the siege and sent the rebels to Hell,' her grandfather finished. 'I am not so far removed from the world that I do not hear stories that are worth hearing.' His left eyebrow lifted. 'A child out of wedlock, hey? And what did Sir Francis make of that, I wonder?'

'We had made our vows,' Bess said, her hackles rising. 'The ceremony was all arranged and we would have been wed before little Francis was born if not for the country turning on their king. We had my father's blessing.'

'Indeed.'

The servant hurried in with two wooden cups, presenting one to Bess before delivering the other into a trembling hand that had been outstretched since Bess had heard the man's steps across the hall boards.

'So your mother raises two boys and one is a hero, the other a traitor,' Lord Heylyn said, putting the cup to his lips and slurping the warm wine. 'That's what you get if you marry without regard to breeding.' He let that hang in the air between them and Bess got the sense he was testing her, perhaps willing her to take umbrage.

Well, she would not bite.

'My mother married the man she loved. As I would have done had Emmanuel lived,' she said simply. 'My brothers are not the boys you remember but grown men. They follow their own paths. As for Tom, it is true that he has fought with the rebels, God save his soul, but he has suffered terribly. Hatred and the hunger for vengeance blinded him, Grandfather, as hatred is wont to do to men.'

This barb was well aimed, it seemed, for the old man's eyes flickered and narrowed further still, and a faint tremor ran through his body from leg to face.

'You are here about *them*, aren't you, Elizabeth? Your boys,' he said, bringing the cup to his lips again, inhaling before slurping more spiced wine. 'Those devils used to thieve my apples. Damned natty lads.' He dragged his shirt sleeve across his mouth, leaving a faint red stain on the linen.

'I need your help,' Bess said, looking into the flames that leapt in the hearth. And suddenly she felt like a fool on a fool's errand, for why would this old man, whom she had not seen since she was a little girl, deign to help her? Was she even now (and a mother too) the same callow fool who had encouraged Tom to court Martha Green when she should have condemned the courtship? And look what had come of that.

'Why would I help you?' Lord Heylyn asked. She could feel his eyes on her like hot coals, though she yet watched the fire. 'Your mother turned her back on me many years ago, before you were a mewling red monster at your wet-nurse's breast. She's not lacking in gall, your mother, but I *am* surprised she thought sending you here would avail your family anything. I would have said she'd too much pride for that.'

Bess felt as though one of those withered apples were lodged in her throat. She feared that by calling on the earl she might be betraying her mother.

'My mother does not know that I am here,' she said. 'No one does.'

'And the boy shivering in my hall?'

'A friend. Joseph Lea. The son of a tenant farmer and now musketeer in the Shear House garrison.'

The thick brow above the earl's left eye lifted. 'What elevated circles you move in, girl. You really *are* like your mother.' Bess did not deny it. 'She will spit fury when she learns you are here,' he said, a glint – like the scales of a fish just beneath the water – flashing across his old eyes. 'I would like to see her face when she finds out.'

'Will you help me?' Bess said again.

'Help you?'

'See my family whole again.' It will never be whole again, she thought, fixing her eyes on his. But there was a wound that might be healed. 'I will bring Tom back. I will see my brothers standing together again as they should be. As they always did.'

'And you think I can help you in this? You are misguided, girl.' He drained the cup and reached over to place it on a table, wincing with the movement. 'Your mother chose Rivers over me.' He sat back, swiping the air with a big hand, so that Bess got a glimpse of jewelled rings. 'That was done long ago. You have come here too late. I have no need of you, girl. Wine!' he roared, slamming a hand onto the arm of his chair. 'Where the devil are you, Merrett, you damned saunterer? And a member mug. I need to piss!'

'My father is dead. Does he yet cause you offence?'

'It is nothing to me,' he said, though his eyes said different.

'Then I have wasted my time,' Bess said, standing.

'Sit down, Bess,' her grandfather said.

'Why? I have work to do and our business is concluded.'

'Sit down.'

'Why, my lord?' she said, the title all but spat.

'Because I have not finished looking at you, girl,' he said, patting the air with a hand. 'How do you suppose to lure the young wolf back into the fold? And what will you do with him if you manage it?'

Bess held his eye and, deciding she had nothing to lose, sat back down.

'You are a wealthy man, Grandfather.'

'Wealthier than I appear,' he admitted. 'But I have found in times of war no prudent man should beat the drum about his fortune. Not unless he wants to piss his money away on muskets and horses for soon-to-be-dead men.'

'I want you to buy Tom a royal pardon,' she said, the very idea sounding preposterous now she had given it voice. 'Such things must be possible. For a man of your standing.'

But to her surprise the old man did not laugh or scoff. He steepled his ringed fingers as Merrett came in with a leather pitcher and a chamber pot, which he tried in vain to place surreptitiously behind his lord's chair before refilling his cup. Then he came to Bess but she shook her head.

'I played the part in King James's court,' the earl said then, almost grinning. 'Hell's beast but there were some young blades back then.' He drank. 'Most are long dead now of course. But his son,' he said into his cup, 'his son is a different man. I know him not.'

Bess made to rise again but her grandfather's hand bid her wait.

'For all that His Majesty has requested me at court many times. You are not the only one who wants my money, Elizabeth.' He pinned her with those deep eyes that must once have made women's hearts flutter but now rested upon plump cushions. 'You still have not told me why I would help you.'

'You hold no sway at court,' Bess said.

'My money does,' he riposted. 'Money always commands an audience.'

This was true enough, Bess thought, and so she would answer him.

'You would help me because perhaps you are tired of being alone,' she said. 'Or because you are old and doing good might ease your conscience before it is too late.'

The old man stood up now and picked a log from the basket by the hearth. 'I have been alone a long time, granddaughter,' he said, weighting the last word, 'and am resigned to dying here . . .' he glanced around the dimly lit room, 'in this house.

I want no part in the quarrel that has got men so excited.' He shook his shaggy head. 'The fools do not know what war is, for if they did they would not be so eager for it.' He bent, placing the log in the fire with a trembling hand which he did not remove until the log was just as he wanted it. 'I have seen war and have no appetite for it,' he said, straightening and looking at her again, firelight playing across his face, bronzing his grey hairs and beard. 'Should the rebels beat the King, gain their great victory and turn the world on its head, what would I care? Pray tell, girl. I shall be gone soon enough. I have no family whose place in this world I am bound to preserve.'

'We are your family,' Bess said, unsure if the old man sought her pity or her anger. 'You cannot undo what was done long ago, but you *can* help me. Together we might, God willing, give my mother back her sons. Tom and Mun are enemies and should not be. Your blood runs in their veins, Grandfather. Help me bring Tom back before he is killed in some muddy field or strung up for a traitor.' The words sickened her but she could not hide from the fate Tom was courting. She feared her mother could not survive another such tragedy. Or perhaps Bess feared for herself. 'If Tom knew the King would pardon him he would come over to us,' she said, realizing that she still gripped the now empty cup in her right hand, 'and we might be a family again.' She did not know if this last was true, but she had to try to believe that it was, had to make her grandfather believe it, too.

Still staring at her, the old man scratched his cheek. 'You remind me of her,' he said, then he walked to the back of the room and stood with his back to Bess as the fire ate into the new log which cracked and spat in the silence between them. She thought he was studying the books, several of which she recognized from her mother's library at Shear House: tomes by Sir Thomas Browne, John Donne, Ben Jonson and Robert Herrick. But when he turned back to her he was holding an apple, one of the hundreds from the crowded racks below the books. 'It takes about twelve years to grow an apple tree from a pip to its first fruiting,' he said, examining the apple as though he had never seen one before. 'It is a labour of love. It requires enormous patience.' He thrust his old thumbs into the apple where the stem emerged, splitting the fruit into two equal pieces. Then he pressed the halves together so that the apple looked whole again.

'I will help you, Elizabeth,' he said, putting the apple to his nose and inhaling. 'I will buy your brother a pardon and you will give me your word that your mother shall never know that I have had a hand in the thing, or that you were ever here.' Bess nodded and for the first time a smile found its way onto the old man's lips. 'Of course,' he went on, 'yours will be the hardest task, scouring this bleeding land for sight of the lad.'

'I'll find him,' Bess said, excitement flaring in her blood at the reversal.

'Perhaps you will. I will have a useful man accompany you, for the road will be dangerous. No place for a young woman.'

'I have Joe,' Bess said, glancing towards the door.

'That wet-nosed boy out there? Nonsense. The man I am thinking of is resourceful and reliable. He will be your escort. Your . . . bodyguard.' He tossed the two halves of the apple into the fire. 'I would protect my investment,' he said, walking to the door as the apple hissed and bubbled in the flames. 'Merrett! Have the guest rooms prepared. My granddaughter and her skinny pup will be our guests tonight. And send someone for Dane! I don't care if he's drunk, up to his ogles in some whore's notch or swinging from a gibbet, but I want him here by noon tomorrow.'

'My lord, thank you,' Bess said as he walked back over to his chair by the fire. He bent and picked up the chamber pot, waving his other hand at her, a grimace nestled amid his unkempt beard.

'Now give me some peace, girl,' he said sharply. 'For I need to piss.'

CHAPTER FIVE

'WELL, I WOULDN'T WIPE MY ARSE WITH IT,' TRENCHER SAID, slamming the newsbook down onto the rough-hewn table and taking a lit taper from Robert Dobson who, his pipe clamped in his mouth, began digging filth out from his fingernails with a ballock dagger. The big-bearded trooper seemed not in the least interested in anything that was going on. '"Communicating the intelligence and affairs of the Court, to the rest of the kingdom"?' Trencher mocked, voicing the statement written beneath the newsbook's title. 'I've heard more truth in a cow's fart.'

Weak dawn light seeped in through the farm kitchen's window. The manuscripts which the secretaries had been so busy working on the night before still lay on the desks beside ink pots and quills, though the men themselves were absent.

'Unfortunately, Trencher, not everyone shares your opinion of *Mercurius Aulicus*,' Captain Crafte said, glancing at Tom as though seeking some assurance that the men in the room were really the right sort for the job at hand.

Tom did nothing to persuade him that they were, said nothing to smooth the lines etched in the captain's brow. Let the man work for it.

With one hand Matthew Penn pulled up a stool and with

the other grabbed the newsbook and brought a candle closer. He opened the printed pages and started to read. He had barely begun when Weasel cuffed him across the back of his head.

'Come on then, you cunny! Tell me what it says,' Weasel griped. 'We didn't all have a rich father and fancy schooling.'

'You wouldn't understand if I told you, Weasel,' Penn said, rubbing his sore head and running a finger beneath the words printed in long blocks up and down the newsbook's pages.

'What your friend means to say,' Crafte said to Weasel, who seemed to have lost interest anyway and was busy scratching at an angry red boil on his cheek, 'is that the half-truths and bare-faced lies printed therein are not worthy of consideration.' Crafte walked over to the table and snatched up the newsbook, holding it aloft as much to get everyone's attention, Tom guessed, as to push his point. 'This is our enemy, men. This flimsy, insubstantial binding of ink and paper does our cause more harm than that devil prince and all his Cavaliers.'

'It's just paper,' Dobson said with a shrug of his heavy shoulders. 'What 'arm can it do?' Tom sighed inwardly at that, knowing he was about to hear the same sermon Captain Crafte had delivered the previous night. So he took the opportunity to pull out and study the crude map of Oxford the captain had given him. It was just lines and street names but the captain had said he must memorize what he could, for he must return it before setting off rather than risk being caught with it and giving the game away.

'Just paper you say?' Crafte enquired. 'This is a concoction of vile squibs, mockery, satire and grotesques, all deployed to propagate the King's cause and pour scorn on ours. This damn thing and its editor John Birkenhead lampoon us.' He tossed the newsbook back onto the table and Penn looked about to pick it up but then thought better of it. 'The pulpit and the press,' Crafte went on, sweeping a hand through the air, 'they are the bellows that fan the flames upon the world. We may have the pulpit but the King has the press and the press is the greater weapon.'

'Can't kill a man with paper,' Weasel put in, a bony hand caressing the hilt of the hanger scabbarded at his hip.

Crafte gave a bewildered shake of his head and looked at Tom. 'Would you care to clarify, Thomas?' he asked. 'I fear your friends here can barely reach my ropes, let alone pull them.'

'Ropes?' Penn said, glancing at Tom, who gave a slight shake of his head in a gesture that said *don't ask*, then waved the map at Trencher in a gesture that told him to pass over his pipe.

'Thank you, sir, but I'll let you carry on,' Tom said, 'for if these men choose to walk with me into the lion's den and place their heads between the beast's jaws, I would have them blame you not me if it turns out badly.' He drew on the pipe and exhaled, watching the smoke drift up to join the haze hanging around the roof beams.

Crafte sighed and turned back to Weasel. 'The destructiveness of such a newsbook stems from its eloquence. Do you see? From its ability to project its disembodied voice, to travel long distances, to swarm over and infest the kingdom.' He pointed down at the tatty-looking sheets still lying on the table by Matthew Penn. 'The threat of *Mercurius Aulicus* lies in its capability of addressing a greater audience than manuscripts or the human voice. For John Birkenhead's printing press spits out a thousand or more exact copies every week!' He rolled his slight shoulders as though his own clothing were horribly uncomfortable. 'Can you imagine?' Clearly Weasel could not. 'They are paper bullets and they harm us—'

'Which is why,' Tom interrupted, tired of the speech, 'I am going to Oxford. I will silence John Birkenhead's printing press.' He looked at Will Trencher, who gave the slightest nod confirming that he was in no matter what. 'We destroy the press, we silence the lies that plague our efforts.'

Now he had everyone's attention. Dobson was scratching his

bearded cheek with his dagger's point, brows bunched over dark, deep-set eyes. 'You think you can walk into the enemy's new capital and go around blowing things up?' he asked, looking from Tom to Crafte and back again.

'I'll have more chance with some help,' Tom replied matter-of-factly. It was important to appear confident if he was to hope for volunteers. But then, he *was* confident.

'A handful of men, good men, have more chance than one alone,' Captain Crafte said, 'but more than that and the more likely you are to get found out.'

'It will be dangerous,' Tom said.

'I'm with you.' Trencher picked a shred of tobacco off his tongue and flicked it away.

'Why would we leave the soft warm bosom of the army,' Weasel asked through a grimace, 'to put ourselves in harm's way like that?' He glanced at Dobson who shrugged broad shoulders and looked to Tom. 'Just so as I'm clear,' Weasel went on, 'you want us to steal into Oxford, which has got more bloody Cavaliers than rats, and risk being shot, or worse strung up, for the sake of that bunch of arsewipe.'

'We might bump into His Majesty himself, Weasel,' Trencher said, 'and you could offer him a drop of General Balfour's brandywine in exchange for his surrender.'

Weasel shot Captain Crafte a guilty look, then glared back at his loose-tongued friend, who smiled conspiratorially.

'I'll admit it is an audacious scheme,' Crafte said, taking in all the faces before him, before settling again on Weasel, 'but perhaps not too bold for a man who would dare thieve his own general's liquor.' Weasel blanched at that but Crafte paid him no mind. 'The newsbook is printed in Oxford for the consumption of cuckolds and fools,' he said, 'and in that city it seems least sense goes furthest.'

'There's ten pounds in it for each man if we get the job done,' Tom said, sensing Crafte's surprise, though the captain's face showed no sign of it. There had been no mention of money when Tom had suggested his accomplices for the mission, but he knew that for Weasel and Dobson at least, silver's lustre outshone duty's.

'A generous reward to be sure,' Crafte said in answer to the eyes now on him, 'but surely a pittance against the satisfaction of serving your Parliament and your country.' Seeing how the captain had seamlessly endorsed his promise of reward, Tom cursed himself for not promising twenty pounds each. 'Thomas here has vouched for your zeal,' Crafte said, lingering a moment on Trencher whose face now looked granite-hard with the dawn light falling across it. 'And that means something coming from a man who lay torn and bloody all night amongst the dead at Edgehill and yet stands before me now, willing to take the fight to the enemy once again.' He flapped a hand. 'But if your livers are too pale for such a task I will recruit others. The earl himself has recommended several men from his own guard with assurances that their valour is beyond question.'

'Valour aside, Captain,' Matthew Penn said, pulling his neat beard between finger and thumb, 'what happens to us if we choose to decline your kind invitation to silence this John Birkenhead and his printing press? I presume your ambition relies on secrecy.' He glanced at Tom then looked back at Crafte. 'If even a whisper of it reaches Oxford the plot is dead.'

Crafte nodded. 'If you turn down this offer to help Parliament you will be placed under arrest until the deed is done,' he said simply.

'Ballocks,' Dobson muttered.

'When you were a wee snot-nosed brat did you ever poke a wasp nest?' Trencher asked Weasel, thrusting an imaginary stick towards him. Weasel nodded. 'Well, this will be fun just like that was.' He looked at Tom, the slab of his face shifting, suddenly making him look younger, less fierce. 'When do we leave, Black Tom?'

'And your friends, Trencher?' Captain Crafte asked, encompassing the others with a sweep of his arm, 'must I lock them up and seek other confederates for you amongst the earl's men?'

'That won't be necessary, Captain,' Trencher said. 'These lads are being coy now but that is just on account of you being an officer and a gentleman and a friend of the Earl of Essex to boot. They're coming with us, all right.'

'We are?' Dobson said, his bird's-nest beard jutting belligerently.

'Yes you bloody are,' Trencher said.

Mun shivered in the pre-dawn dark. At last the feeble flames had eaten through the frost that sheathed the deadfall they had gathered and now the branches cracked and spat, challenging the spiteful cold. Mun had not wanted to make the fire. The reason they had been so successful, he knew, was largely their maintaining the element of surprise. They would track their quarry – recruiting parties, supply trains moving between Blackburn and Manchester – sometimes for days, always keeping downwind so that neither smell nor sound gave them away. Then, at his word they would strike out of the freezing dusk, falling upon their prey with savage joy like a starving wolfpack upon sheep, and the enemy died. But they had been out here for weeks now, sleeping under hedgerows, foraging on the move, and some of the men were beginning to suffer. He could see it in the clench of their jaws and the shoulders curling over their chests. They were filthy and unkempt, only briefly coming alive through the terrified elation of battle, and then retreating back into themselves once the blood-letting was over. Of the thirty-six men he had started out with, four had been killed and three had been wounded too grievously to remain with the troop. These men had ridden back to Shear House, their eyes full of shame at having to leave their comrades. The remaining thirty, himself included, had become hard, had been tempered like a sword forged in flame and cooled in the plunge, so that Mun was proud of them the way a man is proud of his best hunting hound. Yet he knew he must give them something. Knew too that a fire did more for a man than heat his bones: it revived his spirit. And so a fire blazed now, shielded from the west wind – and at least partially from sight – by a hillock that rose up towards the vast, black, star-flecked sky. His wolves hunched around that fire, some talking in low voices, others silent, their eyes feeding on the flames. All were swaddled in their cloaks and blankets, augmented by those pilfered from dead men who need fear the cold no longer.

Mun looked east, his own eyes fixing on the sentry who stood with his back to the troop, peering out into the dregs of the night.

'Move, damn you,' Mun whispered, wanting even the slightest gesture that would tell him the man was not asleep on his feet. All around, the heather stirred so that the moor seemed to Mun like an ocean, ever shifting, restless and alive. The sentry, a strong young stonemason's apprentice by the name of Tobias Fitch, crossed his arms to beat some warmth into his shoulders and Mun nodded, satisfied, then began up the hillock to relieve O'Brien from his watch.

'Still limping then?' O'Brien said, gazing up at the sky, barely turning as Mun came up.

'Just habit,' Mun said, gripping the short neck of his Dutch coat and pulling it tight against him. He had stripped the woollen coat from a dead rebel officer four days previously and now wore it over his buff-coat. 'I barely feel it now,' he said, remembering the brief but savage fight. A small troop of rebel dragoons had been scouting the land south-west of Bolton and had been approaching a farm when Mun and his wolfpack had swept down on them in a wave of steel and death. In the fray Mun had taken a sword blow to his left shin but luckily the dragoon's hanger had been blunt, had not even pierced the skin. Though it had left an angry bruise and in truth it still hurt like the devil.

'I'll wager you've chipped the shin bone,' O'Brien said, still staring at the night sky.

'Go and get some sleep,' Mun said, huffing into his hands. He wondered if this winter was ever going to end. If he would ever be warm again.

'Have you ever wondered,' the Irishman said, 'how it is that so many stars blaze through the heavens, vanishing in half a sparrow's fart, and yet there never seems to be fewer stars.' He swept a gloved hand across the vast sky. 'I've seen ten or more fall while I've been up here. Where do you think they go to?'

'You're supposed to be looking out for rebels,' Mun said.

O'Brien bent over and began rubbing some life back into his legs. 'I'll make sure Goffe relieves you in an hour,' he said, lifting his hat and scratching his head.

'Let him sleep. It's nearly dawn and I'm awake now anyway.'

The Irishman shrugged his broad shoulders and turned to make his way back down towards the fire and the ground sheet and blankets waiting for him. 'You'll see nothing, mind. No one is daft enough to be out here at night,' he said. 'We're safe as the dead.'

'I'm not looking for men who might kill us,' Mun said, scanning the bristling moor, the chill wind in his face, causing his eyes to water. 'I'm looking for men whom we might kill.'

'I'll send Goffe up in an hour,' O'Brien said, raising a hand as he picked his way back down the hill, the edges of the fire-light spilling the colour back into his red breeches and russet cloak.

And two days later, Mun got his wish.

It was by Mun's reckoning late afternoon. Before long the rooks and crows would be winging back to their roosts. Not that there were any birds to be seen, nor deer nor fox nor rabbit, nor any other living thing, because the weather was so foul. Freezing rain lashed the heath, running down men's necks, soaking hats and cloaks and souls. It had even worked through the leather of Mun's boots so that his feet were going numb. The wind came in sharp gusts, one following another like waves on the sea, snatching the last stubborn brown leaves from oaks and whipping them high into the freezing day.

'I'll be glad to get out of this wee draught,' O'Brien said through a grimace, nodding ahead to the woodland that stood on the rising ground like a bastion against the elements. 'Being cold is one thing. Jesus knows being wet is no fun. But both together and it'll wipe the smile off a butcher's dog.'

'Let us hope that whoever they are they've already got a blaze going and some meat over it,' John Cole said with a predatory smile, for they were not riding to the woods simply to get out of the storm. Earlier in the day they had come across a party of peat-cutters from a village near Pennington, who had told of a mounted column, some twenty to thirty men heading south towards Leigh.

Like all peat-diggers they had been lean, hard-looking men, bent over in their wide wet trench, treading spades into the turf, and their having no possessions worth stealing made them doughty enough as Mun and his ragged troop had ridden up. But their leader, a grey-bearded man, the creases of his face black with earth, was no fool and answered every question Mun asked of him. The man could not be sure because the column had been a distance off, but some of the riders, he said, had seemed to have orange scarves about their waists or across one shoulder. And orange was Parliament's colour.

And so Mun had turned his troop south and the day had turned vile and it had not been long before they had picked up the tracks the column had scored into the soft earth. Amongst the hoof prints there were wheel ruts, which had pleased the men for two reasons. First, it meant that the column could not outrun them, and second, it meant that the chances were their cart carried something worth having.

'With any luck they'll have a barrel or two of ale,' Allen Godfrey said, rain dripping from the wispy tuft sprouting from his chin, 'or better still beer.'

'In Heaven, boys, there is no beer,' O'Brien sang in a deep, round voice, 'and that is why we drink it here.'

Mun smiled. 'You think you're going to Heaven, you Irish rogue?' he asked, looking ahead, eyes ranging along the treeline, for if the column knew they were being followed the trees would make a good place to spring an ambush.

'And why not, I ask you?' O'Brien said. 'It is my aim to get into Heaven a full day before the Devil knows I'm dead.' There were a few low chuckles at this and O'Brien gave young Godfrey a smile and a wink as Mun raised a hand to halt the troop.

The trees ahead were mostly oak, birch and beech, and their leaves being gone there was little cover in which to hide, but that did not mean there were not men with loaded firelocks behind the wide trunks or hidden amongst the pollarded boughs.

Mun swept the sodden cap off his head and stuffed it into his left bucket-top boot. Then he took his helmet from its leather wrapping behind his saddle, sweeping his long wet hair back before putting it on and tying the leather thong beneath his chin with freezing fingers.

'Shall we take a look, O'Brien?' he suggested, tapping his heels against Hector's flanks and drawing his sword, for he did not trust his powder to be dry. The stallion tossed his head and moved off, hooves trudging through downtrodden russet bracken.

The Irishman had already put his helmet on. 'I'll save you a drop, lads,' he said, urging his mare forward and pulling his poll-axe from its scabbard against his saddle, 'if I'm not so drunk that I forget.'

Entering the woods Mun noted the slant of the rain and checked the wind's direction.

'It's sweeping behind us,' O'Brien said, bringing the poll-axe up towards his own face, 'then coming up in a twist right into our faces.' He lifted his buttocks and farted loudly. 'An awkward, if not damned impossible wind to stalk in.'

Mun leant over, forcing a globule of spit through pursed lips. The wind dashed it off past his right ear.

'At least they won't smell us coming,' he said, which would have been a very real risk had the wind been blowing the stink of his thirty unwashed troopers into the woods.

A handful of wet leaves slapped into O'Brien's face and he cursed, pawing them away. 'With any luck we'll hear them before they hear us,' he said.

Mun nodded. Squinting against the whipping wind his eyes scoured the wood either side of the new tracks that led into its depths. A pair of ravens croaked somewhere out in the gloom and the wind began to keen. Despite the lashing rain, old wind-blasted snow lay frozen on the leeward side of beech and oak trunks. There was no sign of danger, nothing to suggest the column they were tracking even suspected it was being followed. But Mun could not risk his men. They had fought like devils for him, endured cold and hunger and filth, and he would not lead them into a trap.

'They'll thank you for it,' O'Brien said, and it occurred to Mun that the Irishman was becoming altogether too good at reading his thoughts. 'As my da used to say, a hundred times careful is better than one time dead.'

'Remind me how your father died, O'Brien,' Mun said, tearing his eyes from the woods to look at the Irishman.

Beneath the dripping rim of his three-bar pot O'Brien's eyes widened. 'He was labouring on a castle in County Clare when a cartload of limestone upset,' he said. 'A wheel hit a divot, as they do. Da put his shoulder into it, thought he could stop the thing tipping.' He shook his head. 'The daft bastard. It crushed him.' He shrugged. 'He was a wise man, my da, even if now and then he forgot that he was.'

'At least there's no fear of you forgetting that you're a wise man,' Mun said. The Irishman frowned at that, trying to pick the insult out of it, and Mun was about to turn and ride back to his waiting men when a blur half a stone's throw away caught his eye. It was a stoat, pure white but for its pitch-black tail, dashing across their path and then stopping dead, its head turning every which way. Then the creature must have caught the scent of its prey for it sprang away and vanished down some unseen hole.

'That little bugger's coat would have been fit for the King,' O'Brien said, red brows arched. ''Tis not often you see a pure ermine like that. I'd call that a good omen, if I wasn't such a God-fearing man.'

'It will be dark soon,' Mun said, glancing up at the leaden, rain-filled sky. 'We need to hit them now before they make camp and set a watch.' He had been wondering if it might be better to wait until nightfall and attack his prey then, but he knew that driving rain makes men careless, for they are too busy being miserable. Besides which, while it was still on the move the column's own noise, along with that of the wind and rain, would cover his approach until they were upon the enemy.

'It'll be a steel job.' O'Brien gestured with his poll-axe. 'Half the firelocks won't bloody fire in this mess.'

Mun nodded, clicking his tongue and turning Hector back towards the rain-flayed moor. Where his wolves were waiting.

CHAPTER SIX

'THEY'VE SEEN US,' JOHN COLE SAID, PULLING HIS SWORD FROM ITS scabbard. It was a brutal-looking weapon, its curved blade ending in a falchion-type point, and Mun had seen Cole kill with it many times.

'Hold!' Mun looked left and right along the crescent his troop had formed so that they could sweep in on the enemy and hit them all together. 'Wait for my word,' he said, peering through the gathering gloom at the column up ahead, roughly mapping the route Hector would take when he gave the order to charge. The wood thinned here, larger trees – oaks, beech and elm – giving way to patches of dogwood with their last stubborn blood-red leaves and old berries, and slender birch. Which was why this was the place to strike, for horses could gain momentum here. Blades could slice down.

Mun's heart was pounding. Suddenly he was no longer cold, could not feel the freezing damp against his skin.

'We've got to do them now!' Cole hissed.

'Shut your mouth, Cole,' O'Brien growled.

The long note of a nuthatch pierced the moaning wind.

Mun could feel the blood coursing through his limbs; it thrummed as though full of bubbles, as though it were simmering up to the boil. But still he did not give the order.

'What are we waiting for, a bloody invitation?' O'Brien mumbled to his right. 'They'll be preparing us a nice welcome.'

Mun ignored his friend. 'Who's got good eyes?' he called, the rain drumming against his helmet, Hector's breath pluming upwards like that of all the other horses.

'Milward,' a trooper named Henry Jones called back. 'His eyesight is so good he reckons he can see the future.'

This raised some laughter but from throats not bellies, the sort that winds men tighter like a spanner on a wheellock, rather than dispersing tension.

'Tell me what's happening, Milward,' Mun called, his own eyes fixed on the rear of the column one hundred paces away that was a confusion of movement. Noise too, Mun supposed, but most of that was being caught by the storm and hurled up into a world of tempest and wind-whipped leaves.

'They're waving a banner but I can't make it out.'

'I can see the bloody banner!' Mun barked, yanking his reins, curbing Hector who wanted to be released to the madness. He knew every moment wasted could mean the death of one or more of his men, but something was staying his hand.

'Permission to cut them up, sir!' a trooper called Rowland Bide called.

'We go now, Mun, or we'll lose men,' O'Brien hissed.

So Mun hauled his heavy sword from its scabbard and held it aloft for all to see. He pressed with his left knee and tapped the foot against Hector's hip so that the stallion performed a side pass and he heard O'Brien offer up a prayer to the Virgin.

'For God and King Charles!' Mun yelled, and Hector neighed like a prince amongst horses and all along the bowed line naked steel glowed dully in the rain.

And then he heard it.

'Hold!' he yelled, his left hand holding his reins tight as Hector whinnied in complaint.

'Hold, damn you!' O'Brien roared to those men who a heart-beat before had given their spurs and now fought to halt their mounts. The Irishman glared at Mun. 'Bloody drums?' he said. 'With a troop of horse?'

Mun was hauling Hector left and right, the beast snorting and squealing as Mun kept snapping his head round to front, straining to see through the hammering rain what was going on in the clearing up ahead. The men of the rebel column had dismounted in the way of dragoons, their horses being led to their rear whilst they arrayed themselves amongst the trees, finding what cover they could. But not a shot had been fired and Mun assumed that his enemies' firelocks would be just as unpredictable as theirs in this downpour.

Then two men came forward, each beating a drum which he wore high up on his left side, suspended by a leather belt over his right shoulder.

'It's the Parley so it is,' O'Brien said through gritted teeth, fighting to control his own mare.

'I know what it is,' Mun growled, for he had been with the King's army long enough to recognize the calls of war, those distinctive rhythms that beat out amidst the chaos of battle, relaying orders that were otherwise lost in the snarl of it all.

'So are you going to talk to them?' O'Brien asked, thrusting his poll-axe through the deluge towards the enemy. 'Or are we going to ride in there and gut the whoresons?'

Mun cursed under his breath. His indecision had already cost them the advantage. He could not know exactly how many men made up the rebel column and he had lost the element of surprise. If he gave the order to attack now he would lose men. And their blood would be on his hands.

'Yes, I'm going to talk.' He rammed his sword back into its scabbard and urged Hector forward. 'If it's a trap, kill the bastards, Clancy,' he said, as rain lashed against his helmet, running in streams off the lip in front of each cheek piece, and along the rim, pouring down onto the neck of his buff-coat. And the drummers walked towards him, the deeply resonant beat of the Parley almost bewitching in that gloaming world in which a damp fog was rising, beginning to curl amongst the trees. The air was cloyed with the sweet scent of rotting wood and the tang of the wet metal against his face, as he walked Hector towards the drummers, not looking at those men but rather beyond them, trying to get an idea of his enemy's strength.

Then the drums fell silent and one of the drummers stopped but the other kept walking. Mun recognized in the man an air of steadiness, a quality required of drummers who, if they were to panic or run, could fatally compromise their regiment's cohesion.

The only sounds now were the hiss of the rain and the whinnies and snorts of horses, as Mun walked another fifteen paces and then stopped, leaving the drummer to make up the remaining ground.

'God and the King!' the drummer declared, holding Mun's eye as he pushed the big drum round onto his back and gripped the sticks in an easy fashion across his waist. 'Sir Edmund Rivers, I presume.' He gave a curt nod of greeting, the face behind the neat beard firm, showing no sign of fear.

Mun was taken aback. 'Who are you?' he demanded. 'How do you know me?'

'I am Sergeant Cuthbert Boxe, drummer in Sir Jacob, Lord Astley's Regiment of Foot,' the man said, and the rain was not so loud on Mun's helmet that he did not hear the hard edge of pride in the drummer's introduction, as good an indication that the man was telling the truth as Mun could hope for.

'Then you are supposed to be in Oxford with the King, Sergeant Boxe,' Mun said, picking out the man's comrades amongst the birch trees and brambles up ahead, seeing none of the orange scarves the peat-digger had spoken of.

'We have been looking for you these last four weeks, Sir Edmund,' Boxe said. 'Naturally we went to Shear House first. Lady Rivers fed and watered us but could not say where you were, only that you were out hunting.' The ghost of a smile flashed in the drummer's eyes. 'My master assumed that fox was not your prey.'

'Lord Astley assumed right,' Mun said.

'Not Lord Astley, sir. We are under another's command. Temporarily.'

Mun shrugged. 'Whilst Essex recruits in London and His Majesty waits out the winter in Oxford, Lancashire remains the battleground. We bleed the rebels at every opportunity.'

Boxe's montero-cap was soaked through, water running from it into his beard, from which it dripped in a fast rhythm the drummer would have been hard pressed to mimic.

'Will you give up the hunt long enough to speak with my master, sir?' Boxe asked, cuffing rain and snot from his nose.

'That depends on who your master is,' Mun answered.

Boxe's brows knitted together. 'Truth be told, I haven't a bloody clue,' he said, 'save to say he told me to tell you that you have met more than once, and that you have a mutual friend.'

'That's it?' Mun asked. Hector snorted and Mun understood the stallion's derision.

Boxe nodded. 'If you would be so kind as to follow me, Sir Edmund, I will take you to my master.'

'What's in your cart?' Mun asked.

Boxe frowned. 'Provender for man and beast. Some powder and shot. Nothing too exciting. Your Major Radcliffe at Shear House said we would never find you out here. Said that you would find us. So my master had us bring the cart to lure you out. He reckoned it would make us look a tastier morsel.'

'Had you been rebels the cart would have made no difference. I would have killed you anyway,' Mun said, patting Hector's wet neck. 'Have your master bring a barrel of ale when he comes to meet me. You do have ale?'

'We do,' Boxe admitted, almost smiling.

'I will be waiting with my men at the wood's edge,' Mun said, then turned Hector and walked back through the mustering gloom, the blood in his veins slowing and turning cold again now. Because the men they had tracked were not rebels and there would be no butchery that night.

'Prince Rupert is taking the fight to the enemy,' the man said with a sniff, dragging a sopping sleeve across his hook nose. They sat on blankets beneath a crude canvas shelter rigged between four birch trees and Mun regarded the man opposite him. He looked utterly miserable and Mun saw that he was shivering though trying to hide it. 'Whilst the peace talks continue, Rupert strikes into the enemy heartland, determined through his vigour and martial zeal to win political advantage on the battlefield.' Those hawk's eyes bored into Mun's. 'He fights whilst you and your men roam the moor like common brigands.'

'And yet I hear the rebels call *him* Prince Robber,' Mun said, raising a cup of ale to his lips and sipping the bitter draught, savouring the taste of it on his tongue. 'The ones I meet tend not to live long enough to insult me.'

'So I have heard,' Hook Nose admitted with an expression that held neither admiration nor condemnation. All around them Mun's men were busy making what shelters they could, ground sheets and bad-weather gear strung up to keep off the worst of the rain. They talked in low voices, moaning about rust on helmets, back-and-breasts and sword scabbards. They complained about the lack of hot food, decent beer and the want of women, so that Mun thought for all that they looked like a horde of murderous thieves, they sounded just like any other soldiers.

'My men were nervous, I don't mind telling you,' the man went on, shifting out of the way of a torrent of water that was pouring off the canvas onto the muddy ground by his left leg. 'They feared you would simply attack without warning or first allowing us to offer our surrender.'

'I would have done if not for this damned weather pissing

on our powder,' Mun said, choosing not to mention that there had been other doubts, or at least some unexplained feeling, which had stopped him falling on the column as he had on so many others.

Prince Rupert's man sneezed three times, his face gripped in a strange rictus as he anticipated a fourth explosion, which never came. Mun had recognized him straight away, unlike when last they had met. That had been at Oxford and the man had been in Rupert's company the night the Prince had given Mun leave to ride north home to Shear House which was then under siege. But Mun had seen him once before that, on the road to Lathom. Lord Denton's son Henry and some others had dragged Minister George Green from his house, accusing him of being a secret but practising Catholic. Mun, Tom and their father had tried to stop Denton, but they had failed and Green had been hanged. And worse. And the shivering man before him, this agent of the Crown, had been at the heart of it all, had played his part conducting an exemplary campaign against Catholics and those suspected of spreading papism. Likely he had been at George Green's hanging. On a colder day than this.

'This God-forsaken winter will be the death of me,' the spy said, flexing slender fingers as though he feared he might lose the use of his hands. Just to look at this man, Mun knew he would not trust him. That the Prince's agent was a friend of the Dentons made Mun all but despise him. Their persecution of Minister Green and the horror of seeing him hanged, coupled with Lord Denton's cruel use of Martha when she had sought his mercy for her father, had driven the girl to suicide. This in turn had led Tom to turn his back on his family and his king in the pursuit of revenge.

'The Prince and six thousand men took Cirencester in four hours,' the man went on, 'and marched back to his uncle with one thousand prisoners as well as much-needed arms and provisions.'

'That was well done,' Mun acknowledged with a nod. 'Cirencester gains the King a stronghold between Oxford and his rich recruiting grounds in the north-west and Wales.'

'And allows us to growl at Bristol and Gloucester,' the man added, glancing at O'Brien and Cole who were trying and failing, it seemed, to get a fire going near by.

'Where is the Prince now?' Mun asked.

'When I left, His Highness was rampaging through Hampshire. But now I expect he is striking terror into our enemies in the Midlands.'

'The Midlands? So not all of the King's regiments are bottled up in Oxford waiting for spring.'

'Rupert rides to Yorkshire to meet with Her Royal Majesty who is returned from the Continent with men and weapons,' Hook Nose said. 'On his way north he means to carve himself a corridor, thus ensuring the convoy a safe return journey with its precious load.'

'The weapons?' Mun deliberately goaded.

'The Queen,' the agent snapped waspishly, as though, the weather being foul as it was, he did not need Mun compounding his considerable irritation.

'I still don't know your name,' Mun said.

The miserable man drew his narrow, sloping shoulders even closer together, if that were possible, and Mun felt his own contempt for him bristle across his back like a dog's hackles. Any friend of the Dentons was no friend of Mun's. Despite being near neighbours the two families had never got along; Lord Denton's son Henry had been Mun and Tom's enemy since they were all boys running wild. That made this man a bastard by association if nothing else.

But there was plenty else, Mun suspected.

'My name is unimportant, Sir Edmund.' A full-blown shiver ran from the top of his head to his toes. 'We both serve God and our king, and that is enough.' He smiled then and it seemed almost genuine. 'Even though our methods . . . our roles in this

80

play, if you will . . . are very different. In fact, you might say I am one of those whose talents remain hidden from the crowd. The scenery changes and the players play on.' He lifted his cloak and with two fingers fished inside his doublet's sleeve, pulling out a handkerchief. 'I change the scenery, Sir Edmund. I leave the spilling of blood to others.'

It was clear that that last was aimed at Mun and he accepted the bait. 'I am spilling no blood sitting here with you,' he said, 'so what is it that you want with me?'

'Indeed, let us come directly to the point. The Prince wants you to do something for him. He needs a man he can trust.'

'The Prince barely knows me,' Mun said, 'and I fail to believe he would choose me for any task.'

'The task is of a sensitive nature. We need the right sort of men.'

Mun glanced around, feeling a smile find its way onto his lips. 'Men that look like cut-throats and villains?'

'Just such.' The agent secreted the handkerchief back up his sleeve. 'Your men's wild aspect is what makes them perfect for the purpose.' He looked over to where O'Brien and Cole had at last managed to nurture a flame into life, the feathered kindling beginning to catch. O'Brien, looking like a half-drowned troll, growled a satisfied curse. 'The Prince wanted to ask your friend Osmyn Hooker first but the man was nowhere to be found.'

'Hooker is no friend of mine,' Mun said.

The face before him looked surprised. 'Is that so? And yet the man won you back your estate.'

'I'd sooner trust a mastiff with my meat pie,' Mun said.

'And there's another man who comes highly recommended. A fierce-looking fellow. Captain Stryker.'

'I've heard of him,' Mun said.

'I dare say, but Stryker is already engaged on the Crown's business. So here we are.'

'I am also busy serving the Crown, as you can see,' Mun

said, sweeping an arm across his wolfpack's makeshift den. 'I kill rebels.'

'You were supposed to ride south and join us at Windsor weeks ago. Once Shear House was safe you had your orders to return to your regiment, not skulk around the moors like a rogue hound.'

'The war goes on here,' Mun said.

'I could have you up on a charge for desertion, God knows—'

'Be careful, friend,' Mun said, returning the man's intense stare. 'You are far from your comforts and I do not take kindly to threats from men without name or rank. For all I know you could be the keeper of the Prince's chamber pot.' The man's lip curled at that insult but he held his tongue. 'Until I know that my family and estates are safe from rebels I will continue to . . . hunt.'

The man turned his face and looked out at the gathering dusk. The rain was slowing but the fog was thickening and the air was turning even colder.

'Your brother Thomas is a traitor, is he not? An impulsive young man as I recall.' Mun bristled, clenching his teeth so as not to take this bait. 'I have heard a rumour, and I am certain it is just a rumour, that Thomas Rivers, second son of Sir Francis Rivers who died bravely trying to save the King's standard, was one of those prisoners that escaped from our camp at Meriden.' He frowned. 'You recall? Someone blew up that powder cache and in the confusion the rebels were sprung from their gaol.'

'I remember,' Mun said, holding the man's eye.

'A terrible business,' the spy said, glaring at him. 'The perpetrators were never found and the Prince took the whole thing very badly, considered it a monstrous insult that the miscreants thought they could carry out their brazen act under his very nose and get away with it.'

'They did get away with it,' Mun said, aware of his own heartbeat, hoping that his eyes gave away nothing. For with the help of the mercenary Osmyn Hooker, Mun and Emmanuel had broken the five rebel prisoners out of their gaol that night. They had made traitors of themselves and risked everything. Because one of those rebels had been Tom, and Nehemiah Boone, Mun's captain – another bastard in Mun's book – would have seen Tom hanged the next day and taken altogether too much pleasure in it.

'Indeed,' Rupert's man said. 'I have been considering hiring Mr Hooker to find out who was responsible. He is a very resourceful fellow. When one can find him.' He knows, Mun thought. Or at least he suspects. 'Can you imagine what would happen to the men if they were found? Especially if, as is suspected, they are King's men.' He raised an eyebrow. 'You recall what we did to the traitor Blake, the Prince's personal secretary?'

'I watched him hang,' Mun said. 'He deserved it.'

Hook Nose's eyes flicked from left to right, taking in every aspect of Mun's face, like maggots trying to wriggle deeper inside flesh. 'Enough of rebels and traitors,' he said. 'Let us get back to the issue of *your* duty. Furthermore, if duty is not in itself enough to lure you away from this desolate, freezing land, if that fruit is yet too tart, let me sprinkle some sugar in the pie. If you perform the service that we require of you, your reward will be not ungenerous. I am sure Mr Hooker's services cost you dear, even though I had agreed with him to settle that account.' He tilted his head then, gauging Mun's reaction to that.

That bastard Hooker, Mun thought, for with the rebels beaten the mercenary had indeed duped him into draining his family's silver reserves, just as Mun had suspected at the time. '*You* paid Hooker?' Mun asked.

The agent nodded. 'You only got Hooker and his men be-cause of me. It was my doing.' He wafted long white fingers through the numbing air. 'But that is not important now.'

Mun's head was spinning. He felt nauseated by the thought that this man had been manipulating events all along. Perhaps

Hook Nose had had it from Osmyn Hooker's own lips that it had been Mun who had broken the rebel prisoners out at Meriden, but here was someone who would only use that leverage when he needed it.

Could he even have fashioned the rope that had hanged George Green? Surely not, Mun thought. And yet somehow this man, whose name he did not even know, had manoeuvred him into a position of weakness, something the rebels had been unable to do since Mun had broken the siege of Shear House and begun to hunt them across the moors, forests and valleys of Lancashire.

Mun looked at his men now as they came out of their shelters to add fuel to, and gather by, O'Brien's fire, the rain having all but stopped. They were good men. Mun knew that they would follow him.

Then he looked back at the man before him, who looked nothing much but was as dangerous as a blade in the dark.

'What is it that you need me to do?' he said.

Bess did not like Alexander Dane. The man was arrogant. Or else plain rude. He had arrived at her grandfather the earl's house just after midday and with a pallor that only accentuated the dark circles burrowed beneath his eyes. His breeches, shirt, doublet and cloak had about them all the neatness of having been slept in and his whole appearance slurred of a night drenched in ale.

'By God, man, you're still at your altitudes!' Lord Heylyn had remarked as Dane dismounted from a sorry-looking Welsh cob, snagging his foot in the stirrup and all but falling on his face. He muttered a curse at his horse, which lifted its head and snorted as if to say it had heard it all before, then he bent, placing his hands on his knee, and Bess thought he would vomit. Instead, he spat into the mud, dragged a gloved hand across his mouth and stood up nearly straight, his broad-hat in a worse condition even than Joe's.

'My lord, if you had seen the strumpet I was forced to share my bed with last night you would have downed a cask of the first water just to get over the shock.' Stifling a belch he glanced at Bess and Joe, then looked back to Lord Heylyn, suspicion thinning his eyes as he removed his hat and raked dark hair off his face.

'Your father would be ashamed,' Bess's grandfather said, though he had only just finished a jug of malmsey himself.

Dane squinted at the sky. 'At this hour my father would have still been in his cups with a whore on each knee, my lord, as well you know,' he replied through a scowl, hitching back his cloak, so that Bess could see two pistols tucked in a belt and a brutal-looking sword scabbarded at his left hip. The sword was nothing special but Bess knew enough about weapons to know that the firelocks were of good quality, easily the most expensive items about his person, and that included the cob.

'I have a job for you, Dane,' the earl had said, pulling his own thick cloak tight around himself, his grey-flecked hair ruffling in the chill wind. 'You still owe me, for all you seem to squander every penny that comes your way. This is my grand-daughter Elizabeth,' he said, gesturing to Bess, 'and she means to find her brother, my grandson, who is currently enlisted with Essex's rebels.'

The dark points that were Dane's eyes grew at that, though Bess could not tell which bit of what her grandfather had said interested him more – the fact that she was his granddaughter, or that his grandson was a traitor.

'You are to accompany my granddaughter, however long it takes, and make sure that no harm comes to her. You will have money enough to last, so long as you don't piss it all away.'

'And the boy?' Dane said, at which a flush spread across Joe's face.

Lord Heylyn shrugged. 'He is no concern of mine. Keep my granddaughter from harm. Whatever it takes,' he said, the word *whatever* the ballast of the command.

Dane had seemed indifferent to the task being asked of him, preoccupied instead with the misery of his self-inflicted condition. On top of this he struck Bess as disrespectful, inattentive and slovenly, which made the prospect of travelling in his company not in the least bit appealing. Still, she had Joe, who if anything seemed to like Dane even less than she. Furthermore – and this made her heart sing, threw light upon the world and vanquished a great shadow – she had succeeded in prevailing on her grandfather to help. Somehow she had done that. She would find Tom and Tom would be pardoned. Then they would weave the broken threads of her family back together and make the picture whole again. No, not whole. Never so. But it would be a new beginning.

Thus had they provisioned and set off south from Kingsley that very day with the aim of travelling the ten or so miles to Winsford before dark. Part of Bess wished she had brought her own mare, Chryseis, but she had feared that such a fine-looking horse would bring her unwanted attention and so she had taken a bay called Millicent, who was usually ridden by servants running errands in the village or Ormskirk. Lord Heylyn had provided them with a good-tempered dun mare to help carry provender for man and beast as well as spare furs and waterproofed canvases should they for some reason find themselves sleeping underneath the stars. Dane, Bess noticed, now wore a buff-coat, though made sure it was covered by his bad-weather cloak and a ratty old bear skin which he wore across his shoulders, so that on his short-legged cob he looked more like some grizzled, itinerant pedlar than someone in whose hands you would place your safety.

For the most part the man kept his mouth shut and his thoughts to himself and this was fine by Bess, fine by Joe too, she suspected from the young musketeer's silence. He was sulking, she knew, presumably because he felt his position as her protector usurped, and Bess had given up another prayer, an utterance steeped in frustration, that they might find Tom soon, before such gloomy company made of their venture some sort of purgation.

And yet Alexander Dane's stony-faced silence irked her, too, for how could the man have no questions? How could anyone show such scant interest in her purpose or in the charge commanded of him?

They overnighted in a hostelry in Winsford, the men sharing a room adjoining Bess's, and set off next morning at dawn along the River Weaver's eastern bank, the rising April sun on their left cheeks making white blooms of each breath. Bess had spent the first mile wondering if Dane would exhibit a more affable temperament now that he should have at least recovered from his indulgences of two nights before. But by the third mile it was quite clear to her that the man was simply a boor and even that acceptance was a knife in her heart, because it made her think of Emmanuel, good, joyful Emmanuel, and how lucky she had been to love him and be loved by him.

CHAPTER SEVEN

'I STILL DON'T SEE WHY WE COULDN'T HAVE RIDDEN THE FIRST forty-five miles and walked the last ten,' Weasel griped, sharply tugging the halter of the ass he was leading, as though it were the animal's fault that they were footsore and comfortless. 'Might as well have bloody enlisted with the musketeers.'

'I'd give you a week before you forgot about the match between your fingers, stuck your hand in the black powder and blew yourself to Kingdom Come,' Trencher said, sweeping his cap from his head and mopping his slick brow with it.

'I don't know what you're moaning about, you little runt,' Dobson said to Weasel. 'Try pushing this damn thing half a mile and then let's see what you've got to say about it.'

Tom suspected it was time someone else took a turn pushing the handcart but said nothing, enjoying seeing the big man's pride take him further with it than he ought to have gone. It was dusk and they had been on the road since dawn, so that Tom knew they would have to lie up for the night before long.

'When we get to that oak tree yonder, I'll take the cart,' Guillaume Scarron said, his English thick with French, 'and after me Tristan will take it.'

'He's all right for another mile yet, Scarron,' Tom said, lifting his chin towards Dobson who muttered something foul under his breath.

'Well, this bloody beast stinks like a dead dog left out in the rain,' Weasel said, 'and I've been downwind of it ever since Stokenchurch.' Each man had a knapsack slung across his back in which he carried spare clothing, money, flint, steel and charcloth, a wooden bowl and spoon, a leather bottle and some other essentials for the journey, but the ass was saddled with more knapsacks containing food, blankets and dry tinder. The animal also carried five skins full of small beer, two large mattocks and a pickaxe.

'I doubt the beast likes your stink any more than you like his,' Penn put in, 'yet you don't hear him complaining.'

Just then the ass flared its nostrils, opened its mouth and brayed, startling a pair of pigeons that clapped into the darkening sky and raising laughter from the small band of stonemasons on the road to Oxford. Except, only three of the men were real masons: Guillaume Scarron the master stonemason, and his two companions – one a squat, square-headed carver of marble named de Gombaud, and the other Scarron's apprentice, a dark-haired, fine-featured young man named Tristan. All three were Frenchmen and like many of their profession they spent their lives travelling across England from one great house-building project to the next. But the war had put paid to many such building ambitions and now the three men, originally from the village of Brimont five miles to the north of Reims, found themselves in the employ of one Captain Crafte of Parliament's army and earning more, Tom guessed, for not shaping stone than they would working on some cathedral or lord's hall.

'No horses, no firelocks or swords or any of a soldier's accoutrements,' Crafte had told Tom and his small band of volunteers, 'for you must appear to all the world no different from any company of roaming masons and labourers, though you may of course bear what crude weapons are common to such fellows.'

'No weapons?' Trencher had blurted, turning to Tom, his eyes bulging incredulously.

'We'll not get into Oxford looking like this, Will,' Penn had said, rapping his knuckles against his breastplate.

'We'll never make it to Oxford at all without bloody steel and shot,' Weasel had said through a grimace.

'Once inside the city you will be supplied with arms. Thomas has received the necessary instructions,' Crafte had said, and all eyes had turned to Tom then.

'We're to keep our mouths shut in company.' Tom had laid the greater weight of his gaze on Weasel. 'The masons we'll be travelling with are French and—'

'French!' A yawp from Trencher. 'Why don't we invite the Pope along while we're at it?'

Tom had ignored this. 'By keeping our mouths shut and letting our companions make any necessary introductions, we shouldn't arouse suspicion.'

'The last thing we want is your being recruited into a company of the King's musketeers,' Crafte had explained humourlessly. 'Being French should spare you that particular indignity.'

'I think I'd rather be taken for a Cavalier than a Frenchman,' Dobson had muttered, raising his brows at Trencher.

'It's not too late to change your minds,' Tom had said, glancing at each of them in turn and not caring much either way, for he would go to Oxford whatever their decision, alone if it came to it.

Trencher had folded stout arms over his barrel chest. 'Oh yes, and stay here locked up till you've either clobbered the Cavaliers' newsbook or been strung up by your ballocks?' he suggested. 'No thank you, Thomas. And more to the point, if we've got snail-gobblers running around the country some-one needs to keep an eye on them.' Then he had looked back to Captain Crafte and held out a meaty palm. 'Where's my damned mallet?'

Next day, Tom, Trencher, Penn, Weasel and Dobson had

been introduced to Guillaume Scarron and his men. Captain Crafte had found the masons at a sandstone quarry in Godstone village some thirty-something miles to the south-east. The Frenchmen had been living in a draughty, timber-framed, bracken-roofed lodge built into the semi-circular, scarred wall of tawny stone, and the main reason Crafte had chosen them for the mission – other than their being French – was that they had appeared the least drunken of a very drunken company. It was not hard to imagine the scene that must have greeted Crafte, for Tom had seen such a travelling band working on Emmanuel's house in Shevington. That ruin had belonged to Cockersand Abbey, before King Henry had changed all that, and Tom had not disagreed with his father's assertion that the masons labouring in Emmanuel's employ might be reckoned the lewdest and worst-conditioned fellows that one could expect to meet.

'They will drink more in one day than three days' wages will come to,' Sir Francis had warned Emmanuel, 'and you must all but take up your crop to rouse them from their drunken stupor.'

And now Tom and the others were to imitate such men so as not to provoke suspicion amongst any that they should meet on the road to Oxford and on entering the city.

'At least it's not raining,' Penn said cheerily, slapping Dobson's back, so that a cloud of yellow stone dust puffed up from his tunic. 'I've got no drill and no corporals yapping in my ears and that's good enough for me.' In the meadows either side of the worn track, sheep bleated, dogs barked and shepherds whistled. Clusters of men and women were still out in the fallow fields spreading manure and others were strung out in lines, bent over, dibbing peas and beans by the last of the light.

'If you don't mind looking like a crump-backed bloody shabbaroon,' Trencher remarked, taking a swig from his leather flask. For Crafte's ruse was more elaborate than simply having Tom and his companions dress in dishevelled, dust-ingrained breeches and doublets. Like all the stonemasons Tom had seen, the three Frenchmen were lopsided in appearance, Scarron most of all, the muscles of their mallet arms being overdeveloped from years of hard use. So Crafte had made them wrap swaths of linen round their upper right arms and shoulders beneath their shirts to create the masons' disproportional bulk. Scarron and de Gombaud wore tough leather gloves, but the rest had bound their hands in grubby linen rags or thin leather strips and all had rubbed stone dust into beards, faces and hair, so that Tom thought the only apparent characteristic they did not share with the real masons – one which afflicted Scarron more than the other two, he noticed – was the cough that announced itself all too often, caused by years of breathing the airborne gritty powder of the quarry.

Dobson let go the cart's handles and the thing thumped down, rattling the assortment of mauls, gavelocks, kevels, and chisels within the canvas knapsacks stowed in the cart bed. Scarron cursed at the tools' treatment, but though he was a big man he was not a killer like Dobson and had the sense to know it.

'Done my bit and more.' Dobson pushed big hands into the small of his back, looking up to the sky as though waiting for the Divine to reward him. Instead, a murder of rooks and crows swept above them eastwards in a dark riotous cloud, heading for their roosts. The sun had gone and the sky was grey blue and streaked with cloud the colour of cooked salmon flesh.

'Give it 'ere then, you big girl,' Trencher said, but Scarron raised a palm and went muttering to the handcart, lifting it with the fluid ease of long practice and setting off, shaking his head with Gallic disapproval.

'You're welcome,' Dobson growled after him, sharing a look of disgust with Weasel, who hawked and spat a green string onto the track.

'Hard to think of war with springtide in the air,' Penn

announced, slapping the bulbous end of his wooden club against the leather-bound palm of his left hand. They all carried some such crude weapon as protection against outlaws and every ten or so paces Penn would toss his club so that it turned once end over end then catch it neatly. It was a habit which Tom had been tiring of for the last two miles. 'That was a winter I'll happily forget,' Penn went on. 'Froze my nutmegs off a dozen times.'

'Old Jack Frost did well to find your gingamabobs, lad,' Trencher replied, shooting Tom a grin. But something else had caught Tom's eye: a smithy, perhaps a mile away on the near edge of a clutter of dwellings spreading northwards along the fringes of woodland. There was barely a breeze to talk of but what there was came from the west, bringing with it the faint ring of hammer on anvil and dogs barking. Smoke curled into the sky, a dun smear against amethyst, and far away figures could be seen making their way back towards the village, some of them driving sheep or cattle.

'Crafte never said we had to sleep under hedges, did he?' Dobson said, his own club – a three-foot length of ash with a six-inch nail through its end – resting on one massive shoulder. 'No point in waking damp as a whore's crotch if we don't need to.'

'Aye, a bed of clean straw is all a weasel needs,' Weasel said, knuckling snot from the end of his pointy nose. 'Not much to ask.'

'We can't risk it,' Trencher put in. 'I'm surprised we've not met any King's men as it is.' He nodded towards the settlement. 'But if we go upsetting any locals we'll have a troop of dragoons on us in the time it takes to fill a piss pot.'

'Then we won't upset any locals,' Dobson suggested with a shrug.

'Trencher's right,' Tom admitted reluctantly, for he would have chosen a bed or some old straw in a barn over another night under the stars. 'The less attention we draw to ourselves the more chance we've got of getting into the city. We don't need people asking questions. Not unless your French has improved since we left Richmond, Dobson.'

'Can't be so hard if this lot can bloody speak it,' Dobson grumbled, at which de Gombaud muttered a filthy oath which Tom was relieved none of his companions understood.

'We'll overnight in those woods. Keep ourselves to ourselves,' Tom said. 'We can't be many miles from Oxford.' He looked up to see the first stars pulsing like embers immeasurably far above the streaks of grey cloud. 'It won't rain tonight.'

'It rains much in England,' Tristan said, the young Frenchman's first words of English since leaving Richmond.

'If you don't like our rain why don't you bugger off back to France?' Weasel suggested, at which Tristan pursed full lips and scratched his short black beard as though he was considering doing just that.

In time, they were into the woodland and looking for a good place to make camp a fair stone's throw from any of the smooth mud tracks that spider-webbed through the woods. Rooks squabbled high up amongst the branches of beech and oak, but otherwise there was a stillness, in large part due to the lack of wind but also, Tom sensed, because it was the twilight hour, when the daylight creatures make themselves scarce and those of the night have yet to venture out. He and Scarron hefted a corner of the handcart on their shoulders whilst Trencher and de Gombaud held a handle each out above their heads because this was easier than pushing the thing over root tangles, deadfall and brambles. And by a big storm-felled elm from whose prostrate yet still living trunk sprouted a row of healthy new branches, they made camp for the night. As it had fallen the tree had wrenched up its roots along with a great circular clot of mud and this whole mass had mossed over, creating a wall behind which they could shelter. Penn soon had a fire going and small beer was being poured into cups and even the ass seemed happy enough relieved of its burden and tethered the other side of the fallen elm. Pipes were thumbed full of tobacco and lit and Tristan, who it turned out had no small skill for concocting something almost delicious from basic provisions, had won himself two new friends in Dobson and Trencher by the time the last light seeped from the world and the woods were given to the night.

And none of them had thought there would be blood.

Tom was woken by someone prodding a finger into his right shoulder. He opened his eyes to see de Gombaud's square face much too close to his own.

'I don't sleep,' the Frenchman whispered, so that Tom could smell tobacco on his beer-soured breath. 'Not enough to drink,' he said, answering Tom's glaring eyes as to why he was not snoring along with the rest who lay beneath blankets, their feet towards the fire that still popped and spat, working its way into a thick oak limb. They had not set a watch; had not thought it necessary, but Tom now suspected he'd got that wrong. 'People are here,' de Gombaud hissed, eyes wide, jerking his chin off towards the direction in which the great elm had fallen. 'They are . . . sneaking. Don't want us to listen them,' he said, tugging an earlobe. Tom pushed himself upright, noting that Trencher on his left and Penn on his right were as still as the dead. His heart was buffeting his breastbone, his lungs clenching on their breath to allow his ears to scour the night. Then, without another word and still crouching, de Gombaud brushed past Tom's left shoulder and scrambled over the fallen elm out of the reach of the fire's glow and was gone.

'Will, wake up,' Tom growled, grabbing hold of the two-foot-long cudgel he had carried in his belt since Richmond. The smooth ash was warm in his hand and he felt anger bloom in his gut, rising and spreading through his limbs with the promise of violence. 'We've got company, Will,' he hissed, knowing it was true though he had yet to hear or see the interlopers in the flesh. In a heartbeat Trencher was awake, his club in his hands, and Tom was waking Penn when the unmistakable click of a firelock being cocked stopped him cold.

'Don't move. Don't even piss yer breeches or ye'll be pickin' bits o' brains out yer muzzles.'

'Ballocks,' Dobson muttered, sitting up and scratching his bushy beard and taking in the sight before them. Five men stood in their camp, their wild-looking faces sheened by the fire's copper glow. The one who had spoken had a face as thin as a hatchet and looked as though a stiff breeze might knock him down. But he was the one holding the pistol and to Tom's eyes his thin arm looked steady enough that if he pulled the trigger Tom's insides would adorn the fallen tree behind him.

The other outlaws were armed with crude-looking blades but for one who held a blunderbuss, a weapon to inspire fear because, although it was short like a handgun, its bore was almost an inch, greater than a musket's.

'What do you want?' Tom said. 'We have nothing worth stealing.'

'Talk again and we'll kill the lot o' ye and piss on yer corpses,' Hatchet Face said, the skin stretched tight across his cheeks so that he looked like a living skeleton. Tom glared but held his tongue. 'My friend's dragon has seven balls down its throat,' the outlaw said, jerking his pistol across towards the grey-haired thief holding the blunderbuss. ''Tis his greatest pleasure in this world to fire the thing. He'd rather wave that thing around than put his cock in a nice warm notch, so ye don't want to be givin' him any reason to tickle its trigger.'

The grey-haired man hawked and spat a gobbet into the fire, where it sizzled as he grinned like a fiend waiting at Satan's elbow for a sinner of his own to torment.

Hatchet Face gestured for one of his other accomplices – a boy, perhaps even his son from the look of his long thin face – to go and see what treasures might be waiting for them in the handcart and he hitched across the clearing all but dragging a lame leg behind. The other two took this as their cue and edged closer to their victims in a move that spoke of long experience, their blades pointing threateningly, and Tom saw that all of his companions were awake now, rubbing eyes and trying to make sense of their situation.

'Tools,' the boy said, opening a sack to let the fire's glow reveal its contents. 'Hammers, chisels and the like.'

'We're stonemasons,' Scarron said. 'Our tools are all we have. Without them we cannot work.'

Hatchet Face turned his pistol on the Frenchman. 'Ye speak when I tell ye to speak, ye foreign bastard.'

'There's nothin' else, just tools,' the boy said disappointedly.

'We can sell 'em,' another outlaw said, his sword favouring Dobson and his ballock dagger pointing at Tristan who was closest to the wall of roots and earth ripped up from the ground.

Hatchet Face shot the man a withering look for stating the obvious, then looked back to Tom whilst gesturing with the pistol's barrel towards the empty bedroll between Dobson and Scarron. 'Where's yer friend, hey?'

'He's got the shits,' Tom said, as though that was answer enough, and the thief glanced off into the woods over Tom's head, teeth worrying the crooked line of his lips. Then he swept the filth-stained cap from his head and held it out like a beggar expecting charity.

'We'll have yer coin and finger rings if ye please,' he said. 'Nipper, load that ass with them tools and we'll be on our way.'

'Let's tear them apart,' Trencher growled under his breath beside Tom and from the corner of his eye Tom saw the big man's hand clench around the haft of the club by his side.

'Not yet, Will,' Tom murmured, his blood simmering in his veins, demanding savage action. But his limbs were rigid, awed by the promise of death whispered by the muzzle aimed at him, and so he denied his blood's appeal. And yet they must do something, for without their tools they stood far less chance of gaining employment in Oxford.

'Joe, do the honours,' Hatchet Face said, offering the up-turned cap to the man beside him, who nodded and took it, starting at the end of the line with Penn who, still sitting, emptied a fistful of coins into the cap.

The thief straightened his sword arm so that the blade's point was a hand's span from Penn's face.

'If that's not all of it I'll stick this cheese-toaster into your belly and give it a good twist,' he threatened theatrically, giving the impression that he had delivered the line many times before.

And then de Gombaud came back.

The Frenchman burst from the trees behind the man with the blunderbuss and the thief turned just as de Gombaud swung something two-handed – a pickaxe – and there was a boom as the spiked curved head erupted from the outlaw's back.

Hatchet Face fired wild and Tom felt the ball whip past his head as he scrambled to his feet and swung his cudgel at the fool who had just wasted his one shot, cracking the thief's skull open with the ferocity of the blow and sending him sprawling.

'Come here, you scab!' Trencher roared, throwing himself after another outlaw who had turned to flee, and Tom looked across to see the other swordsman backing off from Scarron, Weasel and Dobson who were edging towards him brandishing their own crude weapons.

'The boy!' Tom growled but Penn was already leaping the elm to chase after the lad who had limped off into the woods. Trencher knocked his opponent's sword aside and swung his club up, taking him beneath the chin with a loud crack of bone and spray of blood and teeth, and another splintered report announced Dobson's blow to the back of the last man's skull. The impact had likely killed him but that didn't stop Weasel and Scarron pummelling his body until it must have been no more than a bag of blood and broken bones.

Vaguely aware of Trencher beating a man to death, Tom walked over to where Hatchet Face lay. The man was moaning pitifully, his whole world reduced to a swirling maelstrom of confusion and pain, and Tom hated him even more now because it was all over far too quickly and Tom's blood-lust had not drunk deeply enough.

'Got the little runt,' Penn said, a hand snarled up in the boy's lank hair, hauling him back into the clearing. 'I've seen old timber-toed veterans run faster,' he said with a grin.

'Is that your boy?' Tom asked Hatchet Face. The man moaned incoherently. His eyes were rolled back into his cracked skull to show only their whites. 'Is the lame boy your son?' Tom asked again and this time the thief moved his head in what might have been a nod. Tom leant in close so that his mouth was against the thief's ear and he could smell sweat and fresh blood. 'I'm going to cut his throat open,' Tom said. Hatchet Face gurgled and groaned and it was a subtly different sound, different enough that Tom guessed he had understood.

He pulled the knife from Hatchet-Face's own belt, stood and walked over to where the thin-faced lad stood pissing in his breeches. Weasel glanced at Penn and grinned wickedly. Penn frowned, gave a slight shake of his head and turned away.

And Tom cut the thief's throat.

CHAPTER EIGHT

DE GOMBAUD WAS DEAD. THE GREY-HAIRED THIEF WITH THE blunderbuss had been quicker than he looked and turning on the Frenchman had given fire just as de Gombaud's pickaxe spike had punched into his chest and out through his back. The thief had died instantly but at such close range his fearsome weapon had done for the stonemason, spewing a spray of lead that had exploded fully half of the Frenchman's head away in a spatter of bone and gore. And yet somehow the man had lingered a while with his brains exposed to the night and his left eye, cheek and much of his jaw gone. His body had endured until just before dawn, clinging to life that was far beyond its ambition. Then, with them all gathered around, the dying man's young companion Tristan weeping silently, de Gombaud's chest had risen, fallen, and had not risen again.

'He was a brave man,' Trencher said to Scarron whose hands were slick with his friend's blood. 'Things would have gone worse for us if he had not stuck that old scab.'

'On the up side you and the lad here will have his share,' Dobson put in, the sentiment genuine, it seemed to Tom, though Scarron shot the trooper a glance of loathing that had Dobson shrugging his massive shoulders.

To break up the ground they used the pick which de Gombaud

had wielded to such effect and then they buried the mason in his own furrow. The outlaws they dumped in one shallow hole, covering the disturbed earth with a large bough cut from a nearby birch. Then they had cleaned the blood from their clubs and knives, broken their fast on bread, cheese and beer, and set off, with the sun spilling shafts of pale dawn light through the trees, guiding their way westward to Oxford.

A mile from the walled city, above whose church spires and pinnacles, quadrangles and high-walled gardens hung a lazy pall of brown-grey smoke, they piqued the interest of a small troop of Royalist horse.

'Dragoons,' Weasel spat as the riders trotted towards them, the metal fittings of their arms and tack glinting in the light of the rising sun.

'It's about bloody time,' Penn said. 'I would not have liked to think this whole charade was for nothing.' It was his turn pushing the handcart and he lacked the strength of Dobson or Trencher and was drenched with sweat despite the dawn chill.

'We'd have been sniffed out before now if we weren't dressed like this,' Tom said, feeling sweat bead between his own shoulder blades and slicken his palms now that their ruse would be put to the test. The patrol coming towards them must have been one of many such roving the countryside, guarding the city that was now, for all intent and purpose, the King's new capital and home of the royal court. 'Just remember to leave all the talking to Scarron and Tristan.' Tom felt horribly vulnerable without sword or poll-axe, firelock or armour, and knew that if things turned bad he and his companions would die too easily.

'Aye, we've got one less French tongue to wag for us now,' Trencher put in. 'You'll be all right, Weasel. One look at you and they'll presume you're a simpleton, a bloody numbskull, dumb as a stump. You too, Dobson, come to that, but the rest of us will have to do our best to look as French as our friends here.'

'Now would be a good time to stop talking, Will,' Tom growled under his breath as the dragoons covered the last hundred paces at an easy trot, their mounts steaming in the dawn air.

'Who are you?' a sergeant barked, reining in but not bothering to bring the carbine to bear which hung on a belt buckled over his right shoulder and under his left arm. 'What's your business here?' The man's bay mare looked a decent animal to Tom's eyes, better than dragoons could normally expect, though its mouth was ill-used by the bridle, suggesting that the sergeant was either cruel or not a good horseman.

Scarron stepped forward, presenting himself as spokesman for the company. 'My name is Guillaume Scarron and I am a master stonemason.' He spoke with a pride that was as genuine as the thick muscle layered on his right arm and shoulder. 'I am the owner of many sought-after templates,' he said, his accent smooth as dressed marble, 'and drawings of both ancient and the very newest designs from France.' He swept his bulky arm round to encompass Tom and the others. 'These are my companions, skilled men all.' He threw a thumb back towards Dobson. 'Except for that bearded ox. But stone will not lift itself, hey?' He smiled but the dragoon sergeant was in no mood for humour.

'You all bloody French?' he asked, deep-hooded eyes raking over each man before him. There were sixteen in his troop, armed with an assortment of matchlocks and carbines for which powder flasks hung from bandoliers. Fewer than half wore buff-coats.

'Qu'est-ce qu'il dit, Guillaume?' Tristan said, which was cleverly done, Tom thought, and Scarron snapped at the young man in French to hold his tongue at which Tristan made a good show of mumbling foreign oaths.

'They don't speak very good English, Captain,' Scarron said.

'I'm a sergeant not a bloody captain,' the dragoon said as some of his men chuckled. Some of the dragoons were talking amongst themselves, allowing their mounts to empty their bladders of steaming piss or crop the grass either side of the mud track.

'My apologies, Sergeant,' Scarron said. 'I can draw a plan as well as any Italian. I can fine carve a rose into a stone fireplace that you would believe smells as sweet as the rose in your lover's hair. But I know little of soldiers and war.'

'Why have you come to Oxford?' the sergeant asked. Tom saw that most of the dragoons armed with muskets had not even bothered to light their match-cord, which gave him hope that their deception was at least well conceived. Indeed, glancing at his companions now he was quite taken aback, for they did in truth make for a coarse, almost feral sight.

'Oxford has the King,' Scarron replied with a shrug, 'the King has enemies. The King needs walls.' The sergeant gestured for one of his men to dismount and check the canvas-covered contents of the handcart behind which Penn stood picking his nose as though he hadn't a care in the world.

'A wall ain't no fancy French fireplace,' another dragoon said with an unkind smile, 'so I wouldn't be expecting your two shillings a day, master mason. You and your company will be lucky to make a shilling after a day on the walls.'

'Nevertheless, we do need masons,' the sergeant said, 'and labourers,' he added, glancing at Dobson who affected an air of dumb incomprehension with consummate ease.

'Just tools, Sergeant,' the dismounted dragoon called, pulling the drawstring to close the sacks. 'Kevels, mauls, wedges and such.'

The sergeant nodded. 'Beden, Holt, escort these men to St Edmund's Hall and make sure they report to Smithson on the east wall.'

'Yes sir!' a dragoon replied, and with that the sergeant yanked his reins for no good reason, the bit savaging the mare's mouth – proving he was both cruel and a fool – and the column rode off in the direction from which Tom's company had come, leaving two dragoons, seven masons and a sorry-looking ass in their wake.

'And tell Smithson he owes me a quart of Adkinson's wettest for sending him proper masons for his section of the wall instead of the usual dregs,' the sergeant called behind him. 'Of the first water, mind! Or I'll send them to Harding up at the New College wall. Tell the old muckworm I'll be along with my thirst this evening and shall expect settlement.'

'Yes sir!' the older of the two dragoons called again. 'Come on then, Frenchies,' he said, turning his piebald gelding back towards the city, 'let's have you and that fine beast of yours earning an honest crust sweating for the King of bloody England.'

'Guillaume Scarron and his masons are at His Majesty's service,' the stonemason said with a nod of his rough head.

Dobson shouldered Penn aside and lifted the handcart's handles and Tristan pulled the ass's halter at which the beast brayed in protest, and the ragged bunch of men with their lopsided bulk, their skin and hair ingrained with stone dust and rough hands wrapped in leather or linen strips, walked on over the plain towards the imposing Magdalen Tower, with its thrusting pinnacles, that had clearly become the city's eastern watch-post. They would pass the earthworks that had been thrown up along the divided stream of the River Cherwell, which were guarded by the King's musketeers and patrolling troops of dragoons and harquebusiers. Then on across the Magdalen Bridge. That would take them into Oxford.

'You've brought your own tools, Frenchy, that's what I like to see. And good tools, too, by the looks. Take my advice and always leave one eye fixed on 'em or some thieving scoundrel will be limping off with a mallet-shaped cock filling 'is breeches. I've seen it more times than I can remember. If your men are as good as you say, they can spare one eye for your tools.' Smithson spat into the mud. 'We lucky sods are repairing an old wall here, not carving laurels in some earl's window jamb or a bishop's bloody ceiling boss.' He held up a thick, gnarly finger. 'But no fighting or I'll have the guards down on you quicker than it takes to shell a snail. They'll get tenpence a day,' he added, nodding towards Tom and the rest, 'you'll get a shilling, maybe more if I use you on some of the other jobs I've got on and you prove you know your business.'

'You will get no trouble from my men, monsieur,' Scarron said, 'and I can assure you that I know my business.'

'Aye, well, we'll see. You can start today, there's plenty to be done.' And this was evident enough from the looks and sound of men carting stones here and there and of others up on scaffolding set against the long stretch of wall that extended north for two hundred paces before angling west.

'We'll start tomorrow,' Scarron said, to Smithson's surprise. 'I have promised them a day to enjoy this fairest of cities.'

Smithson narrowed his eyes and folded his arms tight against his broad chest. 'You won't get a better offer anywhere else in the city,' he said.

Scarron smiled and made a show of looking up at the east gate which spanned the road by which they had come into Oxford. 'They just want to look around, I assure you. Tristan, tell Smithson the rhyme.'

The dark young Frenchman, who had been watching two pretty, well-dressed young women walking towards St Peter's, beamed white teeth.

> 'At North-Gate and at South-Gate too
> St Michael guards the way,
> While o'er the East and o'er the West
> St Peter holds his sway.'

Smithson looked about as impressed as a man could who had heard the same poesy as many times as he had woken piss-proud and hungry.

'He can't speak much English but for some reason he likes that rhyme,' Scarron explained with a shrug of his stout shoulders. Tom had heard the verse before and knew it spoke of the four churches, one on each of the four roads that passed through their own gates into Oxford and met at Carfax in the shadow of St Martin's church. 'So I promised them they could see the city before unwrapping their tools,' the stonemason said with a matter-of-fact air.

Smithson looked up at the sun which had risen above the old east wall to wash the city and the King's loyal subjects in clean spring light. 'If you're happy to give up a day's pay for half a day's work that's your loss,' he said, shaking his head and walking off to bark at a group of hapless-looking labourers who had spilled a dressed stone from its handcart.

That had been that. And Tom was in Oxford.

Being French stonemasons had got them in but now that they were in they would be assumed to be loyal to King Charles and as such could move about the city freely. Tom was relieved now to see the rough gravelled streets thronged with traders, labourers, soldiers and whores. With liveried servants on errands and water-bearers and children chasing each other through the crowds or playing Scotch Hoppers in the mud. For he and his company would be no more conspicuous than any others of those taking refuge, earning silver any of a hundred ways, in the King's new capital. Of course none of them, not even the two real masons, would show up at the east wall ready to work for Smithson on the city's defences. Scarron and Tristan had done their jobs and were free to go, to head back to Captain Crafte to collect what they were owed: each their reward plus an equal share of de Gombaud's, whose saving of the tools had likely saved the whole mission but who had paid for it with his life.

The Frenchmen had said their goodbyes and taken the ass and the cart and by now would be wending their way to the heart of the city where the four roads met. Then they would take Cornmarket Street and leave Oxford via the north gate and Tom suspected he would never see them again. Perhaps they would be attacked again by outlaws who saw a cart full of opportunity and an ass laden with knapsacks and only two men guarding them, but that was their own affair now. For Tom the real work must begin and he must not fail.

'So what now?' Trencher asked, turning towards the sudden roar flooding out of a tavern whose door had banged open. A young soldier stumbled out onto the refuse-strewn mire of Tresham's Lane and bent double to spew his guts into the filth. A woman's high-pitched cackle cut through the bawdy laughter pouring out into the day, and Tom was struck by the thought that perhaps the revellers had been at The Fighting Cocks all night and that if so the soldiers and folk of Oxford seemed little concerned about Parliament's rebel army or the war that yet gripped the country.

'Now we need black powder and ale,' Tom said.

'Not a good combination, lad, didn't anyone ever tell you?' Trencher replied, swiping off his filthy cap to scratch the side of his bald head where a few grey bristles sprouted.

'Any black powder will be stashed somewhere tighter than an ant's arsehole and guarded like the King's damn crown,' Weasel blurted.

'Keep your voice down, you paper-skulled idiot,' Trencher growled, at which Weasel pulled his head down into his shoulders and glanced nervously around, which was more conspicuous than his original offence.

'The munitions are kept in New College Tower. That way,' Tom said with a nod behind them towards the north-east.

'And you think we can walk in there, steal a few casks of black powder from under the bastards' noses and walk out again?' Dobson joined in, his great beard jutting belligerently as he spoke.

Tom shook his head. 'I think you can steal ale. Or better still, buy it,' he added, handing Trencher a small scrip bulging with Captain Crafte's coin. 'Three of you, three barrels. If they're scrawled with the maker's mark or some tavern's name so much the better. If not we can see to that later. Leave the powder to me and Matt.'

'You want the barrels empty?' Dobson asked hopefully.

'In your bloody dreams, Dobson,' Trencher said.

'Stash the ale somewhere near the chapel of All Souls, where Mousecatchers' Lane meets The High. Then meet us at sunset by the south porch of the church of St Mary the Virgin.' Tom shot Trencher a warning look. 'Keep them out of trouble till then, Will,' he said.

'So where are you two going?' Weasel asked, his close-set eyes narrowed as though keen to confirm that he, Trencher and Dobson *had* got the best of the jobs, for surely procuring black powder could not be as gratifying as procuring ale.

'We're going to a hostelry to find a whore,' Tom said.

Tom sensed Penn's head snap round and even Trencher's eyes were round as shillings at that, for like the others Trencher was in the dark regarding the finer points of Captain Crafte's plan.

'You mutton-mongers!' Dobson blurted. 'You get to bang Cupid's kettledrums while we're working? How is that fair?'

'Just stay out of trouble,' Tom said, 'and meet us at sunset.'

'Aye, well, you two enjoy your notch,' Dobson growled as Tom and Penn turned to make their way back north up Alfred Street. 'And save some for the rest of us!'

The Spotted Cow had not been easy to find. Tom and Penn had followed several winding lanes then a dark, narrow alley on whose dank walls someone had scrawled, long ago by the looks of the faded white paint, *Hell's Passage*. But rather than leading to Hell it had led to a grubby, noisome hostelry which was thronged with patrons despite the stench, which told Tom that either the ale was good or the whores were.

When at last he had been able to gain the landlord's attention, Tom had asked for two cups of beer and a whore named Hester. A plump, red-faced, scowling man, the landlord had nodded purposefully, thrown two drunks off a table in a dark dingy corner (because they weren't buying flesh) and told Tom he would have to wait because the girl was busy upstairs. And so they had waited, ears full of the incessant burble of the congregation, eyes on their mugs or a pretty girl but otherwise oblivious to the soldiers and students, idlers and drunks, as though they were regulars of the Cow. And now Tom watched a wild-haired, wide-hipped girl descend the stairs opposite, lacing up her stays with nimble ease as she came, and he knew from Captain Crafte's description that it was Hester. Evidently the whore had been well informed too by the landlord's boy, for she came directly up to their table and looked both men up and down.

'Which one of you two handsome gentlemen wants his quim first?' she asked. 'Or are you the sort that'll share a dish?'

Feeling Penn grinning beside him Tom asked the girl if she had any cards. 'I'm fond of Ruff and Trump,' he said.

'I prefer Laugh and Lie Down,' Hester replied, completing the pre-arranged protocol, and Tom nodded and leant forward. 'I'm here to see The Scot.'

Hester straightened the front of her full skirts, fingers brushing at a drying stain on the woollen cloth.

'I know where I might find him,' she said, lifting Tom's cup and taking a draught. She dragged a bare arm across plump, wet lips. 'Do you gentlemen want some company whilst you wait? I can get you two of the other girls.' She smiled, handing the beer back to Tom. 'They ain't got what I've got but they're good girls and clean.'

'We have all we need,' Tom said, taking the cup, and Hester nodded, turned and threaded her way through the throng towards the door. And one hour and three cups of beer later they met The Scot.

Captain Crafte had said nothing of The Scot other than that

he would supply the black powder and then be the one to see them safely away from Oxford when the job was done. But Tom did not need Crafte to tell him that the man now sitting opposite him was every inch a soldier. Though he was not a big man, his face was hard and unforgiving, reminding Tom of the effigy of some long-dead knight sculpted into a sarcophagus lid. But for the eyes. The eyes were big and alive and blazed with the zeal of a man who has lived amidst death.

'They get younger,' The Scot said. 'They'll be sending bairns and bantlings to do men's jobs next.'

'You know why we're here?' Tom asked.

'Nae, laddie,' The Scot said, raising his cup to his lips and downing a wash of ale. 'I neither know nor care what they've got you sticking your neck in the noose for, but I've done what was agreed.'

'Then you must have risked your own neck,' Tom said. 'With respect you risk it now by sitting here with us, for I'd wager you were at Kineton Fight and cannot have killed every man who saw your face.'

The Scot's eyes widened still further as though his mind recalled the events. 'Aye, I was there and at Brentford too, under Philip, Lord Wharton.' Tom saw Penn wince and glance about to see if anyone had reacted. It seemed that no one had. 'And I've made enemies in Germany and the Lowlands and even in Monymusk, Aberdeenshire, in my own damn parish,' The Scot went on, not caring who heard. 'But I've friends, too, laddie, and some of them are in this stinking hole now and would kill any man who so much as offended my eye.'

Tom found himself liking the soldier, admiring his cold in-difference to danger even though it could get them all hanged for spies.

'Where is it?' Tom asked.

The Scot jerked his chin at Penn. 'This one got no tongue?' he asked, turning those callous eyes on Tom's friend.

'I'm just here for the beer and the laced mutton,' Penn said, holding the man's eye long enough to hint at a belligerence that defied his affable grin.

'Spoken like a true stonemason,' The Scot said with a satisfied nod, then looked back to Tom, leaning closer now. 'You'll find it stashed with a farrier at the north end of Grope Lane. The man's a simpleton and won't give you any trouble. I'll be waiting at the footbridge that crosses the Cherwell north-east of the city. I'll wait as long as I can but I'll be gone before first light, with or without you.'

'We'll be there,' Tom said. The Scot nodded, finished his ale and slammed the cup down, then stood from the table and left without another word.

'So what now?' Penn asked, his eye drawn to Hester who stood at the foot of the stairs hoiking up her full breasts so that the white flesh bulged clear of her low-cut bodice. 'Seems we've got some time to kill waiting for dark.'

'Even if we had the silver,' Tom began, nodding at Penn's right shoulder made thick and bulky by the linen wrapped round the arm beneath the shirt and doublet, 'a crump-backed labourer like you paying for a wench like that would raise eyebrows, even in a flea-pit such as this.'

Penn looked crestfallen, a condition exacerbated by the emptiness of his beer cup.

'What are your orders then, general?' he asked, head tilted, one eye still watching Hester.

'Now, Matthew, we find out where John Birkenhead drinks,' Tom replied straight-faced, 'for a Fellow of All Souls and editor of the King's newsbook does not drink here.'

CHAPTER NINE

'YOU WOULDN'T KNOW THERE WAS A WAR ON,' JOE SAID, WATCHING A line of women working in the field beside them, faces obscured by broad-hats, the hems of their skirts and their white hands caked in mud. They were setting seeds in neat rows and none even deigned to glance up at the riders making their way south along a road churned by hooves and wheel-rutted. 'Mind, they're late to be planting peas. S'pose the war might account for that,' Joe suggested. 'Perhaps they had meant to leave it fallow. But now, what with the way things are . . .'

Bess had thought the same thing, had been surprised not to see more evidence of the great struggle, more debris from the conflict that had stripped her own family of so much. She had watched men and women spreading manure across the fallow fields and ewes suckling their young. She had seen livestock being herded from home pasturage to the communal pens and women tending fruit trees and she had resented it all. For how could the world go on as normal when somewhere, perhaps in many places throughout the kingdom, men were killing other men? Brothers, fathers and sons were being butchered, their carcasses left as carrion, unburied, without the meagre comfort of a prayer said over them.

'You think they should be cowering indoors?' Dane put in,

uncharacteristically joining a conversation. 'Do you resent them for trying to survive?' Bess felt a pang of guilt clench in her chest at that, felt annoyed with Dane for putting it there.

'I think they are lucky if this cursed war has not touched them,' Bess said. 'And if it has, I pity them, whichever side they are on.'

Dane looked back towards the bent-over women. 'The first army that marches past this field come the harvest will leave nothing behind but the worms and maybe not even them. Those folk know it but they'll still break their backs now. The world is sliding into chaos and they plant peas.' He shrugged. 'I admire them for their hope if nothing else.'

'I pray this war will be over before the harvest,' Joe said.

'And you believe your prayers will make any difference?' Dane asked, looking straight ahead.

'Yes, Mr Dane,' Joe said, sitting tall and rigid.

'Then you are a fool, lad. Even if you promised me a thousand hands clasped in prayer, I'd sooner take two hands on two good firelocks.' Even the way the man rode, casually swaying from side to side on his sorry-looking horse, annoyed Bess.

'You do not believe in prayer, Mr Dane?' she asked.

'I do not, my lady,' he said, deliberately baiting her by not calling her Bess as she had told him to. 'To my ear, praying is too much like begging.'

'Praying is nothing like begging,' Bess snapped, annoyed with herself for reacting to the man's nonsense.

'Whatever you ask in My name, this I will do,' Dane said, 'that the Father may be glorified in the Son. If you ask anything in My name, I will do it.' He leant over in the saddle, hawked and spat a gobbet onto the mud track.

'Book of John?' Bess asked, surprised to hear the man quote from the Scriptures. Even Joe had raised an eyebrow though he did not turn his head from the road before them.

Dane nodded. 'I'd wager a barrel of good wine that my mother could recite the whole damn lot of it.'

'Do not let the Puritans hear you talk of gambling, drinking and the book of God's True Law in the same breath,' Joe advised, still not looking at him.

'I do not think Mr Dane spends much time in the company of godly men, Joe,' Bess said.

Dane did not contradict her, nor did he give some frivolous reply, and from his absent air she saw that his thoughts were elsewhere.

'Line after line she knew by rote,' he said. 'My father would have her deliver whole parables to guests at our table.' He grimaced. 'I was a bantling with ears stuffed full of damned prayers.'

Bess did not know what to say to that and neither did Joe have anything to add, and so they continued into the grey day, the empty sky blending into the colourless earth like an ashen veil. It was a windless day and Bess watched a lone bird of prey coursing low over the fields, gliding and twisting, unhurried yet resolute. Her stomach ached with loss. It seemed like forever since she and Joe had left Shear House and she wondered how little Francis was. Was his wet-nurse feeding him enough? She imagined her mother's fury, or worse still sadness, and supposed she might have sent someone out to find her, end her folly and bring her back to Shear House.

The hen harrier was covering the ground in sharp sweeps and turns as it came towards them, its wings forming a V so that she noticed their tips were black, as though they had been dipped in the ink pot that still sat on her father's writing table at home. Then suddenly the bird rose and twisted over them, making no sound at all in the still, moist air, and was gone, lost in the grey.

Where are you, Thomas? her mind whispered. *Where are you?*

It was raining now: a lashing deluge that had seemed to come from nowhere and soaked them to the bone even as they threw capes around themselves and rode slump-shouldered as though by making themselves smaller they might escape the worst. They had meant to ride further, perhaps making another five miles before dusk and thieves or treacherous footing made it too dangerous to be on the road, but the rain made such an imitation of twilight that when Dane suggested they stop at the next village neither Bess nor Joe had protested.

'It will be good to get by a fire,' Joe said, clenching and un-clenching cold hands on the reins.

Bess agreed wholeheartedly, though did not say as much. She had been shivering for the last three miles but had resolved to clamp her teeth shut and say nothing rather than be seen as the weak one. She *was* the weakest. She knew that, of course: weakest not only by virtue of her sex but also because hers had been a life of privilege and she was unused to hardship. She could change none of that. But not to reveal her weakness by showing that she could not endure what the men could endure, nor, God forbid, to engender their pity – that much was yet within her control and it would take more than a week of being saddle-sore, cold and tired to erode her purpose. Had she not watched her mother, attired for war in Mun's old back-and-breast, ride out on her grey mare Hecuba and bleed the villains besieging Shear House? Had Lady Mary not stood with Major Radcliffe's musketeers when all had seemed lost and the rebels were closing in?

If Mother has such steel in her spine then perhaps I do too, she dared to ponder.

'What village is that?' Joe said, breaking the spell of her thoughts and nodding through the gloom. 'Stone? Some other place?'

'Matters not, so long as neither side of this damned quarrel has soldiers billeted there,' Dane called above the seething rain, water cascading from the rim of his broad-hat. 'We have her ladyship's money,' he said with a sour glance at Bess, 'and they . . .' he dipped his head towards the cluster of thatched houses ahead, 'they have food, fire, ale and . . . agreeable company.'

Was that meant as an affront? Bess wondered vaguely, or was the man's *agreeable company* alluding to some village harlot? 'Are you afraid of the King's men?' she asked, steering her mount around a deep hole in the road that was fast filling with water.

'Not afraid, my lady,' he said, 'but I have no desire to get myself recruited. And believe me, if some jackanapes sergeant lays eyes on young Joseph here, he'll be whipped off to fill some poor tosspot's boots in a company of musketeers before you can blink. He's got that lamb to the slaughter look and don't say you hadn't noticed.'

'I have fought,' Joe said, eyeballing Dane. 'I've killed a man.'

Dane removed his hat and looked up at the sky, letting the rain hammer against his face and cascade through hanks of dark hair. 'Killing is the easy part,' he said, rain spitting from his lip. 'It's the not being killed that takes practice.'

'Well, it seems you have perfected the art simply by being a man of no conviction,' Bess said, sorry for Joe who clearly felt at a disadvantage in Dane's company. 'For you do not fight for the King?'

'I do not,' Dane admitted. 'Nor can Parliament claim the honour of commanding my sword arm.'

'It would seem that modesty is another quality to which *you* may not lay claim, sir,' Bess said.

Dane shrugged, water spilling from the cape about his shoulders. 'Modesty perhaps not, but honesty? That you will not find in short supply here, madam.'

Bess cocked an eyebrow at Joe but the young man was staring at Dane, his disapproving glare laced with a dash of awe. 'You think yourself so skilled at arms?' Joe asked him.

For the first time since they had set off from Lord Heylyn's house Dane smiled, and to Bess's surprise it was a comely smile, much warmer than the rain beating upon her broad-hat. 'Oh

I am a fucking killer, Joe,' he said. 'And neither the King nor Parliament shall waste my talent in a mad rush on the field or a disease-ridden camp.'

Bess's menfolk had waded into the fray, had stood in the storm of lead. But not all men were men of honour. Perhaps he is a coward, she thought, watching Dane sway on his cob like a boat wallowing in a swell.

'And neither shall I freeze to death in the pissing rain,' Dane muttered, as the village emerged from the hissing downpour and the horses nickered softly at the prospect of a warm stable and dry fodder.

'That at least is one ambition we share,' Bess said, inhaling the sweet, resinous smell of the smoke slung above the village like a dark pall in the still air. Instinctively she tilted her hat to partly obscure her face, for men on the road were less worthy of remark than a woman and the last thing they needed was an abundance of questions.

'Turn around and go back!' a voice bellowed out of the gloom. 'There's a fork in the road a half mile back. Take it and go around.'

Dane stopped his horse and Bess and Joe did likewise, as the body to whom the voice belonged materialized.

Dane clicked his tongue and the cob ambled forward.

'Are you deaf, sir?' the man asked, booted feet squelching in the mud. Bess moved up too and saw that the man who had challenged them was not alone. It seemed a whole welcoming committee had turned out.

'Clubmen,' Dane murmured to Bess, who noticed that every man in the assembly brandished some sort of crude weapon, from cudgels and flails to sickles and scythes, though none so far as she could see owned a pistol or even a sword. Most had wrapped scarves around their faces so that only suspicious eyes showed beneath the sodden rims of their hats, but the band's spokesman was bare-faced, *his* eyes marked more by intelligence, Bess thought, than by fear.

'We are not deaf, sir,' Dane replied, holding his hands out wide in an unthreatening gesture, the rain bouncing off his palms, 'simply in need of a roof over our heads and a plate of hot food.'

'You'll find neither here,' the man said. 'Now go. We do not welcome outsiders.'

Dane leant over, turning his face from the crowd towards Bess. 'Remove your hat if you want a hot dinner, my lady,' he growled. Bess did not remove the hat but she did push the brim up away from her face and she saw several pairs of eyes flicker in her direction. 'We will give you no trouble and have coin to pay for your hospitality,' Dane said to the man, in whose right fist and left palm sat a smooth cudgel, recently oiled so that the rain rolled off it or sat on the bulbous head in fat drops.

One of the other men leant in to their leader to speak, but against the rain's hiss and the patter of it striking the muddy track, Bess could hear none of what was being said.

'How do we know you are not the King's spies? Or Parliament's?' the spokesman asked, pointing the cudgel at Dane and sweeping it across towards Joe and then Bess. 'Come here to eye up our resources or count the men you will return to conscript against their will? We have had crops and property seized before now,' he added to a chorus of sullen ayes from his companions, 'sometimes by soldiers, other times by deserters.' His lip curled. 'We have all heard the fates of other villages, of wives and daughters raped and of the depravities which attend armies and make rabid dogs of young men.'

'I can assure you, sir, that I have no love for armies whichever ensign they march beneath, and neither do I have a heart for the quarrel, which I have so far managed to avoid. We want bed and board,' Dane said, 'wine if you have it. At first light we will be on the road again.'

'Show me,' the leader of the clubmen demanded. 'Your coin.' He glanced at Bess but she kept her eyes downcast so as not to encourage him. 'You must understand that trust in strangers is a little thin on the ground these days.'

'Thin as cat piss,' another man announced, having hauled down his scarf to cuff snot from his nose. Bess's horse snorted impatiently, its breath fogging in the wet air.

'We need to know you can pay,' the leader said, 'that you will not creep off before sun-up like some conscience-stung adulterer.'

'Of course,' Dane said with a nod, then reached into the hidden layers of his clothing and pulled out a leather purse, letting its weight speak for itself in the palm of his outstretched hand. For good measure he gave it a shake so that the coins within clinked gently. There were more murmurs within the group and Bess noticed arms and hands relax, the flails and scythes looking like agricultural tools again rather than the weapons of desperate folk.

'You can stay one night,' the leader said. 'Then you'll move on and you will not speak of this village to anyone.'

'Agreed,' Dane said, and though it irked Bess to have him speak for them all, she was more keen to be under a roof.

'You may eat together but you will sleep apart,' the other went on, then gestured to Bess, 'unless this is your wife?' Bess almost felt the flush in Joe's face at the clubman's presumption that Dane, if either of them, would be Bess's husband.

'The lady is this young man's sister,' Dane said. 'We are bound for London to bury their brother who was recently killed fighting in Parliament's army, may God receive his soul.' Bess flinched, not at the lie but rather at the tale's propinquity to her own tragedy.

'And you?' the clubman asked Dane.

Dane blinked once, slowly, as though behind his eyelids was some fond but bitter memory. 'Their brother was my friend,' he said with a pathos that could have seen him on some Southwark stage.

The clubman nodded. 'The war is an open sore upon this

land. But it will not infect us here.' He gestured to his companions with his cudgel. 'We happy few, we band of brothers,' he said, the quote by Bess's reckoning utterly lost on the other clubmen, 'will defend our liberties and livelihoods against all comers.' He singled out a broad, squat man who gripped two sickles, one in either hand. 'Take them to Greenleafe's. Tell him I sent them.' Then he turned back to Dane. 'You'll be well fed and watered and Greenleafe's boy will see to your horses.'

'I wouldn't have the mutton pie,' one of the others put in, pulling the scarf down to reveal his grin, 'not unless you like dog.'

'The mutton tastes like dog?' Joe asked, the first time he had spoken.

'The mutton *is* dog!' the man said, stirring a damp peal of laughter from the others.

'You will pay for three rooms, which will be found for you by the time you've eaten,' the clubmen's leader said.

Joe shook his head, rain flying from his broad-hat's rim. 'I will not have my sister left alone, sir,' Joe said, the steel in his voice impressing as much as surprising Bess.

The clubman nodded. 'Very well, as you two are kin you may share a room, though you'll still pay for three.'

'Agreed,' Dane said, then clicked his tongue and his cob moved off, feet squelching in the mud. Bess and Joe started forward too, all of them following the squat man with the sickles who was already on his way back to the village.

'One more thing,' the clubman said, his band dispersing, tramping off to get out of the rain. 'Your weapons. Folk here are not used to swords and firearms and I will not have you terrifying them.'

They stopped and Joe looked at Dane who nodded, drawing his fine flintlocks and flipping them over in his hands to give them butt-first to a spotty-faced stripling who held them gingerly, as though afraid they might go off at any moment, and then passed them to his leader. Then they handed over their swords, Dane his plain rapier and Joe his short hanger, to another of the drenched clubmen who took them in one hand, his scythe in the other.

'And your blunderbuss, lad.' Joe hesitated then, reluctant to give up the weapon with which he had for many freezing nights stood sentry outside Shear House and without which Bess had never seen him. 'Unless you want to turn around and ride four miles through this pissing rain to the next village.' The clubman shrugged, as though he cared not either way.

'It's all right, Joe,' Bess said. She had begun to shiver again now and could barely remember what it felt like to be warm and dry. Frowning, Joe lifted the blunderbuss on its belt over his head and gave it to the spotty youth, who grinned this time, gripping the weapon as though he wanted nothing more than for it to roar.

'Powder and shot, if you please,' the clubman said, and Joe reached for the bag of musket balls strung on a belt across his other shoulder but Dane stopped him with a raised hand.

'No, sir,' he said to the clubman, 'we shall keep those things with us.' He pointed at the spotty young man who was still grinning and pointing the blunderbuss at an imaginary foe. 'I wouldn't want the lad there to shoot his foot off.'

The clubman held Dane's eye for a long moment and then nodded, lifting the pistols. 'I shall hold them for you till the morning. Now go and get yourselves dry.' They moved off again, drawn by the scent of wood smoke and the promise of a hot meal. 'And spend that coin,' the clubman called after them.

According to the short, squat man who had led them through the deluge to the alehouse on the muddy bank of the Trent, Allen Greenleafe and his wife had both been servants at the nearby Shugborough estate for upwards of twenty years. But a fall whilst replacing old slate on the house's roof had left Allen lame and Cecily sick with worry that, she being frequently struck with colds, they would spend their last years on God's earth starving and miserable. But in recognition of their long and faithful service (and more likely, said the squat man, because he had known Allen wasn't up to the job and should never have been sent up on the roof) their employer, the lawyer William Anson, had come to their rescue. Anson had bought the Greenleafes the modest cottage in which Bess, Joe and Dane now huddled by a roaring fire which raised a stink from their wet woollen clothes.

'A simple fire is the most wondrous of life's free pleasures,' Joe said, his smooth cheeks flushed with drink. 'Well, other than going for a piss when you're bursting.'

He suddenly looked at Bess, horrified to have spoken thus in her company, but she smiled gently and looked back into the flames and the awkwardness was swept away by the raucous, barking laugh of another of the Greenleafes' guests, one of three men at a table behind them who nursed their ale pots protectively, pipes clamped in their lips. In one dark corner a young cooing couple sat oblivious to all, and in another corner two old men seemed asleep but for the occasional gruff comment or squeaking fart. Two dogs – an old spaniel and a thick-haired mongrel – lay asleep near the fire, their heads on their paws and the mongrel's back legs twitching so that Joe said it must be dreaming of chasing rabbits.

'Either that or it's a nightmare about being put in a pie and served up as mutton,' Dane suggested, and Bess hushed him lest he offend their hosts. 'You are quite right,' he mumbled into his mug. 'We haven't seen where we shall sleep yet.'

The air was thick with pipe and hearth smoke, the stench of wet clothes, wet dog, old sour beer and the more pleasant aroma of cooked food. In the little kitchen adjoining the parlour the Greenleafes were clattering pots and scraping scraps, and Bess felt renewed and strong, confident that a full belly and a good night's sleep would brace her for another day on the road come rain or shine. Avoiding the mutton pie, they had wolfed down a meat and onion stew, cheat bread and pancakes spiced with cloves, mace, cinnamon and nutmeg. Their outer garments hung drying on a frame by the fire and Allen's home-brewed ale was disappearing almost as fast as the man could pour it, though that was mostly Dane's doing. Bess wondered how a man could drink so much and yet still stand on steady legs, as Dane did now, having risen to go back out into the rain to check that their horses were being well looked after.

'Order another jug, lad,' he said to Joe. 'As it appears there are to be no other amusements,' he added, scratching the scalp beneath his long black hair, 'we may as well drink properly.'

'You will both make for poor company tomorrow,' Bess said as Joe signalled to Allen that their cups were empty, and Dane opened the door, so that for a brief moment Bess could hear and smell the rain that was still sheeting down outside.

'The less he says the more I like him,' Joe said, thumbing back towards the door, and Bess nodded in agreement with that as Allen Greenleafe appeared with more ale.

'Make sure you fill it,' she said, pointing to Dane's cup and thinking the man could stew in his own juices next day for all she cared. 'To the brim if you please.' And Joe laughed at that, his face suddenly full of a boy's mischief that warmed Bess's heart.

By the time the other patrons had emptied their last cups and disappeared into the damp night Bess was struggling to keep her eyes open, Joe was blind drunk and Dane was . . . Dane. Allen Greenleafe had insisted on all accounts being settled before they were too drunk to count their coin, but Bess guessed the man was simply canny enough to want his money before his guests saw their sleeping chambers. Her suspicions were vindicated when Allen hobbled over and began banking the fire, which was their cue to retire to bed.

'You two are upstairs,' he said to Bess and Joe with a jerk of his grey-bearded chin. 'There are two rooms up there and yours is the one that doesn't have Mrs Greenleafe snoring in it. You, I'm afraid,' he said to Dane, 'are in the barn down the lane by the mill.'

'I'll sleep here,' Dane said, nodding at the rush-strewn floor and the two dogs that still slept on.

Allen shook his head. 'No you won't,' he said. 'Not with your thirst. You'll find Hogg's barn dry and . . . spacious.' He turned back to the fire and continued shovelling old embers onto the logs that still burned, smothering the flames. 'You won't be the first to bed down in there and we've had no complaints before.'

'From the cows?'

'Now look here,' Allen said, turning back to face them, trailing his lame leg, his face clenched with offence.

'I jest, sir,' Dane said, raising a hand. 'Give me a jug to take to bed and I shall not care where I sleep.'

Which left Bess and Joe climbing the stairs, knapsacks over their shoulders, candle lamps held out before them, and pushing open the door to the bedchamber they would share to maintain their pretence of being brother and sister. The lie in itself had been a good idea, Bess knew, for it lent credibility to Dane's tale of them travelling to London to bury their brother. But neither she nor Joe had yet brought up the subject of their sleeping in the same bedchamber and now here they were, in a small bare room, the door closed behind them.

Just weeks ago she would have dismissed as absurd the very idea of sharing a bedchamber with another man, let alone this young man, a tenant farmer's son and now soldier in Shear House's garrison.

She watched him spread his bedroll and blanket out on the floor beneath the small window in the far wall and she knew he must be feeling as embarrassed as she. Perhaps even more so. Then he cleared his throat and turned, as though he had heard her thoughts. 'I could sleep just outside the door,' he suggested. 'I know Dane said I must not leave your side, but we're in no danger and I'd be just out there.'

'Don't be silly, Joe. You wouldn't have the room to lie flat out there and after all that riding you must get a good night's rest.' She felt her brows arch. 'Things are not as they were,' she said, thinking of the chaos that nowadays reigned in the kingdom. 'Besides, the folk back home need never know, for I am sure of your discretion and you may be assured of mine.'

He nodded. 'I shall never breathe a word of it,' he said, fiddling with his shirt sleeves.

'There then, we have our agreement. Now, if you would step outside whilst I get ready.'

'Of course,' he said, making for the door.

'At least we are not in a draughty barn with the rats.' Bess could not help but smile at the thought of Dane bedding down somewhere out there on such a gloomy wet night.

'He will be happy enough with his bed partner,' Joe said, raising an imaginary cup to his lips.

'No one else would have him,' Bess said, and Joe's smile was full and strong. Then he left, shutting the door behind him, and again Bess thought, as she took off her damp coif and bodice, how glad she was to have the young man with her.

By the time she called him back into the bedchamber she lay cocooned within the blankets, arms tucked close against her body, looking up at the whitewashed ceiling upon which the glow from her candle danced. She tried to ignore the sounds of Joe undressing, instead listening to the rain scattering upon the roof and the wind that was steadily building beyond those poor walls. It was painfully embarrassing to have a man lying on the floor in her room, but then all she had to do was think of what her brothers must be enduring and her discomforts were as nothing and her toes could uncurl themselves. She felt dry and warm and safe. And she could not know that beyond the Greenleafes' walls sharp steel was glinting dully in the wet night. And men were coming for her.

*

Bess woke to what for a heartbeat sounded like a drumroll of thunder, but which she then knew to be boots thumping up the stairs.

'Joe!' she said, as the bedchamber door crashed open and men stormed in, one of them kicking Joe in the face as he tried to rise.

'Don't you touch him!' Bess screamed, scrambling backwards so that her shoulder blades pressed against the cold limewashed wall.

'Shut your mouth, woman,' one of the men growled, turning savage eyes on her.

'Get hold o' him,' another man barked, gesturing at Joe who lay in a dazed heap half illuminated by what little moon-glow seeped through the window's thick glass.

There were five of them and two carried swords: Dane's and Joe's swords, Bess saw, though they looked somehow less dangerous than the weapons which the other men gripped.

'You!' she said, recognizing the squat man who had brought them to the Greenleafes'.

He clutched one of his sickles and pointed it at her. 'I'll have that pretty tongue if you don't hold it still,' he threatened, and Bess's heart bucked at the realization that none of the men had their faces covered now. They have no fear of being identified later, she thought, dread filling her soul like ice-cold water.

'Search it proper,' a scrawny old man growled at two others, a man and his son by the look of their copper hair, who were on their knees rifling through her and Joe's gear.

'You come here, to our village,' the squat man said, hauling Joe up, one fist fat with nightshirt, the other clutching the sickle's haft, 'with yer firearms and yer money.' He thrust Joe against the wall and brought the sickle blade up. But Joe launched his knee into the man's belly and slammed a fist into the side of his head and the squat man doubled. Then the older man with copper-coloured hair sprang up and swung his club, catching Joe's left temple and sending him spinning, blood splattering up the white wall.

'No!' Bess screamed and now there was a man on top of her, clawing at her linen nightdress, ripping it like some frenzied animal. She felt hot spittle on her naked breasts, was vaguely aware of a man grunting at another to *stop the whore scream-ing*, and the next moment she felt the pressure of a hand over her face and mouth, smelt tobacco and faeces on those molest-ing fingers.

She writhed and thrashed, every sinew in her body enraged, trying to resist the irresistible. She knew they were beating Joe, could hear the dull blows of them kicking him, but she was consumed by her own terror now.

Francis! her mind screamed, *my boy!* Not just terror. Fury, too, at these animals. Fighting for her life she opened her mouth and bit into the hand and the man screamed, then the back of his other hand smashed into her face. Blood was in her mouth. Not her own, she realized with crazed joy, seeing the fleshy wound on her attacker's hand.

'Hold her still, damn you!' someone growled and then she felt hands grasping her legs, knew they were being forced wide. Knew what was coming.

No! 'No!' she yelled, frenzying, kicking as though her life depended on it, for she knew that it did.

'There it is,' one of them growled, touching his throat. Stroking it hungrily. 'Feast yer eyes on that.'

They had got her legs wide now, the dead weights of their bodies pressing down on them, and she felt a bristled cheek scratch her inner thigh, felt hot breath on her private parts.

'Makes you hungry, don't it?' the squat man said, his ugly face joining the others. Down there.

Is Joe dead then?

'Out of my way, Jonas,' the squat man said, pushing the others aside.

'You said I could go first,' Jonas protested.

'Get off, Jonas, or I'll tell Phyllis,' he spat, and with that Jonas squirmed up the bed and clamped a hand on her right breast, grinning like a dead fox.

Francis! My baby!

Knuckles gouged into her cheek, the blow blinding her, and now there was a hand around her throat, squeezing, the finger ends in amongst the cords and sinews, digging deep.

Then something about the air in the room changed, seemed to shiver, though she did not know what was happening until the squat man's head jerked back and a knife slashed open his throat, spraying her with hot blood.

Suddenly her legs were free, the weights that had pinned her to the bed gone as her attackers reeled in the face of this vicious threat.

Dane! Dane spun, caught the arm that was swinging the club at his head and plunged the knife into the man's eye socket, yanking the blade free and turning again even as the man with the copper hair slumped to his knees dead. The hanger swept through the gloom and he twisted aside, clutching his own cloak and hauling it up, snaring the short sword amongst the woollen folds and wrenching it from the clubman, as he scythed the knife across the man's throat, instinctively ducking a swipe from another club.

'Gut him, Nate!' the one with Dane's own rapier squawked. 'Gut the bastard!'

The younger copper-haired man had picked up the squat man's sickle so that he had that in one hand and his club in the other. He stepped forward and Dane flew at him, catching the sickle blade on his knife and slamming his head into the man's face. The young man staggered back, blinded, flailing his weapons before him in a desperate defence. Dane went for him, suddenly dropping to the floor with a flurry of knife strikes that made the man mewl as he dropped in a pile, his hamstrings cut.

'I'm sorry!' the last man shouted. 'They made us do it. I

never laid a finger on her. Or him!' He gestured down at Joe who was half-sitting against the wall, eyes glowing white.

'You want to kill me with my own sword?' Dane asked, as though he found the idea almost amusing, beckoning the man on with his knife. Gore was dripping from the blade, Bess saw. 'Well here I am. Come.'

The man shook his head and Bess saw the wet stain spread down the legs of his breeches as he wet himself. 'I won't fight,' he said, then threw the sword at Dane's feet.

'Then you might as well stand still,' Dane said, striding up and plunging the knife into the man's chest and twisting it savagely so that the blade lacerated the heart. He pulled it free and wiped it on the dying man's tunic, then turned to Bess.

'We should go,' he said. Behind him the man's eyes rolled in his head, his legs buckled and he thumped to the floor.

Bess could not move. She was paralysed.

'Up you get, lad,' Dane said, extending a hand to Joe and hauling him to his feet. Joe pulled away and raised his hands to show he was all right, though his legs were unsteady and his face was a blood- and snot-smeared mess.

'Must I carry you, Bess?' Dane asked, turning back to her. She knew he would.

'No,' she said, climbing from the bloodied blankets, trembling fiercely. Five men lay dead or dying. The walls were spattered with blood and there was the smell of faeces again but this time it was sharp and offensive.

'How did you know?' Joe asked.

'They came for me too,' Dane said, 'that ugly lad who liked your gun and some others.' Bess shuddered to think what scene awaited whosoever went into the barn down the lane. 'We should go.'

Bess nodded, steeling herself for flight, then dressed hurriedly, as did Joe, as Dane crouched by the man whose hamstrings he had severed.

'The man that spoke for you on the road yesterday,' Dane said in a soft, even voice. 'Where will I find him?'

The clubman was sobbing, teeth bared in savage pain, blood pooling on the boards around him.

'Tell me and I'll kill you cleanly,' Dane said. 'Don't tell me and I'll cut off your balls and walk away.'

The man pulled a hand from the boards and looked at it. The palm was slathered in thick, dark blood. 'The last house on the bend. By the church,' he whimpered.

Dane nodded, then took the man's hair in his fist, pushed the head back against the wall and sliced open the windpipe, so that Bess heard a soft gush of air and then a foul frothing, choking sound.

She watched the man die. Part of her didn't want to, but a stronger part would not let her tear her eyes away. 'Shouldn't we just get away? As fast as we can?' she said. Once the other villagers knew what had happened they would want revenge. They were likely already coming. Looking at Joe she doubted he could put up much of a fight.

'Not without my pistols,' Dane said.

For some reason Bess closed the door behind them, shutting in all that death so it could not follow her, and down in the tavern stood Allen and Cecily Greenleafe, his arms around her protectively, their faces masks of horror.

'It was none of our doing,' Allen muttered. 'We knew nothing of it.' From the looks of them they had been rudely awakened too and Bess preferred to believe they had played no part in the betrayal.

'As fine a drop as your ale is, Mr Greenleafe, you will understand if I do not call on your hospitality again,' Dane said, leading Bess and Joe out into the night, his sword arm ready. But when they got outside all was quiet, the village in darkness and the rain falling softly now, a drizzle whose scent Bess inhaled gladly to cleanse her nose of the stench of death.

The horses were as they had left them and within moments

they were walking them up the lane towards the church behind whose steeple the moon glowed when not obscured by black cloud.

Bess desperately wanted to gallop away, to flee the place as fast as her mare could carry her. But Dane said they were wiser to move quietly, at least until they had paid their last visit, and Joe had nodded his agreement, so she had held her tongue. Now she all but twisted her head off her neck, looking through the dark for attackers she was sure must come. Her heart was thumping and her arms and legs ached where the men had gripped and mauled her, but what were bruises compared with their intent?

They would have raped me, she thought, the idea itself as cold as death and like ice in her veins.

'Wait here,' Dane said, dismounting and handing his cob's reins to Bess. She nodded and watched him walk up to the house as though he were calling on a neighbour for some flour.

On the third time of thumping his fist against the door it opened and there stood the clubmen's leader in his nightshirt, bare-legged and barefoot, his smooth cudgel in his hand and a frown beneath a thatch of dishevelled hair. Bess could not hear what was said but she saw the man peer around Dane at them, his mouth open and his frown plunging deeper. Then he disappeared and Dane leant casually against the doorframe, yawning and rolling his shoulders as though they were stiff. The clubman soon reappeared with the two pistols and Joe's blunderbuss, handing them to Dane with a shake of his head, then he watched Dane walk back up the short path and hand Joe his firearm before mounting.

'He looks surprised to be alive,' Joe said as they turned their horses south and their backs on the clubman. The young man was hunched over, one hand on the reins and the other clamped upon his ribs. They had kicked him. Those savages. 'You don't think he knew what the others had planned?' In the dim light Bess could make out the lumps on Joe's face, but even in total

131

darkness his voice – all thick and swollen – would have told its own tale, and she shuddered to think of the pain he was in.

'I'd like to think those merry-begotten shankers came up with the idea all by themselves,' Dane said. 'He'd have been with them otherwise and might have made sure the job was done properly.'

'The black-hearted devils,' Joe muttered, glancing behind to make sure they were not being followed.

Dane shrugged. 'We came here uninvited. They knew we had coin. That was my fault. They saw my pistols and the blades, useful things if you're trying to protect your village. They could have sold our horses and bribed some recruiting officer to turn a blind eye.'

'How many came to the barn?' Bess asked, a shiver running through her right down to her feet.

'What does it matter? Fools and boys, that's all.'

Bess felt Joe beside her tense at that.

'I am sorry, Bess,' Joe said, looking at her though his eyes would not bind with hers. 'I did nothing to help you.'

'Oh, Joe, what could you?' She shook her head, aching with pity for him. For his shame. 'There were so many of them and we were asleep.'

'Next time try sleeping in front of the door so the wretches can't open it,' Dane suggested unhelpfully, earning a scalding look from Bess in the ensuing heavy silence. 'Ah, you did well, lad,' Dane went on, and for a heartbeat Bess was surprised. 'I think some of the turds hurt their feet on your head.' He grinned at Bess and though the night had been drenched in blood and a knot of terror still gripped her heart, she laughed. And Joe laughed too.

CHAPTER TEN

THE CLOTHES DID NOT FIT WELL. THE BREECHES WERE TOO BIG and even the stockings were on the baggy side. The shirt and slashed doublet were too tight, despite Tom's having lost much of the muscle that had filled him out before the war, before wounds of the body and of the mind had taken their toll leaving only taut flesh on strong bones. But the high bucket-top boots were a good fit and the other accoutrements of a gentleman – the falling band, the silk cuffs pinned to the ends of the doublet sleeves, the cape of purple felt that matched the breeches, and the expensive broad-brimmed beaver – did enough, Tom hoped, to throw the eye off the ill-fitting parts.

'Well, Matt, what do you think?' Tom was buckling up the wide leather baldrick from which a fine rapier hung, its hilt decorated with chiselled heads of King Charles and his queen Henrietta Maria against a fire-gilt ground. A nice touch, Tom thought.

'You'd fool me and I'm no fool,' Penn said. 'As much as it turns my stomach, you could pass for one of the King's fart-catchers dressed like that. Might even get a blush out of Her Majesty.'

'I wouldn't go as far as that,' Tom said, 'but I think it'll do.' What he really thought was that he felt more like a Rivers than he had for two years, though he resolved to snuff out that notion before it could catch and burn him. And yet to better pass as a gentleman perhaps it was as well that he feel like one again.

He and Penn had found the farrier on Grope Lane and the dim-witted fellow had grinned and handed Tom a sack and inside had been the clothes, all arranged by The Scot. The cape and the hat had been on the trestle beside the bag, so that Tom guessed the farrier had tried those on for size. He could imagine the overgrown fool prancing around his workshop in them, and now they were imbued with the acrid stink of burnt hooves.

'The smell will wear off,' Penn said now, 'once the breeze gets into you. I'm more afeared the farrier will wonder what's in those casks and prise the lid off one. Strange idea of The Scot's to put black powder in a farrier's workshop with red-hot coals all about.'

'The powder was well covered,' Tom said, recalling the oiled canvas that someone had draped over the four barrels. 'Whoever finds they're short of black powder is not going to think to look there. The Scot knew what he was doing.'

'You think he'll be in there?' Penn asked, looking at the Fox and Hound tavern, nestled as it was at the western end of Holywell Street amongst a great upspring of tall, crowded houses: three- and four-storey buildings topped with attics and cock-lofts, on narrow plots.

'He'll be there,' Tom said, looking west across the city that was falling into darkness. Here and there candle lamps were being lit as folk left their places of work and thronged the thoroughfares. The south side of the street was dominated by New College, but beyond that, less than two hundred yards away, was All Souls, so that if John Birkenhead, editor of *Mercurius Aulicus*, did indeed take his ale in The Fox and Hound, he was a man who did not stray far from his desk. And Tom had no reason to doubt the young student who had furnished him with the information. Leaving his scruffy companion to linger in the shadows of Mousecatchers' Lane, Tom had strolled into All Souls and there regarded a group of young, studious-looking men loitering in the cloister to the north of the chapel. Introducing himself as an old friend of Birkenhead's, Tom had asked one of them, a pustule-afflicted youth with long curly hair, where the man could be found.

'Mr Birkenhead possesses a thirsty wit, which must be served or nought is writ,' the young man had replied pretentiously and loud enough to get a laugh from his friends. He had grinned, evidently pleased with his own wit, and gone on to say that Birkenhead and Peter Heylin, one of the other writers of the newsbook, could be found most nights in The Fox and Hound, quills in hand and stooped over papers stained with the tears of the beaker. 'They are assiduous fellows, ever inventing new ways to mock the rebels and exalt our cause.' *Our cause.* That had sounded strange to Tom, coming from a pus-faced stripling who had never gripped a hilt or ridden into the blood-fray.

'Fetch the others and I'll go in and look for Mr Birkenhead,' Tom said now, tilting his beaver so that its rim partially obscured his right eye and a small portion of his face, for it was not impossible that he might be recognized amongst followers of the King. 'Leave the powder where it is until I bring word. The ale too,' he added, 'if Dobson and Weasel haven't rinsed their guts with it.'

Penn nodded and headed off with the leisurely, rolling gait of a stonemason tavern-bound after an honest day's work, and Tom glanced up at the hanging sign upon which was painted a white hound in full flight after a leaping red fox. And then he pushed open the tavern door, releasing the roar of revellers into the dusk, and stepped inside to find his prey.

It did not take long. The student's information was good and a casual question to a serving girl confirmed that the short, dignified-looking man with a neat tuft of beard and a well-groomed moustache sitting against the back wall of the tavern was in fact John Birkenhead. He was alone, too, no sign of his fellow editor, which would make things easier, Tom thought, as he shouldered his way through the drinkers and the thick haze of tobacco smoke towards the thorn in Parliament's side.

'John Birkenhead, I presume,' Tom said, smiling, feeling the smile in his eyes too, for the game was on and his blood was up.

The neat little man, yet to turn thirty by Tom's reckoning, looked up, deftly turning over the paper he had been writing on, and half smiled half frowned in the way of someone at a social disadvantage.

'You know me, sir?' he asked, standing.

'Admire you, sir, but do not know you,' Tom replied, sweeping his beaver from his head and half bowing before gesturing for permission to sit on the empty stool. Birkenhead nodded, his palm directing Tom to take his ease. An empty cup on the table suggested that Peter Heylin or someone else had occupied the stool only recently and might return, so Tom knew he must be quick.

'Though through your work I feel as though we are old friends,' he said, 'and hope I'm not too presumptuous.'

Birkenhead's smile slipped its bridle now. 'Not at all,' he said. 'I am honoured to know that you appreciate our endeavours, Mister—'

'Rivers,' Tom said, his heart hammering in his chest because he knew that he had lit the fuse with that one word and must now stay to see whether the charge exploded or began a more complex ignition.

'Rivers?' Birkenhead sat back, tugging his short beard with his ink-stained thumb and forefinger. 'I only know . . . knew of one Rivers: Sir Francis Rivers who died a hero at Kineton Fight. And then there're his sons of course. Edmund is one. I believe the young hero won his spurs that very day and was knighted on the field. And the other boy . . . well—'

'Tom Rivers at your service,' Tom said, extending his hand for the other to shake, the smile on his own face feeling like a stranger.

'But you are known, Tom,' Birkenhead said, wide-eyed, his natural curiosity pulling him in towards Tom like a fish to the fly. 'You fought for the rebels at Edgehill. They say you lay with the dead. Spent the night on the field with the ghouls and ghosts as the souls of the dying left their tortured bodies.'

'Everything you have said is true, sir,' Tom said, giving the smile some shade now. 'But there is much more to say.'

'Indeed?' Birkenhead's top teeth worried his bottom lip, his eyes devouring the young man before him, taking in the delicate lace trim of his falling band, the fine fabric revealed by the slash in the doublet, the scars on the face and the long sand-coloured hair. 'And you have now come over to us?' he asked, gesturing to a serving girl to bring two cups of beer.

Now Tom affected a solemn expression, giving a slight shake of his head as though hinting at the deep shame that tortured his soul just as mercilessly as any pain that had tormented the wounded and dying left on the field at Edgehill. 'I have seen loathsome things. Seen soldiers commit ungodly horrors on their fellow man.' He looked down and realized that the fingers of his right hand were cradling the stub of his missing ring finger. 'I lay with the corpses at Edgehill, plenty of them dead at my hands, and such horrors will prey on a man's mind. I have walked a dark path, Mr Birkenhead, but I have emerged into light.' Tom shuddered then and could not have said if it was part of his act or genuine.

'The rebel son of a slaughtered hero,' Birkenhead mused, leaning back once more, his whole hand cupping his bearded chin, pulling the bristles to a neat point over and over, as he eyed Tom. His mind, though, was clearly elsewhere. 'And now drawn back to the standard his father died trying to protect,' he muttered.

Tom let Birkenhead absorb his own words and leant back to allow the girl to put two cups of beer down on their table.

'I thought you might print my confession,' Tom suggested eventually, 'allow me the privilege of declaring my penitence, that His Majesty's loyal subjects may, with God's help, deign to forgive me my sins and accept me into the ranks of the righteous.'

Tom had the sudden fear he had overplayed it, for the words had tasted so dry on his tongue. But the editor of *Mercurius Aulicus* was lapping it up like a cat in a dairy.

'It need not be much, just a few words, a concise piece so as to not infringe on your other texts, for we must not dull the blade's edge,' Tom said with a curl of his lips. 'I will gladly pay. Furthermore, my brother Sir Edmund Rivers is a great admirer of your newsbook. I'm sure he can be persuaded to contribute to its continued production. Running a printing press must be a costly business.'

'Indeed it is,' Birkenhead said, eyebrows arching, 'and yet it is worth every penny for my press hurts the rebels more than any cannon or regiment in the King's army. But . . . but . . .' he said, placing his elbows on the table and pressing his palms together as though about to pray, 'we can do better than a few words. Bless your heart, boy, but this is the tale of The Prodigal Son, wrought again in fire and glory for our age. This tale of loss and redemption is just what my readers need. It will ignite in their breasts, Tom, it will leap from tongue to tongue and spread through London like a great fire.'

'So you will publish my story?' Tom said, raising the cup to his lips and sipping the beer.

'It would be an honour, Tom Rivers,' Birkenhead said, eyes narrowed as though he feared their lustre would belie the grave expression he had affected. 'It cannot have been an easy matter to decide to bare your soul and seek to make recompense for your foolhardiness.' He pointed a finger that was ink-black to the knuckle. 'But your story will persuade other young miscreants that it is not too late to abandon Parliament's hopeless cause and come over to the King. Perhaps we might persuade your brother to contribute to the piece.'

'It's possible,' Tom said, then nodded resolutely. 'Then I shall call on you again next month when I return to Oxford.'

'You're leaving?' Birkenhead's eyes were wide enough now.

'I'm afraid I must,' Tom said. 'I'm to ride north with the Earl of Northampton and earn *my* spurs by helping to turf the rebels out of Lichfield. I will prove my mettle.'

'But my dear boy, our story will not wait a month,' Birkenhead announced, pushing his cup to one side as though the time for such pleasures was past. 'We must strike now, while the block is inked. You must come with me to my workshop and together we will put the flesh on the bones of your remarkable story.' He stood, his small frame rigid with purpose, those editor's fingers thirsting for ink.

Tom frowned. 'At this hour?'

'At no other, Tom,' Birkenhead said, head dipped, one neat eyebrow arched. 'What say you? Do you have a story to tell, lad? Shall *Mercurius Aulicus* help reclothe you in the honour a Rivers deserves?'

'I am in your debt, sir.' The grin stretching Tom's lips was as real as the cup in his hand. He downed the last of the ale in one great wash. 'And at your service,' he said.

Tom did not turn round. He did not need to. He knew that Penn was following them, could sense eyes on his back as they walked through the shadow-played city, north up Mousecatchers' Lane and then east at the junction onto New College Lane. The plan had gone better than Tom could have hoped and he had not had the opportunity to step out and tell Penn that he had made contact with John Birkenhead, but it had not mattered and Penn was tracking them.

'What about the night watch?' Tom asked, avoiding a great puddle which would by the looks have reached halfway up his boots had he not at the last seen its surface glistening in the moonlight. There were other folk about, some merry with drink, but most were observing the curfew.

'The men of the watch know me, Tom,' Birkenhead said, 'besides which, since His Majesty and the army moved in, the curfew has been more . . . relaxed. Take this parish,' he said, throwing an arm out towards the timber-framed houses, the halls and colleges whose windows glowed dully against the newly fallen night, 'these days it's full to the rafters with noblemen, knights and gentlemen. Such as they do not take kindly to being told by the watch when they must be abed. Especially in time of war. They want their ale, their women and their games.'

'And they don't mind the stink?' Tom said.

'The smell is from the ditch outside New College and is, I'm sorry to say, noisome to the whole town,' Birkenhead said. 'But there are some five thousand souls now quartered in the city and all those . . . expulsions have to go somewhere.' He smiled. 'I assure you that you'll hardly notice it by tomorrow.'

They followed New College Lane a little way south, but before it snaked eastwards, becoming Queen's Lane, Birkenhead led Tom through a pitch-black passage and across a patch of grass and mud to a low, stone-built building behind which loomed the great bulk of All Souls chapel, whose sharp spires rose like silent sentinels keeping watch over the college.

'I dare say you expected something rather more grand for the home of *Mercurius Aulicus*, scourge of the rebels and organ of our cause,' Birkenhead said, turning the key in a stout iron-studded door and then pausing to look at Tom, one brow hitched. 'But we've got corn piled in the law and logic schools, wood, grain and hay cramming the colleges, and even the town hall is bursting with provisions in the unlikely event that we are besieged. And so we must make do with what we have. Not what you're used to, I'm afraid,' the editor said, pushing open the door.

'I have grown used to many things that I had not thought to,' Tom replied, and no longer able to resist the urge he turned and took one look back along the street but saw no one.

'As have we all, Thomas,' Birkenhead said thoughtfully, then swept a short arm into the room, inviting his guest to make himself comfortable. Then he locked the door behind them. 'A strange thought, is it not, that our king lodges at Christ Church not half a mile from where we stand now?' Birkenhead said, using what little light there was by the window to see as he struck flint and steel, showering sparks onto a swatch of charcloth in a clay dish.

'I'll wager the King says the very same about John Birkenhead,' Tom said with a grin, and the editor gave a short bark of a laugh just as the charcloth caught in a little burst of yellow flame. In no time his candle was burning and he took it up and neatly went from lamp to lamp until the workshop was illuminated and Tom could gain an appreciation of it.

'I have never seen one before,' Tom said, genuinely impressed by the great wooden machine that stood in the middle of the workshop. Seven feet long, three feet wide and seven feet tall, with its great screw and windlass, its frame in which the text-blocks were placed and inked and another two frames which were even now covered with paper ready to be folded down onto the inked type.

'My fellow editor calls it a glorified wine-press,' Birkenhead said, standing and staring at the contraption as though it still awed him. 'And yet even Mr Heylin, who appreciates a fine drop as much as the next fellow, will assert that the nectar of our endeavour is more intoxicating to man than any French wine.'

Tom's muscles had begun to tremble the way they did before a fight, and the thought that the King of England himself and all his loyal knights were only a few hundred strides away did nothing to calm him. He ran a hand along the smooth flat bed, recalling what Captain Crafte had said about the printing press being a weapon more powerful than any cannon, an opinion which Birkenhead clearly shared.

'For we deliver what folk across the land crave. News of the King and the cause and of the base villainy of the rebels,' the editor said, as Tom took hold of the hand-smoothed lever that had been hauled across countless times to lower the screw and transmit the pressure through the platen. 'I will gladly give you a demonstration afterwards,' Birkenhead said, beckoning Tom across to the desk behind which he was pulling up his chair to sit, 'but first, Tom Rivers, we must write our story.' He took up his quill and dipped it into the ink pot. Then he froze and looked across the room, his eyes fixing on Tom's. 'But it was appropriate to celebrate and be glad, for this, your brother, was dead, and is alive again. He was lost, and is found,' he said, then grinned. 'I must admit the Gospel of Luke is my favourite.'

And Tom drew his sword.

'If you're a God-fearing man now would be the time to make amends,' Tom said, striding towards the editor, candlelight glinting off his rapier's blade.

'My God!' Birkenhead exclaimed wide-eyed.

'That's a start,' Tom said.

'What is this? You mean to kill me?'

'I mean to do more than that,' Tom replied. 'I'm going to blow up your press, Mr Birkenhead.' He held the rapier's point an arm's length from the man's neck. 'Unless, of course, you can prove here and now that your precious words are a match for cold steel.'

'You're still a rebel,' the editor said, dropping the quill and slumping back in his chair as though resigned to his fate. 'You have played me like a prize carp, Rivers. I am humiliated.'

'That's the least of your worries.' There was a knock at the door. 'Open it,' Tom said and Birkenhead walked over with his key and unlocked the door with a trembling hand, stepping back as though afraid of what might be on the other side. And he looked no less perturbed when Dobson walked in brandishing a club, his face all bristle and scowl as he glared about the room like a bear looking for hounds to rip apart.

'It's just us,' Tom said and Dobson nodded, glancing at Birkenhead with an expression that was half disappointment, half indifference, then turning to step back out into the night to help the others, who were unloading barrels from a handcart.

'So you're the quill-driving bastard who mocks us,' Weasel gnarred at the editor whilst rolling a barrel across the tiled floor, 'and this is the machine that vomits your lie-ridden papers,' he said, placing the barrel beneath the printing press's flat bed.

'In thy foul throat thou liest,' Penn said, rolling his own barrel and setting it against Weasel's. Then he snatched up a page of *Mercurius Aulicus* that had been set aside because the ink had smudged. 'An honest tale speeds best, being plainly told,' he said, ripping the paper into pieces and tossing them aside.

Birkenhead raised his neat-bearded chin defiantly. 'Bloody thou art, bloody will be thy end,' he said, his riposte also plucked from Shakespeare's *Richard the Third*, or so Tom suspected. 'And you call me a liar, yet you, sir, and your fellows are all other than what you purport to be.'

A fair point, Tom thought, given his own performance, and his companions' being begrimed with stone dust when none had ever shaped a stone.

'Slit his throat and shut him up, Tom,' Dobson growled, bringing another barrel in.

'Where's Will?' Tom said.

'He's keeping an eye out,' Dobson replied, nodding towards the door as he put his barrel in the room's far corner, which meant it must be one of those that contained ale not black powder. To Tom's eye they all looked the same but he trusted the others knew which were which.

'The night watch came sniffing,' Weasel said as though he had read Tom's mind. 'Suspected we were up to no good moving ale around in the dark. But when we gave them a barrel, thanking them for keeping the streets safe for honest folk, their questions seemed to run dry.' He grinned, revealing small pointy teeth. 'A curious thing.'

Tom nodded, not dwelling on how close they had clearly all come to being discovered. 'Get over there with your contraption,' he said to Birkenhead. 'We need rope.'

'Got some,' Dobson said, heading for the door. 'Used it to lash the barrels down.'

A moment later Trencher came in with a length of rope, having left Dobson on watch outside in the dark. 'I wanted to see this here printing press before it goes up in smoke.'

'You won't see drier timber,' Weasel said, pouring black powder from a flask in a trail across the floor. 'We didn't need all this damned powder nor the risk of getting caught with it. That press'll burn like a witch dipped in wax.'

'We could not risk someone seeing the fire and putting it out,' Tom explained, taking the rope from Trencher.

'Aye,' Trencher said, staring at the printing press with an expression of reluctant admiration, 'and I'd wager a nice explosion is Captain Crafte's way of answering their arsewipe newsbook. Get on with it, lad,' he growled to Weasel who had evidently pilfered a chisel from Guillaume Scarron's tool cart for he was using the thing to punch a hole in a barrel which lay on its side and had been wedged to stop it from rolling away. 'If we get caught they'll string us up, pull out our guts and send pieces of us to each corner of the land.'

'Don't do this thing. This is a base act, Tom Rivers,' Birkenhead said, jerking, straining against the rope tying him to his press as Tom tested his knots. 'This is unworthy of your blood,' the editor dared, eyes wide with terror now, saliva churned white at the corners of his mouth, his whole body trembling.

'What do you know of blood? Hiding here with your books and your ink. Weaving lies whilst other men die in the fields. Whilst they who were hale and strong are butchered like beasts and sob for their mothers.' Satisfied with his knots Tom put himself face to face with the editor and glared into his tear-filled eyes. 'We are at war, Mr Birkenhead. Real war, not some squabble of words and pathetic lies. And you have lost this fight.'

'Your father would be ashamed,' the editor spat, dredging up some courage or hate in the face of death. 'He would turn in his grave.'

'My father has no grave,' Tom said, and with his knife he cut Birkenhead's falling band from the neck of his doublet, cut it down and rolled it, stuffing it into the editor's mouth and tying the ends behind his head.

'We're done,' Weasel said, standing to admire his work. The powder trail would have stretched forty feet if it had been poured in a straight line. But it was not straight. It followed a saw-blade pattern which would slow the flame and give them enough time to get clear of the workshop before the three barrels exploded and the printing press with them.

'We've a better chance of slipping out of the city alone than as a group,' Tom said as the others gathered round. 'The Scot will be waiting for us to the north-east by the river. There's a footbridge. If any of us do not make it the rest must go on. The Scot won't wait for sunrise, he'll be gone and any of us left on foot in the valley will soon be rounded up by King's men. So we go no matter what.'

'I love you all like brothers,' Weasel said, 'but that's not nearly as much as I love not swinging on the end of a rope. When The Scot rides east Weasel will be squinting at the sun.'

'Good luck, lads,' Trencher said, gripping each man's arm in turn and finishing with Tom's. 'May the good Lord see us safe out of Oxford while the King's curs are pissing on this fire.'

'Off you go,' Tom said, then walked over to Birkenhead's desk and took up a candle lamp. 'You too, Will. I'll see you at the bridge.'

'If you have no objections, Tom, I'd be the one to light the fuse that makes charred splinters of that thing,' Trencher said, gesturing at the printing press. 'That'd be something to tell my children's children when I'm old and they're readying to put me in my eternity box.'

'You're already old,' Penn put in, grinning wickedly.

Tom nodded and handed Trencher the candle, at which the big man's face lit up like a flame in the gloom, and rather than leave the workshop then, all of them were compelled to stay and watch the powder lit.

There was a flare of orange flame and a bloom of white smoke and the little blaze fizzed along its jagged course. And the small company scattered like leaves on the wind and vanished along the lanes, passages and amongst the messuages into the night.

All except for Tom.

Tom fumbled with the key in the lock, his chest thumping, fighting every instinct screaming at him to get as far away as he could, and then the lock clicked and the door was open again and he was inside. There was no time. Surely. He sawed at the rope which bound the editor to his printing press, the knife's handle slick with sweat, as the furious seething flame scuttled ever closer. Only ten feet of unburnt powder remained. Seven feet. Five.

'Move!' he roared, a fist snarled up in the man's doublet, all but hauling him across the room, through the thick, stinking smoke towards the door. Then out and down onto the grass, faces in the mud as the flame met the charge and the whole lot exploded like God's wrath.

Birkenhead's eyes were white orbs of unspeakable terror glowing in the moonwashed night, as Tom lifted him to his feet. 'Run, you bastard, or I'll cut your throat,' Tom snarled, and they hurried down New College Lane, then Queen's Lane, as the first shouts were raised in the darkness around them. Then, just past the church of St Peter-in-the-East, Tom shoved the smaller man up against a stone wall and pressed his knife against his white throat. 'Make a sound and I'll kill you. Understand?' Birkenhead blinked rapidly and nodded and Tom cut through the gag in the editor's mouth and threw the thing over the wall. 'Now you're going to help me, Mr Birkenhead,' he said, giving a smile that was cold as death on his own lips. The shouts were getting louder and now Tom heard the scuff of boots and the jangle of swords and kit, knew men were coming up Queen's Lane towards them and must surely be upon them in a matter of heartbeats.

'Up you get,' he growled, lacing his fingers, creating a stirrup into which he invited Birkenhead to put his foot.

'Over there?' the editor said, nodding at the stone wall that was a little over six feet high. On the other side were trees and bushes and no doubt graves. 'Now,' Tom said, 'and don't even think about running,' he added as the man stepped into his hands and grabbed the top of the wall while Tom lifted him up. Up he scrambled, neatly for a man of words, and Tom followed, fingers clawing at the damp stone, his arms hauling his body up until he could throw his right leg over the wall and then jump onto the grass below. Just as the night watch clattered past, hurrying north up the narrow walled lane towards the confusion of shouting and fire. Towards the chaos.

CHAPTER ELEVEN

'WILLIAM, LORD DENTON AND HIS SON HENRY. WHERE WILL I FIND them?' Tom asked. He had taken a huge gamble by saving John Birkenhead's life in exchange for information, but he knew there was a chance that Denton, his hated enemy, was in Oxford with the King. Where else would he be? And hadn't Birkenhead himself said that Oxford was nowadays *full to the rafters with noblemen, knights and gentlemen*?

'I do not know a Lord Denton,' Birkenhead managed, the words squeezed through a throat constricted by fear.

'You know him,' Tom said. 'The King and his court are here. Lord Denton is here.' Tom glanced round and through a gap in the bushes saw the weak glow of candlelight through one of the church windows. But they were safe enough amongst the trees, for anyone curious enough about the tumult to investigate would be drawn away from them and towards Birkenhead's flaming workshop at the college.

'Why would I tell you? Why in God's name would I help you?' the editor said defiantly, so that Tom admired him, for all the good it would do the man. 'You devils and traitors have destroyed my press and you will slit my throat the moment I have told you what you want to know.'

Tom grabbed a fistful of the man's shirt and brought his

knife up to his bulging left eye. He could feel the editor trembling, could smell the terror on him.

'Let me assure you, Mr Birkenhead, slitting your damned throat would be a mercy. If you do not tell me where Denton is I will cut off your ballocks.' His mind recalled an image of George Green, Martha's father, as they mutilated him, slicing off his private parts and casting them into a fire. 'I will cut off your nose and carve the letters on your face so that the world will know you for a seditious libeller. And I will not kill you but will let you live in misery and abasement.'

'I would still decry the rebels and their base villainy. I would still serve my king,' the editor said, but even his short beard was trembling now, so that Tom knew his threats had taken root.

'Denton,' Tom growled, pressing the knife's blade against the man's nose.

Birkenhead held as still as his quivering flesh would allow and blinked slowly in place of a nod.

'New Inn Hall. Lord Denton lodges at New Inn Hall. He has been appointed to oversee the establishment of the new Royal Mint.'

'That comes as no surprise,' Tom said, hatred for Denton welling in his gut and souring his mouth. Bats whirred above them, dark streaks against the smoky, moon-silvered sky. Some creature rustled in a nearby bush but did not show itself.

'It's half a mile from us.' Birkenhead nodded westward. That sounded good in Tom's ears. A chill ran up the back of his neck at the thought of bloody vengeance being within his reach at last. He was suddenly aware of the painful throbbing in the stub of his ring finger, could feel his pulse in it, and his mind's eye summoned Denton again standing beneath his ensign on the plain below Edgehill. Before Tom had been shot and beaten down to the blood-churned filth.

'What has the man done to you?' Birkenhead asked, professional curiosity getting the better of mortal fear.

'Just take me to Denton,' Tom said, turning the editor round and pushing him through the trees.

Rather than go back north past All Souls and Birkenhead's workshop, and risk the editor being recognized by the crowds that Tom presumed would have gathered there by now, they headed south and crossed over High Street. They stuck to the shadow-shrouded gravel back streets, the ancient litter-strewn lanes and even a stinking, unpitched cartway, but steered clear of Christ Church College, for that was where the King himself had his chambers and Tom had no wish to run into His Majesty's soldiers.

Up ahead a college door creaked open and a man stepped out into the road. 'Who goes there?' he challenged them, a candle lamp flickering at the end of one spindly arm. An ancient sword wavered at the end of the other.

'Get back inside and lock your door, old man. The rebels are here,' Tom growled, marching past with Birkenhead. By the flickering light of the candle Tom saw a shock of white hair and a wizened face in which the jaw had all but unhinged.

'Rebels? In Oxford?' The man's rheumy eyes blinked incredulously. 'Fate stands now upon the razor's edge,' he murmured, then vanished, and there was a slam of door and clicking of locks and Tom and Birkenhead had the street to themselves once more.

'Old fool thinks it's the fall of Troy,' Tom said.

'Are you not Achilles full of wrath?' Birkenhead accused him.

'My horse was called Achilles,' Tom said, a sudden pang in his chest as though a cold hand had clutched his heart. And then they came to the church of St Peter-le-Bailey where a knot of men were angrily debating whether or not to ring the bells in response to the earlier explosions.

'What news?' a man called to them, silencing the others with a wave of his cane. He was portly and well dressed, his beaver sporting three white plumes.

'Some sort of accident near All Souls,' Tom replied. His talk

150

of rebels had made the old man scuttle back inside and lock his door but these men would ring the bells and call out the regiment, which would make it harder for Tom and the others to make their rendezvous with The Scot.

'It was no accident, sir,' the man replied, crossing the street towards them, thrusting his cane into the mud with each step. 'The watch have caught a damned Roundhead trying to slip out of the city!' He flapped a hand. 'Like a damned eel, may they stretch his neck and watch him do the gallows jig.'

'Keep moving,' Tom hissed at Birkenhead, whose shorter legs were struggling to keep pace with Tom's long stride. 'Then good luck to us all, sir,' he said to the portly man, who pulled his plump neck in as though offended at being all but ignored.

'You think we should pull on the damn ropes? Wake the town?' the man called after them.

'I do not!' Tom called without turning, as he and the editor paced on up New Inn Lane, Tom ignoring the shouts of sergeants and officers coming from the castle whose imposing dark bulk dominated the western skyline off to their left.

Tom cursed under his breath. Which of them had been caught? Trencher? Penn? Some small part of Tom hoped it was Trencher. It was an ignoble and dark hope and Tom was ashamed of it. Trencher and Penn were the nearest thing to friends he had in this life, but he knew that the big, granite-faced man was tough to the marrow. Trencher burnt with a hatred for the Royalists and if anyone could hold his silence long enough for the others to get clear it would be him.

'If you do not go now you will never get out of the city,' Birkenhead said.

'Hold your tongue or I'll cut it out,' Tom growled. *They do not know there are more of us*, he thought. The explosion could have been the work of one man, someone within Oxford who hated the Cavaliers, some Puritan zealot with a love of black powder.

But damn ill luck that one of them was caught.

New Inn Hall was, in the main, a grand-looking, stone-built affair with a slate roof, several broad chimney stacks and leaded windows. But what held Tom's eye were the four sentries, two either side of the main entrance and all alarmingly well armed. Each had a good buff-coat, two firelocks thrust into his belt and a curved hanger or Irish hilt at his left hip.

'Your rebellion exacts a heavy price and not just in blood,' the editor said in a low voice. 'The university's silver plate has been requisitioned. It goes through that door, is melted down and comes back out as crowns to pay the King's army.' He grabbed Tom's arm and Tom rounded on him and wanted to thrust his blade into the man's neck. But Birkenhead held his ground. 'Think, man!' he hissed. 'It's the Royal Mint. There will be more soldiers inside. You will get us both killed.'

Tom's heart was a raging fireball in his chest, burning with the need for vengeance, so that a part of him believed he could slaughter those sentries and anyone else who got in his way. But another part of him, probably the same cold, calculating part that had hoped it was Trencher who had been caught by the Cavaliers, knew that Birkenhead was right and that he would die before he even got a chance to spill Lord Denton's blood.

'Will the soldiers know you?' he asked.

Birkenhead shrugged. 'Perhaps they have seen me around the city. Perhaps not. They will know my words if not my face.'

'Then get us in there,' Tom murmured. From the corner of his eye he could see that the guards were looking over at them, more than likely growing suspicious.

'How?' the editor said under his breath, eyes imploring Tom to see sense and give it up.

'Just do it and do it now, or you'll greet the new day a corpse.' Birkenhead exhaled slowly as though gathering himself, then nodded and they crossed the road towards the soldiers, who bristled and drew their firelocks, no doubt put on edge by the explosion to the east.

'What is your business?' one of them challenged.

'I am John Birkenhead, the editor of *Mercurius Aulicus*, and I would speak with Lord Denton.'

The soldiers were wide-eyed. 'We just heard tell that a rebel blew your printing press to shivers!'

'Which is why I need to speak with Lord Denton,' Birkenhead said sharply, 'for we must have a new press built immediately and the college plate must pay for it.' He lifted an ink-stained forefinger into the air and Tom hoped that the sentries could not see the tremble in it. 'We must print a newsbook without delay to show the rebels that their base sabotage has come to nothing.'

'Was anyone killed?' another soldier asked, tucking his firelock back into his belt.

'Just fetch Lord Denton before I put your teeth through the back of your skull,' Tom snarled, at which the young soldier blanched and looked to his fellows for support that never came.

'Lord Denton is not here,' the first soldier said, looking from Tom to Birkenhead and back to Tom. 'He's been gone some four or five days and I cannot say when he will be back.'

The words struck Tom like a musket butt rammed into his gut; his hand found his sword's grip and he resolved to drown the night in blood.

'Tell Lord Denton I will call again,' Birkenhead said, his tone suggesting that he suspected the soldier of some duplicity. 'Come, Thomas, we have work to do,' and Tom felt a tug on his arm and looked round as if in a dream, saw the editor's eyes pleading with him to follow, and before his reeling mind caught up with itself he was walking south, back down the moonlit street, as a peal of bells assailed the night.

'I could not do more,' Birkenhead said in a small voice. Then a door slammed and Tom turned back and saw two men step out of New Inn Hall. It was dark and the men had their backs to him as they walked north, their features hidden by broad beavers and night's veil. And yet none of that mattered and Tom's breath caught in his throat. For he did not need to see the broader man's face to know who he was. It was all in his bearing and gestures and the way he held his shoulders as though inviting any who dared to get in his way. Tom had known this man almost all his life.

'Come with me if you want to live,' he said to Birkenhead.

The editor turned his face up to the sky, to the moon-silvered smoke slung low over the city, some of which might have risen from his own beloved printing press, and offered up a prayer. And then they began to walk north.

After Henry Denton.

Henry Denton and his companion did not follow New Inn Street onto the wide thoroughfare of Thames Street. Not that the small troop of musketeers from the King's Oxford Army gathering there could have stopped Tom from following Denton if he had gone that way, for the promise of blood had sluiced away all sense of caution now.

Henry had lusted after Martha. Tom had always known that. Much worse was that Henry had stood by whilst Lord Denton had defiled her. And after that he had joined in the ritual humiliation when Tom had been helpless and rage-filled, face-down in the freezing mud outside Baston House. When Henry's father had pissed on him.

And as for fear, Tom could not recall the last time he had felt that. Anticipation, yes, and certainly the blood-shivering thrill that filled his limbs before a fight – as it did now – but not real fear. Yet for all that he was vaguely aware that it was fortunate the two men had turned right into a darker, meaner lane that led to Cornmarket Street.

'You think one of them is Lord Denton?' Birkenhead asked, his tone suggesting he would be deeply offended to learn that the sentry had indeed lied to him.

'Not William,' Tom said, never taking his eyes off the man thirty paces ahead, who was richly clothed in voluminous blue breeches and an expensive blue doublet that was slashed to reveal the fine lining of white fabric underneath. He wore the red sash of the King's service and sported two red feathers in a silk scarf around the crown of his broad beaver. 'His piss-proud son Henry,' Tom said, thinking that running the new Royal Mint was a job to which the Dentons would take like pigs to mud.

The man next to Henry glanced behind him, aware of company, but Tom touched the brim of his hat and the man turned back round, reassured that the two men following had no malevolent intent. Both men laughed and Henry passed his friend a bulbous flask, slapping the man's back and growling some drunken malediction.

You won't be laughing soon, Tom thought, wishing he had a good poll-axe or an Irish hilt rather than the rapier that had been provided to complement his disguise, for he knew Henry was a fine swordsman and Tom would rather assail them with brute force and aggression than engage two opponents at once in a fencing bout.

'And you have a grievance with Master Denton?' Birkenhead enquired but received no answer as Henry and his companion waded into a throng of women who had coalesced out of the darkness. 'It would seem the young man is a flesh-monger,' the editor said, 'with an appetite for Jack whores and harridans, for there is no decent notch to be found round here. So I am told.'

Tom recalled a summer's day many years ago when he and Mun had come across Henry and his cronies in Gerard's Wood beating a crippled boy. Henry had taunted Martha Green too. He had declared that she would open her legs for a farthing, *but seeing as there are three of us, I'd happily stretch to the price of a quart of good ale.* Those foul words echoed now across the years, piercing Tom's soul like a thin blade: a blade he twisted himself by conjuring Martha, his once beauti-ful love, in his mind's eye, her skin turning blue as she hung lifeless at pain's end on a rope beneath the old bridge across the Tawd.

Henry's companion turned, the wench clinging to him cooing in his ear, and wafted a hand at Tom the way a man might shoo a fly. 'You wags will have to wait your bleeding turn,' he called, enough slur about it to suggest that they had been enjoying the favours of the beaker. But Tom gave no reply as he and Birkenhead approached, the editor's unease palpable in the night air.

Several churches' bells were ringing now, alerting the city to the furore, or perhaps celebrating the capture of a traitor. A stone's throw north musketeers were gathering, readying to sweep through the streets in a night patrol. The men of the watch were bristling and there was a growing thrum in Oxford, as though, having heard the explosion at All Souls, folk were venturing outside to taste the night for themselves. At the end of the street the Saxon tower of St Michael at the north gate imposed itself on the gloom as God's witness to Man's sin. But none of this seemed to concern Henry Denton and his friend.

Henry too turned towards them, thrusting a ringed finger into an ear and waggling it theatrically. 'Your lugs full of dung?' he barked. 'My friend told you to wait, sirrahs.' His other hand was snarled up in a mass of black hair, beneath which a hard-faced woman half grinned, relishing the covetousness she had provoked. 'I will not be rushed when buying quim.'

'Take your time, friend,' Tom said, lingering in the shadow of a garden wall. By contrast Birkenhead was cast in the glow of the near-full moon that hung in the eastern sky above the old Saxon tower beyond Cornmarket Street. Tom could feel the editor's eyes on him, could sense the man's cold fear. And his indecision.

'Stay where you are,' Tom growled at him, never taking his eyes off Henry and the other man, a rougher sort by the looks but a soldier certainly, given the age and wear of the leather baldrick across his right shoulder and the nicks and dents on the wrist and knuckle guards of the pattern sword hanging from it. A ballock dagger hung above his crotch from a belt, its wooden grip worn smooth. Tom fixed on this man's eyes. 'Your taste in friends is worse even than your taste in women,' he said, nodding in Henry's direction. 'Leave him to his whores and be gone.'

The man glanced at Henry, who was busy assessing and comparing the attributes of three women who were fawning over him with the ardour and insincerity of the hungry.

'Do you know who he is, whelp?' the man snarled at Tom, throwing one hand Henry's way, the wine flask hanging from his index finger. The promise of violence – a look Tom had come to know well – flashed in the eyes beneath the hat's rim. 'His father's a lord, you insolent cur.'

'I know Henry Denton better than you, you scab-faced bastard,' Tom said. 'Henry is a fartleberry hanging from his father's arse.'

The insult cut through Henry's preoccupation and he turned, shrugging off one of the whores who sought to hold his attention. A gust blew from the south bringing the tang of blood from the offal and filth which the butchers in the Queen Street shambles emptied daily into the street. To Tom it was also the smell of battle. He inhaled deeply.

'You are drunk. Now fuck off!' Henry's companion swigged the last drop from his flask and hurled it at Tom, just missing, so that the vessel shattered against the wall in a spray of clay shards. He turned back to the gaggle of whores and gestured for Henry to do the same.

'Leave us, ladies,' Tom snarled from the shadows. 'You'll get no silver from these men tonight.'

'The lad's tired of life!' Henry's friend exclaimed, turning. His sword hissed against the scabbard's throat and he came at Tom with the naked blade. 'Your stubbornness will get you killed, whelp.'

Tom hauled his own blade free and lunged but the man parried, his heavier blade knocking Tom's rapier wide, and brought the sword scything back so that it would have opened Tom's belly had he not stepped back and thrown his left arm across himself, catching the other's sword on his knife where blade met guard. Taking the strain Tom threw his right foot forward and slammed his forehead into the man's face, sending him staggering.

A whore screamed. 'Fetch the watch, Clemence!' another shouted as they dispersed like crows shooed from a hanged man's gallows.

'You're a dead man!' the soldier snarled through teeth daubed in the blood that was flooding from his nose, but anger had made him reckless and he came at Tom with a series of wild hay-making strokes that Tom avoided with keen eyes and fast feet, backing off until his opponent's sword was out wide. Then he whipped his rapier up, slashing the man's face so that he screamed in agony and reeled, dropping his sword.

'I saw you die!' Henry yelled, his own fine sword pointing at Tom accusingly, whilst his friend staggered, clutching his face, then fell to his knees, blood cascading through his fingers and soaking his cuffs and sleeves. Tom had caught a glimpse of the wound: a deep slash that had opened the soldier's face from his neck to his right eye. 'I saw you die,' Henry said again, paying his friend no heed, fixated as he was on his old enemy. 'We saw you killed at Kineton Fight!'

'I came back from the dead, Henry,' Tom said.

Birkenhead had thrown himself against the garden wall which he now all but clung to, the whites of his eyes glowing against the inky dark.

'What happened to Martha . . .' Henry's mouth twisted, as though he hated himself for what he was about to say. 'None of that was my doing. My father—'

'Your father will bury you two days hence, Henry,' Tom said, fighting the urge to fly at the man and tear him to bloody meat with his bare hands. 'He will stand by your grave and know his line is extinguished and then I will kill him too.'

Tom might not have felt real fear since he had become a killer of men, but he recognized fear when he saw it and he saw it now in Henry's handsome face.

'Kill him, Henry!' his friend screamed, on his knees drenched in blood, the gore-slick hands at his face shaking wildly with pain and shock. 'Look what he's done to me! Kill him!'

'This time there's no coming back,' Henry snarled, finding his courage, remembering his own prowess. 'You'll be food for the maggots, Rivers. Just like your hanged whore.'

Tom flew at him and their swords sang out in the night, the ring and scrape of steel barely keeping time with the deadly dance of the blades. Strike, parry, riposte, Tom's left arm bent as a counterbalance by his right cheek, the hand still gripping his knife. But Henry's skill was more than a match for Tom's fury and he fluently turned each parry into an attack, so that Tom knew he was in the fight of his life. And though they were evenly matched in height, Henry's was the longer blade, giving him a greater lunging distance and a murderous advantage.

The first flurry ended as suddenly as it had begun and both men stepped backwards, their guards raised, Tom sucking air into his lungs and knowing he needed to close the distance between them. He launched himself at Henry again, his front foot kicking back and his rear leg thrusting forward in an explosive pass, his arm straight and strong, the rapier's point impelled towards his enemy's face, but Henry threw his back foot across his body, turning side-on, and the point of Tom's blade hit nothing and then Henry was upon him and Tom's body worked instinctively, his blade meeting every thrust and driving the deadly point wide, the balls of his feet barely brushing the ground as he made of himself a moving target. The weapons kissed and rasped and Tom knew Henry was the better swordsman but he twisted and parried and somehow kept the death-dealing point of his enemy's blade off him.

Then Tom stepped backwards out of reach and dragged a forearm across his head, blinking away sweat and turning his face enough to spit but keeping his gaze riveted on Henry. Henry almost grinned, for he knew that Tom had made a mistake by putting space between them, knew that Tom's best chance, the explosive pass, had failed. Now Henry's longer blade would finish it.

'On a horse you were a nuisance, Rivers,' he said, whipping his blade left and right, cutting the air with sharp breaths. 'But like this . . .' Now the predatory flash of teeth in the moonlit shadows. 'Like this . . . without your brother . . . you are nothing.'

Small, still careful steps brought Henry a little closer, their sword points overlapping now by a hand's span. Perfect striking distance.

'The watch!' Birkenhead cried, and Tom was aware of men's voices, a commotion behind him on New Inn Street. 'Cease this madness before it's too late!'

'Kill the bastard!' Henry's friend screamed, one eye bulged and mad with pain, bloody hands still pressed against the savage wound as though he was ashamed of it.

Come on, you arrogant pig's bladder, Tom thought, aware now of flamelight spilling across the ground round his feet and along the garden wall, chasing away the shadows and illuminating Birkenhead's wan face. Then Henry lunged to show how the pass attack *should* be done, but Tom dead-parried the blade and struck, his rapier's edge slicing into Henry's forehead, then punched in with his left hand, plunging the knife into the side of Henry's neck.

'You're a dead man, Henry,' Tom spat in his face. Then he hauled the knife out and would have stayed to watch his old enemy piss his breeches and gasp his last pain-racked breaths, but to stay was to die.

And so he ran.

For a while they chased him like a hound pack on the scent

of a fox, west past the old Saxon church and the run-down tenements, on through damp passageways, then south-west along the paved streets of the colleges. Their yells sometimes sounded close enough that they must surely be on him, their torches drowning him in their accusing light. Other times the voices were more faint, swirling in echoes off grand college walls and lost to the night. But Tom never stopped to take stock, instead letting his legs eat up the ground, his boots splashing through filth, the wind gushing past his ears and his heart hammering with exertion and the thrill of the chase.

He did not know when they had at last given up the hunt, or at least when he had outstripped them, but by the time he had weaved his way back to the north-west of the city there was no sign of pursuit. And yet by now the night watch would know that what they had been alerted to was no drunken brawl over whores. John Birkenhead would have revealed Tom's identity and his part in the destruction of his precious printing press. He would have reported that there were other rebels involved too, though there was every chance the Royalists had already gleaned as much from the man they had captured trying to slip out of the city. All of which meant they were still searching for him.

Furthermore, Tom was certain that regardless of what information they had pulled from the man they had caught, they would have alerted the soldiers at the city's gates, effectively sealing Oxford until they knew the extent of the threat. Even if the others had escaped after the explosion, Tom knew he would never now make it out of the west gate through which they had entered the city that morning. Which was why he had followed his nose. Behind him was New College, from which he could hear sergeants bellowing orders and a drum beating the Assembly, dragging soldiers from their quarters to protect the gunpowder stored there. In front of him was the north-west section of the old city wall, against which stood scaffolding and piles of rough-dressed stone that glowed dully in the moonlight, indicative of the overall shoring up of Oxford's defences of which Tom had seen evidence across the city. But immediately in front of him, between him and the wall, was a stinking ditch, the same that had assaulted his senses earlier that night and to which Birkenhead had assured Tom he would grow accustomed. He had not grown accustomed to it and the stench was almost overwhelming at such close proximity, but he had gambled that of all the possible ways out of the city, this one would not be crawling with Cavaliers. The reeking trench, into which the people of Oxford's foul waste was tipped, was somewhere all but the rakers avoided, either deliberately or subconsciously. Tom's gamble had paid off and even the night watch had not thought to come here. Yet.

That was the good news. The bad news was that there was no bridge across the mire. The trench extended east and west for as far as Tom could see in the dark. He could not go west because that was towards New College and the sound of soldiers and drums. He could perhaps go east, try to find a way round – for surely there was one – but that way stood the west gate and the heavily defended Magdalen Bridge. Besides which, he was running out of time. It was likely the Cavaliers had sent additional patrols out to sweep the surrounding countryside, in which case there was a good chance that The Scot and his men would have given Tom up as lost and were even now riding south-east towards the dawn.

He turned at a sound, pulling his sword from its scabbard, but it was only a flea-bitten dog searching for scraps amongst the scrub. He turned back towards the ditch and the wall beyond, plotting his route up the scaffolding, hoping he would find a rope or some other means of climbing down the other side.

Then, his blood still thrumming from the fight and the chase and the thrill of being alive whilst his enemy was not, he plunged into the stinking filth.

CHAPTER TWELVE

'THAT'S A SIGHT TO GET A MAN'S MOUTH WATERING,' O'BRIEN SAID, looking across a fair meadow whose yellow cowslips glowed unnaturally bright in the weak dawn light, to the close-cropped pasture beyond and further off still, where a throng of beeves stood hemmed in by fence and hedgerow. The morning's fog lay thick across the land like a blanket yet to be thrown off, and all was still and quiet but for the relentless shrieks of buzzards soaring high above and the forlorn replies of their unseen chicks. 'There must be enough beef there to feed a bloody regiment,' the Irishman said, using his teeth to pull the stopper from the neck of his powder flask.

To the west of the cattle enclosure stood a copse of mist-threaded birch and hazel just as Prince Rupert's agent had told them it would. According to the spy, behind that screen they would find a timber-framed barn that had seen better days, and inside that they would find . . . well, that had been a little harder to swallow, and yet here they were.

For two days they had ridden south-east, avoiding all towns and villages in favour of the fields, drovers' paths and trackways, like the shadow of a hawk skimming the ground. The Prince's agent had been sceptical of Mun's troopers' ability to get the job done when he had discovered that there were only thirty of them, and yet he had nevertheless insisted that they undertake the business, that Mun repay his past assistance and future silence. Besides which he could not deny the success Mun's wolfpack had enjoyed preying on rebels amongst the rolling hills, rugged rough pastures and the wild uplifts of Lancashire's massifs. Furthermore, he knew as well as Mun that being so few was what would make it possible to travel across country without drawing attention, which was what they had done, skirting towns such as Tunstall, Burslem, Hanley and Stoke-upon-Trent, and others whose names none of them knew. Only once had they ridden into a settlement: the large village of Tutbury, where Mun had spent some of the silver Hook Nose had given him on meat and ale, deciding that if he was to risk his men's lives in an enterprise not of his choosing, he would at least see their bellies full and their thirst slaked. Albeit O'Brien was still hungry judging by the gurgles emanating from his stomach as they stood considering their next move, while two hares boxed madly amongst the yellow flowers a stone's throw away.

'You really think this Lord Lidford would keep a siege gun out here in the middle of nowhere, where any gimblet-eyed pedlar might stumble over it?' O'Brien asked, putting a ball and wadding in his wheellock's muzzle and ramming the whole lot down before replacing the scouring stick beneath the barrel.

'I doubt his wife wants the thing sitting in their parlour, Clancy,' Mun said. 'And if it's as big as that sly bastard says it is, no one is going to run off with it. No one apart from us.'

'I suppose there's some sense in it,' O'Brien said, looking up as a flock of geese passed overhead, boasting of their adventures in wild, far-away lands. 'I knew this girl from Mullagh, County Clare. Cleona Dalaghan.' The Irishman shook his head. 'Christ, she was ugly. She had teeth like the Ten Commandments, all broken! One Christmas we near hung *her* and kissed the mistletoe.' He grinned. 'Bigger than me she was, a grand doorful of a woman. Her shadow had its own shadow! Still, she was a generous wench and even the few who hadn't flattened some straw with Cleona Dalaghan were never to wonder what her tits looked like. Why is that, O'Brien, you ask?' Mun hoisted an eyebrow and O'Brien cupped his big hands over his chest. 'Because those apple dumplings of hers spent more time out of her bodice than in it. Like your man's gun, hiding in plain sight.'

Perhaps that was it, Mun thought, for nothing would draw attention to Lord Lidford's prize possession – a gun he had won in a card game according to Rupert's man – like soldiers and defences. Better to hide the thing where no one would think to look, specially in time of war. And yet an old barn still seemed an unlikely place. 'We're not going to get any wiser standing here reminiscing about your old sweethearts,' Mun said, turning and walking back to his men who were waiting by a thick snarl of blackthorn and bramble amongst whose white flowers a thousand spider webs glistened with dew.

A little while later Mun and eleven of his men were walking through the birch copse, sword blades held low as though they were cutting through the last of the morning mist still cloaking the ground. He had left four with their horses and sent the remaining fourteen, mounted under John Cole's command, to the oxen, with orders to round up the beasts and anyone they found guarding them.

'No killing,' Mun said now, the barn appearing through the trees. It was no wonder that they had not seen the building before, for the birch bark and the barn's old limewashed walls were almost the same colour, so that Mun wondered if Lord Lidford had planted the trees for that very purpose. Then they were through and there it was, fitting Hook Nose's description down to its knee-height stone base and the roof that was for the most part straw-thatched, but for the eastern end which had been re-covered in the recent past, and hastily too by the looks, not with straw but with fern and gorse.

But the large double doors of good solid oak looked out of place against the rotting daub walls, almost ruining the overall image of neglect. It was like a man arriving at a horse auction on a tired nag to give an impression of modest means, only to betray his wealth by having not swapped his best saddle for another. O'Brien's raised eyebrow said that he had noticed the incongruity too as Mun nodded at him to lift the beam that held the doors shut. It thumped onto the ground an inch away from crushing Godfrey's foot.

'Keep you on your toes, whelp,' O'Brien said, shooting the lad an awkward glance before pulling the big doors open. 'After you, Sir Edmund,' he said, and, sword in hand just in case, Mun walked into the rotten-smelling dark.

'Open the door right up,' Mun said behind him, for the entrance faced east and the dawn light, pink with the blush of spring, flooded in, chasing the disturbed gloom to the barn's corners where it gathered thick as pitch. To his left against the wall stood an old cart in which some creature had made a nest. Cobwebs laced the wheels, filling the holes between the spokes and shivering slightly in the breeze coming through the open doors. Immediately in front of him was what remained of last year's hay, a large loose mound of dusty fodder that still held the scent of a summer past. A flap of wings above drew Mun's eyes up as a pigeon moved noisily to another beam. Other birds cooed softly in the darkness through which shafts of light poured from holes in the thatch and walls.

'You afraid of rats, Edmund?' O'Brien asked, nodding at the sword in Mun's hand. But Mun ignored him and began to plunge the blade into the hay pile, filling the air with dust that made the big Irishman sneeze.

'Well, lads, what are you waiting for?' Goffe said, joining Mun and poking the dry old fodder with his own hanger.

'I've got something!' Trooper Godfrey called from the dark at the rear of the barn. 'Here in this straw!'

'All right, don't wet yourself, lad, we're just here,' Goffe said.

O'Brien put both hands into the straw and a moment later his teeth flashed in the half-light. 'I love them that love me; and those that seek me shall find me,' he said, throwing off the straw like a dog digging up a bone.

The gun was draped in canvas but even then and in the murk it was clearly a monster.

'Fetch the others,' Mun said to Godfrey, 'and tell them we'll need at least ten oxen.' The young trooper nodded and ran off, all but tripping over his sword scabbard with the excitement of it.

'We'll never move it,' O'Brien said, scratching his thick bristles.

'We've got no choice,' Mun replied, lifting the canvas and pressing a palm against the cool iron.

'I'll make us a torch so we can see what we're about,' Harley put in, turning to go back outside.

'You'll do nothing of the sort, you paper-skulled pillock,' O'Brien said, clouting the man's right ear. 'There's likely to be black powder hereabouts, cully. Bring a flame in and . . .' he spread the fingers of both hands, 'you could scare the wee birdies,' he said, pointing up to the rafters.

Further exploration of the barn revealed ten kegs of black powder and yokes and harnesses for sixteen draught animals. All in all the rotting old place was a treasure trove; the only thing of which there was no sign was the forty-seven-pound iron balls that such a beast would cough to pummel castle walls and put terror in men's bellies. But that was not Mun's problem.

'You say this Lord Lidford is in Oxford with the King?' O'Brien said, frowning at Mun. 'Why in God's name is all this not being used against the rebels?' He slapped the gun's muzzle. 'She looks almost a virgin, like she's barely been fired.'

'She's a he,' Mun said, pointing at the carriage. Upon one smooth elm cheek could just be made out the name someone had given the cannon. 'Goliath.'

'A fitting name for the beast,' O'Brien admitted, 'though he's hardly making them quake with fear tucked away in here with the rats and mice.'

'Perhaps Lord Lidford has not yet decided whose side he is on,' Mun suggested. 'He has no affection for Rupert. The Prince's man told me that even if the Prince could provide the Earl of Essex as wadding Lord Lidford would not allow him to fire his precious gun.'

'Which is why we're stealing it,' Tobias Fitch caught on, the mason's apprentice sharing Godfrey's enthusiasm for the business.

'Easier said than done, lad,' O'Brien said, glancing at Mun who recalled the appalling sight of the royal artillery train hauling itself through the mud on the way to Edgehill. 'I still say we'll never move it. Not far anyway. Not without more men.'

'I thought a good Irishman was worth three or four Englishmen,' Mun said, walking out of the barn and into the dawn. There was no sign of any other folk around, which was good.

'That's true enough,' O'Brien admitted, 'but with that being the case we still need another three Irishmen.'

Two hours later and with the help of the oxen they had hauled Goliath from his resting place. Revealed in all its glory the gun had the men slack-jawed and wide-eyed. None had ever seen a gun like it, for being a full cannon it was even bigger than the demi-cannon which now stood sentinel at Shear House. Goliath was mounted on a complicated affair, a carriage constructed from different woods and one and a half times as long as the length of the gun's bore. Its wheels, like the side-pieces, were of elm and were half the length of the barrel in diameter. But its proportions and how the thing was made was not what interested Mun. What was of infinitely more importance was that the oak spokes and the axle trees, the planks at the fore-end, and every other part, were all present and in apparent good order. The old cart was sound, too, and the powder casks were loaded onto it and covered over with the canvas that had cloaked Goliath. Another two oxen were brought from the enclosure to pull this and those beasts were the lucky ones, Mun thought, for the cart and its contents weighed next to nothing compared with the gun carriage.

'What are we going to do with them?' O'Brien asked, nodding towards the three boys, not one of them a day over seventeen, whom Cole and his men had found guarding the oxen. Two had been armed with clubs and the third, a yellow-haired, ruddy-cheeked boy and the eldest of the three, had been brandishing a poorly made firelock for which he admitted, crimson-cheeked, having neither powder nor shot.

'We'll leave one man behind to guard them and keep an eye out until sundown,' Mun said, 'by which time we should be at Lichfield and the Prince should have his gun.'

Of them all Goffe had the most experience of oxen and so Mun had put him in charge of the beasts. The farmer-turned-soldier had assumed his responsibility earnestly, as though he relished the reminder of his former life, and not for the first time Mun was glad to have the man with him.

'It'll be painful slow, Sir Edmund,' Goffe said, checking the lead pair's harness whilst the oxen lowed and swished their tails agitatedly, 'but if we ta' care w' shall get there in one piece. It's nay plough, and new to me,' he said, lifting his helmet to scratch his red hair, 'but they're good animals.' Then young Godfrey came up and presented Goffe with a long slender hazel switch he had cut from the copse, and the farmer whipped it through the air and gave a reluctant nod.

'It'll do, youngen,' he said, then turned to Mun to show that all was set and his animals were ready to set off. Mun nodded back and gave the command, turning Hector west, away from the morning sun. The oxen moved forward, moaning, and the gun carriage creaked into life, the wheels turning over the muddied ground, and Goliath lurched, bound for Lichfield and Prince Rupert, the King's loyal nephew. Scourge of the rebels.

Mun sent John Cole and two others cantering west to ride as a vanguard a mile in front of the train. Another trooper rode just ahead, his job to choose the route that would make for the easiest passage, given that Goliath weighed, by O'Brien's reckoning, the better part of seven thousand pounds. Other than the man they had left back at the barn, the rest of Mun's troopers were split between those walking beside the train keeping each pair of oxen in check, and those mounted and leading the riderless horses.

'This all feels like an idea not even good enough to be terrible,' O'Brien said, twisting in his saddle to regard the train over his shoulder. He and Mun rode side by side heading up the lumbering column. 'I've seen men walk faster to their own hanging.'

'Just keep your eyes peeled,' Mun said, though he felt exactly as the Irishman did. Their success in the last weeks had come from their speed and manoeuvrability, from being unencumbered and lean. They had been a wolfpack all but living off the land, ranging far and wide. Killing at will. Now they were slow – painfully, cumbrously slow. They were just thirty men and a stolen gun that was so big as to be only useful for siege work. And there were twenty miles of open land between them and that siege.

'His Highness the Prince must have Lidford's gun if he is to break Lichfield,' Rupert's agent had said that night they had huddled beneath Mun's rude shelter as the rain seethed in the dark. 'And so Lidford's gun he shall have.'

But it was slow. The ground was soft but not too wet, so that only occasionally did the gun carriage's wheels need to be dug free, though that did not stop the men moaning when they did. Goffe was busy, covering twice the distance of any other, up and down the train with his switch, barking gruff commands in a language only the oxen understood. Where they could they kept to trackways and the well-trodden paths where the grass had long worn away and the ground had been compacted over the years. But this meant they were exposed and there were plenty of folk who watched them pass. Despite the war, men and women still worked in the fallow fields, spreading manure and their stinking cesspit waste, ploughing the filth into the soil to make it ready for the next year. They watched, leaning on spades, putting down handcarts and lifting their eyes from the plough lane to spy, and yet none of them approached, which was hardly surprising given the column's ragged, almost feral appearance. An appearance that was more help than hindrance, Mun knew, just as Hook Nose had said it would be. For the passing of such a gun would not go unnoticed. The folk of Seal and Acresford and of all the other unnamed villages between them and Lichfield would spread the news much quicker than they would the manure. Better if Mun's name and the allegiance of his troopers were not a constituent of that news, for he would be hard pressed to explain why he had stolen the gun from a lord who was even now with the King at Oxford.

And yet their anonymity did not stop Mun's stomach rolling over itself when he heard a trooper yell from the train's rear that a rider was coming hard and fast from the east and that it looked to be Walter Cade, the man they had left at the barn.

'The lad must be missing me already,' O'Brien said, the face behind the beard betraying his concern.

'Don't stop!' Mun called to Goffe, then nodded at the Irishman, pulling Hector round, and the two of them trotted back down the column to meet the rider. Mun looked up at the sun which was directly overhead. Midday, then, and he guessed they had only come some seven or eight miles.

'It's Cade,' O'Brien confirmed, but Mun knew it already for he had come to know how each of his troopers sat his horse, would recognize each man's riding style and perhaps even their horses too.

'Rides better than he shoots,' Mun remarked.

'Aye, he wouldn't hit a hole in a ladder.'

Cade was flying, hunched low in the saddle, his face obscured by the peak of the single-bar pot which he had stripped from a dead rebel corporal. And Mun felt his heart hammering in his chest as fiercely as the hooves of Trooper Cade's mare pummelled the ground, because he knew that someone must be on to them.

'It's not as though there'll be any hiding from whoever is sniffing our scent,' O'Brien said, which was true enough, for the oxen had disturbed the ground and the gun carriage's wheels had cut two deep ruts which stretched back east as far as the eye could see.

Mun wanted to wait until Cade had reined in and caught his breath, wanted to maintain a façade of equanimity as a professional officer should. But he failed.

'How many?' he yelled as Cade made up the last fifty paces and hauled on his reins and the mare screamed, biting at her foam-flecked bit and tossing her head so that her mane flew.

'Four,' Cade said, spitting a wad of thick saliva, his chest within his buff-coat heaving, labouring for breath. 'Four,' Cade said again. 'They must have seen the oxen were gone and they came to the barn.' The sweat-lathered beast wheeled round and round and Cade held the reins loosely, allowing the horse to calm down in its own time.

'Only four?' Mun said. 'Are you sure?'

Cade nodded. 'Aye, and you said no killing,' he said, as though all four would be dead now if Mun had not given that order. 'I left the lads where they was and came hard after you.'

Mun looked back the way they had come. No sign of pursuers. Yet.

'They'll be along, sir,' Cade said, wiping spittle off his beard with a filthy hand. 'Could be they're gathering more men.'

'There's a coppice back there, no more than half a mile,' O'Brien said, nodding back along the churned track. 'What say we prepare a welcome for our guests.' He winked at Cade. 'It's clear that your fellows are after an introduction.'

'We're King's men, O'Brien,' Mun warned. 'I'll not kill our own, if that's what they are.' I've done enough of that, he thought sourly.

The Irishman raised both palms and perfected a look of childhood innocence: the kind employed by children who have already been caught stealing apples. 'Being Irish doesn't make me a savage,' he said, 'but we can't stop, can we?' He thumbed back towards Goliath lumbering on further up the track. 'So better not to meet with any surprises, eh? A few of us in that copse, waiting nice and quiet. Then a polite greeting if someone happens along. What's the harm in it?'

'Then we'd better be quick,' Mun said, turning Hector back towards the train.

CHAPTER THIRTEEN

MUN HAD PICKED NINE MEN AND THEY HAD GALLOPED BACK TO A coppice of hazel, hornbeam and beech, and there waited hidden from the track by the young shoots upon which spring leaves were beginning to burst from their buds. Ten was not many, but to leave fewer men with the cannon would be to invite suspicion of an ambush from any who followed within sight, and likely slow the train's progress further. So ten would have to be enough, at least to put the fear of God into those they fell upon and send them tearing off back the way they had come.

They did not have to wait long.

'They only managed to scrounge two more,' O'Brien remarked disappointedly as they watched the party of six canter along Goliath's tracks towards them. 'We could have sent that lot running back to their mothers by ourselves, Sir Edmund. Still, I'd wager that shiny whore-monger doesn't lack lady admirers. Have you ever seen a thing so pretty that didn't have tits?'

Mun's eyes were also on the man riding in the middle of the group, for he wore a cuirassier's three-quarters armour that covered the entire upper body as well as the front half of the legs down to the knee. On his head was an open burgonet helmet with its distinctive fin on top, and the whole ensemble

glinted in the sunlight, making him look like some long-ago
hero from a story.

'They're brazen enough,' Tobias Fitch said, 'coming after us
like this.' The young apprentice already had a mason's broad
shoulders and thick arms so that in his forge-black back- and
breastplates and pot he looked every inch the warrior.

'Aye, makes you wonder what they intend when they catch
up with the gun,' Trooper Milward said, pulling his hanger
half out of the scabbard then thrusting it back in.

Hector snorted, one foreleg pawing at the ground, the stallion
sensing in his master the potential for imminent violence.

'Do not give fire,' Mun said as his men readied themselves to
explode from their hiding place. 'Show them steel and teeth and
they'll turn tail.' *I would if I saw us coming fast*, he thought,
aware more than ever of their wild appearance: their unkempt
beards and hollow cheeks, their assortment of blades and arms,
most of which had been stripped from defeated enemies and
bore the marks to prove it.

Their pursuers were well armed too by the looks and the
cuirassier and at least one other rode fine-looking horses: well-
muscled Cleveland Bays of over sixteen hands that would in
mere moments, Mun thought, be bearing their masters off in
great haste.

'As wild as you whoresons can look, if you please,' O'Brien
said through a grimace, and was met by eight wolfish visages
and eyes blazing with that intoxicating mix of thrill and fear.

'Now!' Mun gave Hector the spur and they erupted from
the thicket, shouting wildly, their mounts' hooves thumping
the earth and flinging clods into the air. 'Yargh!' Mun yelled,
the thrill seizing him in its maw. This was the flame to his soul
and he loved it, pulling his heavy sword from its scabbard and
holding it out wide, a promise of blood and death unleashed
unto the day.

And four of the six riders ahead of them hauled on their reins
and turned their mounts off the track, spurring off south-west

in sheer bloody fright. But to Mun's amazement the cuirassier and one other turned towards them and drew their own swords and charged.

'Mad bastards!' O'Brien bellowed. And Mun wanted to warn his men again not to kill, but they were committed to the charge and the two fools had signed their own death warrants and Mun's men would have to do what needed to be done.

In all that fine plate armour the cuirassier had fallen behind his companion and Mun on Hector had outstripped his men, so that he saw at least a chance, if only a slim chance, to avoid blood.

Forty yards.

Twenty.

Mun pushed his seat bones down into the saddle and sat up straight, thrusting his heels against the stirrups to slow Hector, but the other man did not slow, could not slow perhaps, and the blade at the end of his arm was bouncing madly. But Mun and Hector moved as one and Mun got his own sword up so that the two blades struck with a great ring of steel and the impact was too much for his opponent who was thrown back in his saddle. The man tried to cling on but couldn't and some twenty yards behind Mun he fell in a sickening crump of flesh, bone and war gear.

'Quarter! Quarter!' the cuirassier roared, exhibiting much better horsemanship than his companion and bringing his own Cleveland Bay back to the trot just as Mun's troopers came on him, enveloping him in a mass of horseflesh and blades. 'I yield, damn you!' the man yelled, hurling his sword at O'Brien so that the Irishman had to duck or be struck by it.

'Don't touch him!' Mun barked over his shoulder, riding back towards the man he had spilled from his saddle. Was he dead? He was not moving. Mun knew it was all too easy for a man to break his neck or his back in such a fall. 'Bloody fool,' he murmured, dismounting and patting Hector's neck, whispering praise and thanking the stallion for his fidelity.

'Leave him be!' someone called and Mun turned to see the cuirassier on his feet hurrying over to them. 'He's my son!'

'Then your son is a damned fool,' Mun said, seeing now the face of the young man on the ground before him. 'But he's alive.'

'You want me to restrain the lobster?' O'Brien asked, nodding at the man whose armour clanked with every move.

Mun shook his head. 'Let him see to his son.'

'The others ran, Father, the damned cowards,' the lad said, wincing as he pushed himself upright. Beneath his helmet blood was trickling from his forehead down the side of his aristocratic nose and his eyes were round with shock. He wore good back- and breastplates over an expensive-looking buff-coat.

'But you didn't run, son,' his father said, crouching awkwardly in his armour to undo his son's helmet strap and ease it off his head.

'He's but a cub,' O'Brien remarked, seeing the young man's face properly for the first time.

'And he needs to learn to control a horse properly or he'll get himself killed before he can grow a man's beard,' Mun said.

The cuirassier stood and marched over to Mun, whose men were watching, their pistols drawn. 'Who are you, sir?' the man demanded, removing his elaborate burgonet helmet which was gilded with patterns of swirling leaves. His short white hair was swept back and his white brows made a hawk's wings above eyes that were rivet heads of cold indignation.

'My name is not important,' Mun said, cringing inwardly. *I sound like that clandestine bastard*, he thought, recalling the man who had somehow persuaded Mun to do his bidding.

'Damn your insolence!' the cuirassier spat, his short white beard trembling with rage. The silk ruff at his neck spoke of a fashion long gone, completing the image of a soldier from a different age. 'Who is your master? Whom do you serve, your king or Parliament's traitors?'

'I am Sir Edmund Rivers and I serve His Majesty King

Charles,' Mun said, unwilling to play the game of secrets any longer. The other man did not so much as blink, which led Mun to assume that he had not recognized his name.

'Well, I have been soldiering, Sir Edmund Rivers,' the white-haired man said, smacking his left hand in its iron gauntlet against his own beautifully incised breastplate. The other hand was gloved only in leather so as not to hamper the loading of pistols. 'I have been soldiering in the Low Countries while this kingdom has been crumbling like bones in the grave. I have been in England but weeks, yet I see all too clearly that common folk have run amok and knights have become thieving thatch-gallows laying hands on whatever they come across.' Behind him his son was gingerly climbing to his feet and using his lace falling band to wipe the blood off his face. 'Where in God's name, sir, do you think you are taking that gun and those beasts?' He pointed up the track where no more than a mile away Goliath continued his slow lumbering progress west.

'What has that to do with you, old man?' Mun said, losing patience with this man who clearly did not appreciate how lucky he was that he and his son still lived and breathed.

'What has that to do with me?' the cuirassier blurted, eyes wide beneath his beetle-brows. 'You insolent devil! That's my damned gun!'

Mun heard an Irish snort escape then and nor was the perpetrator contrite when Lord Lidford spun and called them all thieves and scoundrels before turning his fiery gaze back on Mun. 'You steal my gun and my cattle, then you try to kill my son. You are more of a villain than any of Parliament's rebels!'

'Your son tried to kill himself,' Mun said, glancing at the young man whose cheeks flushed red with embarrassment for his reckless charge. A brave lad, though, Mun thought, for he could not have been a day older than seventeen and four other men had turned tail and fled for their lives. 'Besides, I thought you were in Oxford with the King.'

Lord Lidford flinched. 'You *knew* it was my gun?'

'I'd heard a rumour,' Mun said, glancing at O'Brien. The Irishman was leaning over his saddle's cantle, clearly enjoying the exchange. For the first time Lord Lidford seemed lost for words. Mun shrugged and took hold of Hector's bridle, rubbing the stallion's muzzle affectionately. 'You were supposed to be in Oxford and I was supposed to borrow your gun.'

'I have not been to Oxford for more than five years and then only to conclude some business before I took ship back to the war.' Lord Lidford swept an arm back towards his son who, now that he was on his feet, looked hardly the worse for his fall other than the cut where his helmet had gouged his head. 'I was at my estate. I have just buried my wife, Sir Edmund,' he said, all but sneering Mun's title, 'and my son just happened to be out riding, taking stock of my cattle, when he saw more than half my beasts gone, along with the lads I pay to look after them.'

'That devious bastard,' Mun murmured under his breath, recalling Rupert's spy assuring him that Lord Lidford was with the King in Oxford.

'You will turn that train around and return my gun to me,' Lord Lidford said flatly, then turned to walk back to his horse.

'No, sir, I will not,' Mun said. 'The gun stays with me. It is going to Lichfield.'

'How dare you?' Lord Lidford exclaimed, his right hand falling on his sword's hilt.

'Don't be an idiot . . . my lord,' O'Brien growled, flapping his hand at the man, warning him to remove his own from his weapon or else face the consequences. Beneath his white beard and moustaches Lord Lidford's face bloomed crimson with rage, though his hand came off the weapon's hilt. His son stood statue-still, nonplussed, eyes riveted to his father as though he had never seen him in such a compromised position.

'You will come with us, Lord Lidford,' Mun said, 'for I will not have you rounding up men to try to hamper our progress.'

'I shouldn't worry. His friends are halfway to bloody France by now, their arses playing a merry old tune,' John Cole said, raising a few chuckles from the others.

'We go to fight,' Mun said, stepping into his stirrup and hauling himself up onto Hector's back, 'and your gun will be more useful aimed at the rebels than it would be sitting in your damn barn. Fitch, Jones, disarm Lord Lidford and his fool son. Keep them on a short leash. If they give you any trouble, kill them.'

'You heard Sir Edmund,' Fitch barked, dismounting. 'Your swords, gentlemen, if you please.'

'The King will hear of this!' Lord Lidford protested, unbuckling his belt and handing it with its scabbarded blade to the broad-shouldered, broad-grinned former stonemason's apprentice.

'I have no doubt he will, my lord,' Mun said, turning Hector with his right knee and a click of his tongue and walking him westward after Goliath. 'I dare say His Majesty would be cheered to hear that you have brought your cannon to aid his nephew in reclaiming Lichfield for the Crown.'

And with that Lord Lidford had the sense to hold his tongue.

The rest of the slog to Lichfield was arduous and ponderous and uneventful. Three miles east of the city one of Prince Rupert's troops of dragoons came upon them and if Mun's allegiance was not immediately obvious, one look at Goliath told the dragoons that the ragged men had come to help prosecute the siege. Their captain, a smartly attired young officer with impeccable breeding and a penchant for ostrich feathers, judging by the plumes – two blue, one white – trimming his wide-brimmed hat, appeared less than impressed by Mun's troop. This Captain Assheton had ridden up, swept his hat from his head to unleash a mass of curls, and demanded to know to which regiment they belonged.

'Looks like a damned owl in an ivy bush,' O'Brien had muttered.

'I command here,' Mun had replied coarsely, choosing not to

mention his own title though he knew it would likely smooth his way, 'and I answer to no man but His Highness the Prince.' Captain Assheton had raised his eyebrows and eyeballed Mun, his dragoons bristling behind him. But then he had curled his lip and nodded, assuring Mun that he would provide safe escort to Lichfield, for the rebels, he said, were like toadstools and liable to spring up where none had been before, so that caution was advised. Mun knew that it was not his mention of the Prince that had blunted Assheton's bellicosity but rather that the captain was enough of a soldier to recognize fighting men – dangerous men – when he saw them. He must have been awed by Goliath too and likely wondered how such a powerful gun was in the hands of so few.

It had not rained, thank God, for that would have made moving Goliath impossible, but the day had grown overcast and now the grey, rain-filled clouds were brewing a storm and blending into the dusk as they rode into the town.

'It'll be pissing on us before we can find warm billets, a wee drop and a fond welcome,' O'Brien grumbled, ignoring the gawping faces of musketeers and artillerymen who had gathered thick as hounds on a bone around the cannon.

'I'm sure Captain Boone will be overjoyed to see us,' Mun said through a half smile, knowing full well that the Irishman's idea of a fond welcome involved rather more assets than their captain boasted. He inhaled the myriad smells: some terrible, but all strangely comforting, of a camp full of soldiers. His mind bore him back to the last time he was with the King's army, at Oxford, and that memory was closely followed by a pang deep in his chest which he tried to ignore. For being back with the army dredged up events much darker than the rain clouds which threatened them now. He could all but see his father in his neat buff-coat and high boots, adorned for a war he would have preferred no part in. He could almost reach out and grab Emmanuel, wrist to wrist in the warrior's way: Emmanuel who had been braver than any man and eager for the fight. Yet both of them were dead. And Mun fought on.

'Ours must be bigger than anything they've got here,' young Godfrey suggested, thumbing at the artillery sergeant who was thrusting his halberd this way and that, barking at his men to get Goliath moved to the main battery further west. Godfrey was sitting his dappled grey mare as proudly as if he had brought the five loaves and two fish to feed the multitude, as were several other of his men, Mun noticed, albeit they gladly relinquished responsibility for the cannon to those who had been prosecuting the siege.

The oxen began lowing again, complaining at being made to pull the encumbrance further still when they had already hauled it twenty miles and thought their labour done for the day. 'Fresh beef, lads! Dinner on the hoof compliments of Lord Lidford!' O'Brien called out, earning a look from Lord Lidford that would have taken the skin off a rabbit.

'These cattle and this gun are mine!' Lord Lidford countered from his saddle, his voice cutting through the din of cattle and men and musketry near by, 'and if any man mistreats either, if any man so much as salivates in front of one of my animals I shall have his hands cut off. Do you hear?' Some of the seasoned musketeers grumbled obscenities and Lord Lidford's son, whose name Mun had learned was Jonathan, had the decency to look embarrassed, for all his puffed-up chest and defensive posture.

'What did I tell you?' O'Brien grumbled, catching the first spits of rain in an upturned palm as he and Mun, relieved of the cannon, led their column towards the immense imposing pile that dominated all before it. To Mun's eyes the cathedral resembled more of a challenge to God's authority than a grand demonstration of His glory. Its three great spires proclaimed a martial power more than a hopeful, spiritual endeavour; looked for all the world like spear points thrusting for Heaven's belly. Which was fitting, he thought, knowing the blood that had been spilled within the cathedral's shadow over the last weeks. For having neither walls nor a castle, the Earl of Chesterfield had established his garrison in the Cathedral Close which was encircled by a high wall, and there he had held out against Lord Brooke's Parliament for several days before his inevitable surrender. Now, the rebels held the Close. The besiegers had become the besieged.

'Looks as if our lot took a battering,' O'Brien said as they drew nearer. Even in the dark Mun could see the damage Parliament's cannon had wreaked amongst the towers and spires.

'They still shouldn't have given it up,' Mun said, taking in the sight of Prince Rupert's forces gathered behind their siege lines, sheltering behind ruined walls and in the shells of houses, milling behind earth-filled gabions, keeping their match dry, smoking their pipes and resigning themselves to another night out in the open. 'Because now we've got to take it back again.'

'O'Brien, you red Irish devil, is that you?'

O'Brien grimaced. 'If we turn round now, Sir Edmund, we can ride out of here before it's too late.'

'I fear it's already too late,' Mun said, feeling a smile tug at his lips at the sight of Richard Downes and Vincent Rowe threading their way through the soldiers, the rain and the gloom towards them.

'No, it's not me, Downes,' O'Brien replied, showing a palm, 'I'm just a Heaven-blessed handsome Irishman who happens to look like your old friend O'Brien, though I'll confess 'tis a strange thing that two men should share such good looks.' He reached down and gripped Downes's wrist and then Rowe's, the four of them grinning like fiends, and as they greeted Mun in turn he felt warmth bloom in his chest, vanquishing dark thoughts. For it was a fine thing to be reunited with his brothers-in-arms, men with whom he had shared the fear and the frenzy and the madness of battle.

'You tosspots are still giving the rebels cause to piss in their boots and regret taking up arms against their king?' Mun asked, noting that young Vincent Rowe had a more steely look in his eyes nowadays. Perhaps they all did, he thought.

'I'm not so sure we've been keeping those traitorous bastards from their sleep,' Downes said, gesturing back towards the Cathedral Close, 'but I'll wager we've got the men of Lichfield keeping a close eye on their women.' He gripped Rowe's shoulder with a filthy, powder-burnt hand. 'Even the whelp here has been swinging his nutmegs around the town. As fortune would have it we've been knee-deep in quim since you two buggered off and left us in Oxford.'

'Now I know you're lying,' O'Brien said, nodding at Rowe, 'for youngen's got a face like someone set it on fire and put the flames out with a spade,' at which they all laughed, for Vincent Rowe's high cheekbones, full lips and dark eyes made him handsome enough to turn many a girl's head and cause husbands to tighten their grip on their wives.

'The boys will be glad to see you back,' Rowe said, rubbing Hector's muzzle like an old friend.

'And how's our good friend Captain Boone?' O'Brien asked.

'Still alive. Still a bastard,' Downes said.

'Now now, Trooper Downes,' Corporal Bard said, appearing from nowhere and nodding in greeting to Mun and O'Brien. The guard of his three-bar pot was pushed up, exposing his skull-like face. 'Good to have you two back with us,' he said. 'Do I take it there are no more rebels in Lancashire? Rumour is you and your farm lads have been hunting 'em down like the bloody plague.' His eyes ran the length of the column behind Mun but it was impossible to know what the man was thinking.

'There are still plenty of Parliament men up there, Corporal,' Mun said, 'but I heard that Captain Boone has been heartsick ever since I left.' He shrugged. 'I couldn't think of him suffering like that and so here I am.'

Bard hawked, turned his head and spat a wad of tobacco

and phlegm into the mud. 'And you happened across a bloody great gun on your merry way,' he said. 'A bloody great cannon no less.'

Again Mun shrugged, glancing at O'Brien, who smiled. 'It was just sitting there by the road, Corporal,' Mun said. 'Seemed a shame to ride on by and leave it to the enemy. We thought His Highness might find use for it.'

'The cannon is mine, Corporal,' Lord Lidford said, walking his Cleveland Bay up, so that Mun noticed Bard taking in the fine horse with its large, white-star-marked head and well-muscled withers, before he fully appreciated the man upon it.

'And who might you be?' Bard asked, the respect he would usually have afforded a man in full cuirassier's armour blunted by the man's apparent lack of a sword.

'Insolence everywhere I turn,' Lord Lidford announced despairingly and Bard looked up at Mun for an explanation that Mun did not have the time or patience for.

'I must speak with the Prince,' Mun said, peering through the torch-lit night towards the siegeworks before the Cathedral Close.

'Aye, I expect you must, Sir Edmund,' Bard said, as though the title still tasted curious on his tongue, 'but I warn you His Highness has cursed you more than once since Oxford. You were supposed to join us at Windsor once you had broken the rebels attacking your house.' He raised one eyebrow. 'Perhaps you forgot,' he suggested, scratching one hollow cheek upon which the bristles were thick and grey. 'Besides which, he's been in a foul mood since we got 'ere.' He thumbed back towards the rebel defences which Mun now saw were surrounded by a moat. 'Getting that lot out will be harder than getting a quart of ale out of Walton,' he said, which made the point well for Humphrey Walton was a known niggard though he always seemed flush with coin for whores and gambling.

'I suspect my cannon might cheer him,' Mun said.

'Aye, it might,' Bard admitted, glancing again at Lord Lidford and the young man at his shoulder and cocking his chin in their direction, wanting an explanation. But Mun did not want to get into it and so he ignored the corporal. Bard shrugged. 'Downes, Rowe,' he barked, 'now that I've found you why don't you make yourselves useful for once in your miserable lives? Get Sir Edmund's troopers' horses picketed and find this lot billets and ale.'

'Why don't we find them each a woman, a warm bed and a suckling pig while we're about it?' Downes dared, earning himself a look from Bard that promised cold horrors.

'Let's not go spoiling them,' Bard replied, 'they ain't bloody heroes. And I'm no military genius but I reckon that there cannon would be a great deal more use if they had brought shot for it.'

'Don't ask for much, does he?' O'Brien grumbled.

'You haven't changed a bit, Corporal Bard,' Mun said, dismounting, impressed that even in the dark with the cannon being taken off by the artillery sergeant and his men, Bard had known from the way the cart rode that it could not have contained shot.

'I'm older, Sir Edmund,' Bard said, 'but I blame that on the damn rebels.'

'We're all older,' Mun said.

'Praise the ripe field not the green corn,' O'Brien said, as Rowe took Hector by the bridle and Downes took O'Brien's mare and the horses blew and nickered excitedly for they knew they would soon be fed.

'Lead on, Corporal,' Mun said.

'Aye, off we go then,' Bard said, turning back towards the looming cathedral as Mun and O'Brien, Lord Lidford and his son Jonathan followed through the siege lines that smelt of wet wool and tobacco smoke, the latrine pit and, more faintly, the sharp metallic and earthy scent of burnt black powder.

To find the Prince.

CHAPTER FOURTEEN

BESS HAD NEVER SEEN LONDON BEFORE. SHE HAD HEARD ENOUGH about it – too much if truth be told – from Mun who had visited the capital several times and then from Tom who had been full of it all after his time there with his father and brother before the war. They had told her that London was a great monster, spreading out beyond the confines of the medieval city, stretching from Stepney in the east to Westminster to the west. They had told her that London was home to four hundred thousand souls, though she had not been able to conceive of so many people and had listened to their stories with a quiet detachment, as though they talked of a foreign country which she, in all likelihood, might never see with her own eyes.

'The streets flow like rivers,' Mun had said, 'and like a river in which it is impossible to touch the same water from one heartbeat to the next, there flows an endless tide of faces which once seen are never caught sight of again.'

'All the country is stuffed into London,' her father had said once on returning from the place, 'so that soon England will only be London and the whole country left waste.'

And yet none of their talk had prepared her for it. Because it was not the same place any more. She had been struck by its size, its vastness, but where were the multitudes thronging the streets which her brothers had spoken of? She had been awed by the palatial buildings of the Strand and made dizzy by the grand classical piazza of Covent Garden, its space so at odds with the random and haphazard arrangement of London's winding streets, alleyways and courtyards. She had been horrified by the atrocious housing of the poor labourers and apprentices and desperate migrants who massed in London like flies on a corpse, their appalling and unsanitary living conditions like nothing Bess had ever seen or imagined.

Yet London was but a shadow of itself. Even Bess, who did not know the city, could feel that. If London had been an open hand before the war, now it was a closed fist, scalded by the conflict, withdrawing from it like flesh from the flame. Absent was the feverishness she had expected to see but should have known she would not, for with the King and his court removed to Oxford, London's apprentices off fighting, other men having been conscripted, and those folk that remained burdened by Parliament's new taxes, parts of the city had a stillness about them. The great law courts, the chancery, and the King's Bench at Westminster had seemed all but abandoned and now, as they crossed the bridge into Southwark, Bess could tell that Dane sensed it too, that there was a cloud over the city as thick as any you might see on a cold day when the coal fires belched their smoke into the sky. Dane's eyes had lingered on the boarded-up shop fronts and the lifeless trading and livery companies which would normally have buzzed with craftsmen and manufacturers.

'It is a pity you and the boy should see London like this,' Dane said now, careful to step around a pile of fresh dung as they led their mounts southward down Long Southwark. 'This damned war has ripped out the city's heart and soul.'

And yet to look at Joe Bess would have thought he was gazing upon St Peter's gates. The young man had never before been north of Preston or south of Wigan, so that he had turned dumbstruck the moment they came into the city. Was dumbstruck still, and they had been in London two days.

'I'll wager one can't even find a comely whore any more with so many Puritans wagging a finger around Westminster,' Dane said.

'Then you can blame the rebels for your loss,' Bess muttered as soon as an old white-haired brewer had trundled out of ear-shot on his cart.

'I blame both parties,' Dane replied, letting go the bridle to sweep his unkempt dark hair back off his forehead, tying it with a thong as his little Welsh Cob walked dutifully behind.

Without the lank hair to obscure his face, his cheekbones and strong dark eyebrows announced themselves, and Bess considered that some women might think him handsome, at least until they knew the man for a boor and a drunkard.

'Royalist and Parliamentarian garrisons have spread like a pox over the country,' he said. 'Every town along the Thames from here to Oxford is choked with them and London suffers for it.' They had been approached by so many starving, wild-eyed beggars that Dane now walked out in front just ahead of Bess, his hand never far from his sword. Joseph guarded the rear, though his blunderbuss and Dane's pistols were well hidden amongst the blankets carried in sacks upon the dun mare's back. 'The normal trade routes are tightly controlled or blocked completely,' Dane said, 'and London is hungry. But Parliament is hungrier. It milks the city's merchants as much as – perhaps more than – did the King.' He grimaced then and Bess caught a glimpse of the other Dane, the man who had slaughtered those clubmen with terrifying ease. The killer. 'Parliament's war chest fills and men's bellies do not.'

They stopped at the junction of St Olave's Street to let a troop of dragoons trot past, their horses' hooves clipping and scuffing off the cobbles, and Bess could not help but study the riders' faces, struck by the notion, absurd as she knew it was, that one of them might be Tom.

Then Dane glanced at her and she looked away, afraid

that he might in that brief moment have read the hope in her eyes.

He had.

'It will not be so easy, Bess,' he said.

'What will not be easy?' She felt the blood come to her cheeks.

He shrugged, dropping the issue, then clicked with his tongue to lead his horse off again. 'It's not just the fighting men that will feel this pinch,' he said, to Bess's relief. 'With Parliament's navy blockading Newcastle the coal is not getting through, so come next winter London will freeze. And nor will the brewers and the glass-makers, the potters and the smiths earn their crust with no coal to burn.'

'And yet I suppose some of Parliament's taxes will be spent here on clothing and equipment for their armies?' Bess suggested. 'Some of the shoe-makers and felt-makers will be up to their necks in orders.'

'True enough,' Dane admitted. 'But still. You do not know London. If you did it would bring a tear to your eye to see it in this condition.'

'Have you been here many times?'

He nodded. 'On your grandfather's business.'

Bess was not ready to ask what kind of business that was, for Dane was talking courteously and that made a pleasant change. Besides which, whatever business her grandfather had the man involved with, it was unlikely to be delivering candles to St Paul's Cathedral or alms to London's poor. Better to leave that conversation for another time.

'For a man who has displayed no allegiance in the conflict, who would rather sink his head in wine than serve his king, you surprise me,' Bess said. 'You are less ignorant of the world than you would have folk believe.'

'Folk believe what they want,' he said. 'Or what they are told. As for myself, I have no wish to die for either my king or my parliament. Each wants to rip out the other's throat and I will not get between them, for when it is over and one of them has its *victory* . . .' he almost spat that word, 'there will be a mountain of corpses, Miss Rivers. My intention is to be not amongst them.' He reached inside his tunic, drew out a flask and pulled the stopper, then took a long draught and winced as though whatever it contained was sour. 'I want good wine, good company, and now and then a spirited wench to share my bed. Until such time as I may once again enjoy those simple pleasures, I must attend you on your wild-goose chase.' He thumbed back towards Joseph, who fortunately could not hear their conversation for the rumble of cartwheels and the clatter of hooves. 'I must play the nursemaid to you both to earn my pay.'

Bess flinched at the offence, angry at herself for having thought he might be capable of civility. 'You are rude, sir,' she said, glaring at him, wanting to tell him how poor and pale a version of a man he was compared with her Emmanuel who had been brave and honourable. 'You are rude and I wonder that my grandfather should have anything to do with you.' She looked ahead, seething inside yet knowing she needed the man. That much had been made clear already. 'The moment we find my brother you may slope off to seek whatever debauchery pleases you. I shall tell my grandfather that you earned your coin.'

'I will tell him myself when I deliver you back to him,' Dane said. And Bess bristled at his impertinence but bit her tongue rather than bite back. Even that young rebel Captain Downing who had besieged Shear House had been as a gentleman compared with this rogue. For all his faults the rebel had been a man of honour. But Downing was dead, too, just like Emmanuel. He had fought bravely and given his life for his cause, and a selfish and ignoble thought occurred to Bess then: that if Emmanuel had been a little less honourable, a little less brave, he might still be alive and they might be married. And little Francis might have a father.

*

Bess sat at a small table that was chipped, stained and littered with tobacco, looking around the smoke-filled room at the other patrons of The Leaping Lord. Joseph was still outside seeing to the horses and Dane had gone to find the latrine, and Bess tried her hardest to not look as though she had never been in such a place before. Not that the half-dozen smoke-wreathed old men and the dogs on the rush-strewn floor took any notice of her. Two of the old men were playing dice, three were mumbling over their cups and one was alone and looked to be either dead or fast asleep. As for the dogs, one had come to sniff at her skirts when she first walked in, but had lost interest and wandered off to flop back down with a yawn.

The last time she had seen Tom, when the snow had lain thick on the iron-hard earth and Mun had fetched their brother down from Gerard's Wood, she had found him much changed. She had heard how he fought at Kineton Fight, how he had been wounded in the battle and mutilated by looters as he lay with the corpses in the aftermath, frozen half to death. He had told her of the kind family who had taken him in and nursed him back to health and how they and other good folk had been ill-used by the King's men. They had talked by the fire long into the night as Tom's bones thawed, and he had mentioned The Leaping Lord, had to Bess's astonishment told them that he had worked there for room and board, hefting barrels and cleaning tables.

Come the morning Tom had gone, been driven off bloody and beaten by the men of the Shear House garrison. Now Bess touched the grubby table before her, as though tracing upon it the ghost of her brother's hand, as though she could connect with him through it.

The smell of tobacco and wood smoke was undercut now by the sweet aroma of food, a pie perhaps, wafting from the kitchen, and Bess realized she was hungry.

'What will it be?' a young woman asked, jolting Bess from her thoughts. She looked up to see a face that she knew would draw men's eyes for all that she doubted women would call it pretty.

'Wine. Whatever is good,' Dane answered before she could, appearing behind the serving girl and still lacing his breeches to his doublet. 'Three cups. Our friend will be along soon.' The young woman nodded and walked off, parting a haze of pipe smoke that was lit by a shaft of dusk light coming through a window.

'At least the lad can manage looking after the horses,' Dane said, sweeping his misshapen broad-hat from his head and pulling up a stool to sit opposite Bess, 'so he's not entirely without use.'

'Don't be cruel,' Bess said. 'He may not be a killer but that is a virtue not a fault.' She leant in so that she would not be overheard. 'Joseph volunteered to escort me even though the major of the house will punish him when we return. He risked his own position for me—'

'Because he is in love with you,' Dane interrupted, and Bess felt a wave of guilt wash over her. 'But of course you know that,' he added, one dark eyebrow arching. 'Why else would you have a wet-behind-the-ears boy along for the ride if not for the fact that he was the only one foolish enough to volunteer? Because he worships you and will prove it by getting himself killed for you if the occasion presents itself.'

Bess was appalled by this but Joseph was coming and so she shushed Dane with a glare.

He paid no notice. 'Does he even know how to fire that blunderbuss?' he asked.

'Would you have me show you, Dane?' Joseph asked, standing tall behind him, his own eyes hardening.

Dane waved a hand but did not turn round. 'Sit down, lad. We've wine coming. I dare say it won't be up to much but it'll be better than nothing.' But Joseph did not move and so Dane twisted round on his stool and sighed wearily. 'Sit down, will you? You're drawing attention to yourself.' In truth no one had so much as looked their way, but Joseph glanced at Bess, who gave the slightest nod of her head, and sat down between them, scowling.

I am in the company of children, Bess thought, as the serving girl came back to their table with three cups and a tall jug of wine. She placed all on the table and turned away, but Bess, thinking there was no reason to delay – particularly given her tiresome company – seized the moment and called her back.

'You want some food?' the young woman asked, gesturing at a young boy to come forward with a pitcher and basin for them to wash their hands. 'We don't have much in but I can do you a dish of quails and sparrows and we have a handsome rhubarb pie.'

'Maybe a little later, thank you,' Bess said, nerves like moths fluttering in her stomach. 'I am looking for someone and hope you might be able to help. A young man who has lodged here,' she said, not mentioning that Tom had worked there cleaning tables, because the notion was still almost incomprehensible to her. 'His name is Thomas. Tom to his friends.'

The woman started, the indifference on her face replaced by concern. Bess saw something else in those worldly blue eyes too. 'And who are you?' she asked, glancing at Dane and Joseph, taking them in properly for the first time. 'I've not seen you in here before.' She folded her arms across her large bosom in a pose that embodied London itself, cautious and defensive.

'I am Thomas's sister Elizabeth,' Bess said with a smile that felt awkward on her face, 'and these are my travelling companions, Mr Dane and Mr Lea.' Even if this woman knew Tom, and it was clear that she did, Tom might have said anything about his family, might have said he despised them. 'We have ridden over two hundred miles to find Tom. The last time I saw him he told me he had stayed here on occasion.'

'That is true,' the young woman said. Dane had washed and

dried his hands and now Joseph was washing his as the young boy held the heavy basin. 'But he's not here now.'

Though she had not dared hope Tom would be lodging at The Leaping Lord still, Bess's heart sank at the confirmation.

'He was here some weeks ago. Haven't seen him since and don't expect to neither.' In Bess's peripheral vision she saw the surprise on Dane's face, as though the man was amazed they had come even this close to finding Tom.

'How is . . . was he?' Bess asked. 'I'm sorry,' she said, 'forgive me. What is your name?'

'I'm Ruth,' the young woman said. 'I run the Lord since the landlord passed recently. Just after your Thomas left, as it happens.' She ran a hand through greasy blonde hair. 'At least, I'm running the place until the real landlord Mr Sayer comes for his rent.' She picked up the coins which Dane had spread on the table, putting them in a purse at her waist. 'He was much changed, your Thomas,' she said.

Your Thomas too, Bess thought but did not say.

'This damned war changes them all,' Ruth said. Her skirts were too big for her and there were dark pools beneath her eyes, so that Bess suspected she was either ill or exhausted from taking over the running of the inn after the landlord's death.

'Mistress, 'scuse, mistress!' Another grimy-faced lad had appeared and was half looking back towards the kitchen. 'Cook needs to see you,' he said, knuckling his snub nose. 'Think he's burnt the pie again.'

Ruth swore, shaking her head, and Bess put a hand on her arm before she could walk off. 'Can we speak later?' she asked. 'About Tom.' Ruth's last words had been like a nail in Bess's heart and yet she needed to hear more, though not in front of Dane and Joseph. 'We shall be lodging here tonight if you have rooms.'

Ruth seemed to consider this, locking eyes with Bess as though she were looking for Tom in her.

'We have rooms,' she said. 'Snout will show you to them. I'll be up when the last one has buggered off,' she added, thumbing back towards the table with the two men playing dice. 'But don't hold your breath. I've much to do.'

'We're going to need more wine,' Dane said, handing her the jug, which surprised Bess because she had not yet touched a drop. Ruth did not look surprised though. She nodded, took the jug and headed off to the kitchen.

It was late when Ruth knocked on Bess's door. Now the two of them sat in the gloom, Bess on the end of her bed and Ruth on a small creaky stool, the darkness shifting with every draught that rippled two sooty candle flames. Bess was suddenly aware that her hands were twisting together as though she were washing or warming them, and her teeth were digging into her bottom lip. She was thirsty too, even though she had recently finished a cup of small beer.

'He had been wounded at Kineton Fight,' Ruth said, 'like so many of them.' She held a clay pipe between finger and thumb, a tendril of smoke rising lazily from its bowl.

'Yes, I saw him after.' Bess recalled Tom's pitiful state when Mun had brought him shivering into the house: his hollow cheeks and the ridge of his collarbone against his shirt. The stub that was all that remained of his ring finger since the looters had cut it off. 'He came home,' she said. 'Briefly.'

'This was his room sometimes.' Ruth looked around as though seeing the room for the first time. Then her eyes came back to Bess and suddenly Bess knew what she had seen in the woman's face earlier.

'We were lovers,' Ruth said, and though Bess had known it the revelation shocked her to her core. She had thought Tom still grieving for Martha Green, but the notion of her brother being with this tavern wench, not just for a quick fumble as was men's wont, but that there might have been more between them . . .

196

'Does the thought so horrify you?' Ruth asked.

Bess knew she had stiffened, felt that her muscles were rigid. 'It's just that my family . . . our family is—'

'Rich,' Ruth finished for her. 'And I am a lowborn shoe-maker's daughter. And yet Thomas chose me, chose this flea-ridden inn over his family and your grand house.'

'He was grief-stricken. Angry,' Bess said, knowing her own anger showed in her hot cheeks now. 'You know nothing of us. Of our family.'

'I know about Martha,' Ruth said softly. 'I know that Tom loved her. More than he could ever love me. I know how she died.'

Bess felt her stomach sink. It seemed wrong that this stranger should be familiar with her family's tragedies. It was strange hearing her talk of Martha.

'You needn't fret, for he doesn't love me,' Ruth said, her gaze slipping from Bess for a moment. Then she lifted her head and the challenge was back in her eyes. 'So your family can have no worries of another unlucky match.'

'But you love him?' Bess said.

Ruth hitched her bodice higher over the white flesh of her bosom and smiled. But there was only sadness in it. 'What does it matter what I feel?'

Bess's mind fumbled for words. 'These are hard days,' she said. 'My family has suffered much. As for myself—' but she stopped then and shook her head lightly, unable to bring herself to talk of her father and Emmanuel. This tavern girl already knew too much of their business. 'My only desire is to find Thomas and bring him back to his family,' she said.

'Thomas serves a noble cause. He is needed,' Ruth said. She drew on the pipe and parted her full lips, allowing the smoke to coalesce in front of her face.

'His only cause is vengeance,' Bess said. 'He seeks only blood and will get himself killed if I cannot persuade him to come home.'

'You would have him fight for the King like his brother,' Ruth accused.

'I would have him not fight at all,' Bess replied honestly. 'He has fought enough. They both have.' Ruth gave an almost imperceptible nod at that, as though she too was weary of this war that should have been over one way or the other. 'I left my boy. He is just a babe and every day apart is a knife in my chest. I must find Tom and return to my son.' And with those words, and because she had been in the company of men but was now with a woman, Bess felt tears flood her eyes. They spilled down her cheeks and Ruth, who Bess supposed must have thought her a privileged, weak-hearted fool, stood up and came to sit beside her on the bed.

Ruth raised a hand and swept Bess's hair back from her face, tucking it behind her right ear. 'You must miss your little one terribly,' she said.

Bess did not answer. She was trying to gather herself. She felt ashamed to be laying her heart bare before this stranger. And yet, Ruth was not a stranger. Could not be if Tom had shared so much with her.

'He left to rejoin his regiment,' Ruth said, pulling her hand away, watching a tendril of pipe smoke curl up into the darkness as Bess dabbed her eyes with the heels of her hands. 'I told him to stay here. He could have joined the Trained Bands, served with the city garrison. I would have taken care of him.' She shrugged, then offered the pipe to Bess who shook her head. 'The army is camped at Richmond. At least that's where our boys were the last I heard. Lord Essex will move against Reading next.' She raised an eyebrow. 'You ought to be careful around here. Your friends could find themselves recruited, or worse, if anyone finds out who you are. You are a long way from home, Miss Rivers.'

'I am not afraid,' Bess said.

'That's as may be,' Ruth said, her eyes sharpening, 'but I don't want you staying here again.'

Bess nodded. 'We'll leave at first light.' Their eyes remained locked for a long moment before Ruth stood and went to the door. There she stopped and turned back and Bess would have sworn there were tears in her eyes now.

'I hope you find him,' Ruth said. Bess nodded and tried to smile as Ruth closed the door behind her, causing the candles to gutter. Then Bess was left alone and she sat for a long time simply looking around the small, grimy room, wondering how her brother had felt in that same place, having turned his back on them all. She let her eyes roam across the ceiling cracks and the stain in the plaster on the wall opposite. She examined the dark knots in the creaky floorboards and the tiny holes in the woodworm-riddled bed head, her eyes drinking in every detail because in doing so she felt a little closer to Tom.

In the morning they left The Leaping Lord, bound for Richmond, and when they found Sir William Balfour's regiment they spent five shillings and sixpence on bribes, two shillings on one corporal alone, for the privilege of traipsing through the camp unchallenged seeking any information they could get.

But no one knew anything about Thomas Rivers.

The pistol's muzzle dug sharply into his back between the shoulder blades, forcing him forward, and then again so that he turned glaring, his fists balled at his sides.

'It's not worth the trouble, Sir Edmund,' O'Brien said behind him, having already been shoved into the kitchen of the derelict house that was to be their prison. 'There's nothing to be done now.' The Irishman put a big hand on Mun's shoulder and squeezed hard enough to get Mun's attention.

'You're not as stupid as you look, O'Brien,' Captain Boone said through a grin, his pistol aimed at Mun's chest. Behind the captain Corporal Bard stood stone-faced, a wheellock at the half cock across his chest.

'Come on now, Mun,' O'Brien said, 'I'll have no one to talk to if Captain Boone puts a hole in you.' He frowned. 'Then again, I've never known trouble like I have since making your acquaintance. And me being an Irishman, too!'

Mun held Boone's eye, promising hurts he could not deliver being unarmed and at the wrong end of the captain's firelock. Yet if Boone only knew that Mun had facilitated the escape of five rebel prisoners – Thomas Rivers amongst them – and had even helped kill Boone's corporal Scrope in the process, he would surely murder Mun where he stood even before someone could fashion the noose.

'You stole a man's cannon and that man not just some cur rebel but a baron and friend of the King,' Boone said as though he was at a loss to imagine why anyone would do something so foolish. 'You'll be lucky if you don't find yourself at the end of a rope. Your collar day is coming, Rivers, and I'll be right at the front of the crowd to watch you dance.'

Mun held his tongue and stepped back into the ruin, from which most of the roof timbers had been plundered for fuel or some other purpose, so that the earthen floor was puddled and what rushes yet remained were filthy and rotting.

'By all means attempt an escape,' Boone said, gesturing with his pistol to the kitchen's crumbling east wall that stood about the same height as O'Brien. 'My men will be on the other side and they have orders to shoot you if you try to leave us.'

'I wouldn't give you the pleasure, you whore-born jackanapes,' Mun said.

Boone laughed, easing the cock down to the priming pan. 'Those spurs which His Majesty gave you after Kineton Fight,' he said, nodding down at Mun's boots, 'give them to me and I will petition the Prince on your behalf. I give you my word.'

Now it was Mun's turn to grin. 'The Prince would sooner take advice from his damned dog than from you,' he said, 'and as for your word, it is piss on a nettle, you vainglorious lick-spittle bastard.'

Boone's lip curled beneath his long moustaches. 'Enjoy your comforts, Sir Edmund,' he spat. 'You too, you Irish bloody hang-in-chains. You'll be going into the hole tomorrow.' He grimaced. 'And those pretty spurs will be no use to you down there.' Then he gestured to Bard who opened the door, allowing Boone to step out into the night.

'It ain't personal,' Bard said to Mun, holding his eye for a heartbeat, just long enough for Mun to nod curtly to show he accepted the sentiment. Then the corporal closed the door behind him leaving Mun and O'Brien standing in the dark. It was raining, but barely. Mun had known heavier dewfall, his face now turned up to the sky. Now and then he could see stars through the cloud and the pall of smoke rising from Lichfield into the damp night.

'It's not so bad,' O'Brien said, glancing around. 'I've slept in worse than this.' He sniffed, cuffing his nose. 'Mind you, we'd have done better keeping on the right side of Captain Boone. Not that he's got a right side,' he admitted. 'My da used to say keep in with the bad man for the good man won't harm you.'

'I'd sooner keep in with the Earl of Essex than that bastard,' Mun said.

'His Highness the Prince could have given us a warmer reception if you ask me,' O'Brien grumbled. 'We've been getting our swords dirty up north while half the King's bloody army has been sitting around on their arses and what do we get for our troubles?' He kicked a lump of charred roof beam across the grimy floor. 'A drink would have been a start and we could have talked about the rest.'

'What could he do?' Mun said. 'You think he was going to admit to having us steal the baron's bloody cannon?'

'Why not?' the Irishman asked with a sullen shrug. 'A prince trumps a baron.'

'He may be a prince but he's not an Englishman and unless Boone was talking from his arse Lord Lidford is known to the King.'

When he had first laid eyes on Mun the Prince's teeth had flashed in the candle-lit gloom. But then he had noticed the man beside Mun in the fine cuirassier's armour, noticed the stone-cold fury knotted up in the jaw, the man himself constrained by decorum not deference, and the royal smile had vanished.

'The last time I saw you, Baron, we had just kicked the Spanish out of Breda and the Dutch were writing songs about us.' The Prince had been genial but not friendly. 'Poor old Goring, eh? He's never danced since.'

'Sod Goring! I was almost strung up and flayed alive for *letting* you join the storming party, your highness,' Lord Lidford had said icily. Mun got the distinct impression that the Prince had been meant to enjoy a secondary role in whatever fight they were recalling, and furthermore that it had been the baron's job to make sure that this remained so.

The Prince had wafted the tallow-smelling air with long fingers. 'We were young,' he said as if that explained all, as if he were not still young.

'And now I have but recently returned, my shoes yet brine-stained, to serve His Majesty, and I find this gang of thieves making off with my beasts and my own cannon. I expect an explanation.' Lord Lidford had been angry and haughty but not fool enough to openly accuse the Prince of ordering Mun to steal his gun and the oxen to pull it. Yet the unspoken words were loud enough and Mun knew that in the following frosty silence the Prince had been on the verge of hurling black powder into the embers rather than keeping the peace. Yet he had resisted and now Mun and O'Brien were locked up, their punishment for stealing the good baron's cannon that they must climb into the tunnels even now being dug beneath the outer walls of the Cathedral Close.

'I do not have the luxury of time to make use of your cannon, Baron,' the Prince had said, 'for you neglected to bring me shot for it.'

'I did not *bring* you the gun at all,' Lord Lidford sputtered.

'Indeed you did not.' Prince Rupert's eyes were accusing

then. 'And now Essex lays siege to Reading and I may not tarry here. Sir Edmund, you will bring down the rebels' wall and by doing so earn my forgiveness. And you will use the baron's black powder to do it.' He turned back to Lord Lidford. 'You did at least bring powder, Baron? May we be grateful for that?'

Lord Lidford had simply stared, the ire coming off him like heat.

'Yes he did, your highness,' Mun had said.

And so now Mun and O'Brien were locked up in a collapsed house while the rest of their troop drank, smoked and ate, enjoying what scant comforts Prince Rupert's besieging army could provide.

'I'm not fond of small spaces,' O'Brien said. 'Ever since I was a wean and me and my brother Jack borrowed the parish coffin.'

'We should have stayed up north,' Mun said, thinking that mud and cramped darkness was an odd reward for bringing his prince a cannon. There was a long silence. Somewhere men were singing a bawdy song about weak-willed wives and strong red wine.

'Well?' Mun said.

'Well what?' O'Brien asked, as though he had not been filling the space with silence just for the opportunity to fill it with the rest of his tale. 'Ah, now then, I thought you were never going to ask,' he said, then nodded towards the source of the music. 'But Jesus and Mary there's not a singer among them! That's the tune the old cow died of, heavens above! I shall have to give them a proper song later.' He coughed into a fist. 'So where was I? Ah, the parish coffin. It was a daft idea thinking about it.' Mun had no doubt that it was. 'We wanted to know what it felt like to be dead.' The Irishman looked at him accusingly. 'Don't be telling me you never wondered the same.' Mun was not sure how to answer that and so he didn't. 'Jack said the only way we could truly know, short of leaping from the bell tower or running each other through with a pig sticker, was to lie down in a coffin and for the whole night too. Lucky for us our uncle was two days since bereft of life. As cadaverous as it's possible to be. Just dropped dead one day still clutching his jar, but then my da always said Uncle Eamon was mostly in the field when luck was on the road. We waited till they had hauled him from the box and dropped him in the ground, as was only good and decent, then we lingered by the empty coffin which stood upon joint stools in the chimney in the hall, deliberating as to which one should have the honour of visiting the afterlife.' Those broad shoulders lifted again. 'The job fell to me, me being the bravest and most intrepid.'

'Your brother was older than you, wasn't he, Clancy?'

'Aye, so he was. How did you know?'

Now it was Mun's turn to shrug. 'Pray continue.'

'Our kin were off drinking to Eamon, giving him a proper send-off. No one missed us sprats. The bells were still pealing and the hall still whiffing of rosemary when I was in the box with the lid on. Jack said he'd give me tuppence if I stayed in it all night. Of course the little fartleberry never had tuppence, which I should have well known. But he'd have been the poorer if he had.'

'You lasted the night?' Mun asked.

'Aye, I did.'

'And you know how it feels being dead?'

'I know how it feels to have a shit for an older brother,' O'Brien said, going over to the east wall and stepping up onto the rubble until his eyes were just shy of its ragged top. 'Walton, is that you out there?' There was no reply, just the sounds of singing and officers barking at their men, and the occasional crack of a musket in the dark: men taking pot shots for want of something to do. 'Walton, you merry-begotten tosspot, I know you're the other side of this wall. I can smell the rag water on your breath, you miserable shanker.'

'I'm not allowed to talk to you,' Walton said.

'If I'm going to crawl into a bloody hole to win this damned war for His Majesty the least you can do is be courteous.' O'Brien shook his head as though there was simply no accounting for some folk's manners. 'This tunnel me and Sir Edmund have bravely volunteered to wriggle through, who's dug it?'

'Fifty men up from Cannock Chase,' Walton said. 'The Prince had them drain the moat and now they've got the tunnel almost to the bastards' walls.'

'So they know their business? The diggers?' O'Brien said.

'I should bloody hope so,' Walton replied. 'They're bloody miners.'

'You hear that, Mun?' O'Brien clawed at his great red beard. 'It doesn't sound so bad.'

20 April 1643

His lungs felt as though they were filling with scalding liquid and his mind was screaming at him to get out. To crawl back the way they had come before it was too late. Before he suffocated to death or drowned in the filthy freezing water that was a foot deep and getting deeper as more seeped into the slick cavity.

'Jesus, I'm stuck.' He had never heard fear in O'Brien's voice before but there was fear in it now.

'You're not stuck, Clancy. Keep going,' he managed, fighting the panic surging in his own veins, flooding revulsion and terror through his limbs and loosening his bowels. 'Move, damn you. We're nearly there.'

But they were not nearly there. They were on their bellies, Mun in front of the Irishman, pushing themselves along, straining to keep their canvas-wrapped powder kegs out of the water as much as was possible. There were others in that cold black hell, several of the Cannock Chase miners following up behind with their own powder kegs, and perhaps those men were not half paralysed with fear and fighting for every breath. Perhaps being men who plied their trade beneath the sod they were as comfortable as moles. But perhaps not. Whatever, Mun found no comfort in company. Down here where the air was scant, where it was more precious than King's gold or victory or love, every man was alone and Mun felt it deep in the marrow of his bones. At least the timbers propping the shaft felt strong enough whenever he brushed against one in the dark, so that he must hope the Cannock men knew their business as well as he knew his own.

'How far?' O'Brien growled, his voice intimate in that too small space.

'Just a little more,' Mun said, feeling his flesh begin to tremble though he knew not whether it was through fear or cold. The water *was* cold. 'Can you see that light up ahead?'

'I can't even see your boots and yet they're in my face,' O'Brien rumbled.

'Just keep going,' Mun said, as much to himself as to his friend. Up ahead, twenty yards away, maybe more, the over-bearing dark was disturbed. A halo of non-dark eked out a frail existence and so Mun steeled himself to the task, the toe ends of his boots digging for purchase in the clay, gouging furrows, the flesh within them numbing as he pushed on, now and then half choking, spitting foul water that spilled into his mouth.

I can't breathe.

Not far now, he told himself. Get to the end. Place the charges. Set the fuses. Then back, quick as a wet rat slipping through the gutter.

His arms trembled with the strain of holding his cask above the rising water, the muscles bunched and burning. If he dropped the cask he might well ruin the powder and then he or some unlucky Cannock man would have to squirm through one hundred feet of filth with another cask to make right his mistake. So he would not drop it. His agonized arms would not fail him.

He could hear O'Brien grunting with effort for the tunnel was narrow, and if Mun's own face was as much in the water as out of it then the big Irishman must be in a worse hell still. For with his broad chest and shoulders he must feel like a bung in a bottle neck.

'Ten feet. No more,' Mun growled, and received no reply but for laboured breathing: his own and that of O'Brien and, faintly, the few men further back.

Thank God the tunnel was getting ever so slightly wider, so that he managed to get the cask up onto his right shoulder, the lanolin stink of the sack pricking his senses awake from their half-death, then pull himself along by repeatedly digging his left elbow into the freezing filth. He could see candles now which the miners had set in clefts scooped in the earth, but the little flames guttered and choked and threatened to fail.

Soon back above ground, his mind whispered. *Back with the living.*

Then he was in the chamber which the Cannock men had dug and he could reach out and touch the foundations of the Cathedral Close's walls, press freezing fingers against the slick stones that bore the tool marks of the miners' excavations. In the earth below these foundations, four feet beneath the stones, they had dug a channel for the explosives.

'I'm suffocating,' O'Brien said. 'Can't get a breath.' Suddenly the Irishman was beside him in the chamber at the tunnel's end, his own cask easily out of the water, his prodigious strength unflagging. His unblinking eyes, though, glowed white in that near-grave and were swollen with terror.

'The worst is over,' Mun said, knowing it to be a lie for worse was to come. Once they had lit the fuses. 'Give it to me.' Mun had already placed his cask up on the rough wooden platform which the miners had erected to keep the charges clear of the water. Now he took O'Brien's and placed it beside his own. 'Go on, get out,' he growled.

'Ballocks,' O'Brien growled back, edging up so that they were almost level, their combined mass all but filling the cramped alcove. 'You'll need help with the fuses.'

'Get out, Clancy,' Mun said, seeing black spots before his eyes, the fear threatening to overcome him.

'Fuck off,' O'Brien said.

'You're too damn big and too damn slow,' Mun hissed. 'Once these are lit we need to be gone. I won't have you lying there like a stopper in a flask leaving me at the back when this lot goes off.'

'But you can't do all the fuses.'

'I can help,' another voice said.

'Who has match?' Mun asked. He had brought his own lit match coiled round his right wrist but it had long since gone out when keeping the end burning had seemed less important than keeping his head above water. It was too wet to relight now.

'I have two, both lit,' the same voice came back from somewhere behind them, followed by the sound of the man blowing on his match to back up his boast.

Mun locked eyes with O'Brien, who passed up another powder keg from a Cannock man further back. 'Go back. I'll be right behind.' For a heartbeat, by the frail faltering candlelight he saw pure turmoil in the Irishman's eyes. He knew his friend would sooner half of Lichfield came down on his head than that he leave Mun to finish the job alone. But then a grimace showed white against O'Brien's mud-smeared beard and he nodded and cursed, his reason to remain negated by the man behind who anyway had the only burning match and would need to come up to the foundation wall with it. That the Irishman was down there at all with his fear of confined places . . .

'If you're not back . . . above ground . . . before I finish the Lord's Prayer . . . I'll be back to drag you out by your feet.' With that O'Brien pushed himself deeper into the meagre chamber, careful not to disturb the casks, and there contorted, bringing his mud-slathered knees up to his chest. Awkward as a cow on a crutch he got himself turned round and began to crawl past Mun, who sucked in his belly for every half an inch was needed, back towards the narrow shaft.

The next man behind squirmed into the space left by the Irishman and went to crouch in a dark corner, his wrists up by his begrimed face, blowing now and then on the match coiled round them so that the lit ends glowed menacingly before dulling again. Five more powder kegs were passed along by the Cannock men and Mun painstakingly set them side by side on the low trestle beneath the slick, stone-flecked earth and the wall's foundations.

He could not lay a trail of powder, for the dampness underground would likely ruin it, besides which there was no dry surface on which to pour it. Also, he could never lay a trail long enough to give him the time to crawl back out before the explosion. Instead they would have to hope that at least one of the young man's match-cords remained lit long enough to ignite the one charge that would blow up the whole cache.

The canvas-swathed keg O'Brien had brought down was bone dry and so Mun chose this for the heart of the detonation, with his knife cutting the sack open and digging a hole into the lid until the tip of the blade fetched out a spill of black powder.

He nodded to the match around the Cannock man's wrists. 'Give me both of them,' he said. The others, their work done, were already backing out of the tunnel boots first, eager to be far from so much black powder, candle flame and lit match.

'Shhh!' The man put a finger to his lips and Mun froze, holding his breath, his heart clenching. Then he heard the wet percussion of picks stabbing into pebble-flecked earth. There was a sudden crumbling of soil to Mun's left and immediately a musket's muzzle appeared and there was a tongue of flame and there must have been a crack but Mun did not hear it. He was on his back in the water. The musket ball had hit him, he knew that much. But he did not know where it had struck him for though he had felt the blow he felt no pain. Yet.

A face appeared through the hole and then the Cannock man scrambled through the filth, pulling a knife from his boot, and Mun saw the man's arm rise and fall, saw a flash of blade and heard a man screaming.

'The fuses,' Mun growled, pushing himself up onto his knees. Now the pain. Searing agony in his thigh, the mud slathered on his breeches sheened with watery blood. 'Cut them shorter!'

'But we won't have time—'

'Just do it!' Mun threw himself onto the bloodied rebel, grabbed hold of his bandolier and hauled him further through the hole until the body stuck fast sealing it. 'Hurry!'

The other man *was* hurrying, pulling the match-cords from his wrists, blowing on them, taking his blade to them and sawing them shorter. He held them up and Mun nodded, half lying on the dead man, holding on for all he was worth, his cold hands numb to the steaming blood on them. He could hear the muffled shouts of those on the other side of the hole and suddenly the corpse was convulsing, jerking like a fish on a hook as his comrades took hold of his legs and tried to draw him back through the breach. But Mun held on. 'Set them! Do it now!' he yelled and the other scrambled over to the trestle, his eyes wild, and pushed the unlit ends of the match-cords into the hole which Mun had dug into the cask lid.

'It's done,' the Cannock man said, blowing on the fuses.

'Now go!' Mun was losing his grip on the dead rebel, the men on the other side beginning to win the tug of war.

The other man muddled over on hands and knees and took hold of the dead rebel's coat.

'Get out!' Mun growled.

'No,' the man said, and then Mun saw the begrimed face properly for the first time.

'You damned fool!' Mun said, for not only was the other no Cannock man, he was barely a man at all, but rather Lord Lidford's heedless boy. Who seemed determined to get himself killed. 'What are you doing here? Get out!' Mun screamed at

Jonathan, whose face was a snarl, his fists full of the dead rebel's felt tunic. 'Go now or die.' The corpse lurched violently but together they held on. Mun heard a man curse savagely and the body went still.

'You're shot,' Jonathan Lidford said.

'Go, you goddamned fool,' Mun said. 'There's no time.' The rebels had given up and were no doubt scrambling back up their shaft on the other side because they knew what was coming. Jonathan let go of the dead man and slewed off and Mun exhaled, cursing in pain.

Then he was moving, being hauled backwards, a strong arm under his right arm and across his chest. He tried to call the boy a bloody idiot but the words were garbled. He was cold, had lost sensation in his legs. It's the cold water, he thought, the black spots filling his vision again. But he knew it was more than the cold water, knew it was because his warm lifeblood was leaving his body, draining into the Lichfield mud so that he would soon be as dead as the coffin-buried corpses in the earth above him.

He tried to dig his heels into the mire, wanted desperately to speed the progress back up the tunnel because he somehow knew that the fool boy would not leave him and so would be blown to pieces or buried alive when the burning match met the dry black powder.

If the match was still alight.

The boy is stronger than he looks, he thought. *I wonder how short he cut the fuses.*

Then the world shook and there was a boom, but a muted one like a far-off cannon's roar, and a blow like a kick to the stomach. And then there was nothing.

CHAPTER FIFTEEN

WHEN TOM HAD COME EXHAUSTED AND STINKING TO THE FOOT-bridge across the Cherwell north-east of Oxford he had thought The Scot had gone, ridden east into the dawn, and thus that he was a dead man. But then he had seen shapes moving in the gloom, men and horses milling and the glint of helmets and tack against the silver tideline of the coming daybreak.

'It's done?' The Scot had asked simply, whistling a signal for his sentries to come in from their positions in the scrub to mount up.

'It's done,' Tom had replied, pulling himself up into the saddle and scanning the faces around him. Trencher's face was a slab of granite and in a heartbeat Tom knew what was coming.

'Weasel,' Trencher said. 'Heard it, didn't see it. The place was crawling with dragoons.'

'There was nothing to be done,' Penn put in, holding Tom's eye. Beside him Dobson bristled as though the violence in him clamoured to be unleashed in spite of there being no recourse now other than to escape Oxford before the King's men rounded them up or flayed them with lead and steel. 'But you know Weasel,' Penn said. 'He'll swallow his own tongue before he tells those damn nigits anything.'

'He'll bloody swing is what he'll do,' Dobson said, grimacing.

'After what we did to their precious printing press they'll make him dance.'

'Shut your mouth, Dobson,' Trencher gnarred, giving the bigger man a murderous glare. Dobson shrugged casually but said no more. Yet Tom knew that Dobson was right for all that he had not wanted to hear it. Weasel, with whom Tom had shared ale and food and ridden into the fray at Edgehill, who had been his brother of the blade, would now die strangled and pissing down his leg at the end of a rope. If the Cavaliers did not bring him down before death and cut him open and pluck out his still throbbing organs.

There was nothing Tom could do, nothing he could have done differently, that would have changed the outcome for Weasel. Or if there was there was nothing to be gained by raking the ashes of it now as they rode south-east, the wind in their faces, across a land stirring towards the new day. After some fifteen or so miles they made camp in woodland near the village of Watlington. The Scot's men shared their food with them and lent them rain cloaks to sleep under and some time later they woke stiff and damp and moaning to Tom that he still stank like a sewer. Then they rode east twenty miles into the rolling Chiltern Hills and the village of Great Kingshill, where they rendezvoused with a column of horse coming from London bound for the new Parliamentary headquarters at Thame. The day was bright and warm for the time of year and the sun made a silver ribbon of a river in the valley to the south as they watched The Scot make his introductions to a Colonel Bartholomew Haggett.

'Most of 'em look green as snot,' Dobson remarked, un-impressed.

'Most of them look as if they're knocking at death's door,' Penn said. The column comprised some seventy-five men, all harquebusiers, plus the men leading three carts, two pulled by oxen and the third by draught horses.

'What are they moving?' Dobson asked, nodding at one of

the carts whose cargo like the others' was covered by canvas that was lashed tightly down.

'I can tell you exactly,' Trencher said. 'Silver and coin. Twenty thousand pounds' worth to be specific.' He nodded towards one of The Scot's troopers, a spotty lad who was begging two others to return the lump of cheese they had clearly stolen from his knapsack. 'That is if we're to believe young Banister over there.'

Penn's mouth slackened and Dobson became suddenly still, his dark bushy brows hoisted.

'What?' Trencher protested. 'You think I share a man's bottle and his fire and don't have the good manners to enquire after his business?'

'We're going to hold their hands all the way up to Thame,' Tom said, making sense of it. He could understand why The Scot had not told them about the convoy – being loose-tongued about that much silver was never a good idea – but Tom was angry nevertheless, for he would rather be southward bound, not least so that the others could claim their reward from Captain Crafte. Instead they would be going north again and west to Thame.

'That's enough silver to pay all of us, Essex's whole bloody army,' Penn said.

'Doing God's work is its own reward,' Trencher said. 'I don't need coin for killing Cavaliers.'

'Need it for ale, though,' Dobson said.

'True enough,' Trencher admitted. 'Killing Cavaliers is thirsty work.'

'You kept that quiet, Will,' Tom said, cuffing water from his face. He was on his knees amongst nettles by a foam-flecked brook, washing off the stubborn filth from the ditch through which he had scrambled to escape Oxford.

'I only found out last night, besides which I knew you ladies would get all giddy when this little trove turned up.' He coughed into a fist. 'Well, not you, Tom. I expect your lot would spend all that on a good family feast.' Tom gave that comment the look it deserved. 'Anyway, I got the impression that young Banister's tongue was ale-greased and I didn't want to land the poor lad in trouble with The Scot.'

'He *must* have been well oiled to find you good company,' Penn remarked.

'Sod off,' Trencher said.

'I would have sent a bloody regiment at the least with that much silver,' Dobson said. They were all still watching The Scot and Colonel Haggett. And the carts that were filled with treasure.

'And bring two regiments of the King's horse down on them?' Tom said and Dobson considered this, scratching his black beard. 'Fewer than a hundred and there's a good chance they'll be ignored, better still unseen.'

'Still one hellish gamble,' Penn said and Tom agreed that it was, then noticed one of Haggett's men bleeding from the nose. Others were coughing, some violently.

'How far is it to Thame?' he asked, standing and raking his wet hair back from his face.

'Can't be more than fifteen miles,' Trencher suggested, 'but those carts will make it seem like fifty.'

'Those carts are not the problem,' Tom said, 'at least for now. You're right, Matt, Colonel Haggett's men are unwell. I'd wager some of them will be in the ground before we get this silver to Thame.' All eyes turned to Haggett's men, who were ragged-clothed and unkempt and seemed struck by some malaise that had them leaning against tree trunks and propped up on deadfall.

'Soldiers usually stand a little taller and straighter when they meet men from another regiment,' Trencher said, 'but that lot are a shambles.'

'They do seem to lack professional pride,' Penn, a lawyer's son, observed. 'Could be typhus fever. That'll have a man coughing his guts up.'

Even their horses' coats, Tom noted, were dull, their tails and manes tangled and thick with dust. By contrast The Scot's thirty men looked hard, battle-tested and ready for a fight should a fight come along.

'Colonel Haggett must be relieved to have the company,' Trencher said, 'if his lads are fever-racked.'

'We've done our job,' Dobson said. 'Those bastards in Oxford will be wiping their arse cracks with charred scraps of their damned newsbook for the next month. We could be back in London the day after tomorrow spending Captain Crafte's money on women and wine.'

'Our orders were to ride back to London with The Scot,' Tom said. 'So it's Thame first and then London.'

'That because you'd never disobey an order, Tom?' Penn asked through a grin.

Tom half smiled at that. In truth he would happily ride back to London regardless of Captain Crafte's orders. He would half drown himself in beer and perhaps find a whore to share his bed, for he had killed Henry Denton and *that* was *his* victory. *Mercurius Aulicus* and the destruction of the printing press that spawned it meant nothing to him, though what Crafte would do when he discovered that John Birkenhead was still alive Tom could not say.

'What say you, Will?' Tom asked, 'shall we see this bounty safely delivered to Thame?'

Trencher had removed his battered old pot – part of the war gear The Scot had supplied when they had joined him outside Oxford – and was rubbing a patch of bristles on his mostly bald head where the pot had raised an angry red welt.

'We do the Lord's work and that's the truth of it, but that coin will buy us the tools to do it. Powder and shot, blades and blankets. I'd have us do our bit in seeing it delivered into righteous hands and put to good use.'

Penn nodded. Tom looked at Dobson and the big man turned and glanced at one of Haggett's men whose hacking cough, sweat-sheened face, and hand clutching his swollen abdomen marked him as a dead man walking. 'Well I'll not ride all the way back to London like some friendless Devil-driver preaching to the damned rabbits and crows.'

So they would remain with The Scot and his thirty troopers and Colonel Haggett and his seventy-five ragged men and turn their horses north again to escort three wagons brimming with silver to Thame.

And the next day, as they lumbered on, the carts' wheels sinking into the ground or wedging behind grass-covered rocks, the first of Haggett's men died.

The man had been in his forties, a shoe-maker before taking up arms to fight for God and Parliament. It was the same man, Tom realized, whom he had seen bleeding from his nose the previous day.

'He shook all night like a wet dog. I 'eard his teeth chattering and couldn't sleep for it,' another trooper had said as they stood gathered round the stiff body whose legs stuck out the bottom of a shelter half-heartedly put together using a fallen ash trunk and a wet-weather cape. 'He won't be the last neither,' the man went on, sharing a forlorn look with another ashen-faced trooper.

'There are worse ways to go than in your sleep,' Trencher observed, 'and the Lord will receive him gladly as a righteous man and a holy soldier.' Some of Haggett's men ayed and nodded in thanks to Trencher, grateful for those words, and Tom saw the fear in their eyes, because if the Lord truly *was* recruiting then the chances were their names were next on the roll call.

They hastily dug a grave and laid the dead man in it – with most of his belongings, for they feared, despite their godliness, that some ill luck might yet cling to his knapsack and his shoes and spare clothes, his tinder box, leather bottle and spoon. Though they evidently believed that ill luck could not adhere to coins, for the man's five closest friends shared out the three shillings and fourpence they found in his purse. The same must be said for his rusty hanger and his wheellock for they took those too.

Corporal Mabb, a grey-haired, grizzled trooper, told Christopher Allingham – for that was the dead trooper's name – that he was sorry for not putting him in consecrated ground but that he hoped the man would understand that they could not be hefting corpses around the country. Though again it was the cause of death and not the inconvenience of it that put fear in men's bellies. Colonel Haggett himself said a prayer, most of the words drowned by the raucous clamour of nesting rooks above, the birds seeming to disapprove of the rites. Or perhaps, Tom considered, they were warning them that whatever disease had carried Allingham off was still lurking amongst those beside his grave.

Then they took the road north-west through a valley of arable land and pasture, the rising ridges on either side thickly crowned with beech woods. Now and then they saw farmers and shepherds hurriedly moving their flocks further up the hills towards the trees, the lambs and calves that were being weaned from their mother's milk bleating timorously as they were swept along. Late that afternoon they watched a man and boy up on the east ridge cut a cow's throat. Leaving the beast on its knees, its blood washing down its chest onto the cropped grass, the farmer and his boy rounded up the rest of his animals and moved them off. Panicked by the sight of soldiers the farmer hoped his sacrifice of one beast might save several, and perhaps it was a ploy that had worked for him before. Yet he need not have killed the cow, because Colonel Haggett had already made it clear that God's soldiers did not prey on honest men like common thieves. And so despite his men's grumbling and The Scot's barely concealed ire, they left the cow where it lay and moved on through the valley.

'Well, that farmer and his brood will be eating like kings

for the next week,' Penn had said, as chafed as the rest to be turning down fresh meat.

'It was likely an ancient beast anyway,' Trencher had replied, trying to make the others feel better, 'and we'd have spent a tooth or two on the meat.'

The Scot sent two of his troopers galloping on to Thame, their task to warn Essex of the convoy's approach and request an additional escort to see the silver safely in. He and his men now headed up the column, riding half a mile out in front to reconnoitre the ground. Tom had volunteered his party to ride as the convoy's rearguard and Haggett, a careful-looking man with close-set, studying eyes and a yellow tinge to his clean-shaven skin, had seemed grateful and accepted. The colonel knew many of his men were afflicted and in such state were unlikely to be as vigilant as they should be. Tom suspected that Haggett himself was unwell for he was sweating profusely, had armed the grease from his forehead three times while they spoke, and yet he would not diminish his authority by admitting any such infirmity. In truth Tom had wanted to keep his party away from Haggett's men as much as was possible and presumed that that had been The Scot's thinking, too. Nevertheless, even lagging behind the column they could not put far from their thoughts the sickliness that was eating its way into those guarding the treasure carts up ahead. The breeze was northerly and it bore their barking coughs and their ragged hawking of blood and phlegm. Even from a distance Tom could see that many of Haggett's men were almost lying in their saddles, their heads lolling beside their horses' necks.

'They'll be digging more holes tonight,' Dobson said gruffly, as ever unafraid to give voice to other men's thoughts. Neither Tom, Trencher nor Penn disagreed, though in the event it still sent a shiver scuttling over Tom's flesh when the next man died.

For an hour the long shadows of their horses had tracked them along a thick boundary hedge which was bathed in a cheerful copper glow, so that the black shapes flowed smoothly through and over the briars, searching and caressing. Then one of Haggett's harquebusiers fell from his horse like a sack of grain and never moved again. From the way the man fell Trencher surmised he had likely been dead for the last two miles and that his horse, knowing it, had decided enough was enough. It was the last hour of the evening sun and swarms of gnats brought out by the day's warmth danced in their thousands, hovering above the track so that the men had to close their eyes and mouths to ride through them. Ahead, the whole valley and the sheep pastures on either side were glazed in a gold and crimson light that washed around Haggett's dying troop on a cooling breeze.

This time they did not bury the man. The convoy did not even stop, for the payroll was more important than putting a soldier in the ground with the simple rites and prayers a good Protestant deserved, and later Tom heard that Haggett had announced that they would return and recover the body for a proper burial once their duty was discharged. Tom would have bet the price of a good buff-coat that the crows and the worms would strip the body of its flesh long before the bones ever got beneath the sod.

Now, as they in the rear rode past the dead man, left where he had fallen for his firelocks and helmet were still with his horse, Tom saw that his mouth was bloody and his breeches were fouled. Others up ahead were now and then dismounting to void their bowels in the long grass and Tom muttered, to the cruel God who would have men suffer so, as much as to his companions, that he would rather be hacked apart by sharp steel than die of some fever or gut rot.

That night they made camp amongst trees at the foot of the northern scarp of the Chiltern Hills. They lit no fires for fear of drawing attention, which did nothing to help the men's spirits which were, as Dobson remarked, lower than an old whore's apple dumplings. Several of Haggett's troopers were by now in the fever's maw and gripped by a muttering delirium. They were picking agitatedly at their blankets and at imaginary objects, their faces sickly sheened, hair lank. Some, unable to get to their feet or simply oblivious, must have fouled themselves for the stench began to waft through the camp, Trencher remarking its strange similarity to pea soup.

Rather than lie in his blankets listening to their moans and coughs, their stink in his nose, Tom decided to keep watch, moving halfway up a rugged bluff through which sharp boulders had burst in a long-forgotten time. And it was then, by the light of the rising moon, that he saw a trooper walk his horse into their camp. Tom had not yet been asleep and his senses were on edge, disquieted perhaps by the disease preying on the convoy, and even in the dim light he recognized the man as one of The Scot's harquebusiers, one of the two whom he had sent on to Thame that morning. The trooper must have ridden past them, picked up the tracks left by the heavy carts and followed them back into the woods.

Tom could not hear what the man was saying to the sentry who had challenged him, for they were some thirty paces away and their voices were low and muffled. But something told him that the man's returning so soon, and alone, did not bode well and so he picked his way back down the bluff and followed the soldier.

'Can't sleep, eh, laddie?' The Scot said to Tom, stepping into a shaft of moonlight arrowing through the trees. He greeted his trooper and sent another man to fetch Colonel Haggett. 'I cannae say as I'm surprised. I'd sooner get ma head down in ma hoond's basket than lie there listening to this troop o' the damned coughing up their innards all night.' He wore a smock over his buff-coat and gripped his scaled buff-leather gauntlets in his right hand.

'I saw your man come in,' Tom said, 'and would know what news he brings.'

'Aye, well ye might as well hear what reason Trooper Foster has for being back with us so soon when ah'd have wagered a

221

shilling on him being up to his neck in Thame ale and notch by now.' The Scot beckoned Tom closer with a wave of his gloves.

'What is it, Sir John? What's going on?' Colonel Haggett forced himself straighter as he approached. Clearly he had not been asleep either, though his eyes were sunken into pools of shadow and his face glistened sickly.

'We're gaunnae find out, Colonel,' The Scot said, 'but I dinnae think it's good news.' He turned back to Trooper Foster and flicked the gloves at him in a gesture that said *spill it then*.

'We got within a mile or two of Thame and ran into the enemy. A troop of dragoons,' Foster said, glancing from The Scot to Colonel Haggett, his begrimed face a taut knot. 'Only we thought they'd be our lot, being so near Thame, and it wasn't until we got close enough to smell 'em that I said to Lucas that they looked like bloody King's men. Soon as we turned round they gave fire and chased us and Lucas must have been shot for he went down, his horse too. If I'd have gone back for him they would have got me too, so I flew like the bloody wind.' He bit his lip. 'Sir.'

'Aye, you being full o' holes and us being none the wiser wouldn't be very helpful,' The Scot said, glancing at Haggett. But the colonel had his fingers at the bridge of his nose, pressing into the eye sockets as though he feared his head was about to explode.

'How far did they come after you?' Tom asked the trooper.

'Not far. Not a mile,' Foster replied. 'But at dusk I saw another column of the bastards. Musketeers, cuirassiers, pike, cannon, the whole bloody lot marching towards Thame.' He looked back to his commander, all but snubbing Colonel Haggett, who anyway seemed too unwell to care. 'If you had not stopped here,' he said, gesturing to the trees all around, 'you might have driven the carts right into their arms.'

'But it is not possible,' Haggett managed, cuffing sweat from his forehead and forcing his eyes to focus on The Scot. 'We would have heard if the King was moving against Thame. The last we knew His Majesty was in Oxford and that devil Rupert was besieging Lord Brooke's garrison at Lichfield. Who could be bringing an army to Thame?'

The Scot shrugged. 'Perhaps what the lad here saw was just a patrol.' He grimaced. 'Some of my lot can be a little theatrical with the truth.'

Colonel Haggett shook his head. 'Cannon is cannon,' he said.

'Aye, it is that,' The Scot admitted, turning his hard face to Tom. Somewhere near by an owl was hooting, perhaps warning other night creatures of the presence of men amongst the beech and oak. 'What would ye do, laddie?' he asked.

'Why would you ask him?' Colonel Haggett blurted, turning pain-filled eyes on Tom. 'What does he know about command?'

'Keep the heid, Colonel,' The Scot said, raising a hand. 'I know the lad's got balls. I heard the thunder and saw the lightning he sowed in Oxford and that gives him the right to a say by my book.'

'We can't take the carts back out into the open land,' Tom said, feeling the colonel's eyes boring into him. But he did not care, for what need he fear from a dying man, colonel or no. 'We move the silver deeper into these woods. If we can,' he added. 'We hide the carts. And we wait until we know what is going on out there.' He nodded north-west.

'Aye, that's the only thing to do if ye don't want to finance a new palace for His Majesty,' The Scot said to Colonel Haggett. The sick man closed his eyes and swayed and Trooper Foster put out a hand to steady him but Haggett dismissed the offer, composing himself. Foster looked at Tom and shrugged.

'My professional advice, Colonel,' The Scot remarked, stressing the word *professional*, 'is to do as the lad here says and stash the coin. Yer men are nae fit. Any trouble oot there on the road and they willnae give a good account of themselves. So ye stay here and hope no one follows our tracks into the trees.'

'My orders are to deliver this payload to my commanders at

Thame.' Haggett forced the words through a clenched jaw that Tom suspected mirrored his other end. The man was fighting to control his bowels.

'And how will ye deliver the payload if ye dinnae have it?' The Scot asked. Then Haggett threw up a hand and stumbled off, getting behind a fallen trunk and pulling his breeches down just in time.

'Meanwhile,' The Scot went on, as close by – much too close as far as Tom was concerned – Haggett's bowels squirted their foul mess between his boot heels, 'I will take my men intae Thame, aroond the enemy, or through them if we must, and come back with a regiment to see yer charge safely delivered.'

'I need your men here! Protecting the carts!' Haggett called, his face a rictus of misery.

'Ye need me to ride on and bring back men who are not walking in breeches filled with their ain shite!' The Scot exclaimed cruelly, to which Haggett's agonized guts gave their own answer, which was answer enough, for the colonel knew that The Scot was right. 'Two, three days, ye'll stay in the trees, covering the silver with branches and such. Ye'll be safe and so will the stash. As for your men's affliction, we cannae do nothing aboot that.'

Tom did not know the man's rank but suspected he was a major, which was below a colonel, and yet it was all too clear who was in charge now.

'What's going on, lad?' Trencher asked, appearing out of the moon-burnished gloom and making a fist over a great yawn. The Scot nodded at Tom then he and Foster strode off to make arrangements, leaving Tom and Trencher absently watching a colonel shit like a storm.

'We're staying put, Will,' Tom said, wondering whether Haggett would survive the night, let alone until The Scot returned with men from Thame.

'Then I suggest we four make our own little camp thirty feet away from this sorry lot,' Trencher said.

'Fifty feet is better,' Tom said.

A short while later, as the moon made its way west and night still held sway, they watched The Scot and his thirty men slip out of the camp like wraiths and ride off into the night.

Mun knew that if it were not for Jonathan Lidford, Lord Lidford's foolhardy son, he would be dead. The boy had hauled him along the shaft, through the freezing water and the filth and out into the daylight, like an eager hound pulling a rabbit from its hole. But before that he had finished setting the fuses, whose smouldering ends had crawled inexorably towards the powder kegs. Then any man living, rebel or King's man, had fled from that coming terror as ignobly as the basest beast whose only instinct is survival. The last thing Mun remembered was a great, gut-kicking boom as their mine had exploded, collapsing the earth around it and bringing down the outer wall of the Cathedral Close. With that defence ruined the rebels had had no choice but to surrender.

'The honour in this victory is yours, Sir Edmund,' Prince Rupert had said, the smile on his clean-shaven face reminding Mun that the Prince was barely older than himself, twenty-three or twenty-four at the most. This was the first time Mun had opened his eyes and been able to keep them open and now they were filled with the Prince's imposing frame. He had come directly from some or other fight by the looks, his breastplate spattered with blood and his helmet sprayed with mud. Yet his strong, handsome face seemed full of joy as though he had come hot from the hunt having been led a merry chase before at last running down the fox.

'Though you don't look like much of a hero,' the Prince said, 'lying there in your bed and smelling like a dungheap.' He grinned. 'I knew you would get the job done. I'm a good judge of men.' Mun thought of the man's former secretary who had been betraying the Prince for months before he was at last discovered and hanged at Oxford. 'I knew I could rely on you to make the breach.'

'It was a brilliant idea, your highness,' Mun croaked, reaching for the cup beside his bed and pushing himself upright to take a sip. The room had no window and was dimly lit with tallow candles whose flames streaked soot up towards the whitewashed ceiling.

'Yes it was, Sir Edmund, I shall not be falsely modest,' the Prince said, cocking an eyebrow. 'It is the way we would bring down walls in our fights with the Spanish. Much more effective than a cannon without the right shot, don't you think?'

Mun tried to smile but managed only a grimace.

'You were lucky, Mun,' the Prince said and Mun could not remember the man using his familiar name before. 'My surgeon operated on you while you were dead to the world. He took the ball out of your leg. Either your flesh is hard as Lichfield rock or else the man that shot you was mean with his powder, for the ball barely scratched you.' He slapped his own outer thigh. 'My man cleaned the whole mess up and did a job with the needle and thread that your own mother would be proud of.'

'When?'

'The day before yesterday.'

It did not feel like barely a scratch. Mun's right thigh was a searing bloom of pain, but he did his best to keep the discomfort from his eyes. He felt beads of hot sweat bursting from his scalp and running through his long hair and he hoped the fever would not last.

'Lord Lidford's son, your highness,' Mun said, 'I thought he was one of your Cannock men.'

'Ah yes, Jonathan. A headstrong young gentleman. When Lord Lidford discovered that the boy was down in that hole he became apoplectic. I wasn't certain whether he was simply angry that the lad was down there or furious because he was down there with you.' The Prince's slender finger and thumb stroked his prominent chin, the finger tracing the dimple over and over. 'You did steal the man's cannon, Sir Edmund.'

Mun raised his own eyebrows now and was about to mention the spy who had ordered him to steal the cannon, then thought better of it. It was difficult to accuse a man if you did not even know his name. Besides which, Mun suspected that Hook Nose's purpose in life was to provide the Prince with plausible deniability, though he likely had his own ambitions too.

'Is the idiot all right?' he asked.

'Oh, the boy is fine,' the Prince said, wafting a hand and walking over to the fireplace on whose mantel he had left his cup of wine. The fire was lit and as Mun's mind began to clear he realized with relief that he was merely hot and not feverish at all.

'For some reason my surgeon wanted you to sweat,' Prince Rupert said as though reading his thoughts. Then he waved the matter away. 'I heard you knocked the boy from his horse and him at the gallop too. He came to no harm from that either it seems.' He grinned. 'Must get his hardiness from his mother's side.'

'Hardy he may be, but any sense the boy was born with has long been knocked out of his skull,' Mun said, 'or else why would he crawl into that damn hole with us if he did not have to?'

'I dare say even being buried alive is preferable to riding about the place with that uppish old goat of a father.'

Mun could not disagree with that. 'So the town is ours?' he asked.

The Prince nodded, sipping his wine. 'The rebels surrendered the day after you brought the wall down.' He raised the cup. 'Oh, they fought in the breach a little, made a good show of it for a brief while, but their fate was sealed by your brave subterranean action, five barrels of black powder and the digging done by my Cannock men.'

'And now?' Mun asked.

'I have received word from my uncle. I am to march from here without delay to the relief of Reading, which I can assure you is the singular reason these dogs are getting such generous terms from me. Then straight to Oxford.' The cup was held out wide indicating the Lichfield rebels, who had no doubt paid for their insurrection despite the Prince's talk of generous terms.

'Am I to rejoin the troop now?' Mun asked. 'I suspect Captain Boone misses me terribly.'

'I'm certain he does,' Prince Rupert said, 'but Captain Boone will have to be patient a little while longer.' Those brown eyes fixed Mun now and any trace of the smile that had curled those full lips was gone. 'Oh, don't mistake me, Sir Edmund, your honour is intact and what's more you are to be rewarded for your recent brave action . . .' He made a steeple of his long hands and pointed its pinnacle at Mun. '. . . but I have another task for you. One more befitting your talents than burrowing through the mud like a worm.' His strange accent made 'worm' begin with a 'v'. Then the Prince turned and went to the small room's door, opening it so that the candles' dirty flames drew towards the man who suddenly filled the threshold.

'You're still alive then?' O'Brien said, a grin nestled in his great red beard.

'Alive and well, O'Brien, but you won't get me underground again unless I'm in a coffin. And properly dead too,' Mun added, the pain in his thigh receding at the sight of his friend.

'O'Brien, bring in our visitor,' Prince Rupert said, 'for I have concluded that Sir Edmund is hale and hearty and longs to be out of that bed.'

'Your highness,' O'Brien said with a nod and turned to beckon another man, so that in no time at all the room seemed even smaller for having the four of them in it.

'Sir Edmund,' the newcomer greeted him, blazing eyes fixed on Mun's own. Every instinct told Mun to get out of that damned bed, for being in it in the presence of a prince had been bad enough but with this granite-faced man it was even worse.

But he did not know if he could stand, besides which he knew he was filthy and stank.

'My friends call me The Scot,' the man said, a single-bar pot under his left arm, his right hand resting on the hilt of the sword at his hip.

'What do your enemies call you?' Mun asked.

The man's unforgiving expression changed not at all. 'The Scot,' he said. Prince Rupert's lips twitched but never broke into a smile. 'His Highness has offered me yer troop, the lads ye brought down from yer home turf,' The Scot said. 'Ye an' all if you're fit enough to ride.'

'You don't get my men without me to lead them,' Mun said, bristling. Nobody, neither prince nor major (or whatever rank The Scot held), would take his men from him while he lay grubby as a Cannock miner in his bed.

The Scot raised a placating hand and turned to the Prince. 'I like him,' he said, a smile spreading across his face like a frost-cracked rock.

'And so you should,' Prince Rupert announced, 'for not only did Sir Edmund set the charge that opened yonder breach, taking a hurt for his trouble, but he is the man who rescued my uncle's ensign at Kineton. Sir Edmund rode right up to the rebels who were carrying it off and unleashed his pistols on them.'

'I only heard o' Captain Smith,' The Scot replied.

'Well, Sir Edmund is a modest man,' the Prince said, 'and does not seek notoriety, only the recognition deserved by a loyal knight.' Did Mun detect a barb in that meant to snag The Scot's conscience? If so The Scot seemed oblivious. 'But the evidence of his bravery is in front of your eyes,' the Prince went on. 'There, see.' He pointed to Mun's spurs which sat beside his scabbarded sword and helmet on an ancient-looking chest at the foot of Mun's bed. Mun had taken the spurs off his boots before crawling into the tunnel for fear of them snagging in the earth. 'My uncle the King gave Sir Edmund those spurs on the field after his gallant action.'

'And this is the same man you sent crawling through shite like a damned rat, your highness?' The Scot said. It was more of a statement than a question, as though he was bemused at how heroes were treated in the King's army.

'I did not trust any man more to do the job,' the Prince lied. Or perhaps that *had* been the truth. Who knew with Prince Rupert? Mun thought to himself.

'I stole Lord Lidford's cannon and brought it here,' Mun admitted. 'And no doubt having me down in the ground with all that black powder and lit match was the next best thing to watching me hang. I'd wager Lidford blames me for his having a fool for a son, too.'

'It would seem the boy is headstrong,' the Prince said, removing his lace falling band for it had dried blood on it, though apparently not his own. 'That he has no fear.' Mun had heard men say the same about the Prince.

'He's headstrong and a fool, of that I'm sure. But he saved my life,' Mun said.

Prince Rupert wafted the besmirched collar at Mun. 'Sir Edmund gripes because he is yet in some discomfort, but he likes the boy really. For all that the lad nearly unseated him when they met.'

Mun did not credit that comment with a reply.

'So ye thieved the man's gun, eh?' The Scot said.

Mun shrugged. 'He wasn't using it.'

'That'll do me,' The Scot said with a curt nod. 'Can you ride?'

'I have not yet even tried to walk,' Mun said, shifting uncomfortably, pain thrumming in his right thigh.

'Walking is nae the issue, Sir Edmund, unless ye want tae walk ninety miles on yer ain.'

'I can ride,' Mun said.

'You see,' Prince Rupert said, unpinning the lace cuffs from the ends of his doublet sleeves, 'I told you Sir Edmund was the man for the job.'

CHAPTER SIXTEEN

THEY HAD RIDDEN THE HORSES HARD, SOUTH PAST BIRMINGHAM, which Prince Rupert had burnt after overcoming fierce resistance, then on through the shadow of the great Kenilworth Castle that rose up to dominate the Warwickshire landscape as it had done for centuries. They had kept their distance, though, as the castle had been garrisoned by rebels since the aftermath of Kineton Fight. Then on to Banbury where they spent the night in the castle, for though the townsfolk were mostly for Parliament its castle had been won after Kineton and was now held for the King. Mun's Lancashire men combined with The Scot's and Prince Rupert's men made a body of one hundred and twenty hard, experienced troopers and each man had looked to his mount before he had taken food or rest for himself. Several of the horses, including O'Brien's, were reshod by an enormous farrier and his wide-eyed apprentice. The lad had all but begged Mun to let him ride on with them, for he had seen nothing of the fighting and wanted a taste of it. But Mun had told the lad that his job in the forge was just as important as fighting, more so, for even the likes of Prince Rupert would be nothing without his cavalry. At which the apprentice had nodded with resignation and no little disappointment.

Mun had found that his right leg hurt more in the saddle

than out of it, for on foot he could keep his leg straight, but on horseback the wound stretched and contracted, the searing pain only dampened by the malmsey which he rationed, having filled two bottles before setting off from Lichfield. And yet you would have thought O'Brien the one who had been shot, for the Irishman's red bird's-nest beard could not conceal the misery etched in his face.

'My arse is never going to forgive me. It's raw as a skinned coney,' he complained, lifting his buttocks from the saddle and gingerly rubbing them. The column had slowed to a walk whilst The Scot and a trooper named Foster discussed the route, pointing to woods and the river beyond that flowed past the north side of a sizeable settlement. 'I'm beginning to miss that tunnel and all its comforts.'

Mun handed him a bottle which the Irishman accepted with a solemn nod, taking a long draught of the strong wine before dragging a hand across his mouth.

'We must have ridden seventy, eighty miles in the last two days. Poor Margery's legs are wearing down to stumps,' he said, patting his mare's neck. 'They're shorter by an inch than when we set off, I'd swear it.'

'It can't be far now,' Mun said, knowing how fortunate he was to have Hector, for the stallion was strong and tireless and Mun doubted there was a finer horse in all the fractured kingdom. 'That town beyond the river is Thame.'

'Then that lot must be Essex's men,' O'Brien said, nodding south-west. They could see a small troop of horse riding along the far bank of the river towards the town. But the rebels showed no sign of being interested in them and The Scot raised a hand and pushed it twice towards the south-east, indicating a course that would take them around Thame and Essex's head-quarters, towards Buckinghamshire and the Chiltern Hills.

O'Brien stuck his finger into his mouth and then held it up beside his head.

'What are you testing the wind for, Corporal?' Trooper

Goulding asked – the men had assigned O'Brien that rank, albeit unofficially, and the Irishman had certainly done nothing to discourage them.

'Why, I'm testing to make sure that bleak-faced Scotsman up ahead is still on our side, young Goulding, for I could swear the wind is due a change.' One of The Scot's men evidently overheard for he turned in the saddle and the Irishman affected a look of innocence, pursing his lips and whistling a merry tune, so that the other man grimaced and turned back round.

'They broke good horses to bring the information to the Prince,' Mun said, 'and their arses must be sorer than yours.' In truth he did not trust The Scot entirely. How could you fully trust a man who but three days earlier had fought in Parliament's army? Perhaps the Prince didn't trust him either, and maybe that was why he had convinced him to take Mun and his men south, so that Mun was there to ensure The Scot's loyalty. Mun felt a wan smile curl his lips at that thought, for his own loyalty was not untarnished, the blood in his veins having led him to treachery for his brother's sake. Yet blood was blood. Who knew what had made The Scot come over to the King, but Mun suspected it might be no other reason than the man having come to see that the rebels could not win this war. If this was indeed his reason, was prudence any more contemptible than blind loyalty?

The Scot had come hard to Lichfield with news for Prince Rupert of a convoy out of London bound for Thame. There were, he said, three carts whose twelve wheels bore a king's fortune at barely a walking pace. Twenty thousand pounds in silver and coin. Furthermore, the rebels had put their faith in God and in stealth, rather than in brute force, so that all that silver was protected by fewer than seventy-five men.

'The best bit of it all,' The Scot had said, even then not smiling, 'is that the men are half dead with some disease. We may have to crawl through shite and piss to get to the silver but no one is going to stop us.'

'Their commander?' Prince Rupert had asked. Mun knew he always put as much stock, maybe more, in who led as in who were being led.

'A Colonel Haggett. A damned incompetent,' The Scot had replied. 'Last time I saw him he was all but shitting in his boots. There's four others with them and these you'll be glad to get yer hands on.' His eyes were hard as old ice. 'They blew up the press in Oxford that spits out yer news sheet. *Mercurius Aulicus.*'

'I won't ask how you know that,' Prince Rupert had said, 'so long as you discharge your duty now and claim that coin for my uncle. I will lend you sixty harquebusiers for the job. No, Sir Edmund, not Captain's Boone's troop I'm afraid. I need them myself.'

Seeming content with that arrangement The Scot had gone on to say how he had convinced Colonel Haggett that the King's men were marching on Thame and that the convoy must stay hidden in the woods or else be lost.

With any luck that's where the rebels were still, Mun was thinking now, when a shout went up from the column's rear that a rider was approaching.

Mun and O'Brien walked their mounts out of the column so as to watch the rider, the Irishman murmuring that it had better not be orders coming for them to ride all the way back to Lichfield because if so his arse would have to protest most forcefully. The rider was cantering towards them through a damp patch of mire which they had skirted, and for twenty strides the man's horse seemed unsure, its feet coming up high and its head swinging from side to side. But its master pushed it on, heedless of the treacherous ground, and it was this contrariety between horse and rider that Mun recognized.

'Bloody hell!' he said. 'It's Lidford's son Jonathan.'

'Is he coming to kill you or save your life?' O'Brien asked with a shrug. 'Young men these days don't know what they want if you ask me.'

Jonathan Lidford rode right along the column and up to Mun, who signalled to The Scot that all was well.

'What are you doing here?' Mun asked. The column was moving again and Mun and O'Brien pulled their mounts back round to resume a good trot, moving with their horses' two-beat rhythm.

'I want to join your troop,' Jonathan said, and Mun glanced over to see that the young man's cheeks were flushing red beneath his three-bar helmet.

'God and Mary!' O'Brien blurted.

'I don't want you,' Mun said.

'But I can fight. And I can ride,' Jonathan protested.

'I've seen you kill but I've not seen you fight. As for riding, this big Irish troll beside me rides better and the Irish usually only use horses for eating.'

'Bastard,' O'Brien rumbled.

'Only because he's too heavy for his mare to throw him. 'Twould otherwise,' the young man said petulantly.

'Watch your mouth, youngen,' O'Brien said.

'I don't want you,' Mun repeated. 'Besides which, what would your father say? He'll tell the Prince I've carried you off and I'll end up in some hole again with five barrels of black powder and a short fuse.'

'My father knows. He said I could ride with you.'

'Ballocks,' O'Brien rumbled.

'Your father would never countenance it,' Mun said.

'Maybe that's a reason for taking him,' O'Brien suggested, a smile appearing in the forest of his red beard.

'Why me?' Mun asked. 'Why my troop?'

The hooves beat their pattern on the earth and tack jangled and Mun waited for his answer.

'Because you fight,' Jonathan said, 'and I want to fight too. If I stay with my father I'll never get a proper chance to fight for my king. My father is too protective. I am his only son.'

'Your father doesn't want you to get killed,' Mun said.

'I want to ride with you,' Jonathan countered.

'Ah,' O'Brien interjected. 'Distant hills look green so they do. Only when you're on top of 'em do you realize they're covered in shite.'

'Why now?' Mun asked. 'Why did you not ride out with us?'

'Because you would have forbidden me to come. Likely you would have told my father and he would never let me go with you.' There was a tone to the young man's voice that told Mun that that was not all, that there was something else, and so he waited and sure enough along it came. 'And because first I asked His Highness the Prince if I could ride for him. But he did not want me either.'

'Aha! So we were not even your first choice,' O'Brien barked. 'You've broken me old heart, buttercup.'

'His Highness said I should ride after you, that you would welcome me into your troop as he once welcomed you into his.'

'That crafty German devil,' Mun said, for he knew this had been Prince Rupert's way of getting one over on his old enemy Lord Lidford after having to smooth the waters in the matter of the man's stolen cannon. Lidford would be enraged that his son had ridden off to fight without his consent, but he could not blame anyone for it. Other than Mun perhaps.

'I believe you owe me,' Jonathan dared, keeping his eyes to the front, his big Cleveland Bay tossing her large head.

This was true enough, Mun thought. Though he did not like to admit it, he would have been buried beneath Lichfield if not for this boy.

'Let me play my part in beating the rebels,' Jonathan said, and Mun was reminded of his friend and Bess's betrothed, Emmanuel, who had been brave to the point of foolhardy and eager to do his bit in the war. Emmanuel who had fought so courageously beside Mun's father at Edgehill trying to save the King's ensign and the army's honour. And what had Emmanuel got for his lion-heartedness and his zeal? Not even a proper grave. For the rebels had killed him and Sir Francis on that bloody day and Mun had seen neither again, their bodies having been stripped by looters and lost amongst the corpse piles.

'We can always use another eager soul,' O'Brien suggested, sitting as Margery's inside hind leg hit the ground and rising as the outside leg hit, and grimacing all the while for his sore backside. 'What do you say, Mun?'

But Mun was watching a troop of dragoons milling atop a ridge of high ground to the south-west.

'Brave bastards, ain't they!' Tobias Fitch remarked, his big mason's hand cranking the spanner on his wheellock as he looked up the hill towards the dragoons, who had all dismounted and stood loading their pistols while their horses were led out of sight beyond the ridge.

'We'll see how brave they are,' John Cole said, holding his reins in one hand whilst the fingers of his other hand finished the knot of the helmet strap beneath his bearded chin.

Mun studied the ground between them and the rebels and was relieved to see no rocks amongst the rich green grass and swaying yellow patches of cowslips bowing as one in the breeze. Nothing for a horse to break a leg on or cause it to throw its rider, though charging uphill would be bad enough. Near by, a young rabbit sat transfixed by the men and horses readying for battle, until a rook walked too close and the little creature streaked off for its burrow.

'Are they Colonel Haggett's men?' Mun asked The Scot, who was staring up at the dragoons, shielding his eyes against the sun.

'Ah dinnae ken. If they are then the silver is on the move and Haggett has got some gumption after all.'

'Either way they're rebels,' Mun said, pulling back his firelock's cock halfway. Hector was neighing and baring his teeth, sensing the battle thrill in his master, feeling it himself perhaps.

The Scot nodded. 'You are an eager young blade, Sir Edmund,' he said, half turning in the saddle to address his men. 'Right, lads! Let us introduce ourselves,' he yelled. 'Try to leave one or two of them with their blood on the inside, for ah shall hae words with them. Though ah dinnae think they'll stand.'

'They'll run,' Mun said to Jonathan, 'but we'll catch them and when we do, that is when you'll give fire. When you can smell the tobacco on them.' He supposed that was his answer to the young man's request to join his troop. Jonathan supposed it too for he grinned broadly and leant to plant a kiss on his mare's neck. Mun caught O'Brien's eye and nodded towards Jonathan and the Irishman nodded back with an expression that said, *I'll keep an eye on him*, and all around them men loaded firelocks, encouraged their mounts and steeled themselves to the coming action.

'I hope they don't bloody run,' John Cole said. 'What wi' our horses being done in we'd not mek a long chase of it.'

'They'll run or they'll die,' Goffe put in, his weathered farmer's face impassive as he cinched the belt over his back-and-breast one hole tighter through the buckle.

'Into line!' Mun yelled. The Scot's men were already forming but his own had been awaiting his order and now they moved into their positions almost as neatly as Prince Rupert's own Lifeguard. 'Stay at the rear,' he ordered Jonathan who nodded, his jaw firm and his eyes intense beneath the rim of his three-bar pot. Then Mun nodded to The Scot that he and his men were ready. 'God and King Charles!' he roared.

'God and King Charles!' more than one hundred throats clamoured back, raising a black cloud of *craa*ing rooks into the sky.

They'll give us a volley and then they'll run, Mun thought, looking up at the twenty or so dragoons cresting the ridge. He and The Scot led, the rest of the division forming a killing wave three files deep and in close order as they rode up the hill at an easy pace.

And yet it was still no easy thing riding towards firearms that were pointed in your direction and Mun felt his body contract, drawing into its core like a fist around a shilling, flesh and bones cringing from the coming lead storm. He heard a rebel officer demanding that his men hold their fire and he cursed inwardly, for every moment the dragoons waited made it more likely that their fire would reap lives.

'Ready, boy. Good boy, Hector.' He touched the stallion's flanks with his spurs, the spurs that had once belonged to the King of England himself, and Hector pulled a full length in front of O'Brien bouncing on his right and Cole on his left and even a head in front of The Scot. Mun needed to show that he was unafraid and more than that, that he was eager to get up that hill and teach the rebels that insurrection buys only death. He must lead his men from the front and inspire them by his own example and so he growled an obscenity at that part of him that *was* afraid, and he opened his chest and lifted his chin.

And then the rebels gave fire.

A ball plucked the hem of Mun's buff-coat and another thunked off a man's breastplate near by and the King's men roared in defiance and, heels kicking back, came on at a good trot.

'Fight us, you dogs!' Rowland Bide yelled up at the enemy, but of course they would not fight, for it could be no fight between twenty dragoons and one hundred and twenty harquebusiers. It could only be bloody butcher's work and so the rebels were running back over the ridge to mount their little horses, their token gesture of defiance given.

'Heya!' Mun yelled and Hector put his head down and Mun leant forward, back straight as the creature snorted and broke into a canter, his great muscles defying the slope. Up they rode, yelling now to rebuff fear and to put fear in the enemy, and then the ground evened out and Mun was upon the crest, the wound in his right leg screaming, and there on the reverse slope waited two troops of rebel horse.

'King Jesus! King Jesus!' the rebels screamed and with sudden horror Mun knew that he and The Scot had ridden into the baited trap. He pulled up and straightened, throwing up a hand as Hector wheeled in tight circles, blowing, and the rest of the troop came over the brow and, seeing what awaited them, hauled on their reins.

'I take it that's not Colonel Haggett?' Mun said as The Scot came alongside, his mare tossing her head indignantly.

The Scot shook his head. 'They're fresh out of Thame, I'll wager,' he said, 'and they mean to fight.'

Mun glanced back to see that the two rebel divisions had merged into one which now trotted towards them in neat order, perhaps one hundred and fifty men in two ranks, knee to knee.

'Aye, they mean to fight,' Mun agreed, turning back to The Scot, who yelled at the men to hold and await his command, for confusion and doubt infected man and horse, Mun saw, leaching the battle lust that had but a moment before coursed through their veins.

'We'll not outrun them,' The Scot said, and Mun knew the truth of that. Their horses had not been properly rested for days, whereas if the rebels were out of Thame their mounts would be fresh.

'What say we test their resolve?' The Scot said, his voice raised above the sound of the horses neighing, tack jangling, and now the drumming of hooves upon the earth.

And test yours, too, Mun thought, suspecting The Scot of wanting to prove his new allegiance to The King and the Cause. He nodded, teeth bared, and kneed Hector back round to face the oncoming enemy.

'God save the King!' he bellowed, giving Hector the spur, and felt the muscles in the stallion's hindquarters bunch and explode with raw strength.

'Death to traitors!' Cole screamed, his face a mask of wide-eyed hysteria as he raked back his spurs and charged, and suddenly they were flying towards the enemy.

Carbines and pistols roared at them and Mun heard lead balls punch into flesh and thunk off armour, heard a man grunt and a horse scream and in his peripheral vision saw a man flung back in his saddle.

'Come on, boy!' he screamed himself, not caring that they were outnumbered or that agony and death could be a heartbeat away, and he pulled his carbine round on its belt and shoved the stock into his shoulder, and aimed low into the mass of riders coming to kill him. He squeezed the trigger and a savage hole appeared in a rebel's chest, his buff-coat blooming like a black rose, but Mun had already flung the carbine behind him and hauled his heavy Irish hilt from its scabbard. 'Kill them!' he bellowed. 'Kill the dogs!'

A collective grunt and a chorus of shrieks from horses announced the collision of the opposing forces and suddenly it was man against man and the world was a cacophony of discord. Mun hacked into a face, the blade finding the mouth and cleaving the jaw in two, yet the rebel's eyes stared wildly, madly as though he refused to admit his appalling fate. Mun hauled the heavy sword free, a scrap of bearded flesh clinging to the blade, and thrust the point between the bars of a young man's helmet into the right eye socket and the brain beyond. He yanked his arm back and pressed with his knee, turning Hector because he knew there were rebels behind him.

Steel sang against his sword which he had raised just in time and his left hand pulled a pistol from its holster and fired it into his opponent's chest and the ball punched straight through the metal breast and the man slumped dead.

'Mun!' O'Brien roared, plunging his poll-axe into a horse's skull, so that the beast's legs buckled and it dropped like a rock, spilling its rider into the midst of thrashing hooves where he screamed and was kicked to a pulp, and Mun saw a gout of flame and was flung back, his spine all but snapping. But his steel breast had taken the ball and screaming in mad fury he pulled himself upright and scythed the Irish hilt down onto the arm still pointing the pistol at him, cutting it like a butcher chopping a joint of meat. The rebel screamed but the sound was cut off when his head exploded in a great spray of blood and brain.

'King Jesus!' a man with no armour nor even a buff-coat yelled, swinging his poll-axe whose point punched through young Goulding's backplate into the flesh. Mun saw the young man convulse, his face turned up to the heavens, then topple from his horse onto the ground where he shook, frothing at the mouth.

The Scot was mounted death, working his way through the rebels, his red sword hacking and plunging, killing and maiming. O'Brien was a force of nature, lopping off limbs and felling men like a storm amongst oaks, all his strength behind his brutal poll-axe. Limb stumps spurted crimson gouts. Disbelieving faces passed chalk white in an instant as lifeblood drenched buff leather, horse flanks and the lush grass.

Someone was yelling, ordering the retreat, and Mun knew it was not The Scot, which meant it was a rebel captain, and now he pulled his last pistol free and twisted this way and that, watchful in case a rebel should stab or fire at him on the way past.

'Back to yer dens, cowards!' Goffe screamed, spittle flying, froth hanging in his beard. 'Rogues and bloody bastards, all o' ye!'

'Jonathan!' Mun yelled, catching sight of the boy through the press of men and horses. Jonathan turned in the saddle, eyes wide, sword bloody, and nodded to show that he was unharmed. Mun nodded back, a wave of relief washing over him, as the rebels galloped west, the sound like thunder rolling off across the heavens.

Mun uncocked his firelock and thrust it back into its holster. 'Hold, men!' he bellowed, though he needn't have, for they had won against the odds and knew it, so that no one wanted to push their luck still further by chasing after the rebels.

'God and the King!' a man yelled and two or three repeated the cry. One of Prince Rupert's men was laughing wildly. Other men were cursing. Some were shouting in pain and still others were offering up prayers of thanks because they had survived.

Mun blinked another man's blood from his eyes, wheeling Hector round, taking in the scene: the aftermath of a savage fight that had laid men low in mere moments, like a sudden tempest through a field of winter wheat.

One of his men, Christopher Miller, sat slumped in the saddle, cradling the dribbling stump of his left arm, the severed limb itself lying across his lap, its hand and fingers like a bone-white claw. Rowland Bide, who had been eager for this fight, now lay blood-slathered in the grass, his throat ripped open and the gore bubbling with each breath. He was sobbing for his mother.

CHAPTER SEVENTEEN

IT WAS HARD TO BE SURE BECAUSE THE TREES DISTORTED THE SOUND, but Tom would have said the gunfire was to the north and no more than three miles away.

'Sounds like quite a disagreement,' Penn said, holding the whetstone still against his sword's edge as he listened with the rest.

'Carbines and pistols, not muskets,' Trencher said, 'and maybe three hundred men.' He looked at Tom, who nodded, agreeing with the assessment.

'Not dragoons then. Must be proper horse,' Dobson said. The giant wore rusting back- and breastplates that were too small, over the clothes he had walked out of Oxford in, for The Scot had had nothing to fit him. Tom at least had a buff-coat, though not of quality, and the rapier with which he had sliced Henry Denton's forehead, as well as the knife he had killed him with.

'It can't be a good thing, the enemy being so close,' Colonel Haggett said. Even those men that were sick had pushed themselves upright against saddles, tree trunks and deadfall, coughing into bent arms and wincing against the pain. Some even pressed scarves against the mouths of the delirious to stifle their moans so that they might hear what was happening beyond their woodland den. 'That's cavalry in the thick of it. Man to man,' Haggett said, pressing the knuckles of his two fists together. He was sweat-sheened and his eyes had sunk into his skull but there was nothing wrong with his ears, Tom thought, because he was right about the cavalry.

'Sir, we should move. Go deeper into the woods,' Tom said, nodding west. Above them through the trees the sky looked like a distant seascape, the clouds skimming along like white horses but for one group which were colliding. Around this mass a celestial red stain was spreading. Flowing, Tom fancied.

'But The Scot won't find us if we move,' Penn said, standing and walking over to where Tom stood with the colonel and a handful of others.

'That is why we should move,' Tom said, feeling all eyes on him. 'And we should do it now.' For he had suddenly been struck by a thought. What if The Scot meant to betray them? What if he was even now leading the King's soldiers back towards their camp? After all the man had seemed eager enough to ride off and leave Haggett's beleaguered troop.

'You think he would betray me?' Haggett asked, dragging the sweat-stained sleeve of his shirt across his face. His chest was exposed and Tom could see rose spots against the white skin. Thus attired, his buff-coat and armour lying in a neat pile near by, the colonel responsible for Parliament's silver looked nothing more than a frail, dying man.

'I would if I were him,' Tom replied, holding the man's eye. 'For just think of what he might gain by delivering twenty thousand pounds in silver and coin unto the King.'

'More than his fee for getting it to Essex where it's needed to pay us, that's for damned sure,' one of Haggett's men named James Bowyer said, spitting a wad of phlegm onto a beech's trunk.

'This is the fourth day,' Tom said. 'You think this silver would still be here attended by dying men if Essex knew its whereabouts?' There were some sullen murmurs at that. 'No, The

Scot is not in Thame. He's dead or he's on his way here with King's men or His Majesty himself. But he is not in Thame.'

Either Colonel Haggett believed this or else he had not the strength to argue, for he nodded, shivering now, and flapped a feeble hand towards the carts which sat a little way off draped in thickets and gorse.

'You two,' Tom said to a pair of dozing troopers who seemed healthy enough, as yet untouched by whatever disease was ravaging the others, 'ride to Thame and get word to Essex. Tell him that twenty thousand pounds is at risk of falling into the King's hands if he does not come with all haste to secure it.'

They glanced at their colonel, but Haggett was consumed by his own malaise and did not look up, so they nodded to Tom and went to their horses.

In the distance a last percussive flurry signalled the end of the short but fierce fire fight. Tom turned to Haggett's men, the nearest of whom were already stirring, some of them like corpses into which a cruel God had breathed one last bitter breath. 'Get up!' Tom yelled. 'We're moving. Leave nothing behind and move with care. Do not break any branches, and cover your tracks where you can. If you or your horse shits you will bring it with you.' Then he strode over to the carts, taking Trencher, Penn and Dobson with him, for the draught animals needed to be hitched to the carts and he knew he would get it done faster than Haggett's men would.

'We should mount up and leave this bunch of cursed bastards to look after themselves,' Dobson muttered, slipping a halter over a horse's head whilst Trencher cleared the wheel spokes of foliage. 'If you're right and The Scot *has* turned lickspittle and declared for the King, we'll not get far. He'll smell this lot out like a whore-monger on the sniff for notch.'

Tom thought the big man was likely right, that even if they were careful they would yet leave enough of a trail for The Scot to follow, that so much silver was plenty of motivation to make a good search of it.

'We're not going anywhere, Dobson, except deeper into this wood,' Tom said, then called a knot of Haggett's men over, telling them to put their shoulders against the back of the carts to help get them moving. 'It'll be dark soon and no one will find us in the dark.'

'Not without us having good warning,' Trencher put in with a nod, satisfied that the two oxen before the rearmost cart were hitched and ready to do their jobs. 'You'll stay with us, Dobson, do your duty and serve your country.'

The big man mumbled some or other curse into the thicket of his beard, then clicked his tongue, leading his beasts off deeper into the woods, with Haggett's men – those that were able – helping the carts as they could. But Tom knew Dobson was right, that if they were being hunted there was little chance of not being found, particularly by a troop of men who knew full well in which wood they were hiding, if not now the exact location. If Tom's instinct about The Scot was right he would be better off riding into the dusk and leaving these ill-fated men like sheep for the wolves. There was nothing tying him to Haggett's troop. Better to report back to Captain Crafte, who would surely by now have heard of their success in Oxford and the ruin of the King's printing press. Crafte would also know about Tom's failure to kill the *Mercurius Aulicus* editor John Birkenhead, but that was another issue.

And yet Tom would not leave this troop. It was no sense of duty to the cause, nor even for the sake of seeing the silver used to pay brave men what they were owed. It was something else. Something to do with the fear he saw in these men's eyes, the hopelessness that had etched itself into the faces of the sick and dying and even those who were as yet hale. Now, as one of Haggett's men led the animals up front and Tom pushed the cart from behind, he realized with no little surprise that he needed to protect these troopers for they might not be able to protect themselves. Disease and sickness had ravaged them, so that in place of courage was wretchedness. And it was on this wretchedness that The Scot would prey, if Tom's suspicions were confirmed.

Well, let him come, Tom thought, as the cart's wheels and their own boots flattened bluebells and the smell of damp bog myrtle thickened the air, while they pushed deeper into the wood.

'I am not afraid,' he whispered, wondering how long they had before men came looking for them. *I am a killer.*

Twilight brought the churring of nightjars leaving their nests in the heather and molinia grass to take up residence on branches above the clearing in which Tom and his companions had chosen to make camp for the night. They had pushed west towards the last light of the day and after about a mile Penn had noticed an injured roe buck tucked well into a thicket of blackthorn. From its breathing it was clear the creature's life was ebbing away and even when Tom was but three feet away it could hardly lift up its head.

Trooper Banks, one of Haggett's men, had raised his carbine but Trencher had growled at the man did he want to bring Prince Rupert himself down on them. Then as Tom, Dobson and Penn held the beast still, Trencher took his big knife and cut its throat, afterwards dragging it out from under the thorn.

'This lot will be happy for some fresh meat,' Penn said, but Tom was more interested in where the roe buck had chosen to hide as death stalked it.

'We'll camp here,' Tom said, and with that they had managed, all of them taking cuts and thorns, to push the carts through the mass of blackthorn and hazel into a small clearing beyond, through which a stream ambled. Colonel Haggett had not contested their choice. The man had used whatever strength he yet had to make the journey, albeit in the saddle like those others of his men who were too sick to walk or help with the carts.

Then Tom and Trencher had skinned the roe buck, finding two deep puncture holes in its flesh and terrible bruising.

'Must have been one hell of a fight,' Trencher had muttered, for these fresh scars were clearly caused in battle by another buck's antler.

'Makes you wonder what the other one looks like,' Penn said as the raw, skinned flesh steamed in the crimson-washed gloaming.

'A fallow will seek out an injured or sick deer and beat it to death,' Tom said, 'I've seen it often.' And Trencher had raised an eyebrow at that, his eyes flicking towards the coughing, sweating men setting up camp around them, and not even Dobson had missed the allusion.

Whilst the spitted buck roasted and dripped, glistening above the cookfire, Tom led Trencher, Penn and Dobson out of the camp, Dobson complaining as they left that mouth-watering smell behind. They backtracked along their route into the woods, doing what they could to cover the convoy's tracks, treading-in the more obvious hoof prints and pulling deadfall across the trail, until at last they could do no more in the waning light.

'I'd find us without breaking stride,' Trencher had said, dissatisfied.

'Those arrogant dandy prats ain't you, Trencher,' Dobson had remarked into his beard. 'Bastards can't see past their royal fart-catching noses.'

When night proper fell Haggett was lying in his own filth, holding the right side of his abdomen and groaning. His second in command, a Corporal Laney, seemed all but paralysed by the fear that whatever disease was afflicting his fellows would do for him next. So Tom set the watches, placing four men in a perimeter around the camp, fifty paces out and all armed with two firelocks each so that they would be sure to make themselves heard if the enemy was upon them.

Then, as owls announced the night and the rich green canopy above them rustled in the breeze, Tom and his companions lay down under blankets and oiled skins, their heads on knapsacks, and waited.

*

Tom had taken the last watch, for if The Scot was coming he would come at the first flush of dawn when he could see and Haggett's men would still be half asleep. He had barely slept, his ears sifting the many sounds of woodland at night, all of which were somehow raised to a higher degree so that one could even hear such as a mouse turning over a leaf. He had recalled his childhood and the summers spent in Gerard's Wood, and that thread had led to the last time he had been there. When he had been freezing to death until his brother Mun had found him and taken him down into Shear House where, despite the fire burning in the parlour, his blood had run even colder, for he had learned of his father's death. And of Emmanuel's. Ever since that night he had steered his thoughts from them, from them all, because the wound was so deep and there was not a surgeon alive who could stitch it.

Now the scent of the woods and the silence had summoned thoughts of his old life. His old home. What had become of his family, of Bess and her new child, Francis, and of Tom's mother? What had become of Mun? All this squirmed in Tom's guts, gnawing away as he sat alone and bone-tired, listening to the night creatures and the moans of dying men.

But not so tired that he did not hear the echoing snap of twigs under foot.

He eased himself up from the old stump and took cover behind an ivy-covered ash, wincing at the clicks he made pulling his two pistols to the half cock. Chaffinches and robins were noisily greeting the day. In the distance a cock pheasant called out. Somewhere in the rich green above him pigeons were fighting, their wings beating madly, but he didn't look up, his eyes instead scouring the misty woodland before him.

Another deer perhaps.

Or men with firelocks and cold steel.

Tom cursed himself for not having emptied his bladder before now. Sweat was rising on the skin between his shoulder blades and his mouth was dry. His heart quickened and he felt the great organ thumping in his chest, the blood in his limbs beginning to tremble, raising the hairs on his arms and the back of his neck.

'Where are you?' he whispered into the dawn.

The pistol butts felt good in his hands, though they were poor weapons compared with the pair he had lost on the field below Edgehill: those twenty-six-inch-long man-killers with their octagonal barrels, which had belonged to his father.

Two hundred paces away, beyond the lowest branches of a young oak that were being pushed up and down by the breeze, he glimpsed a flash of red – a tunic perhaps – but then it was gone. Immediately in front of his face two hoverflies held still, inspecting him, their humming loud in his ears, and Tom found he was holding his own breath as he looked past the little creatures for confirmation of what his eyes thought they had seen.

And yet he knew well enough. The Scot was back and he had come for the silver. A crack of twig behind him brought him round to see Trencher creeping towards him, hunched like an old jakes farmer, though no jakes farmer would be gripping a carbine in one hand and a wicked sharp hanger in the other.

Tom put a finger to his lips and shook his head, then nodded back towards the camp, and Trencher understood for he began to step backwards the way he had come, his eyes fixed on a point beyond Tom and the ivy-covered ash. Perhaps one of the other sentries had also seen the soldiers coming through the trees and had already warned the colonel and his men. But perhaps not, and Tom decided the risk of his being seen moving was worth it to inform the troop of the danger, to have them ready to fight if needs be, but preferably to have them stay as quiet as the dead. For this way they might avoid having to fight at all. And so like Trencher he crept back towards the waking men, now and then taking cover behind a trunk or crouching behind a thicket, listening mostly for movement or voices or any indication that either of them had been seen.

When they were at the camp's perimeter he told Trencher to position himself in the thorn and keep watch, and then he slipped through the bramble where they had found the roe buck.

'They are here,' he hissed at the nearest men, one of whom was doing his morning necessary into a patch of bluebells. The yellow stream stopped mid flow and the man looked up into the woods, his pale, dirty face a sudden rictus of fear. Tom strode over to Colonel Haggett who was lying in his blankets staring up at the sky through the gaps in the canopy. 'Colonel Haggett, sir,' he growled, crouching beside the man and shaking his shoulder, 'they are here. Cavaliers more than likely.'

Haggett frowned, his bloodshot eyes glaring at Tom accusingly, but then he seemed to come round and with a quivering hand threw off the damp wool and rose on unsteady legs. The stink of the man's befouled breeches hit Tom's nose.

'Then we must surrender,' Haggett said, the cracks in his lips oozing blood. ''Tis the only course.'

'As yet they do not know we are here,' Tom said, gesturing at Penn and Dobson to spread word through the troop that they were to prepare for a fight. In truth he did not know what he had seen through the trees. Whoever it was could be friendly. But he did not think so. 'There is every chance they will go past. Or turn back,' he said. 'If we just keep our heads down.'

Colonel Haggett shook his head. 'We cannot risk it. We must surrender and let them have the silver. That is what they have come for.' Corporal Laney hurried up, doing up his helmet's thongs as he came, his armour clanking so that Tom cursed under his breath.

'Sir, your orders?' Laney said, at last seeming to find his backbone. Others too, some of them struck with the disease, yet busied themselves with wheellocks and back-and-breasts, jaws set in grim determination to discharge their duty in protecting the carts' precious cargo.

For a moment Haggett watched them, a flash of pride in his

sunken eyes. 'I will not let my men die here,' he said, finding his own resolve albeit a resolve not to fight. 'I will not see my command cut down, these brave men murdered.' He turned those eyes back on Tom, trembling with rage or fever. 'I am no Varus,' he spat. 'My bones will not lie here to be picked clean by birds.' He looked up into the canopy through which dawn light was beginning to filter and then put his hands before his face as though he expected rooks or crows to dive down and savage him with their beaks.

'You would give up the coin without a fight?' Tom said, the accusation of cowardice running like a cold current through the words.

The colonel stared a while longer at the foliage above, then seemed to shudder as though he had been struck. 'Look around you, boy!' He pointed a skeletal hand at three of his men who had not risen but still lay shivering in their blankets, their own night soil gleaming wetly beside them. 'You expect them to fight?'

Tom did not, but there were at least thirty men who *could* fight and if each fired two pistols at the right moment, such a volley might be enough to see off the enemy.

'The Earl of Essex will expect us to fight,' he said, 'and so will the men to whom this silver is owed.'

'Who are you, boy?' the colonel snarled, cracked lips pulled back from his teeth. 'Who are you to tell me what I must do?' He shut his eyes tight against some pain in his head and turned to Corporal Laney who was glancing nervously over Tom's shoulder as though he expected Prince Rupert to gallop into their camp followed by his monstrous hunting poodle, Boy. Instead it was Trencher who forced a way through the blackthorn, grimacing as a barb gouged his right hand.

'They're close,' he hissed, thumbing back the way he had come. 'But they haven't seen us yet. Might go straight by.' He sucked the blood from his hand. 'Might not,' he added.

'I will offer our surrender . . . seek terms,' Colonel Haggett said, bending to pick up his sword, but Tom kicked the weapon away and the colonel stumbled and fell onto all fours, arms trembling and elbows threatening to give way.

Round-mouthed, Corporal Laney raised his pistol but Trencher snatched it off him and shook his head, wagging his finger.

'How dare you?' Haggett said, still looking at the floor, his voice as weak and tremulous as his body.

'You can barely walk, sir,' Tom said, 'and you are not fit to command.' Tom sensed Haggett's men drawing in, armed now and likely to kill him for his insubordination, and he almost smiled at that thought, of his defying this Parliament colonel. Of his being a rebel amongst rebels.

'Take your positions to defend the carts,' he snarled at the troopers, eyes raking them, daring them to defy him. Trencher, Dobson and Penn bristled, weapons raised. Despite their hodgepodge war gear they had all the aura of seasoned killers, something not lost on the nearest of Haggett's men, Tom saw by their conflicted expressions.

'You will hang, boy,' the colonel muttered, then attempted to rise but fell again. Corporal Laney tried to help him but Haggett shrugged him off and lay back on the forest litter shaking, grimacing like an old skull.

'Do your damned work, Corporal,' Tom hissed, 'and get these men into their positions. No one is to give fire unless I give the order, is that clear?' Tom eyeballed the young corporal, who, to Tom's surprise, nodded and turned to his fellows.

'Our charge remains the same,' Laney whispered to the troop, 'to see this coin safely delivered to Thame. *I* am in command now, and you will not give fire until *my* order.' He glanced at Tom then and Tom nodded in acceptance, knowing, or at least hoping, that the young corporal would still look to him when the time came. Then Haggett's men hid themselves as best they could, crouching behind brambles and thickets and the thick trunks of oak and beech. Some, including those too sick to fight, positioned themselves behind the carts which were covered with foliage and at first glance seemed nothing more than a part of the woodland. Corporal Laney all but carried Colonel Haggett, who was barely conscious now, over to one of the carts, and then joined Tom and the others amongst the blackthorn and hazel. Lying on their bellies, carbines, wheellocks and firelocks loaded and cocked, swords unsheathed ready beside them, they peered through mean gaps in the briars at the thick woods beyond, their breathing slowed but their senses keen. Shafts of dawn light cut through a haze of mist rising amongst the trees.

Somewhere a nuthatch's *eeen, eeen, eeen* raised the alarm, the nasal, rising notes warning of new intruders. Then a horse whinnied out there and a man growled at it to be quiet. Tom saw riders. Saw buff-coats against chestnut hide, sword scabbards, helmets and bridle fittings catching the new light. He sensed the men around him tense, sensed fingers exert a little more pressure on triggers. Knew breath was being held captive in stretched lungs.

Hold, his mind told Haggett's troopers, as though they might somehow hear it. *Hold, damn it! Do not fire.*

And then an invisible fist punched him in the gut. The blood in his veins turned to ice.

Mun! His brother, mounted on Hector, was a stone's throw away leading mounted harquebusiers through the woods. The troopers were spread out in loose order, passing almost silently through the trees with carbines and pistols at the ready, heads turning this way and that. *Mun!*

The last days had been dry, so that the carts and horses had made barely an impression on the hard woodland floor, but even so Tom and his companions had done what they could to cover their tracks. And yet here were the enemy, close enough that Tom could recognize his brother and the stallion beneath him. All it would take was a whinny from one of their own beasts and they would be hurled into a storm of fire and lead.

Somewhere on Tom's left a firelock's cock clicked as it was pulled fully back.

'Hold your fire,' he hissed.

'We could savage them,' Trencher growled under his breath and perhaps he was right. They could open fire and some men and horses would die. But the range was still too far for pistols. Besides which, there were not enough of them to unleash a deadly volley. It was more likely that they would simply alert other enemy troopers to their position and eventually, because they could not move the carts quickly, they would die where they stood.

'Hold your fire,' Tom whispered to Trencher, his heart aching as though clutched by a cold hand, because his brother was there: Mun who had likely saved his life when last they met, first by finding him snow-whipped and freezing in Gerard's Wood and carrying him down to Shear House, and then by stopping Major Radcliffe's garrison men beating him to death.

There had also been the time when Mun had killed that big, ugly corporal – a man in his own troop – and soon after that, when he and Emmanuel had risked everything to break Tom out of a gaol, cheating the noose of Tom and his companions.

You are a fool, brother, Tom thought now. And yet a part of him wanted desperately to call out to Mun, wished, for the first time since the war had begun, he realized, that they could be true brothers again. That they could talk of past times and be somehow removed from their situation. But still another part of Tom knew how ashamed Mun would be to see him with the rebels, could almost see the cold scorn that would harden his brother's eyes were they to meet face to face.

Hold your fire, his mind hissed in response to feeling those around him bristle and tense. Then he saw the reason for their unease. The Scot was there too, a little further away than Mun, his men glancing round nervously because they knew Haggett's men could not have gone far with their burden of silver.

'Slippery bastard,' Trencher whispered, his weathered, pugnacious face half obscured by the thicket's new leaves, and Tom wanted to tell him to hold his tongue but dared not speak the words and risk even the dance of his lips giving them away. Thus he kept his body and head dead still, moving only his eyes. As the riders passed their position and carried on west deeper into the woods.

CHAPTER EIGHTEEN

MUN MUTTERED A PROFANITY. THE SOUND OF JANGLING TACK AND hooves scuffing the forest litter was loud enough to wake the dead and he twisted round in the saddle to see one of The Scot's men coming up behind them, pushing his mount through the trees as fast as he dared.

'So much for stealth,' O'Brien murmured, eyeing the forest around them in case the hidden enemy, prompted by the sudden disturbance, should launch an attack. Mun watched as the newcomer rode up to The Scot and conveyed his message, his horse lathered from hard riding and his own chest rising and falling like bellows. 'Bad news by the looks,' O'Brien said, for he too had read the blasphemy on The Scot's lips, and Mun walked Hector over to them as the rest of the troop, seeing their officers in discussion, stopped where they were, pistols and carbines at the ready, eyes scouring the wind-stirred woods.

The Scot turned to Mun, eyes blazing. 'Essex is coming,' he said. 'Haggett must hae had the wit eventually to send a rider to Thame.'

'How many?' Mun asked.

'At least a regiment and more on their heels most likely,' The Scot said. 'Damn it but that coin was ripe for the taking.

Haggett was all but shitting through his teeth the last I saw o' him.'

'That silver's hereabouts all right,' O'Brien put in, 'I can smell it. We can't give up now.'

'Lord Essex is coming up fast, sir,' The Scot's messenger reminded them, pressing an arm against his sweating forehead.

'Keep the heid, man!' The Scot snarled, then turned back to Mun. 'Within the hour these woods will be thicker with men than trees, and all o' them in Parliament's employ. Even if we found the silver and Haggett's lot lying dead beside it we'd still nae get the carts oot and away in time.' He shook his head. 'We cannae bide here.'

As much as he hated it, Mun knew the man was right. To stay amongst the trees was to invite chaos and disaster, and so they would have to give up the silver as lost.

'So we've come all this way, my arse screaming murder, for nothing?' O'Brien growled at Mun, teeth dragging red bristles across his bottom lip as though stopping himself from saying more. Behind him Jonathan Lidford looked crestfallen that the chance of glory was slipping from their grasp.

'Maybe not for nothing,' Mun said. 'We may give up on the silver but in doing so seize the greater prize.' He felt the blood in his veins beginning to simmer now as the scheme wove itself in his head.

'Go on,' The Scot said with a frown, one eyebrow curving suspiciously.

'If your man is right then we have drawn the fox out of his den. Let us draw him further still, out into the open where the hounds may get a proper look at him.'

'Sir Edmund, I'm beginning to suspect yer aff yer heid,' The Scot said, yet there was a spark of curiosity against the flint of his gaze. 'If anyone is the fox it is us, for we are shy of one hundred and twenty men. They are a damned regiment.'

Mun acknowledged this with a wry smile. 'Then let us play the fox well and give the hounds a good run. Is it not a fine day for it?' In his peripheral vision he saw that O'Brien and Jonathan were grinning at each other.

The Scot was not grinning. 'If ye get me killed today, Sir Edmund,' he said, pressing with his left knee to turn his mount, 'be assured I will haunt ye.' He pointed into the air and made circles with his hand to round up the men. 'If it means breaking oot o' Hell to dae it.'

'Blessed Mary, Christ and all the angels!' O'Brien said, still catching his breath from the ride and sweating in the midday sun. 'There must be more than a thousand of the buggers.'

'And the rest,' Goffe said, his ruddy, sweat-sheened face revealing a fear that was natural enough given the position in which they now found themselves. Out in the open, in the path of an army.

'Nothing to worry about, lads,' John Cole put in, rubbing his mare's poll between the twitching ears. 'We're playing at dragoons that's all. We've got the easy job today.'

For they had ridden west out of the woods onto the gently rolling land just south of the Vale of Aylesbury, one hundred and four troopers in a mostly treeless expanse, like a single hawk against the endless sky. And in front of them, like a blanket of cloud throwing its vast shadow before it, was a rebel army on the march.

'Your damned idea, Rivers, your command,' The Scot said as the men milled about them, soothing their mounts with calm voices, checking weapons and muttering prayers up to the pale blue sky. 'I'll not sacrifice my men or His Highness's but I'll play yer game awhile.'

Mun nodded, pulling Hector round to face the troopers, his heart hammering with the thrill of what he could do, what death he could sow amongst the rebels with over one hundred good men such as these were. But this enemy was no troop of horse or column of foot. This was an army. There would be pikemen, musketeers and horse, and so there could be no blood-rushing charge, sword and shot carried into the enemy's heart. Not today. Not unless the rebel horse came at them.

'We are the bait!' he yelled. 'We will draw them close, as close as we dare, and give fire. Then we will retire a safe distance and do the same again, as many times as we can before they grow tired of it. Or until His Highness the Prince joins us.' The Scot had already sent two men galloping off west to find the Prince, who would by now, if they were lucky, be somewhere near Oxford. Rupert would come like a hound on the scent when he heard that a Parliament army was on the move.

'Sir Edmund will command this action!' The Scot glared at his men. 'So keep yer lugs open and yer heids doon.' He glanced across and Mun nodded and turned back to watch the rebel army trudging across the vale towards them.

'How many colours do you see?' he asked O'Brien. The colours were yet furled for the march but their white painted silks were visible against the darker reds and iron greys of the men behind them.

'Trooper Milward, how many ensigns have you counted?' O'Brien bellowed.

'Eight, Corporal!' the young man called back.

'And I'd wager all of 'em as pretty as those fancy drawers your wife wears, Fitch,' Walter Cade teased, stirring a few laughs.

'Jesus, what's that stench?' Fitch riposted. 'Close your mouth, Cade, or that lot over there will think it's the latrine pit and fill you with shit.'

'Cade's already full of shit,' Henry Jones put in.

'Now, now, ladies.' Cole leant over in the saddle, hawked and spat onto the lush grass. 'Let's not get overexcited.' Then, nodding towards the enemy, 'We don't want to scare 'em off,' he said, dragging a hand across his lips.

Mun tapped his heels against Hector's flanks and the stallion moved off towards the rebels; and the whole troop followed, horses blowing and neighing because even they knew that the enemy were coming and that by all rights they should be riding away, not towards them.

Eight ensigns meant eight companies, pikemen and musketeers. Ideally each company would boast one hundred men, but Mun knew this rarely if ever happened in practice. More likely each of those companies coming towards him mustered forty, fifty or perhaps sixty men, because commanders preferred to maintain the numbers of soldiers in each at a reasonable level, even if to do this meant disbanding weaker companies and drafting men into stronger ones. The musketeers would number twice as many as the pikemen whose dark staves Mun now saw bristling above rebel heads.

'They're not short of horse, either,' O'Brien beside him observed.

'It's not the dog in the fight, Clancy, but the fight in the dog,' Mun replied.

'Ah, so it is,' the Irishman said, like Mun assessing the enemy's strength and in particular their horse, for they would prove the biggest threat if they had an appetite for a fight. Parliament cavalry rode on either flank, perhaps as many as five hundred men, two hundred of which were dragoons, two hundred harquebusiers and perhaps one hundred, if Trooper Milward's eyesight was to be trusted, heavy cavalry in the form of cuirassiers, their armour glinting in the afternoon sun.

And still Mun led them north-west, directly towards the seething mass that had marched out of Thame, his mouth drying now and his nerves jangling like the men's tack and sword fittings all around him.

The sound of the rebels' drums beating the March carried to them now, a sound that could put ice-cold fear in a man's gut or even make him piss in his breeches.

'You had better all be loaded, lads!' O'Brien called over his shoulder, a grin nestling in his beard. 'Don't want you telling me after that you forgot in all the excitement.'

It was said only half in jest. Men had been known in their

panic to fire their scouring sticks at the enemy or otherwise charge their firearm incorrectly. Mun had seen troopers, musketeers too, forget the wad so that the ball rolled out of the barrel. He had seen trembling lads fail to prime the pan, seen their shocked expressions when they pulled their triggers and nothing happened.

But all those who rode with him now at a good trot were experienced soldiers, forged and hardened by war, and he did not doubt that they would perform well for him. They were arranged in three ranks, the length of a horse left between each rank, and a good pace, three feet, between the files, which would give them a wide front from which to fire but a weak body should they endure the shock of a rebel charge. Though Mun had no intention of receiving a charge and fighting hand-to-hand. Against so many it would be suicide.

They were close enough now that the enemy were more than a body of rebel musketeers with their matchlocks and stands, buff-coats or simple tunics, bandoliers and broad-hats with orange bands. They were no longer simply Parliament's pikemen presenting a wall of wrought-iron armour – brimmed pots, gorgets, breastplates and tassets – and their great staves: sixteen feet of tapered ash culminating in wicked steel blades. Now, Mun could make out faces within the throng, skin red raw from that morning's shave, jaw muscles tight as knots and eyes steeled by the comfort of relative safety in numbers. He could see hat plumes shivering in the warm breeze, scars on tunics and breeches where they had been oft repaired, mud spatters up bucket-top boots or white stockings, and garters flickering at the knee.

And he could see their cavalry on the move.

'It's just a warning!' Mun called to his men. 'Keep open order and withhold your fire.' The rebel harquebusiers were riding from the flanks to the van, two hundred buff-coated or iron-breasted men placing themselves as a protective threat before their infantry. The dragoons remained on the flanks and for the moment the heavy cavalry, the hundred cuirassiers, stayed on the rebel right, and it was these men that Mun kept one eye on as he led the King's men onward.

'I can smell the scum now,' Henry Jones said off Mun's left shoulder. 'I always say that if I can smell 'em I'm close enough.'

'A little further, Jones,' Mun said, relieved to see the rebel horse out in front, for that was preferable to facing more than two hundred musketeers whom they would be unable to ride down because of the pikes protecting them.

But then the rebel horse facing them divided, forming three troops of sixty-six men in ranks of eleven and files six deep.

'They mean to fight, Sir Edmund!' The Scot called from the rear rank, and Mun grinned because the game was playing out just as he wished.

'We must make them believe we are mad enough to charge home!' Mun replied. 'I want to see them preparing to receive us. I want to see the prayers on their lips.'

'Then you have your wish!' The Scot exclaimed, and Mun knew he had Prince Rupert to thank for that, because ever since the cavalry skirmish at Powick Bridge the Royalist horse had been known for audacious, fearless, even foolhardy aggressiveness. They would carry the charge to the enemy and break amongst them with swords, only making use of their firearms deep in the fray. Mun had been there on that day when they had forged their reputation. He had charged in full career beside Prince Rupert himself and seen the rebels utterly routed, many of them slaughtered by his own hand in what was his first taste of real butchery. Ever since Powick, Parliament's horse had feared them.

They fear us now, Mun thought, even with so many.

'Let them see your blades!' Mun called, and the order of *blades* was repeated throughout the troop. 'But watch the man in your front, for we will not fall upon the enemy but rather give them a volley by ranks and then retire south-west!'

The Scot repeated the order for it was imperative that every man knew what was expected of him.

'Hold your fire!' a rebel officer yelled.

'Aim at the breast or lower, lads,' O'Brien roared, which was good advice however often repeated, for pistols, like muskets, tended to fire high, and Mun hoisted his Irish hilt above his head, the blade promising blood and butchery.

'Hold your fire!' the rebel officer yelled again, holding his nerve.

Fire, Mun willed the enemy. *Fire, damn you!* He gave Hector his spurs and the stallion responded, breaking from a good trot into a canter.

Any closer and they would ride into a hail of lead. The men with him must have known that too, which was why they began to scream and yell, brandishing their blades like madmen, inciting the rebels to give fire too soon.

'Fire!' someone screamed, but Mun already knew the rebels had fired, a heartbeat before he heard the command and the ragged salvo of cracks, as pistols and carbines spat their balls and coughed white blooms of smoke. *Damn fools!* his mind snarled as he glanced left and right to see his front rank intact and savage grins on men's faces.

One hundred paces flashed by, another fusillade erupting from the rebel harquebusiers, and then he leant back in the saddle and pulled on the reins, bringing Hector up. A spray of blood in his peripheral vision told him that someone had been hit, as he swung the carbine round on its belt, gripping it in his right hand, Hector's reins in his left. He gave no order, simply pulled the trigger, and the weapon roared and he could not miss for they were but thirty paces from the rebels, and thirty-four other men gave fire too.

Several rebels were thrown back. Some slumped in their saddles or fell from their mounts. 'Traitors!' Tobias Fitch bellowed and as Mun hauled Hector round to make way for the second rank, he saw Fitch linger a moment to spit at the enemy horsemen.

The second rank, already urging their mounts through the gaps in the first, took aim and fired and more rebels fell. Some of the rebels broke formation in order to return fire but there was no order, only chaos, and by the time Mun's third rank released its hail of shot Parliament's harquebusiers were bloodied and shocked.

'Retreat!' Mun gave the order as he turned Hector and gave the spur so that together they galloped off south-westwards, his world filled with the drumming of hooves against the ground and men's whoops and shrieks of savage joy, and the pounding of his own lifeblood in his head, which was somehow intensified by the three-bar pot encasing it. He glanced over his right shoulder at the rebel harquebusiers who were milling in confusion, some looking to the wounded and others cursing the Royalists or imploring their captains to allow them to give chase.

'Whoa, boy!' Mun yelled, pushing his seatbones into the deepest part of the saddle and his heels into the stirrups, giving the reins a sharp tug. 'Whoa, Hector!' The stallion slowed and tossed its head, neighing, imbued with that same wild thrill that filled them all. The other troopers reined in all around him in a cauldron of steel and horseflesh and exhilaration.

'Load your firearms and do it quickly!' Mun bellowed, but hands were already busy with powder flasks and lead balls, wheellock spanners and scouring sticks, knees gripping their agitated mounts, wide eyes blinking away sweat and now and then glancing up towards the enemy. 'Form up! Three ranks!' Mun yelled, setting himself as a rock around which the avenging tide of steel and shot coalesced. O'Brien pushed into the line beside him and nodded at Mun, his horse biting at the bit. 'Casualties?' Mun asked, powder flask steady as he poured a measure onto the priming pan and closed the frizzen.

'Just one,' O'Brien said, pointing off to their left behind the third rank and Mun twisted to see a riderless horse and a man on the ground beside it, wrapping his red scarf around his bloodied face. 'One of The Scot's,' the Irishman said. 'He'll live but he'll be ugly as a blind cobbler's thumb.'

'Heard a few of us hit,' young Godfrey said, eyes bulging, 'but the balls just bounced off.' Mun had heard the clanks as rebel shot struck breastplates, and some grunts where they'd hit buff-coats, but apart from The Scot's man, no one had received a severe injury.

'They'll not fall for that again,' O'Brien warned, nodding at the enemy who were re-forming into two troops now, their dead and injured and riderless horses being taken back into the body of the infantry.

'They'll be riled. They'll feel humiliated,' Mun said. 'They'll want to show us that they can fight.' With that he squeezed with his legs and gave a gentle kick with his heels, so that Hector began to trot. Back towards the enemy.

Which was turning to face them.

'Well, it would seem that we hae their attention,' The Scot called to Mun from his position in the third rank where he would ensure the troop's cohesion. The third rank being the last to fire, the enemy would be prepared or even counter-attacking, which meant that holding the rank steady was as important as leading the attack. 'They willnae like being stung again. I'll wager they'll send the heavy lot.' He meant their cuirassiers, the troop of heavily armoured men on their big horses.

'Cuirassiers are just as easy to kill,' Mun replied over his shoulder, 'one only has to get nice and close.' So far there had been no sign that the rebel commander would unleash his cuirassiers, and perhaps he would not risk them in such a skirmish as this. But it would pay to keep one eye on them all the same. What Mun had said about killing such men was true enough and a pistol shot from mere feet away did stand a good chance of piercing their armour. But being so close was dangerous in itself. Swords were next to useless against cuirassiers, besides which they would be shooting at you or hacking you to pieces with their poll-axes.

'Keep your heads, lads!' O'Brien called above the two-beat gait of the trot. 'And loosen up would you, Master Lidford? For the love of Christ, lad, you look stiff as a poker.' For all his bravery, or foolhardiness, Mun knew that Jonathan was not a match for his fine Cleveland Bay, all sixteen hands of it. The beast was the same size as Hector. 'That's better,' the Irishman said, 'keep the legs unlocked and your back nice and soft. Damn it but you were making *me* look like a Rivers, and as Sir Edmund will tell you I ride worse than a strumpet on a priest after her last confession.'

Mun grinned at Jonathan, hauling his sword from its scabbard, and the young man grinned back, pulling his own blade free and raising it to the sky.

'For God and King Charles!' Jonathan shouted, and the war-cry was taken up by all three ranks, their horses joining in with cries of their own.

Up ahead the rebel infantry was still settling itself into battalia, having right-wheeled to face the south-west and the fluid threat of Mun's troop. But the two troops of horse out in front were steady now. More than that they bristled with violent intent, eager to restore their honour and blood their enemy. Mun could see it about them even across four hundred paces, and yet he led his men on, the wound in his right thigh beginning to scream again.

'Dragoons!' Trooper Milward called out.

'Keep going!' Mun bellowed, for he too had seen the dragoons in two columns either side of the infantry moving forward, but he would not stop his troop so short. He could not.

'It's only dragoons, lads,' O'Brien hollered, 'neither fish nor fowl and nothing to worry proper soldiers like you.'

The rebel dragoon columns flowed out wide across the vale, taking up flanking positions either side of the harquebusiers that sat their horses patiently in the tall grass that stirred like a lake in the breeze. It was the obvious move from the rebel commander, for even if they remained mounted – as they surely must – those two hundred dragoons would add their firepower to that of their comrades.

'They'll flay us alive, Mun,' O'Brien growled in a voice low enough that only Mun and a few others would hear.

'We will draw them west, Corporal,' Mun replied. *Towards the Prince who will butcher them where they stand*, he thought. *If* the Prince was coming. 'Draw them west for as long as we can. Bleed them as they come.

'Let them fire too soon. Just once more,' Mun murmured, but he knew the rebels would not fall for the same trick again and so, gripping Hector with his knees, he sheathed his sword, his left thumb guiding the blade home, and pulled his carbine round. 'Prepare to give fire!' he yelled, knowing that to ride further would be to spring the trap, and then he pulled up, Hector whinnying in frustration. 'Fire!'

The world exploded, lead shot shredding the air, and a ball smacked into Mun's breastplate again, throwing him back in the saddle. A man beside him screamed, his face torn open so that white bone gleamed and teeth and bloody shards littered his falling band. Horses were squealing and madness was king.

'Up you get,' someone said and Mun was buffeted by another horse as a big hand thrust into the space between breastplate and buff-coat and gripped the iron, hauling Mun upright in the saddle. 'Come on, Sir Edmund, you're all right, laddie.' Mun glanced at O'Brien and then towards the rebels. 'Aye, they're eager to make our acquaintance,' the Irishman said, for the cuirassiers were charging towards them and with them the two troops of harquebusiers. The sound was like the denizens of Hell pummelling fists against the roof of their fiery prison, as Mun leant back, tugging a rein, and Hector stepped gracefully backwards despite the chaos. Those armoured riders were bearing down on them, roaring as they came, and Mun thought his troop must be overrun.

'Heya!' he yelled, his heels pressing Hector's flanks, and drew his two long pistols, gloved wrists pulling both cocks back, and then he sensed a wave flowing with him, heard The Scot bawl at the troop to give fire, and he pulled the pistols' triggers so that they roared like ferocious beasts. He saw armoured men punched backwards and gouts of blood flung from man and beast, and the smoke was everywhere, thick as fog.

'Now back we go!' O'Brien bellowed. 'You too, Jonathan!'

Mun rammed his pistols back into their saddle holsters, pressed a knee against Hector's heaving side and hauled the stallion round. 'Away, Hector!' he said as the stallion's great muscles impelled him into a gallop. And those that could raced off as though a great black cloud of death were on their heels.

'Five men down!' John Cole said, wheeling his mare, letting the beast work out its excitement rather than trying to hold it still. 'Maybe dead, maybe not.'

Mun looked back to where the rebels had stopped and were milling whilst their officers issued commands.

'Seems they dare not stray far from their fellows,' Jonathan said, bristling with the mad thrill of the skirmish, his eyes blazing in his handsome face.

'Your father would kill me if he knew where you were,' Mun gnarred, trying to read his enemy's intentions. The rebels had made a chase of it and Mun had dared to hope they would follow them all the way to Oxford, but then after only some three hundred paces they had pulled up, the pursuit abandoned in favour of prudence.

'That's two more of my men dead, Sir Edmund,' The Scot barked, walking his horse through the press towards Mun.

'And two of mine, sir,' Mun replied, like the ring of sword on sword. The other casualty was one of Prince Rupert's men.

The Scot shook his head, undeterred. 'This game is nae worth the price, lad. Nae for just a regiment o' the bastards.'

'Sir!' a trooper called. 'Sir!' It was Trooper Banister and by his face Mun could not say whether the young man was jubilant or terrified. 'More dragoons are coming up yonder plain. Lots of them and all out of Thame on Parliament's shilling by the looks.'

Mun craned his neck, trying to see north past the great knot of enemy horse and their infantry beyond, but he could not spy Banister's dragoons. Yet he had no reason to doubt the lad.

'That's the Devil's own grin upon your face, sir,' O'Brien said to Mun, slapping his big mare's neck, teeth splitting the bristling bush of his beard.

Even The Scot, who was also tall in his saddle peering north, nodded before giving his men the order to form up once again facing the enemy. For dragoons coming south out of Thame, towards the unmistakable sound of battle, most likely presaged another regiment on the march. Another regiment they could lure onto Prince Rupert's sword.

'P'raps it's Essex's whole bloody army,' O'Brien suggested, thick fingers busy cranking the spanner on his wheellock. 'Never know our luck now, do we?'

'Not so close this time, Sir Edmund,' The Scot growled, turning his mount to get into position for another charge. 'Let us keep a courteous distance and leave them wanting more.'

Mun ignored him. 'Form up!' he yelled, watching the enemy, his heart thumping with wild elation. With pride, too, that such men as these were his comrades in the fray.

Then his loyal black stallion, the finest horse in all the world, bore him forwards. To lure the rebels unto their destruction.

CHAPTER NINETEEN

BY MIDDAY THEY HAD JOINED WITH PRINCE RUPERT, WHO HAD ridden at the head of several troops of horse including his own Lifeguard, towards the distant crackle of gunfire. And neither had His Highness's arrival come too soon, because it seemed that Essex must have emptied Thame of rebels and sent them all south with orders to give battle to the King's men and score a victory in Parliament's name. Mun and The Scot had drawn these men inexorably on, attacking and retreating over and over again, always stinging the rebels enough in pride and blood to keep them marching westwards lusting for vengeance.

'Sir Edmund, it would seem you have been busy without me,' the Prince said, reining in on an enormous stallion whose chestnut coat gleamed against the red and gold embroidered saddle. Sniffing the grass near by, his faithful white hunting poodle, Boy, snapped its jaws at a butterfly that flickered up out of reach.

'We've poked a shit with a sharp stick and raised a stink,' O'Brien muttered beside Mun.

'The devils are eager to make my lord's acquaintance,' Mun said, removing his helmet and wiping sweat-soaked hair from his forehead.

The Prince grinned. '*I* am the Devil, do not forget,' he said, referring to the nickname Rupert the Devil, given to him by the rebels in the early days of the war.

'As I am certain you will remind them, your highness,' Mun replied with a tired grin that was mirrored in the young Prince's face. A mile away the rebel infantry came on in full battalia, ensigns unfurled and rippling in the breeze of the now cloudy day. The monotonous beat of their drums and the sound of yelled commands carried to the Royalists now and then, though Mun knew there could be no pitched battle for the bulk of the Prince's infantry was in Oxford.

'Here they come again!' The Scot, near by, roared, pointing north-east to the seething mass of Parliamentary horse and dragoons which they had been leading on since morning.

'O'Brien,' Rupert said, looking down his nose at the big Irishman, 'Clancy, isn't it?'

The Irishman's face flushed, matching his beard.

'Aye— Yes, your highness.'

The Prince nodded, pulling a rein because his stallion was trying to bite Hector who seemed unimpressed by the beast, his ears flat and his tail swishing. 'Bring your sharp stick, Clancy O'Brien.' And with that Prince Rupert turned his horse and began issuing commands to his officers in readiness to join the game and lure the rebels further still.

Now it was mid afternoon, and having engaged the rebels in a series of rolling skirmishes they were near Chiselhampton and tiring. Mun guessed that they numbered some thousand horse but now, fortunately, some of the Prince's Oxford-based infantry had arrived. Only eight hundred men all counted, but their muskets had made for a welcome sight. He had heard that that morning those men had overrun Parliamentary outposts at Postcombe and Chinnor, but since they were then under pressure from roaming troops of rebel horse the Prince had ordered them to withdraw and hold Chiselhampton Bridge in case a full-on retreat should become necessary in the face of Essex's army.

With his dragoons taking up positions in the surrounding hedges, the Prince was setting his ambush and Mun was reminded again of the brief, mad carnage of Powick Bridge and his stomach would have rolled over itself at that thought if he were not already thrumming with the battle thrill after the day's action.

'You think they'll come this far?' Jonathan asked now, raising the guard of his helmet and dragging an arm across his face, smearing filth and sweat. They were riding back east to face the oncoming rebel horse yet again, which would give the Prince's infantry time to withdraw back to Oxford and the dragoons a chance to prepare themselves. Looking at the young man Mun was struck by how quickly he had become a soldier.

'They might,' Mun said, wincing because the pain in his injured thigh was now too great to ignore. His breeches were stained where blood had begun seeping from the wound. 'They know His Highness is here, almost within reach. Up close the prospect of getting the better of him is too shiny for them to ignore.' A stab of frustration announced itself at the reminder of the treasure that had somehow slipped from their own grasp that dawn. 'But first the Prince will want to bleed them properly. The fools likely think they are winning. Their commanders believe we retreat because we dare not engage.' He lifted the leather flask to his mouth, pulled the stopper with his teeth and then drank. 'Rupert will want to disabuse them of this belief,' he said, ramming the stopper home.

'O'Brien, you Irish arse-berry!'

They looked over and saw another troop of the Prince's Lifeguard joining their right wing and amongst them a grinning Richard Downes, who was giving O'Brien a gesture that would make a whore blush. Beside him were Vincent Rowe, Humphrey Walton, Purefoy, Burke, and the raw-boned Corporal Bard who nodded a greeting at Mun.

'Downes, you seed, breed and spawn of an English whore! May the cat eat you and the Devil eat the cat!' the Irishman called back, earning no few black looks and mumbled curses from the Englishmen around him. 'Now we're all in the shite,' O'Brien grumbled to Jonathan.

'Hey, lad! Your father is looking for you,' Humphrey Walton called across to Lord Lidford's son. Jonathan shot Mun a guilty look. 'He's looking for you too, Sir Edmund.' Walton was clearly amusing himself, but Mun merely raised a hand and flapped it lazily as though he had heard it all before.

'Do me a favour and stay alive,' Mun growled at Jonathan, eyes ranging along the newly arrived troop, preoccupied in searching for the object of his hatred. There he was: Captain Nehemiah Boone, his own hate-filled eyes glaring at Mun as Mun somehow knew they had been since the troops had joined. Given their previous dealings Mun would not put it past Boone to shoot him in the back if the opportunity presented itself.

'No matter how many times I pray that bastard might catch the pox –' O'Brien put the edge of a flat hand against his throat, 'or a halberd in his damn neck, come to that – the good Lord turns a deaf ear.' He shook his head. 'The black-hearted bastard,' he muttered, then quickly turned his face to the sky and thumbed towards the captain. 'Him, Lord, not you,' he clarified.

Then the Prince, having taken a report from a scout who had galloped up with the look of a man who has narrowly escaped ruin, gave the command to halt and form up, for the enemy was almost upon them.

'Where are we?' Mun asked.

'Buggered if I know,' O'Brien answered, the others around them shrugging and shaking their heads.

'About ten miles south-east of Oxford, sir, between the hamlet of Warpsgrove and Chalgrove village,' one of The Scot's troopers answered, and Mun nodded his thanks as he surveyed what was to be the battlefield. Before them a field of corn bristled in the breeze. Elsewhere was pastureland upon which rabbits sat cropping the grass, undeterred by the proximity of men and horses. To the north-east lay hedged fields full of crops and to the south-west a fallow open field of long grass that seemed to roll like gentle waves. At the end of the cornfield, separating the King's men from Parliament's, was a great hedge towards which the Prince was pointing his gleaming sword.

'The insolent dogs are beyond that hedge!' he yelled, 'and as you can see they grow bold.' Mun and his companions watched as several bodies of Parliamentarian horse and dragoons rode down a hill flecked with yellow St John's wort, on their right beyond the hedge, to join their comrades in the enclosed pastureland. 'There are three more troops held in reserve amongst the trees beside Warpsgrove House in yonder close,' he went on, pointing his sword north-east. 'It is possible that we face eleven troops, perhaps six hundred men, and what with their foot being a way off and we being above a thousand, we should make a rout of it.'

'Do *you* think there's more of us, because I bloody doubt it,' O'Brien said in a low voice, scratching his bird's-nest beard. 'Maybe if the foot hadn't buggered off.'

'I think His Highness would want to charge them even if they had three times our number,' Mun answered, walking Hector into the front line just a few places along from the Prince himself. In recognition of their tireless work throughout the morning, Rupert had honoured him and The Scot by inviting their troopers to ride with him in the centre of the Royalist line. To their north the Prince of Wales's regiment made up the left wing and General Percy's regiment had come up on the right. They were arrayed three deep, five foot between each man, so that given their number and the gaps between troops they presented a formidable front some eight hundred yards long.

We are the scythe, Mun thought, looking left and right and

then across the field whose already tall crop swayed gently and brushed against their horses' chests. We are the blade that will cut the rebels down. He had heard young Trooper Godfrey ask O'Brien why they were not leading the rebels back towards Chiselhampton Bridge and the ambush that awaited them. For had that not been the Prince's own plan? 'The rebels are too bloody close now,' the Irishman had replied, 'and might yet fall on the infantry's rear and baffle the whole bloody lot. Bastards might even bring our own horse into confusion before we could recover to our cosy hides. Better to look a nasty dog in the eye than show it your arse, eh, Sir Edmund! Besides which,' he added, getting to the nub of it, 'His Highness loves nothing better than a fight. You see, young Godfrey, every man, even a lanky, long-nosed German, has some redeeming part in his character. Even you, lad.' He grinned. 'Though not even your ma can say what the part is.'

'The lad loves his 'orse,' Goffe had put in, 'almost every night he does.' And this had raised laughter from the men of Mun's troop, men who knew they were about to ride into battle and might meet their deaths in that cornfield.

Now the crackle of firelocks punctured the day as Parliament men sniped through the hedge at the Royalist lines. O'Brien pointed ahead and Mun could make out a cluster of rebel dragoons hacking into the briars with swords, trying to carve a gap through which Essex's horse could pour to give battle.

'We'll be here the rest of the damned day,' O'Brien said, rubbing his mare's ears which were twitching at flies. The hedge was quite an obstacle but not so thick that Mun could not see that a large body of horse had come up to support the dragoons and now faced General Percy's regiment.

But the Prince had grown tired of waiting. 'Yea!' he yelled, his stallion rearing and screeching defiance. 'This insolence is not to be ignored!' Then the beast's forelegs thumped down and the Prince whipped the flat of his sword against its rump and in a heartbeat was galloping towards the hedge.

'Go on, Hector! Go on!' Mun yelled, and gave his spurs so that Hector exploded like a bolt of lightning, his great muscles bunching and smoothing, his hooves pounding their four-beat rhythm like a war drum. Mun did not know who was with him and nor did he care, for he would follow the King's nephew into the flames of Hell and slay Satan himself, such was his fury.

A bullet hissed past his ear and he heard the meaty *thunk* of it hitting flesh and then, in front of him, the Prince leapt the hedge and Hector, being the finest horse that ever lived, gave no pause but surged up and Mun threw himself flat against the stallion's neck. In that held breath Mun saw the enemy below, saw the terror in their faces, then his bones rattled as Hector landed with a gruff snort and barely broke stride, neighing madly. Mun swung his sword, missing a dragoon's face by a hand's span, then he wheeled the blade back round and slashed it at a man's raised arm, lopping the limb off from the elbow, so that the rebel fell away screaming, his raw stump spurting blood ten feet into the air.

'With me!' the Prince roared, wheeling his stallion as terrified rebels fled from him like rings from a stone dropped in a pool. 'With me, King's men!' A bullet plucked the hem of Mun's buff-coat and another whizzed so close that he felt its breath on his cheek as he glanced back to see a handful more men leaping the hedge into the enemy's maw. Through the hedge he could see the vast bulk of his own men thundering off north to find a way round the hedge and he hoped O'Brien and Jonathan were amongst them for he could not see them on this side of the barrier, though there were already dead men in that field.

'My lord, we are too few,' a corporal of the Prince's Lifeguard said, wide-eyed, fighting to get his mount under control, and Mun suspected the man was right for there were but fifteen of them now on the enemy's field. And yet the rebel dragoons had not stood. They were running like rabbits, bits of kit falling from them as they sought the protection of their mounted comrades, some of whom were firing carbines or wheellocks from the backs of their horses. A ball clanked against the Prince's breastplate and his head flew back with the force of it. 'Insolence!' he shouted at the enemy horse across the field. 'You offend the laws of God and man!'

Lead shot shredding the air around him, Mun sat tall in the saddle and trotted over to join those clustering around their prince.

'Like field mice before the owl, hey!' Rupert said, flashing Mun a handsome grin, and just then came the battle-cry of 'For God and the King!' and Mun twisted to see those they had left behind – those who had not risked jumping the hedge – now cantering across the field towards them from the north.

'With me!' the Prince yelled to these men, thrusting his bloodied sword into the air, his stallion gnashing its teeth like some wild monster from a child's nightmare. A dog's barking cut through the thunder of hooves, the cries of men and beasts and the percussive crack of firearms, and Mun looked back to the hedge and a flash of white amongst the brambles. The Prince's hunting poodle, Boy, scrambled through and came bounding across the field towards them.

'Here, Boy!' the Prince called as his men readied themselves for the inevitable charge and the enemy horse across the flower-strewn meadow bristled in their ranks, their commanders unsure whether to attack or flee. Here and there horses whose saddles had been emptied by the rebel dragoons stood cropping the grass as though they had not a care, whilst their fellow creatures, as yet slaves to their masters, shrieked and tossed their heads in fear and excitement.

Some of the newly arrived men cantered towards the Prince and Mun was relieved to see O'Brien, Jonathan and other familiar faces amongst them. The majority, though, led by Lieutenant Colonel O'Neale, broke into a full-blooded charge across the field. Yelling furiously, these hammered into the enemy's right flank, which buckled in confusion, its men caught in fateful indecision between fight and flight.

'Good lads!' Prince Rupert said through gritted teeth, every sinew in his body straining, like a mastiff at the leash, to join the fray.

'Even the dog got here before you, Clancy,' Mun growled at the Irishman, noting that the rebel whose arm he had cut off was lying dead. The grass around the corpse in all directions had been sprayed with dark blood.

'If I'd have followed you, she and me would still be sitting in that hedge back there,' O'Brien growled back, patting his big mare's neck. Then he nodded towards Jonathan. 'Had to all but grab a fistful of youngen's beast's tail to stop him coming after you,' he said, but the young man seemed not to hear, the reins in his fists and his awe-filled eyes riveted on the enemy.

'Like old times, eh, Sir Edmund?' Mun turned to see Vincent Rowe wheeling his mount in tight circles, the horse's eyes rolling, foaming spittle dripping from its mouth as it savaged the bit. 'They said all this would be over by last Christmastide.'

'They also said the rebel horse would never stand,' Richard Downes replied, staring at the mêlée across the field, his lavish curls dark against a bright white lace falling band. 'But they were bloody wrong about that and all.'

The rebel right flank was not running. Rather its men were turning to face the threat of Lieutenant Colonel O'Neale's charge, and Mun winced to see them give O'Neale's men a good volley with their pistols. Troopers were thrown back in their saddles or fell from their horses into the maelstrom of thrashing hooves and were pummelled. Then the rebels gave a second volley and a tremor ran through O'Neale's thrust, though his men fired their own pistols and those who had pushed deep amongst the enemy set about them with blades, hacking like maniacal butchers. Mun watched swords hauled back amidst arcs of blood, saw them plunge again and heard the ring of steel and feral high-pitched screams that were, horrifyingly, the same whether from man or beast.

'Shall we give O'Neale this day's glory?' Prince Rupert yelled, turning fire-filled eyes on the men around him. 'Or shall we attend to these traitorous dogs ourselves and give them a sound whipping?'

'God save the King!' Captain Boone cried and the Prince's men, gathering thickly around him now, took up the call, thrusting pistols or swords towards the hated foe.

'God save the King!'

Mun spurred Hector forward and the whole seething mass around him seemed to explode like a powder keg shown the flame.

'Kill them!' John Cole screamed. 'Kill the maggot-ridden scabs!' And in the time it takes to hurl a terse prayer up to the heavens they were in full flight, the ground beneath them trembling, and Mun was filled with a sudden rush of joy because the enemy, being engaged with O'Neale's men, were not ready to receive them.

This time, as though to show the Prince's stallion that he was the finer beast, Hector outstripped Rupert and Mun found himself the sharp end of the wedge, had only the enemy before him and knew he would be the first to plunge into Parliament's left flank. Twenty paces before impact he swung his carbine round, for he must empty as many saddles as he could to enable the wedge to drive deep and split the foe like an oak trunk.

God, give me courage . . .

Then he smashed into the press of bodies, the impact almost throwing him from the saddle, and a desperate man fired his wheellock at him but the ball screamed above Mun's head because the rebel was young and inexperienced and that was his death. For Mun thrust his carbine against the man's breastplate and pulled the trigger and there was a deafening *crack* and *thunk* as the ball punched deep into the young man's chest, only stopped by his backplate. For a moment he glared at Mun, in that heartbeat his lips curling as though he might cry, then he slumped dead, his hands dropping reins and pistol as he tipped from the saddle.

'Godless devil bastards!' a Parliamentarian officer yelled at Mun, spurring his mount forward into the oncoming tide of flesh and bone, leather and steel. 'Fight me, you whoreson! Fight me!' he screamed, spraying white spittle across the bars of his pot and brandishing his sword as a challenge.

In one fluid movement Mun threw his carbine across his back, drew his left-side pistol and fired and the rebel officer's face collapsed in on itself in a welter of blood and brain. A glancing blow scraped against Mun's helmet and he drew his last pistol, thrust it between his left arm and his side and pulled the trigger, looking over his shoulder as his attacker screeched in agony, Mun's ball having exploded his jaw so that white shards flopped around on sloppy, blood-flinging scraps of flesh. The same instinct had Mun's pistol holstered and his Irish hilt in his hand before the rebel even knew he was dead, and he caught a sword blow on his own blade's forte and pushed it wide, then scythed the broadsword back against the bars of a man's pot. But the bars took the blow and the man, though stunned, brought a pistol up in his other hand.

'Not today, laddie!' O'Brien bellowed, planting his poll-axe into the rebel's horse's head between the eyes. The horse's legs buckled and it dropped like a rock just as its master fired and Mun felt the lead ball rip the air beside him. Mun glanced to his right, eyes filtering the seething, deafening chaos for friend and foe, then saw Jonathan parrying a flurry of blows from a huge bare-headed man wielding the biggest broadsword Mun had ever seen on a battlefield.

'The boy!' he shouted at O'Brien who grimaced and nodded, and together they spurred through the press and Mun took a sword blow on his right shoulder that sent a wave of agony through the whole bone, numbing his fingers, but he pushed on, ignoring his assailant because Jonathan would be dead in moments.

'Withdraw! Back!' Mun recognized the Prince's voice, felt men around him begin to extricate themselves from the fight. The rebels, too, backed off, for both sides had expended their firearms and few men relished the desperate butchery of blades.

'Hold on, lad,' Mun murmured, willing Jonathan to defy the giant a little while longer, for those two were clearly in it to the death no matter what went on around them. 'Go on, Hector!' The stallion ploughed on, unstoppable, buffeting other horses aside, his great muscled neck plunging through the fray. Mun's world shrank, its entirety framed by the steel bars before his face, all sound gone but for the metallic rasp of his own breath that was distilled, made more intense by the helmet.

The blond-haired giant was roaring, battering Jonathan's blade with his own enormous sword, so that the lad was almost out of his saddle yet he somehow clung on, then Mun was there and Hector's great chest smashed into the giant's mare's shoulder, causing the beast to turn, shrieking, so that now Mun and the giant were side by side and the rebel flung his sword arm back, the weapon's hilt smashing into the bars of Mun's pot and sending him flying back over Hector's rump to land in a crash of iron and kit. Mun could not breathe, could get no air into his tortured lungs as his mind tried to make sense of what had happened. Blinking the world into focus he looked up, so far up, to see O'Brien and the giant grappling each other, neither able to free his weapon from the other's grasp, the Irishman's face a knot of rage.

'Fuck off, lad!' O'Brien roared at Jonathan who was trying to manoeuvre his horse round to strike at the giant, whose buff-coat looked to be made from two different coats sewn roughly together. Then Mun heard thunder and everything was a frenzy of hooves and horses' legs and flying turf as the two forces split and galloped away, and though he saw it coming, in a flash of rider and steel, he was too late to warn O'Brien. A rebel hacked into the Irishman's shoulder as he galloped past, a parting blow as he raced for his lines that by rights should have taken O'Brien's arm off. As it was, the impact twisted him horribly and must have stunned him like a fish struck between the eyes but he cleaved to the rebel even as he fell, dragging the bigger man down with him so that they thumped to the ground. Mun felt the impact beneath him as he scrambled backwards to avoid being mauled by hooves as their horses stepped back from the flailing mass.

'Devil! I'll kill you, you Hell-born bastard!' the blond giant bellowed.

Their swords dropped in the fall, the giant was on top of O'Brien, hands clasped around the Irishman's thick neck trying to choke the life from him and growling like a monster. Dazed but moving, Mun stumbled across, fingers working at his helmet strap, then yanked the pot from his head and swung it, cracking it across the giant's head, but the man was berserk and turned, yelling ferociously, and launched himself at Mun, grabbing him and yanking him forward to smash his head into Mun's face. Mun felt the ground strike him but saw only flashing lights in a shifting black sea. Then the pain exploded in his nose and he was coughing, choking on the blood pouring down his throat. His vision returning, though blurred as though he were underwater, he dragged an arm across his eyes, trying to wipe away the tears, and saw Jonathan, dismounted now, swing his sword at the giant. The rebel took the blow on his leather-protected forearm and hammered a fist into Jonathan's face, dropping him.

'In Ireland we've got farm girls who are stronger than you, you ballock-faced gollumpus.' O'Brien was on his feet, unsteady as they were, beckoning the rebel to him with a flap of his own big hand.

The blond giant grinned, spat, and went in for the kill.

A salvo of hoof-beats filled Mun's ears and a trooper reined in beside him, his horse neighing spiritedly. The rider lifted his pistol, pointed it at the rebel's head and fired. Some of the giant's brains slapped into Mun's breastplate and he looked up to see Richard Downes grinning like a fiend.

'Have you lads finished making friends?' Downes asked.

Smearing hot blood across his face Mun saw that, having reloaded, the Prince's men were cantering back towards them to re-engage the enemy. The fight was not over yet and he grasped for Hector's reins though he could barely focus on them.

'I was just about to give the overgrown son of a whore the hiding of his life,' O'Brien growled at all of them. He looked barely able to stand.

Downes shook his head slowly, glancing up towards the enemy lines as he took his powder flask and poured a charge down his wheellock's muzzle. 'I don't know how you gentlemen survived without me,' he said.

It had been a relief to walk across the Magdalen Bridge into Oxford, the King's new capital. Bess had felt pride blossom in her chest when the guards at the east gate had questioned them and she had introduced herself as Elizabeth Rivers, daughter of the late Sir Francis Rivers.

'My father gave his life in service to His Majesty at Kineton Fight,' she had said. 'Sir Francis was killed with Sir Edmund Verney trying to save the Royal Standard.' She had not mentioned Emmanuel. That pain was private to her. But the dragoons had seemed humbled, all but falling over themselves to offer their condolences whilst advising Dane and Joseph where they might find the warmest hospitality Oxford had to offer. That had been three days ago and they were still lodging at The Glove and The Cross, recommended by a young dragoon not so much for its ale as for its nutmeg and cinnamon pancakes and its Banbury cake. It had surprised Bess to discover that Dane had a weakness for sweet treats that almost matched his weakness for drink. 'I had a cousin from Astley near Salford who died for his sweet tooth,' he had said on the first night when, after four days on the road, they had sat down with grumbling bellies to put the young dragoon's endorsement of The Glove and The Cross to the test.

'He died from a surfeit of pancakes?' Bess had asked, sharing a silent look with Joseph, who showed no sign of curbing his own appetite as he tucked into his third pancake.

Dane shook his head. 'His wife made him an apple pie full to the crust with atropine.'

'Atropine?' Joseph had mumbled through a mouth full.

'Belladonna, Joe,' Bess had said, and the young man had grimaced then carried on eating.

'She poisoned poor old Gilbert for his snoring. At least that's what folk said.' Dane had dabbed his lips with a napkin and smiled. 'It's safer not to get married if you ask me.'

'Nobody asked you,' Bess had said, looking to Joseph for support but finding only a boy's grin.

Now, she and Dane sat in the tavern's smoky snug, driven out of the bar by the din of soldiers singing bawdy tales of women and ale. Oxford was alive with music and merry-making. It thronged with soldiers and whores, merchants and the myriad lickspittles, dandies and catch-farts that attended the King's court *like flies attend a turd* was how Dane had put it, so that unlike London, Oxford was a bubbling, intoxicating cauldron of dash and debauchery.

'You would have thought the war is of no concern. Or else that it is as good as won,' Bess said, sipping her weak beer and half watching two men trying to talk a brace of painted wenches into visiting their rooms upstairs.

'I hear His Majesty spends coin from his war chest on masques and plays,' Dane said, 'money that I suspect would be better spent on powder and shot and horses and a thousand other things which they tell me are of use when one is fighting a war.' He was cradling a cup of claret wine and a jug of the stuff sat on the upturned barrel which served as a table.

'More worrying still is that there is talk of forbidding the sale of strong drink in the city after nine in the evening on account of the brawling. There's lots of brawling apparently.'

'Poor man. Whatever will you do?' Bess leant forward and patted his forearm. 'Perhaps you should petition the King. I am sure he will turn a blind eye in your case. Perhaps he'll share his wine with you, after all you have done for our cause.'

Dane drank and dragged a hand across his lips. 'I may not have killed for His Majesty but I have killed for you, Elizabeth Rivers,' he said, holding her eye.

That was true enough and Bess felt a twinge of guilt for how she treated Dane. The man had saved her life. Joseph's too. Perhaps she could try to be a bit more civil to him. At the least, there was nothing to be gained by goading him.

'I never thanked you properly,' she said. 'I am grateful.' The horror of that night was like a cold sweat on her skin.

Dane shrugged, then drank again. 'I wouldn't have got paid if I'd let those men rape and kill you,' he said, and with that Bess gritted her teeth and held her tongue. For a moment at least.

'You are the most ill-mannered miscreant I have ever met,' she said and he shrugged. Then they both sat back, Dane watching a pretty serving girl wiping down a table and she watching the two eager men boasting to the painted women of their heroics at Kineton Fight when it was clear that coin would impress them more. And she wondered how Joseph was getting on.

It had been Joseph's idea to come to Oxford. Well, he had been the one to put the idea in Bess's mind. Still reeling after the disappointment of finding no sign of Tom amongst Parliament's army at Richmond, Bess had not known what their next course of action should be. They had returned to Southwark and visited the Tabard Inn which stood on the east side of Borough High Street, for Bess had remembered her father talking of the place and wondered if perhaps Tom had recalled the same

stories and thus chosen to lodge there. He had not. But the
Tabard was only one among a dingy clutter of inns lining
the thoroughfare leading south from London Bridge towards
Canterbury and Dover. They tried the Spur, the Christopher,
the Bull, the Queen's Head, the George, the Hart, the King's
Head and many more, taking bed and board at some so that
they could ask regular patrons if they knew Tom or had seen
a young man matching his description. With no luck they had
crossed back into the city's heart and searched innumerable
hostelries and weeks passed and they came no closer to finding
Tom.

'We all have a motive, Bess,' Joseph had said eventually,
finally having got used to using her familiar name. 'We all have
a wind that fills our sail.' The young man's cheeks had flushed
at that, which in turn put heat in Bess's own because she knew
that he loved her. 'Yours is to find your brother,' Joseph went
on, 'mine is to help you and do my duty in this war. Mr Dane
here seeks to fatten his purse.' Joseph had glanced at Dane but
the man had not taken offence. 'You must ask yourself what
wind fills Tom's sail, Bess, for you will know that better than
anyone.'

The answer to that had not taken a heartbeat to come to.

'Tom wants revenge,' Bess had said. 'Revenge against Lord
Denton and his son for their odious offences. For their part in
Martha Green's death and for the humiliations they heaped
upon Tom that I will not talk of.'

'And is your brother a man of action?' Dane had asked, one
eyebrow cocked. 'Turning his back on his family and joining
the rebels is one thing, but is he fool enough to go after a man
like Lord Denton in the cold light of day?'

'Where will we find Lord Denton?' Bess had asked, knowing
it to be answer enough.

'I don't know,' Dane had said. 'But it will be easier to find
him than your brother.'

And so it had been, for it turned out that the King had issued a proclamation that a new Royal Mint was to be established and that Lord Denton would be the man to see it done. And this mint would be at His Majesty's new capital. Oxford.

They had arrived not knowing exactly what they would do when they got there, but the theory was better than any other they could come up with. By being close to Denton they might catch word, or possibly even sight, of Tom. Bess had day-dreamed the scenario. She would glimpse her brother strolling through the city's streets and even though he would likely be somehow disguised, heavily bearded perhaps or wearing the red scarf of the King's men, she would recognize him. They would embrace and she would talk him out of his rash plan, dissipate his murderous intention like a fresh breeze blowing through a noisome tavern, and Tom would agree to go back north with her, home to Shear House. Or perhaps they would set off together, there and then, to find Mun so that the boys could make their peace.

They had spent the days watching New Inn Hall, the site of the mint and Denton's quarters, and Joseph was there even now for Bess guessed that he preferred that to being in Dane's company. Besides which, Dane had refused to take the evening watch, saying that his job was to keep Bess safe and he could not do that from a mile away.

'You know Tom, Dane does not,' Bess had said to Joseph, 'so it makes more sense that you should be there, anyway.'

'And the last time I left you to protect Bess the only thing you managed was to bleed,' Dane had added unhelpfully, at which Joseph had stared down at his own hands in shame. That con-versation had been the previous day around noon and they had not seen Joseph since. He had not returned to his room that night and Bess was worried.

'He's young,' Dane said now in answer to the concern that Bess was clearly doing a bad job of hiding. 'He's young and he's in Oxford. You really think he's likely to tell you that he's found some crusty wench who pities him enough to let him share her bed for a night or two? Christ, but the lad might be enjoying himself for once, rather than tending you like some mopsey wet-nurse.'

'Or perhaps it's your company that he finds intolerable,' Bess said.

'Perhaps,' Dane said, reaching inside his doublet and producing a pipe into whose bowl he stuck his little finger to clean out the dregs of his last smoke. His mention of a wet-nurse turned Bess's thoughts to little Francis, her stomach souring with the wrench of their separation.

'You know, it's not much of a plan,' Dane said after a while, breaking the silence between them and reaching for the wine jug. 'It could be weeks or months before your brother turns up here, if he comes at all.'

But Bess did not have the chance to answer that, because two men had walked into the snug. And one of them was holding Joseph's threadbare broad-brimmed hat.

'We have young Joseph,' the narrow-faced, heavy-browed man said, tossing the tattered hat onto the table before them. His companion was broad, toothless and ugly.

Bess's limbs tensed. She felt the blood drain from her face. 'Have you hurt him?' she asked. Beside her Dane placed his pipe next to Joseph's hat and slowly stood, though Bess knew his firelocks would be in his room upstairs. The heavy-browed man hitched his cloak back over the hilt of the sword at his left hip and his companion took a step back, his hand reaching down to clasp the grip of the wheellock thrust into the red sash round his waist. Two men and three women at the next table got up, gathered their drinks and pipes and hurried out of the snug.

'Lord Denton requests the pleasure of your company, Mistress Rivers.' The man glanced at Dane. 'Your friend here is welcome, too, though we insist he hands over his weapons.' With that he moved towards Dane.

'Another step and I'll gut you both,' Dane said, and Bess believed him.

The man stopped, dipped his head and raised his hand, the palm of which was callused from sword use. 'My lord Denton means you no harm, my lady. He knows you are no traitor like your brother. Indeed he assumes you wish to speak with him, for why else would your young friend be sniffing around New Inn Hall?'

'And if we decline your master's offer?' Dane asked.

The man shrugged and looked back to Bess. 'Then young Joe will not be needing his hat back.'

'How do we know you haven't cut the lad's throat already?' Dane asked. 'He might be a callow cub but he's no coward and would not have told you where to find us without considerable persuasion.'

Bess's stomach rolled at that, for she knew Dane was right and that they must have hurt Joseph for him to have revealed that they were lodging at The Glove and The Cross.

'I'll admit he is a stubborn young man,' the heavy-browed man said, 'but in the end he saw that we all want the same thing.'

'Which is?' Dane said.

The man smiled but it had all the warmth of a rapier's hilt. 'Please, come with us,' he said. 'My lord is an influential man. He could have a party of dragoons escort you if you would prefer.'

Bess glanced at Dane and then back to Denton's man, feeling herself nod.

'Your weapons, sir,' the narrow-faced man said.

'You think I'm a damned halfwit?' Dane asked.

'We have no choice,' Bess muttered. 'Think of Joseph.'

Dane muttered a curse. 'You should have left him in Lancashire,' he said. Then he unbuckled his baldrick and handed his scabbarded sword over.

'Looks like the sort that'll have a ballock dagger too,' the ugly man growled.

'And you, my friend, look like the north end of a southbound bullock,' Dane said, conjuring a long knife from somewhere within his cloak. He flipped the knife, caught it by the blade and offered it up. 'Can I at least bring my wine?'

'Leave that goat's piss here,' the other man said. 'My lord has taken the liberty of having a dinner prepared and he is known for his wine cellar.' The smile now was real enough and then he turned to walk out of the snug and Bess and Dane followed.

The evening was warm and Oxford's stinking streets bustled with merry-makers: soldiers, whores, men and women drinking, dancing and singing, and boys and girls up to mischief when they should have been home in their beds. No one paid the small party any notice as they made their way west along High Street and onto Butcher Row, the tang of blood heavy in the air, before turning north into New Inn Hall Street. Bess's heart pounded in her chest. An invisible weight pressed down on her, growing heavier with every step that brought her nearer to that devil Lord Denton. She wondered if William's son Henry would be there too and she did not know how seeing them would affect her, both men having had a hand in her family's ruin. For Tom's joining the rebels was not for any political or religious conviction, nor any other reason Bess could see, but that he sought bloody vengeance on the Dentons, who were firmly for the King, for their treatment of his lost love Martha Green. It was because of the Dentons' viciousness and their machinations that her brother had brought shame upon his family. And yet Bess knew she might now have to bridle her hatred of them for Joseph's sake.

When they got to New Inn Hall Bess barely had a chance to appraise the impressive stone-built, slate-roofed building before Denton's men ushered them past the buff-coated sentries and up the steps to the main entrance. As soon as they entered the candle-lit interior the smell of rich food filled her nose and slickened her mouth which had been dry with nerves but a moment before, and a fat servant in Denton's blue livery received them cordially, leading them into a grand dining room which blazed with candle flame.

Before them stood an oak table bestrewn with plates of roast meats, pies, tarts and custards. There were radishes and hard-boiled eggs, figs, dried apricots, dates and small pots containing ground ginger, cinnamon and sugar. There was wheat bread, several types of cheese and pickles. There were jugs of wine, cider and beer.

And at the head of the table, his grey hair falling in long oiled curls around the golden hoops in his ears, stood William, Lord Denton. Dressed in a fine purple doublet, snow-white breeches and purple silk stockings, Denton looked every inch the sort of Cavalier so reviled by many who had taken up arms against the King. And yet Bess could not help but stare at him, even though the sight of the man disgusted her, made her skin tighten on her flesh. Made her feel somehow unclean.

'Elizabeth Rivers,' he said, more to himself, it seemed, than to her. His cold blue eyes held as fast to her own as a dead man's grip and white teeth dug away at his bottom lip as though he were repressing some base predatory instinct. 'Please take your ease,' he said, gesturing to the chair at the opposite end of the table from where he stood. 'I must apologize for the tableware,' he went on, frowning at the pewter plates, wooden trenchers and ceramic bowls. 'Bit of a hodgepodge I'm afraid, as most of the silverware has been melted down to finance the war.' He blinked but his gaze still leeched to her, those eyes at once consuming and yet somehow distant. Numb.

'Where is Joseph? What have you done with him?' Bess asked. Lord Denton sighed and gave a slight shake of his head.

'What is it with the Rivers children and your impetuosity? I struggle to believe you were brought up without learning the manners befitting your status and yet you are all so graceless. You didn't get it from your father, I'll warrant.'

'Were you civil to Martha Green?' Bess heard herself ask.

'Or her father?' Her throat was tight as a fist on a dagger's grip. 'Were you civil to my brother Tom, my lord?'

'Ah, Thomas,' he all but spat, his lips curling as though it pained his mouth to say the name. 'But let us not get to that yet. I would not ruin my appetite when my cook has gone to so much trouble. Mr Dane, is it?'

Dane nodded. 'Yes, my lord.'

'I hope you are hungry, Mr Dane. I can heartily recommend the broad bean and ox tongue pie.'

'My lady would see Joseph first, my lord,' Dane said, his eyes flicking over to the two other men who were still standing just inside the room, cloaks hitched back, pistols within easy reach. Watchful.

Lord Denton nodded at his men. 'If that's what it will take for you to do me the courtesy of enjoying this table,' he said, 'then so be it.' He held out an arm towards the hallway beyond his two men and the door, wafting ringed fingers.

'Thank you,' Bess said, and she and Dane fell in behind the ugly broad-shouldered man, with the other man and Denton behind them, and made their way back out of the dining room. They passed portraits of scholars and benefactors and several marble busts of unknown men, all strategically lit by beeswax candles. They passed the kitchen, whose door only muffled the clanging and banging of pots and dishes and the conversation of cooks and servants, and came to a wine-cellar door beneath whose arch a man of Lord Denton's height would have to stoop awkwardly to pass.

'I warn you, though,' Lord Denton said, taking up a candle lamp from the table beside him, 'your friend did not help himself at all and has only himself to blame for his current . . . condition.' Bess's stomach tightened at that as the door creaked open and she descended the steps slowly, her eyes adjusting to the dark. But it was her nose that warned her of what she was about to witness. She smelt faeces and the same iron tang of blood that had thickened the air on Butcher Row.

And there in a pool of shadow, his ruined face and gore-streaked naked body strung up by the arms from an old meat hook, was Joseph.

'Bastards!' Dane snarled, turning in a blur, hand down to his boot and then up into the ugly man's belly, and the man grunted, his shoulders rolling over his chest. Dane hauled the knife out and spun, a devil in the gloom, teeth flashing. And saw that the other man had an arm around Bess's neck and his wheellock's muzzle pressed against her temple.

'Don't be a bloody fool!' Lord Denton growled, his own sword raised towards Dane, his candle on the floor beside him. 'I've killed more men than I care to remember and I'd kill you without a second thought. But I'd rather not kill Miss Rivers and I believe you would rather I didn't. I suspect Lord Heylyn would consider your agreement null and void if her brains ended up splattered on that wall.'

Bess was gasping for breath, clawing at the arm crushing her throat, but Denton's man was much too strong and she knew she had no choice but to yield. Either that or be strangled.

'If you harm her I swear I'll kill you,' Dane said, locking eyes with Denton in the nearly dark. Then he dropped his knife to the stone floor and the ugly man, groaning and holding his torn belly, bent and picked it up.

'Tie him,' Denton said to the man holding Bess, coming up and putting his blade against her throat so that the other man could deal with Dane. 'Do it properly.' The man who was gut-stabbed was bleeding but still able to point his pistol at Dane while his companion found rope and began to bind Dane's hands and legs.

Bess looked past them to Joseph, trying to catch sight of his naked stomach rising or sinking, any sign that proved he still lived. Then the knots were done and Dane was helpless, his neck corded with sinew, lips hitched back from teeth, and nostrils flaring as though venting pure rage.

Denton lowered his sword and stepped closer to Bess. 'Your

devil brother killed Henry,' he said, and even in the flame-licked murk Bess saw excruciating pain in his eyes. 'He came here and murdered my son. In the street like some common cut-throat villain.'

Bess shuddered. Tom was no murderer. 'I do not trust your account of it,' she said.

Lord Denton stared at her and Bess truly believed he was going to plunge his sword into her flesh. That she would die there in that dank cellar and never see her son again.

'Secure him down here,' Denton ordered his men. 'I'll have the surgeon brought here for you,' he said to the big man who was clasping his belly and grimacing. Then Lord Denton bent and picked up the candle lamp. Slowly he turned back to Bess, took a deep breath. Held it. Exhaled.

'Now then, Mistress Rivers. Do you think we might go and eat?'

CHAPTER TWENTY

23 July 1643, Bristol

'ONE OF THE LADS SAID IT STANDS IN A HOLE,' O'BRIEN REMARKED, dragging a hand across his mouth and handing the flask to Mun. 'He wasn't bloody fibbing.'

Mun did not answer for he was thinking of all that they had achieved since they had chased the rebel horse from Chalgrove Field. Since then they had all but destroyed Parliament's Western Association army at Roundway Down and the King's Council of War now pressed the importance of securing the routes between Wales, the West Country and Oxford by laying hold of the rebel strongholds of Bristol and Gloucester. Bristol, England's second city and the most important port on the west coast, was to be the first prize and now Mun and O'Brien stood facing east, the sun on their backs as they looked down across the River Frome and into the city. Bristol's houses and churches, its shops, inns, alehouses, streets, alleys and yards were dominated by three hills to the north-west and Redcliffe Hill to the south. To the south the River Avon, around which Bristol had been built, flowed like molten metal, reflecting the July sun. The Parliamentarians had thus decided to fortify the eminences to the north to prevent the Royalists from using them to bombard the city, but this series of forts, connected by lines of earthwork ditches and redans, would not keep Prince Rupert out.

'You can see why the rascals didn't put up much of a fight.' O'Brien nodded down at the city. 'Why they hotfooted it back to their den.'

Mun could. 'I dare say we'd have done the same,' he said, looking along the ditch and rampart running north and south which the rebels had abandoned, though they yet manned several redoubts along its length. 'It would take too many men to hold all this.'

That afternoon they had ridden with the Prince and several others up to the high ground around Clifton church to get a bird's-eye view of the prize. Opposite them now stood Brandon Hill Fort, which would present a serious challenge. An imposing square structure mounting four guns, its defences were eighteen feet high including the palisade.

'The ditch is shallow due to the rockiness of the ground,' Prince Rupert had observed earlier, trying to steel his men to the task.

Now, the cracks of muskets carried to them on the early evening breeze announced that at least some of the rebel outposts fought on, though Mun knew they could not last much longer. One by one they were being overrun and the Prince's soldiers were closing in. 'Must be four miles of wall,' O'Brien said, pointing the stem of his pipe south towards Water Fort on the banks of the Avon. They had left their helmets and back-and-breasts with their horses which stood tethered amongst the abandoned ditches and earthworks, lazily cropping the grass. 'Some respectable fortifications here and there but too many approaches to cover. Too much dead ground.' The Irishman's face was flushed and glistening, rivulets of sweat running into his beard. He shook his head. 'A bugger of a place to defend.'

'It'll be no joy assaulting it, either,' Mun said. For though the Prince had brought eight guns, including two demi-cannon, they had not enough shot: only forty-two for the big siege guns, a woefully inadequate provision for a prolonged bombardment. Neither had they brought Lord Lidford's cannon, for they lacked sufficient draught animals to haul it across the country. The feeding of the army had taken precedence over the pulling of cannon, and Mun wished he could have seen Lord Lidford's face when they had served up his beloved beasts to the wretched rank and file.

So Mun knew they would have to storm the city. But not today. The Prince had ridden off to speak with another officer and so Mun and O'Brien had taken the opportunity to enjoy a smoke and the sun on their faces. A little way off, in a position to threaten Brandon Hill Fort, an officer was barking orders at three dozen bare-chested, sweat-drenched gunners, conductors and pioneers who were setting up a battery of two culverins. Some were hauling stubborn draught animals off to pasture, the beasts lowing indignantly. Others were hefting the fifteen-pound shot up the hill to the platform, piling it up by the guns, and still others were throwing up a protective earthwork, so that Mun was just glad it was they and not he working in that heat.

It was hot and dry, the sky a clean blue interspersed with lambswool clouds. Every scrubby bush, boundary hedge, green tree and grassy rampart was lit by the sun, so that Mun was almost able to put out of his mind visions of butchery and death, his eyes feasting on verdant, unsullied ground and new growth.

'What does their garrison muster, do you reckon? Two thousand?' O'Brien exhaled a ring of smoke and watched it rise. As always Mun was struck by the Irishman's ability to take everything in his great stride, as though the coming fight was to be just another adventure.

'Less,' Mun said, looking north-east to Windmill Fort on top of St Michael's Hill, and beyond that to Prior's Hill Fort, the most northerly point of Bristol's defences. Dragoons and musketeers were massing thick on the heights overlooking these positions, the Prince having ordered them to parade in full view of Bristol's inhabitants in a bid to intimidate the rebels and inspire those yet loyal to the Crown. He swept damp hair back from his face and blotted his forehead on his shirt's cuff. 'Every man, woman and child down there must know they cannot keep us out,' he said, nodding back towards the city.

'Aye, they might know it but that won't stop them trying,' O'Brien said, 'and knowing how keen His Highness is to make an impression, I'll wager we'll be up to our ankles in blood before the week's out.'

Mun grimaced at the thought. With its huge population – some fifteen thousand souls, he had heard – its natural harbour and thriving arms industry, Bristol was the place of greatest consequence of any in England, next to London. It had to be taken.

'We should have secured it at the beginning of the war,' Mun said bitterly, thinking of the carnage that was coming if the city's governor, the Parliamentarian Colonel Nathaniel Fiennes, refused to surrender. But they had not secured Bristol, and the King, even more so Prince Rupert, had eyed the city covetously ever since.

Everyone knew that Rupert had in large part his brother Maurice to thank for being in the position now to besiege the city. Only ten days previously Prince Maurice had led his troopers in the remarkable victory at Roundway Down near Devizes, the Royalist cavalry destroying Sir William Waller's army. That victory had left Bristol open so that at last Prince Rupert might put into action his long-planned assault. Now he had brought the Oxford Army, comprising some four and a half thousand foot and up to six thousand horse, to Bristol, and his brother Maurice had brought the Western Army of three thousand foot and one and a half thousand horse. This combined Royalist force of around seven thousand foot and seven thousand horse, though not quite up to battle strength due to casualties, desertion, and sickness, would prove too much for the rebels. So Mun hoped.

He inhaled the evening breeze and enjoyed the warm sun on his back, as other men toiled or paraded or stood by their posts. For he knew they must have Bristol, which meant he would soon be back in the fray.

Three days later, several hours before dawn and the night still thick around them, it seemed that Hell had been loosed upon the living. Mun sat Hector in the first rank of Prince Rupert's Horse, his own men bristling around him, making, with Rupert's other captains, including Nehemiah Boone, a line that waited for its turn to strike. They soothed their mounts and checked their gear: their pistols and blades, buckles and belts; and tried to make sense of the chaos before them. The attack, signalled by the firing of the two demi-cannon, was supposed to have been simultaneous on all sides of the city so that the defenders would be stretched too thin along their perimeter wall to maintain any concentrated fire. But with the skirmishing continuing through the night there had been some confusion and Prince Maurice's Western Army had gone into action prematurely, at three a.m. according to some young officer's fancy pocket watch. And so Prince Rupert had hastily ordered his Oxford Army to begin its own offensive, the main thrust of which was towards the supposed weak point in the defensive line between Brandon Hill Fort and Windmill Fort.

'Patience, men!' Riding down the line Prince Rupert nodded at Mun as he passed. On his finely muscled horse, with his forge-black back-and-breast and helm polished to perfection, he looked every inch the prince. Those who knew him either in life or reputation knew he was every inch the killer, too. 'Your time will come!' His teeth flashed in the gloom. 'You will be inside the city by dawn!'

Once the foot has been bled, Mun thought, watching several hundred musketeers form up in the dark amongst the ferns and bushes, loading their muskets as they moved. The foot were arranged into three Tertias under Lord Grandison, Henry Wentworth and Colonel John Bellasis, and despite the ragged nature of their supposed simultaneous attack Mun knew that each of these men would know their role in the Prince's scheme.

Elsewhere the fight was on and Mun's eyes were drawn to the south and flashes of flame bursting in the dark accompanied by a rolling salvo of musketry. Prince Maurice's Western Foot were advancing in three columns, he knew, trying to force a breach.

Men were dying out there in the pre-dawn.

A cheer brought him back to his own battle and he watched dragoons go forward under fire, carrying bundles of sticks and dragging carts with which they would try to fill any trenches and ditches that would otherwise slow the Royalist attack.

'This'll be the hottest service we've yet seen, lads,' Corporal Bard announced somewhere to Mun's left, 'so keep your heads down and your wits about you. When we go it'll be a confused bloody shambles, you hear? So you look for your officers.'

'Don't stray, Jonathan,' Mun said, 'stay with me and O'Brien. We'll do this together.'

Jonathan nodded, eyes wide and white beneath his helmet's rim, and Mun could see that even he with all his foolhardiness was afraid.

'You'll be fine, lad,' O'Brien said, leaning forward to take his weight off his mare's back while she voided her bowels. 'Just stick by us and stay in your saddle. It'll be over before you know it.' Tongues of flame lashed out continuously from the rebel line and even in the near dark Mun could tell that there were fewer dragoons coming back than had gone forward.

In front of them the musketeers of John Bellasis's Tertia waited, their tunics and montero-caps, the wooden gloss of their musket stocks or the shoulder buckles on bandoliers illuminated now and then by a nearby gout of flame. Some were fiddling with kit, checking powder flasks or easing serpents forward to make sure the match-cord clamped in them would strike the priming pan. Some were even on their knees praying, and all continually blew on their match to keep the ends free of ash and glowing, though most sought to keep those bright coals behind their bodies or otherwise hidden lest they mark themselves a target for the enemy. But they would have to wait their turn. In front of them John Bellasis himself had gathered a 'forlorn hope', and those unlucky men would form the spearhead of the attack. There were thirty musketeers, six pikemen – their weapons sheathed with blazing rags – and six men carrying grenades, and all would face a fierce fusillade from the defenders on the wall.

'I wouldn't want to be those poor tosspots,' Walter Cade said, stirring ayes from the troopers around him. 'Good luck, lads!' he yelled.

'Aye, good luck and give 'em a good bloody hiding!' another man yelled, as Bellasis raised a hand and started forward with his brave men. Mun saw two of those with the fire pikes go down amidst a hail of musketry, their comrades pushing on through the furze regardless, some of the musketeers firing up at the wall.

'Those lads with the pikes stand out like a dog's balls,' John Cole exclaimed, spitting in disgust. 'You could be one-eyed and twice drunk and not miss 'em!'

There was an explosion as a grenade went off some twenty paces from the wall, its erstwhile bearer cut down long before he could get close, and even in the flame-licked gloom Mun could see from the haphazard course of the fire pikes that the forlorn hope was in disarray. Another grenade exploded in a bloom of flame which illuminated the ditch and timber palisade and several defenders, though again the bomb had fallen short. Bellasis's musketeers were being shredded and rather than stand and reload in sight and range of the enemy some turned and ran back towards the waiting regiments. Others crawled back on their hands and knees, their muskets discarded, choosing shame over death.

'Good boy, Hector,' Mun soothed, leaning forward to talk into the stallion's ear, for the horses could smell blood now and were growing skittish. 'Good boy. Not long now, boy.' Another regiment had come up, its officers roaring commands, tongue-whipping the musketeers into battalia. Behind them hundreds more pikemen were winding rags round their weapons and Mun recognized their commander, Colonel Henry Lunsford, brother of Thomas whom he had met in Westminster Hall before the war.

I was just a boy then, he thought, remembering how Thomas Lunsford had goaded the apprentices during the unrest, how he had seemed to revel in the tumult and how he had been only too willing to unsheathe his sword and spill blood. From the look of his brother Henry and his men they had already seen hard service that night, perhaps to the north at Prior's Hill Fort. None in the King's army could have known, Mun reflected, how those few dissidents stirring up trouble in Westminster would grow into a vast seditious army. An army that threatened to drench the kingdom in blood.

This war has made killers of us all, Mun thought.

'How long do we have to wait, Corporal?' Godfrey asked O'Brien, and Mun saw the sickly pallor of the young man's face, though it was Milward further down the line who was leaning out of his saddle spewing his guts onto the ground.

'Not long now, lad,' O'Brien said, giving him the same lie Mun had given Hector. 'The waiting is the worst part but as soon as we're unleashed the nerves will fuck off, you can trust me on that.'

The drummers had struck up, the Preparative beating out so that the ranks and files of the foot closed to their due distances and made ready to execute on the first command.

Tobias Fitch and Goffe had dismounted to urinate amidst hoots and jeers. Mun drank from his flask, holding the weak ale in his mouth a while before swallowing. His jaw bones ached from clenching his teeth together, but he was aware that Jonathan and others kept glancing at him and he did not want them to think him afraid. And yet, for the first time in a long time he *was* afraid. The night was a dissonant maelstrom that took a man's nerve and shredded it, leaving his guts sour and his mouth dry. Drums and shouting and musketry and the hideous screams of the dying and the shrieks of horses, all a clamorous, dismaying prelude to fate's hand. And yet there was something else that curdled in his belly, something blacker than the fear of coming battle.

He closed his eyes and his mind summoned Bess's face, her golden hair loose around her shoulders and little Francis in her arms. *I will come back*, he silently assured her. *I will not die here this night.*

'Put in a good word for old O'Brien while you're at it, eh?' the Irishman said and Mun turned to see him grinning from ear to ear. 'We'll be off soon and I haven't had the chance to speak to the Almighty myself.'

Mun forced a smile. 'Bringing your name into a prayer would be like taking a whore into a church,' he said, and realized that the drums were beating the Battle now and the foot had begun to move. Not just move, run. They were near running towards the wall, bellowing to put the fear of God into the defenders. A cannon ball ploughed into the throng, the gun's boom following from the direction of Brandon Hill Fort, and four men lay dead or screaming, their dismembered parts lying about them.

Hector was snorting and grinding his teeth. Mun could feel the stallion's back and neck muscles bunching and he tried to soothe him but Hector tossed his head angrily, his ears pinned flat against his head.

'You still glad you joined us, lad?' Cole shouted to Jonathan, cranking the spanner on his wheellock.

'I'll let you know by sun-up,' Jonathan called back, patting his fine Cleveland Bay's neck with a gloved hand. Beyond the bars of his helmet his face was taut as stretched rope, his eyes bright.

'Death to traitors!' Prince Rupert roared, riding his horse up and down the ranks, heedless of the musketry drawn to him. 'Tonight we take Bristol for the King!'

'He's a mad bastard, ain't he?' someone behind Mun remarked, stirring some much-needed laughter.

'I'm just glad he's our mad bastard,' another man said, 'even if he is a bloody foreigner.'

Mun watched Colonel Lunsford, sword and pistol in hand at the head of his men, white plumes dancing on his broad-hat, then lost sight of him as they surged forward. Musketry rolled like thunder, an unending cacophony that might presage the end of the world. The pre-dawn gloom was lacerated by gouts of hellish flame that illuminated the living and the dead and the terror-stricken faces of men. And boys.

Some are but sixteen years old, Mun thought, watching a lad on his knees wailing, though Mun could not see if he had been shot. Another lad had his arms wrapped around his musket as though he were embracing a loved one for the last time, his eyes wide, body shaking madly, flinching with every scream or musket shot.

The defenders were pouring fire into the body of Royalist foot, though from the distances between each musket flame Mun could see that the wall was not heavily defended. The attacks on other parts of the wall all around the city were having the desired effect of thinning the rebel line. And yet here the Royalist tide was faltering.

'What's wrong?' Jonathan asked, nudging his horse closer to Mun to be heard.

'The ditch,' Mun said through a grimace, rubbing Hector's muscle-corded neck, 'it hasn't been filled. They can't get across.'

'Not in that hail,' O'Brien added.

'They're falling back!' someone yelled.

'No, you damned scabs!' Richard Downes screamed, leaning forward in the saddle and pointing his sword at the wall. 'The rebels are that way! Turn around, you flighty arse-rags!'

'Oh ballocks,' O'Brien growled. 'This is turning out badly.'

Prince Rupert was riding amongst the retreating musketeers, yelling at them to stand firm and renew the attack. Mun looked round and saw a hundred or so pikemen by a furze thicket, watching the battle as they waited for the order to advance. Beside the men a fire blazed and spat and when the order came they would hold their cloth-wrapped pikes in the flame and join the attack. But the attack was floundering.

'O'Brien, come with me,' Mun said, pulling Hector round and giving the stallion his heels.

'Where are you off to, Corporal?' Godfrey called after them.

'Never you mind, lad, but I'll be back to hold your hand!' the Irishman yelled.

They rode across the rough ground towards the big clump of furze, where Mun pulled up, soothing Hector with calming words as he eyed the pikemen before him.

'What are you thinking, sir?' O'Brien asked, reining in beside him and glancing at the pikemen, whose eyes were riveted to them.

'Just look big, mean and Irish,' Mun said.

'I can manage that,' O'Brien said, as Jonathan trotted his horse up, the bay tossing her head briskly.

'You said to stay with you,' Jonathan said, glancing at them both, affecting a look of innocence.

'What can I do for you, sir?' a grizzled-looking sergeant asked Mun, eyeing them sceptically, his halberd over his shoulder. Some of his men had downed pikes and were smoking pipes even as the fight raged on near the wall two hundred paces away.

'Give me a pike,' Mun said. 'A short one.'

The sergeant shook his head. 'These pikes are needed and all must be accounted for.'

Mun drew a pistol and pointed it at the man's head. 'Give my corporal a pike. If you please.' The sergeant's eyes bulged beneath his pot's rim and his men looked on with equal bafflement.

'Audley, give the corporal your pike.' The sergeant scratched his unkempt beard as Audley brought his weapon over and rested its butt on the ground by O'Brien.

'Cut it in half, Corporal,' Mun said, still pointing his firelock at the sergeant. The Irishman dismounted, took his poll-axe from its saddle holster and went to work, oblivious of the pikemen around him and the violence coming off them near thick enough to touch. 'You owe me one pike,' the sergeant dared, even with the muzzle of Mun's fine pistol promising him oblivion. 'I don't forget a face.'

Mun nodded, shoving the firelock back into its holster as O'Brien, having hacked partly through, broke the stave in two across his leg. 'Get some rags on the other half too,' Mun said, and this time pikeman Audley came forward of his own volition and proceeded to bind the other half of the stave in rags. When it was done O'Brien handed both staves to Mun whilst he mounted, then held out a hand.

'I assume one of those is for me,' he said.

'Not the way you ride,' Mun answered, walking Hector close enough to the fire that he could, by resting the staves across Hector's withers, light the cloth-wrapped ends in the flame. As soon as they were blazing he backed up, one stave in either hand, his legs alone gripping Hector. He looked at Jonathan. 'You don't have to do this,' he said.

Jonathan grinned. 'I'll decide when I find out what it is we're doing,' he said.

And that was good enough for Mun as he urged Hector forward, breaking into a canter back towards the maelstrom.

'The King and the Cause!' he yelled, riding into the pungent flame-lit fog of musket smoke. 'The King and the Cause!' He spurred past the right-hand edge of the Royalist horse and on across the uneven, gorse-strewn ground into the midst of Bellasis's musketeers. And men cheered him.

Prince Rupert looked up, seeing Mun and with him the chance to turn the tide back towards the wall. 'Ride, Sir Edmund!' he yelled, spurring his own horse into a gallop, cutting across the field towards Mun, men scattering before him.

'Go on, boy!' Mun growled, 'go on, Hector!' And now he saw nothing but the palisade looming as he sped towards it, and tongues of flame flaring down at him, and he gripped the flaming pikes and rode on, Hector snorting furiously. 'Faster, Hector!' Mun yelled, and Hector responded, feet clumping against the earth, and Mun felt a musket ball rip the air by his head, and then with an enormous effort Hector leapt, carrying him over the ditch, Mun's bones rattling when they landed, the stallion's hind hooves gouging the ditch's side for purchase. Then they were up and the wall loomed before them.

'King Charles!' Mun screamed, hefting the short pikes into the night, their blazing ends roaring as he swept them through the air as a beacon for the King's men to see. He glimpsed a musket's muzzle above the wall and half tensed for the shot, then the rebel was flung backwards and Mun turned to see that both O'Brien and Jonathan had fired their pistols from the other side of the ditch. More musket balls were hammering into the earth around him and Hector began to wheel and so Mun hurled the fire pikes against the palisade.

And he heard rebels screaming *fire*.

Then rose the clatter of arms and armour and the Prince was there, having jumped the ditch, his proud horse tossing its head as Rupert grinned savagely and screamed at the musketeers to come and take Bristol. The roar from a thousand throats was deafening as men clambered down into the ditch and up the other side and in the chaos Mun leant forward and kissed Hector's neck, awed by the stallion's bravery and because Hector had carried him safely across that trench without Mun having the reins, which was a thing he knew folk would not believe and yet it had happened. Matchlocks were thundering and men with grenades from John Stradling's South Wales Regiment came forward and lobbed their bombs over the palisade, the explosions making Mun flinch involuntarily. His fire pikes had all but gone out yet it did not matter, for the foot's blood was up and they were falling upon the palisade with hands, halberds and partisans, pulling it down or forcing gaps between the piles.

'Bring up the horse!' the Prince yelled at Jonathan, who turned from the ditch and spurred off back through the musketeers and the pikemen that were surging forward in case the rebels countered with their own horse. Then a great cheer went up as a section of the wall came down, and some men pulled the timbers across the ditch to make a bridge whilst others poured through the breach.

'Sir Edmund! With me!' Sword in hand, his horse neighing madly, the Prince was forcing his way through the musketeers, who did what they could to let him pass. Unable to leave the Prince to face alone whatever awaited them beyond the outer defences, Mun asked another effort of Hector, impelling him through the gap in the palisade.

Then they were through to the dead ground between the city's outer defences and the River Frome. Bodies littered the ground and Mun glimpsed patches of scorched earth from the Welshmen's grenades yet he did not stop, but cantered after the Prince towards a party of musketeers who had made a stand. Perhaps as many as thirty rebels had formed a firing line across a paved street leading towards College Green, their weapons levelled, and in that moment Mun knew he must either ride them down or die with a back full of musket balls.

'Yah!' he cried, vicious with the spurs, drawing his sword as Hector drove on, galloping now, the two of them together. As the night burst into flame and those muskets coughed their hatred and a ball took Hector in his eye. Mun felt the stallion's great strength give out, felt the muscles and sinews release as if cut, and then they were falling. Yet, somehow, and only for a heartbeat, Hector found his feet, found the strength to slow his momentum, before crashing to his knees with a great and weary exhalation, so that Mun was still in his saddle. He pulled his boots from the stirrups and fell to the grass, then scrambled on hands and knees round to the stallion's head and the bloody, gore-filled hole that had been Hector's right eye.

No! 'No, Hector!' He pulled off his helmet and pressed his face against Hector's muzzle, feeling the stallion's hot blood on his lips and cheeks as musket balls whipped through the night around them and the Prince's army ran towards them. Hector nickered softly, his sweet grassy breath and the iron tang of blood filling Mun's nose, and then his head sagged and Mun could not hold on but had to let it slump onto the ground.

Mun could not see for the tears in his eyes and could not hear for the cleaving of his heart. A musket ball thumped into Hector, its force mostly spent so that it only half stuck in the flesh at the point of the shoulder. Slowly, detached as if seeing himself in a dream, Mun dug his fingers in and pulled the ball out, closing his fist around it, feeling its hot slipperiness against his skin.

'The Prince! The Prince is down!' someone yelled and Mun twisted, looking for the Prince, then saw a pistol flash and Rupert standing beside what looked like a small hump in the ground but for the glint of gold in the saddle cloth.

'Pikes!' the Prince yelled over his shoulder. 'Pikes, damn you!' The rebel firing line had dispersed, the musketeers fleeing from the onrushing Royalists. Or from Prince Rupert perhaps. But then Mun saw horse. They were gathered by a line of gabions to the right of the bridge across the Frome, perhaps three hundred troopers, their backs to the river. The Prince had seen them too which was why he was calling for his pikemen, who, with the musketeers, were rushing past Mun now. But those pikemen were in loose order and the commander of the rebel horse saw his chance and raised his sword, roaring instructions as his men prepared to charge.

Mun leant over Hector and pulled his pistols from the saddle, his arms trembling as though the marrow in them simmered, then laid one of the weapons on the ground. With a finger he traced a line from the stallion's left ear to his ruined right eye, then did the same with the opposite ear and eye, holding his thumb on the cross point of this imaginary X.

Because he would not get this wrong. No matter what.

Then he put his lips to the spot, which was just above Hector's blood-beaded white star, and held there. 'My good boy. My brave boy,' he said. 'Goodbye, my friend.'

Pulling away he brought his pistol up. Placed its muzzle on that sweet spot. Turned his face away. Squeezed the trigger.

The pistol's roar stunned him. He dragged an arm across his eyes, smearing blood and tears. His own breathing was gathering pace. His stomach clenched as though he had swallowed a hot coal. He thrust the spent pistol into his boot and picked up his helmet, pushing it down on his head as men of the Oxford Army, who had been flowing past him like a river around a boulder, checked. Because the rebel horse was coming.

A musketeer turned to flee but Mun grabbed his bandolier and hauled him around, snarling at the soldier to be a man and face the enemy. Being more afraid of Mun than of the rebels, the musketeer planted his feet and began loading his matchlock as the ground itself trembled with the rebels' charge and Mun strode towards them, consumed by fury.

'Kill them!' he yelled, drawing his Irish hilt. The Royalist pikemen clustered, trying to form a decent stand and present their weapons, yet were hampered by the musketeers who sought protection amongst them. Then the horse were on them, harquebusiers firing their pistols and slashing at men's faces. Unable to close ranks and lock themselves with one another the pikemen were being butchered and some threw down their weapons and either drew swords or fled. Yet Prince Rupert stood firm in the heart of the fray encouraging his men, and many, seeing him thus, took heart and fought savagely.

A man beside Mun jabbed his pike up at a rider's face but the man saw the blade in time, jerking his head aside and at the same moment firing his carbine whose ball punched through

the pikeman's breastplate and killed him. Mun ducked beneath the horse's swinging head and came up on the rebel's
left, hacking into his leg in a frenzy until the blade got caught
in the bone and the horse turned, shrieking, and knocked him
to the ground. The rider was screaming, his leg all but severed
and Mun's blade stuck fast, when a musketeer came up, his
weapon reversed, and rammed the butt into the rebel's right
side, knocking him out of the saddle. The horse bolted and the
musketeer fell upon its master, pummelling his head to a mush
contained only by the helmet.

Getting to his feet, his neck burning from the whiplash of
being thrown backwards, Mun saw it was the same musketeer
whom he had berated moments before. He looked up at Mun,
eyes wide, a feral grin etched into his face, then hauled Mun's
basket-hilt sword free of the meat and bone and offered it up.
Mun nodded, taking the sword, its weight of more comfort to
him than armour, buff-coat or even pistol. Then the other man
hefted his bloodied matchlock and stalked off to find another
kill.

A musket ball glanced off the left side-bar of Mun's helmet
and struck a nearby captain in the arm as Mun raised his pistol
and fired at a rebel but somehow missed.

'Make way!' someone yelled, 'stand clear!' Mun turned
and saw fire. Men wielding fire pikes lumbered into the fray and
went for the horses, the flames seething in the darkness, and the
horses would not endure it, their eyes rolling, nostrils flaring as
they whinnied in terror.

'Burn the bastards!' a sergeant screamed, thrusting his
halberd into a horse's mouth, breaking its teeth. 'Burn them!'
The stricken horse backed away, tossing its head in a spray of
blood, and whilst its master struggled a musketeer ran up to
him, rammed the muzzle of his weapon into the space between
underarm and breastplate, and fired.

'That's it, lad! Give the shanker something to remember you
by!' the sergeant spat as the rebel slumped sideward, his hand

still gripping a pistol, and the horse sensing the dead weight on its back began to turn in tight circles.

The fire was tipping the balance, Mun saw, for as the rebels fought to control their frightened animals the musketeers swarmed upon them with swords, knives and the butt-ends of matchlocks.

A rebel officer was bellowing at his men to fall back and maybe some of them would have were they not being pulled screaming from their saddles and butchered.

'Now we've got the traitorous scabs!' a man beside Mun yelled, pulling the stopper of a powder flask with his teeth and pouring a measure into the priming pan. 'Here come the bloody gentlemen in their own good time!' The Prince's Horse were coming, funnelling through breaches in the wall, and this was too much for the brave rebel harquebusiers. 'That's right, you bloody run!' the musketeer bellowed, taking a flask from his bandolier and pouring the main charge down the muzzle. 'You run back under the stones you crawled out from!'

Mun's blood yet boiled in his veins. His fury yet grew like a fire feeding on itself and he ran after the retreating rebels, his breathing harsh in his ears, his world shrunk to the vista afforded by his helmet and the craving for revenge.

'Lost your horse, Sir Edmund?' Mun looked round to see Captain Nehemiah Boone leering down at him as he trotted his huge chestnut mare alongside. His sword was in his right hand, glowing dully in the murk. His left arm and the hand gripping the reins were sheathed in a long elbow gauntlet of the type rarely seen any more. Bard, Rowe, Downes and the others were there too but Boone waved them past, gnarring at them to go and kill the King's enemies. 'Pity. A fine horse,' the captain went on. 'I'm only surprised you hadn't got him killed before now.'

Mun ignored him, his eyes fixed on the bridge up ahead where a valorous knot of rebel horse were making a stand so that the rest might withdraw across the bridge into the town. It was a maelstrom of flame-spitting pistols and muskets and the rasping clash of swords.

'You'll get that troop of yours killed too before long. I've made a wager with Corporal Bard to the same.' Mun locked eyes with him then, saw the malice shining there like polished metal rivets. 'A half crown says you'll get those farmers and rogues slaughtered before the month's out,' Boone said. The man's neatly groomed moustaches and beard might have seemed at variance with the predacious-looking teeth revealed now amongst them, but Mun knew Boone, knew he was a killer.

More killer than fighter, he considered through the searing rage that bid him stick his sword through the bars of Boone's helmet. 'Don't tarry here, Captain, you risk missing your share of the plunder,' he said, hungering for Boone to raise his sword or pull one of those pistols from its holster. 'Ah, but of course. You'll wait until the fighting is over. Then when it's nice and safe you'll rob one of your men of his plunder because you're a recreant, merry-begotten bastard.'

Boone's hand went to his pistol.

'Good seeing you in one piece, Captain,' O'Brien called, coming up on his big mare, his poll-axe gripped by its neck in one massive hand. The Irishman's eyes had none of the cordiality of his greeting and he bristled with the threat of violence. Jonathan was close behind with the rest of Mun's troop.

'I could have you on a charge for desertion, O'Brien,' Boone said, his lip curled as his left hand took hold of the reins again. 'But I'd rather not have an Irish devil in my troop in any case.'

O'Brien gave the kind of grin that was almost bloodshed in itself. 'May you live to be a hundred years, with one extra year to repent, Captain Boone,' he said, tilting his head but never taking his eyes off the man.

'A half crown says you'll get them killed, Rivers,' Boone snarled, then flicked his reins, kicked with his heels and cantered off towards the fray.

'Godfrey!' O'Brien called over his shoulder and the young man came forward, grim-faced in readiness for the fight. The rest of Mun's troopers sat their horses patiently as the Royalist army advanced around them, officers roaring orders and all of them still under fire from the rebels who yet held Brandon Hill and Water forts behind them. 'Kindly lend Sir Edmund your horse, Godfrey, then go back and find Hector and keep an eye on Sir Edmund's gear before some bung nipper gets his thieving hands on it. The saddle and holsters alone are worth more than you, lad.' O'Brien locked eyes with Mun, in that heartbeat acknowledging his loss and brave Hector's death, as Godfrey dismounted and walked his dappled grey mare towards Mun, patting the beast's flank as he handed her over.

'What's her name?' Mun asked Godfrey.

'Lady,' the lad replied proudly. 'She won't let you down, sir.'

Mun nodded. He wanted to tell Godfrey that he would bring Lady back safely, but he could make no such promises and so he turned his back on the young man, putting his hands and face to the mare's muzzle, letting her smell him. Then he hauled himself up into the unfamiliar saddle knowing that the stirrups would be about the right length because Godfrey was tall. Lady seemed compliant and trusting, though Mun knew the real test would come soon enough when they rode together into the storm of steel and lead.

'Are we winning?' O'Brien asked, nodding towards Bristol. A shot from a light field piece thumped into a nearby hummock, fired by the rebels still holding out amongst the houses around College Green.

'They should have launched a proper counter-attack when we came through the wall,' Mun said. 'They won't stop us now.'

A corporal cantered up, reining in before Mun, his horse stamping the ground impatiently. 'Sir Edmund,' the man said, nodding respectfully. His face was sheened with blood from a cut above his eye. 'His Highness the Prince requests you join him at the Frome Gate.' He pointed north to a bridge around which another mêlée raged. 'The rebels' resolve is weakening and one good thrust will see us breach the inner defences.'

Mun nodded and told the corporal he would join the Prince presently, then turned back to his troop as the officer cantered off. 'Shear House men to me!' he called into the pre-dawn gloom, raising his sword for them to see through the fog of musket smoke drifting southwards across the field. 'To me!' He had lost men but could not think of that now as the remaining twenty-five troopers gathered around him, the weight of their expectations threatening to drag him under. He could see it in their faces, that need, that hunger to stay alive. Their eyes pleaded with him to lead them well and wisely and, no matter what the outcome of the storming of Bristol, to take them home to their families, for all that they would not shirk their duty here.

And yet his soul burnt, still. His fury raged, still.

'This will be pistol work,' he called, raising his voice above the ceaseless beat of a drum as it drew nearer, 'at least until we get amongst them and they take to their heels.' He pulled out one of his own twenty-six-inch-long man-killers and proceeded to load it. 'Keep to open ground where you can. Stay together. Give them no quarter,' he said, looking up now and then, spending a moment on eyes here, a face there, 'for they will show you none and had every opportunity to yield the town before the killing began.' Those with naked blades had sheathed them and now checked their wheellocks, firelocks or carbines. A blood-soaked musketeer, limping back from the river using his matchlock as a crutch, bawled at them, calling them lace-loving lobcocks and telling them to get into the fight. They ignored him. 'You will take orders from me, from Corporal O'Brien, or from the Prince. No one else,' Mun went on. He wouldn't put it past Nehemiah Boone to order his Shear House men to charge a battery and see them butchered just to spite Mun and win his wager.

'Death to traitors!' Mun roared, turning Lady northward as his men repeated the war-cry, then he rode and they followed him.

And at the Frome Gate they found a slaughter.

Dawn had long broken, the pale light of the new day spilling across Bristol and throwing into shadow those who fought on at the Frome Gate amongst the dead and soon to be dead. Flies were beginning to swarm, drawn by the stench of open bowels and blood and by the heat which the day promised. They gathered hungrily on men's bloodied tunics, befouled the faces of those who had so recently brimmed with life and fear, and massed in exposed wounds, so that the flesh seemed reanimated by some putrid spirit. And as the flies feasted, the storm of steel and lead raged.

The rebels still held Bristol. They had lost the eastern end of the stone bridge and its defences of gabions and earthworks, but somehow yet held the gate into the city which even now they laboured to bolster with an improvised barricade of wool-sacks.

'They cannot hold us!' Prince Rupert had bellowed in the thick of the fighting, walking his new mount back and forth as he encouraged his men and drove them on.

But the rebels *were* holding them.

Mun had led his men up to the gate time and again and each time they had fired their pistols and carbines at the defenders as other men hacked at what remained of the gate with axes or threw up scaling ladders only to be shot or pushed off with pikes, bills and musket butts. Several Royalist officers had been shot and carried off, including Colonel Lunsford who had been shot in the heart and Colonel Bellasis whom Mun had seen take a bad cut to the head. From Mun's own troop a tanner from Parbold called Geoffrey Asplin had been shot in the face and killed, and Thomas Cope, a brewer from Ormskirk, had taken a musket ball in the shoulder. He had been alive and screaming the last Mun saw, but the sheer quantity of blood did not, by Mun's reckoning, bode well for Cope's chances.

Now they were no longer attacking in waves, one troop after another. Instead Mun and his men and those of Boone's troop and others sat their horses behind and amongst the musketeers and dragoons thronging the Frome Gate, firing at will and maintaining a constant hail of lead against the faltering bulwark that stood between them and Bristol's brave but outnumbered garrison.

'We're running out of powder,' O'Brien said, pouring powder down the muzzle of his wheellock and blinking sweat from his eyes. 'Shot too.' He put a ball and wad down the barrel then scoured home the charge. 'And from what I hear Prince Maurice is still picking his nose on the south side,' he said, grabbing the reins one-handed as his horse spooked at an explosion. He calmed her with a soft growl as he took his spanner and steadily wound the pistol's lock.

'We're making hard work of it,' Mun said above the din, aiming his firelock at a rebel who was leaning over the wall trying to shove a scaling ladder off with a captain's leading staff, though it was clear the man was no captain. Mun fired but the ball struck the wall in a spray of stone chips and the rebel ducked out of sight. 'We can no more sustain these losses than can they,' Mun said, glancing at the bodies scattered around and at those wounded being helped to the rear. 'One of us will break soon.'

A cheer went up and Mun looked over his right shoulder to see reinforcements in the form of Colonel Grandison's brigade coming on to the drums in ranks as neat as could be across uneven, furze-strewn ground. Presenting a front some seventy paces across, they were arranged in six ranks of fifty: grim-faced musketeers who to Mun's eye had the look of men who know that they have come to do a job, know that they are expected to change the day. Those horse and foot in loose order before the gate instinctively hurried left or right to get out of the way because they knew what was coming, that to stay was to face obliteration from their own side.

'The buggers will wish they'd opened the doors for us now,' Tobias Fitch called, grinning at the defences, and Mun noticed a musket-ball dent in the man's forge-black breastplate that had not been there before the fight. The former stonemason's apprentice would have been dead had the plate not been of good quality.

'Opened the doors?' O'Brien remarked as the approaching musketeers blew on their matches and cocked them, fitting the cords into the serpents. 'They'll wish they'd killed the fatted calf.'

The musketeers in the first two ranks were trying their match now, making sure the burning ends would reach the centre of the pan.

'Present!' one of Grandison's officers yelled, and the well-drilled soldiers moved the muskets away from their bodies, muzzles still pointing at the sky, powder flasks clacking noisily.

'Give fire!' the officer bawled and the fifty men of the first rank levelled their matchlocks and squeezed their triggers. The sound was deafening and Mun felt Lady tense beneath him, though she gave him no trouble. Then as the smoke hung in the still air like an ethereal rampart before Grandison's men, the front rank fell away to the rear to reload and the next rank stepped forward.

'Fire!' this rank's captain roared and another volley ripped into the Frome Gate and the walls of Bristol. Mun and the men around him watched in awe as each rank came forward in its turn, so that Mun found he could not count beyond ten between volleys. It was impossible for the rebels to present their own firearms in the face of such fury and Prince Rupert knew it. Seizing his chance he ordered his men forward, calling on them to storm the gate in the name of the King. The clamour from Royalist voices was tumultuous. They poured forward unopposed and tore at the barricade like frenzied animals. And they forced a breach. The first two or three were killed for their efforts but then some were through, their own muskets barking, and when he saw that Mun knew it was all but over.

'Forward!' he roared, his ragged voice lost like a breath in a tempest, urging Lady through the throng. He found that the bloodied foot were happy to let him and his men pass, relieved even, to see others going forward instead of them, and then he was on the bridge, glancing down at the bodies in the water as he pushed on. A cold hand clutched his heart with the realization that he was the first mounted man through the gate, but he did not stop and Lady picked her way around corpses and took him down into the doomed city.

And there were the enemy, trying to retreat in good order, loading and firing matchlocks and wheellocks even as they withdrew, from the breach and those spilling through it like blood from a wound.

'They may be short on fealty but they've plenty of courage,' O'Brien remarked, licking dry lips. 'Wait for the order, lad,' he called to Jonathan who had drawn his sword and looked hungry for slaughter. 'You bloody wait.'

Mun looked at Lord Lidford's son and nodded, feeling his own lips pull back from his teeth. These rebels had bled the King's men. They had bled Mun's men. And they had killed Hector. Mun would no more curtail Jonathan's sword arm than he would his own. 'Those traitors would raise arms against their king!' Mun pointed his sword towards a knot of a dozen or so musketeers between two houses in the shadow of the north wall. Two dozen or so garrison men were running east through the streets in the direction of Bristol Castle, but these others and some more brave fools were making a stand. It would be their last. 'Give them your steel! Kill them!' Mun bellowed, then he gave Lady the spur and she responded, showing no fear as she surged into the gallop. Ahead, Mun saw muskets cough their smoke before he heard the report, but he was not struck and the mare carried him on across the baked mud ground towards the enemy.

'Traitors!' Jonathan screamed, outstripping him and reaching the rebels first, hacking down onto a man's bare head and splitting it like an apple. The rebels were reversing their muskets but Mun rode one down even as he slashed his Irish hilt across another man's raised arm, lopping the limb off at the elbow. Then O'Brien was there too, cleaving meat with his ravenous poll-axe, his face all teeth and red bristles.

The King's enemies screamed.

'Mercy! Please, sir, mercy!' a musketeer wailed, falling to his knees amidst the carnage and the flying blood.

'No mercy for traitors,' Captain Boone called, trotting lightly into the fray, and shot the man dead. The man whom Mun had maimed was on his knees holding the spurting stump against his chest, when John Cole rode up, his curved sword raised, and slaughtered him. Mun pulled Lady round and saw that Prince Rupert was establishing a command post at the breach, Grandison's musketeers forming neat ranks and two pike stands gathering like forests, one on either flank, their steel-tipped staves threatening Bristol.

'If the fools don't give His Highness the city now that lot will turn the place inside out,' Mun growled, tasting iron on his blood-spattered lips. But the defenders' spirit was broken now and those that still could were surrendering. Or running for their lives.

'Parley! Parley!' someone was shouting as the crackle of musketry receded and Mun saw an officer coming forward with his company's ensign. 'Parley! Colonel Fiennes requests a parley that he may discuss the terms of surrender.'

'Ours or theirs?' O'Brien joked, making a frightening, gore-spattered sight. Some of the Prince's men cheered and others hurled insults at the rebel officer, who looked exhausted and ashen-faced. All around Mun men took the opportunity to reload in case the fight struck up again, and the Prince rode forward flanked by his own officers and his white poodle, Boy.

'It's over, Clancy,' Mun said.

And it was. At least for now. Prince Rupert had suffered too many casualties already and would waste no more lives if Colonel Fiennes truly meant to end the hostilities. And so Mun patted Lady's neck because she had done well, and he turned her round to make his way back through the Frome Gate.

To find Hector.

CHAPTER TWENTY-ONE

TOM WAS COLD, HUNGRY AND TIRED. BUT WORSE THAN ANY OF THIS he was plagued by the memory of seeing Mun in the woods south of Thame. That had been many moons ago and since then they had marched with Essex's army of fourteen thousand men and relieved Gloucester after a four-week siege by the King. Yet the memory of that near meeting clung to him like a wet shirt and try as he might he could not shrug it off. Now, the monotony of the march and the men's exhaustion being such that they would ride or tramp several miles at a time without uttering a word, Tom's mind would not heed his demands for silence. Again and again it had staged the memory of that day like one of the plays their mother loved so, and Tom had been but a captive forced to endure it.

What twist of fate had set Mun on his trail and brought him amongst those trees where Tom and Colonel Haggett's disease-ravaged troop lay hidden with Parliament's silver? It was only blind luck that Tom had not given the order to fire, that he had not killed his own brother as easily as drawing breath. Or had fate or some other force played a hand in that, too?

He had recognized Mun and with him some tenant farmers and labourers in his father's employ. In Sir Edmund Rivers's employ now, Tom had reflected, noting the hard, blood-tempered look of those riding with his brother. His own blood running cold he had watched Mun's progress down the barrel of his pistol. And he had thought his brother a fool for coming amongst the trees on horseback and more so because he was riding with The Scot, who it turned out was as capricious as the wind. That turncoat bastard.

But he and Trencher, Penn and Dobson had seen that precious cargo of twenty thousand pounds in silver and coin safely to Thame, and Colonel Haggett, who had by some miracle survived the disease that had brought him to death's door, had taken the credit for it. Tom did not care about that, but he did care that a Colonel Lambarde, seeing that Haggett's troop was under strength, had ordered Tom and his companions to join the troop and serve under Haggett until such time as they returned to London.

'With respect, sir, I report directly to Captain Crafte,' Tom had said, holding the colonel's beetle-browed eyes. The thought of serving with Haggett and his ragged, shit-stained troop was anathema. 'Having performed our business against the King's men in Oxford we must return in haste to the captain.'

'What business in Oxford?' Colonel Lambarde had asked and Tom had not wanted to elaborate. Captain Crafte had said that in a war of muskets and cannon his own work was a finely wrought rapier. Discretion and precision must be their watchwords, he had said. But then if telling this colonel would get Tom out of Thame and Haggett's company . . .

'We blew their precious printing press sky high, sir,' he had said, almost hearing again the boom which had shivered the Oxford night.

'Printing press?' Colonel Lambarde's expression had been two parts confusion, one part scepticism. 'And was this printing press . . .' he backhanded the words away with a soldier's scarred hand, 'was it squashing our men, Trooper Rivers? Was it squashing them and were the haughty Cavalier tosspots catching their juices in their silver goblets and drinking of them?' He had narrowed his eyes accusingly, the grey bristles of his brows sprouting aggressively. 'Was that devil prince toasting his victories with those godly, honest men's fluids?'

Tom had thought then that Lambarde was quite mad and in that same thought he had known he would be marching with Haggett's men.

'The Royalist newsbook *Mercurius Aulicus* is a thorn in our side, sir,' he had said, knowing there was really no point. 'It mocks Parliament's cause. One edition even mentioned you by name, sir.'

'This newsbook mocked me?' The colonel pulled his neck in, planting his hands on his hips. His grey moustache had quivered hotly and Tom considered the reaction well worth the lie.

'It said you were too old to fight, sir,' Tom had said, 'that when Moses parted the Red Sea he found you fishing on the other side.'

The colonel's face had flushed red as he sought to contain his anger, like nailing a lid on a cask of exploding black powder. Then he leant in towards Tom and Tom caught the smell of stale tobacco on the man's moustache.

'Listen, lad. And listen well. My men, proper soldiers, are out there dying for our cause, for the rights of Parliament and the liberties of good, God-fearing men and women, whilst you and this Captain Crafte . . . piss your breeches over empty words and idle jests. The Cavaliers' falsehoods are but farts in the wind!' His tongue poked out between his lips and he blew noisily, so that Tom felt the fine drizzle on his face. 'You and your companions will do your damned duty and serve in Colonel Haggett's troop and think yourselves honoured to do it. Good God, man, if not for the colonel, Parliament should have lost a fortune in silver and coin.' He had pointed a finger at Tom then. 'Haggett and his brave men are real soldiers and if you've got any sense at all of what that means you might learn something before you see London again.'

With that Colonel Lambarde had told Tom to report to Haggett, eyeballing him as he left the candle-lit room, and Tom had decided that compared with the mad colonel, Haggett was perhaps not so bad after all.

Haggett's troop comprised sixty-two harquebusiers, seventeen of his original men having died of disease or bullets, or being too sick to serve, and Tom could not help but admire them, be impressed by their resilience. They had been in Thame only a few days before being called into action again, and had even missed out on what few supplies – coats, shoes and knapsacks – had been issued. They had spent weeks patrolling the country around Thame, even on occasion venturing to within a mile or two of Oxford and exchanging salvos with troops of Cavaliers out performing the same task.

Then, still under strength, ragged and weary, they had rendezvoused with Essex's army and the London Brigade at Brackley in Northamptonshire on 1 September and set out to break the siege of Gloucester. Under Sir James Ramsay and Colonel Middleton they had fended off attacks by Lord Wilmot's Oxford cavalry and by 8 September they had occupied Gloucester, having forced the King to break up his siege and withdraw to Painswick. By all accounts it had been a close-run thing and Tom had heard that the city's defenders had been down to their last three barrels of black powder. But Gloucester, now the only major Parliamentarian stronghold between Bristol and Lancashire, was safe and could continue to disrupt communications between Oxford and the Royalist recruiting-grounds of south Wales.

Now Tom and Haggett's men were marching beside a column of pikemen, leading their mounts by the reins to rest them because they were tired and had not been properly fed for two days. The sound of thousands of feet churning the mud, of powder flasks and sword fittings rattling, men coughing and hawking phlegm, insults being hurled up and down the line, the neighs of the horses flanking them and the monotonous beat of the drums – all of it, along with the stench of several thousand unwashed men, accompanied every plodding mile until Tom was no more aware of any of it than he was of what day it was or what village they had passed. It was into this dreary tedium that thoughts of Mun and Bess, and of his mother, poured. Thoughts too of his father who had fallen on the same bloody field as he, but who had not come back from the dead as Tom had.

'I remember the good old days,' Penn said beside him, palming sweat and drizzle from his face. 'When we were proud young bloods with fire in our hearts. With principle and purpose in one hand and a sword in the other. Now look at us.'

'Aye, Rivers, how did we end up in this troop of ragged-arse bastards?' Dobson grumbled, not caring who heard. 'The next time you need volunteers for some shady undertaking remind me to shoot you and save us all the misery.'

'You were born miserable, Dobson,' Trencher said, taking a swig from his bottle and dragging an arm across his brow. 'The day you slipped into the world they took one look at your sour face and locked your mother up. The brothel-house lost money that day.'

Some of Haggett's men laughed at that and Dobson swore at Trencher, calling him a bald, shanker-faced Puritan. 'When you were born, Trencher, a passing cat tried to bury you,' he said, and this got some laughs too, but then a fusillade of musket fire crackled in the distance and the men fell silent to listen.

'Here they come again,' Penn said, as Colonel Haggett gave the order to mount and the men of his troop put on their helmets and prepared for a fight that most likely would not come.

'All this can hang for a proper bed and a night's sleep,' Penn said, getting into his saddle wearily. 'That's all I want.'

'A full belly would do me,' Corporal Mabb grumbled, stepping into his stirrup and hauling his old self up. From his headquarters in Tewkesbury Essex had sent cavalry north across the Severn to Upton as if he intended to march on Worcester.

For a while the feint had worked, the King's army having advanced to Evesham from where it would have a clear march to Worcester. Essex's army, including Colonel Haggett's bone-tired troop, had then slipped out of Tewkesbury and made a forced march south, headed for London via the southern route through Swindon.

Then they had arrived at Cirencester, taking by surprise two Royalist cavalry regiments that were quartered in the town and capturing forty wagon-loads of provisions and arms meant for the King's army.

'That's blown the ruse, I should imagine,' Trencher had said that night as one hundred men, billeted together in one old barn, had hunkered down to sleep. And so it had, for the loss of Cirencester was a blow against the King and now His Majesty's field army pursued them, marching on a roughly parallel route, and the race for London was on. Tom had known that, strung out along Wiltshire's Aldbourne Chase as they were, they would prove too strong a temptation to Prince Rupert, and sure enough the Cavaliers had come, attacking Essex's rearguard time and time again, harassing them like devils. They would appear as if from nowhere, ride within range and shoot on the move, Parliament's ranks making an unmissable target. By the time Essex's musketeers had made ready to fire the enemy was gone, lost to sight amongst the Berkshire Downs, and even if the shot could be made it was at a fast-moving mark and all but impossible. As for the horse, Essex had forbidden them to fully engage the enemy, so all they could hope for was that by riding at Rupert's men they would scare them off. It was frustrating, repetitive work but Tom understood Essex's reasons. The earl could not afford to see his cavalry bloodied against the Prince – as they surely would be if they made a fight of it – before they had even made it halfway to London.

They rode now towards the sounds of musketry, hampered by the undulating landscape, and by the time they came to the part of the column being threatened, the Prince's troopers had vanished once again. Tom and his companions reined in and took in the scene. Some musketeers were firing into a nearby hillock, disposing of charge and shot they had not had the chance to use, for they would not march for miles with loaded matchlocks. Others were falling back into column, cursing the Royalist dogs for cowards. A little further down the line several pikemen lay dead or wounded and the company's colonel, a clean-shaven, red-faced man, was bawling at a captain of horse who had arrived ahead of Haggett's troop.

'Someone's peeved,' Trencher said, nodding towards the colonel, breathing hard after the ride.

'What's the point of bloody horse if it still takes you all day to get from here to there?' the pike colonel was yelling, brandishing a captain's leading staff at the other officer. The staff's erstwhile owner lay dead near by, a gory hole in his face. 'My lads are dying here while you take your merry time and show up when it's all over.'

'My apologies, Colonel, but we came as soon as we heard the shots,' the captain replied, bristling at being upbraided in front of his men.

'Back we go,' Colonel Haggett called to his men, turning his mount and leaving the other troop to their ear-bashing, and Tom rode up to him, bringing his horse alongside as they walked them back up the column.

'Sir, the Prince will dog our heels all the way to London if we let him,' Tom said. 'Every attack slows us, as it is surely meant to. It could be that the King has already overtaken us and that we march into the lion's jaws.'

Haggett pushed up his helmet's three-bar face guard, his close-set eyes latching on to Tom's. 'And what would you have us do about it, Trooper Rivers?' he asked, knuckling at the moustache he had grown and to which he was clearly not yet accustomed.

'We could engage them,' Tom said. 'Bleed them. They come a troop at a time, never in any numbers. Two hundred of us could ride at them, kill some. That would give them cause to think again.'

'Our orders are to stay with the foot, not tear across the downs after that devil prince.'

Haggett did not like Tom. That was clear and neither did Tom blame him seeing as he had all but usurped the man, taking charge of Haggett's troopers when the colonel was racked by fever and in danger of losing Parliament's silver. But to Tom's mind Haggett was too careful. He was not a coward, he had proved that much in the last months, but he was too careful.

'Then they will keep coming and we will keep losing men,' Tom said, frustrated by the colonel's diffidence but knowing he could hardly expect the man to ignore the earl's orders.

'No, Rivers, we will not,' Haggett said, glancing at his men as they passed. They looked tired and ill-fed but Tom knew they would fight. 'Not that I need keep you abreast of my lord Essex's strategy, but we are to cross the Kennet at the first opportunity, keep the river between us and them.'

Tom nodded. It was a sound plan, a better one, truth be told, than charging after Prince Rupert's fearsome cavalry with weary, hungry men.

But then, was it?

'A crossing will slow us further,' Tom said, twisting in the saddle to look south across the downs. 'How far away is the river?'

'Five miles perhaps,' Haggett said, his frown betraying that Tom's point had struck true.

'By the time we've crossed over, the King and every man he has will be blocking the London road,' Tom said. 'We shall receive an ill welcome.'

Haggett closed his eyes and, for a moment, with his sallow skin and gaunt cheeks, he looked like the corpse he had so nearly become. Then those eyes opened wearily. 'Lord Essex knows his business,' he said, then with a click of his tongue and a snap of the reins he trotted off, straight-backed and duteous.

'Obedient as the tamest fireside hound,' Trencher said drawing near.

'You heard?' Tom asked.

'I heard.' Trencher grimaced. 'We're in for a proper fight. Like Kineton, I reckon. When two armies get so close there's no avoiding it.'

That was true enough, Tom knew, for, as they had experienced at first hand, an army on the march was vulnerable to attack. Once two great armies were in such proximity to each other no commander could expect to march away without fighting if his opponent wanted a fight.

'Though, if the earl doesn't have the stomach for it, we could slip away in the small hours, leaving the fires burning. It's worked before now,' Trencher said, the words laced with his distaste at the idea of running from a fight.

'And abandon the baggage train and most of the big guns?' Tom shook his head. 'Even then their horse would catch up and chip away at that lot,' he said, thumbing towards the marching column. 'Piece by piece.' He thought of the master stonemason Guillaume Scarron and hoped the Frenchman was earning good money shaping stone wherever he was. 'No. Essex will fight,' he said. 'He has to.'

'Aye.' Trencher scratched the bristles on his granite-like face. 'And sooner rather than later, too, or his army will be too weak from lack of a decent feed to put up much of a scrap.' He shrugged his broad shoulders. 'I say let's fight the curs and be done with it.'

Two crows flapped up into the sky, *craa*ing loudly, the hard, gnarled notes of their calls sounding as though born of pain. Tom watched them jostle up into the grey banks of cloud drifting south before a northerly that was beginning to bite his face. Yet he felt a bloom of savage heat deep in his gut even as he breathed in the cold air, feeling the September day course through his blood. For he knew the King would be waiting for them.

And there was a battle coming.

*

'I'll wager they cursed the earl when they happened upon that German blackguard and that diabolic dog of his,' Penn said, huffing into his hands and rubbing them together. Somewhere out in the darkness a female tawny owl was hooting, now and then answered by a male.

'Who?' Tom asked, returning to the fire with a bundle of sticks.

'The bloody quartermasters,' Dobson answered, running his ballock dagger over a small whetstone as Tom dropped the sticks and Trencher proceeded to feed them to the flames. 'They thought we had won the race, the stupid bastards. There they were, ambling into Newbury when they stumbled into Prince Rupert and the King's bloody vanguard idling on the bridge. Got Cavalier boot prints on their backsides now, I'll warrant.'

'Which leaves us here in the cold,' Penn said, rounding his mouth and exhaling so that his breath clouded like pipe smoke.

'Another night 'neath the stars,' Corporal Laney added, though he stared up at the black bowl of heaven as though seeing it for the first time. Or the last.

All around them other fires crackled and spat and the sound of murmured conversation filled the night. Essex's whole army, Tom reflected, bivouacked there in that place beneath those indifferent bodies of the firmament, in and around the villages of Enbourne and Hamstead Marshall. Tom could sense the apprehension hanging in the air, the fear and foreboding, the cold unease and the excitement, too, of men who know they will kill or be killed the next day.

He thought of Mun then and felt certain his brother must be in Newbury with the King's army. The chances were they would face each other across the field. It was a dizzying notion that dredged up unwelcome thoughts of their father. And of Emmanuel.

'Just think of it,' young Banks said, the whites of his eyes glistening in the flamelight. 'His Majesty the King just two miles away from where we sit now. The bloody King of England just over there,' he said, pointing north-east.

'A strange thought, ain't it?' James Bowyer said, taking the shoe off his right foot and lying back, holding his stockinged leg in two hands and clenching his foot against the fire's warmth. 'I could fart and with the right wind the King of England would smell it.'

'I'll wager he can smell that stocking even now and asks who has died nearabouts,' Corporal Mabb put in, squatting by the flames, his eyes closed as he relished the heat on his age-haggered face.

Dobson lifted his ballock dagger to his face and looked down its length, then tested the edge against his thumbnail. 'Any of you want a good edge putting on your knife while I'm at it?' he asked without taking his eyes off the blade.

Tom and Trencher shook their heads.

'I rather hope we don't end up that close to the curs,' Penn said, but handed his knife over anyway.

Dobson nodded. 'It always pays to keep a good edge,' he growled into his beard, setting to work on Penn's knife.

Tom doubted knives would be needed in the coming fight, knew that Dobson doubted it too. But it wasn't really about keen blades. Men liked to keep busy before a battle, Tom had learned, because it took their minds away from thoughts of death. Which was why he had not taken Dobson up on his offer. Tom would sharpen his own blades, perhaps later when sleep would not come, as was often the way before a fight. And whilst doing it he would not think of Mun or of his family, or death. Well, not his own death anyway. He would let his mind conjure Lord Denton then let it dwell on him. And he would hope that the chaos-loving God who resided in Heaven and who either fashioned Man's suffering or else did nothing to prevent it, would put that black-hearted bastard in front of him in the coming fray.

20 September 1643, Newbury

'So this is where we shall beat them,' Corporal Mabb said, patting his mare's neck. 'Let your eyes be full of it now, lads!' he called, 'before the fun begins and we all get overexcited. For you will tell your grandchildren about this place. Mark my words. Others will say they were here whether they were or not. But you *are* here, eh? So feast your daylights on these fields and be glad you chose the winning side.' His claw-like hand reached inside his tunic and produced a small bag of tobacco which he opened and brought to his nose, inhaling its fragrance appreciatively. 'And we might as well have a smoke while we're about it,' he said, glancing at Colonel Haggett who nodded his consent. Mabb grinned and pulled out his pipe.

To look at him one would have thought the corporal had not a care in the world, but Tom knew better, knew that as an old head amongst young heads Mabb would serve the troop the way a keel serves a ship, providing the foundation, the spine upon which the strength of the troop depended. What he lacked in youth and vigour Mabb could make up for in temperance, for all that Tom considered the man's optimism ill-founded as he took in what was to be the battlefield, chewing a stale hunk of bread he had saved from the day before. His eyes ranged over a tract of land bounded on the north by the River Kennet and the heavily enclosed water meadows lining its banks, on the east by the Newbury to Andover road, and on the south by the River Enbourne. It would soon be the stage for a scene of bloody confusion. He knew all too well the chaos of battle, when a man is given over to his most base instincts so that he may butcher other men, savage their living flesh with bullet and blade, and watch the terror and regret in their eyes as death claimed them. As his guts soured at the thought, Tom could not help but wonder if Mun was even now making the same appraisal of the field. Was his brother imagining the carnage that would prove yet another stain on the souls of all who survived?

'These fields will soon cradle the living unto death,' he murmured to himself. The earth would be steeped in blood. And yet what choice was there? With the King's army standing astride the route back to his base around London, Essex was doing the only thing he could. He was making a fight of it. And Tom was hungry for a fight. Despite the drudgery of the march and Parliament's army having lost the race to Newbury, Tom had a new-found respect for the earl. Essex had organized his army according to a predetermined plan so that it had marched in the brigade formations in which it would be deployed in battle. That dawn, in the cold damp dark, each unit had known its place relative to another, moving into battalia with the benefit of the earl's leading commanders having surveyed the landscape before nightfall. Though in the event it had been by no means a simple affair, for the ground did not favour the great formations of foot and horse with which commanders had strategized and in which soldiers had trained.

'This will be no Kineton Fight,' Penn had remarked earlier, as the breaking dawn had slowly revealed to the rank and file the landscape before them. The battle lines of both armies ran north–south and what faced them was a terrain of small fields surrounded by thick hedgerows.

'It'll be hard enough for the plodders,' Trencher had grumbled, meaning the infantry, 'but for us it will be near impossible.'

'That's as may be, lad,' Corporal Mabb said, 'but yonder ground will be just as troublesome for His Majesty's horse as it will be for us, meaning they shan't play first fiddle like they normally do. The colonel may put me right,' he said, nodding to Haggett who was out in front of them, talking with another officer, 'but I suspect that due to the terrain we shall be used around the place in small numbers.' He stretched out an arm as though scattering imaginary seeds here and there. 'Same for them buggers. And I reckon they're not so frightening by the score.'

Still, Tom did not like the look of the dew-covered escarpment, in front of him and slowly rising towards the south, eventually to form the broad open plateau known, according to a local man, as Wash Common. He wished brave Achilles were alive still, for the stallion had known no fear and Tom would have trusted his sure-footedness. By contrast the mare he rode now, which The Scot had given him to make good his escape from Oxford, was nervous. Her ears were flat and she was tossing her head, so Tom was trying the same soothing words on her that Achilles had liked.

'Be a good lad, Penn, and take a little ride up there,' Trencher said, pointing up the escarpment, a northern spur of which rose off to their right, the low, newly risen sun shafting light across it yet leaving the near side in cold shadow. From the look of the clouds scudding eastward across the heavens, the new sun's glory would be short-lived. 'Get an eyeful of the merry-begotten curs so we might have a better idea what kind of day it's likely to be.'

Penn responded with the sort of word the request deserved and Trencher shrugged his powerful shoulders as if to say it was worth a try, as a Puritan minister made his way amongst the mounted men, handing out blessings and commanding them to do God's will by smiting the Cavaliers.

'There could well be some smiting done here today,' Dobson said, chewing a wad of tobacco because the time for pipes had passed, Colonel Haggett having announced that any man caught smoking one would be put on a charge. The giant twisted in his saddle, taking in what he could see of Parliament's army, then leant and spat a string of black saliva into the wet grass. 'A rare turn-out is this.'

And so it was. As Tom understood it Essex's fifteen regiments of foot were arranged into four brigades. To the left of Haggett's troop stood Colonel John, Lord Robartes's infantry, whilst to their front, one hundred paces away and a fog of breath hanging above them, waited Sergeant-Major-

General Philip Skippon's foot. Off to Tom's right, set slightly back from Skippon's men and so almost level with Haggett's harquebusiers, Colonel Harry Barclay's musketeers were making ready to light their match, whilst his pikemen rested their staves on the ground, grey blades pointing at the sky. Then beyond that, on the right of the field, though obscured by trees, were Colonel James Holbourne's infantry. Behind Tom waited Essex's reserve including the five London Trained Band regiments. The bulk of the cavalry was divided into two wings, Colonel John Middleton commanding the left and Sir Philip Stapleton the right.

Yet Colonel Haggett's troop of sixty-two men – a meagre number ordinarily but a potentially effective force given the terrain – were nearer the centre than the wings, attached to Major-General Skippon's command as they were. Tom had heard one of the younger men ask Corporal Laney why they were one of only a few troops of horse amongst the main body of Parliament's army.

'Because General Skippon wanted some horse to play with and so Essex gave him us rather than strip the flanks of a decent troop,' Dobson had murmured, earning himself a withering glare from Colonel Haggett.

'One of General Skippon's scouts has reported a strong body of musketeers ahead of their lines over yonder brow,' Haggett had explained in a voice that sounded stronger than he looked. 'We shall ensure their good behaviour.'

'Makes sense to send out a forlorn hope over ground like this,' Trencher had said grudgingly, as a swirling gust had sprayed them with a fine drizzle and brought the clatter of enemy drums. The sound had made some of the men give up a prayer. A trooper three over on Tom's right had thrown up over his breastplate and not a man had chaffed him for it.

Tom had pulled his sword a little way out of its scabbard just to make sure it did not stick. For a forlorn hope of musketeers meant sword work. He would wager a shilling that at the first sight of those men up on the ridge Skippon would send Colonel Haggett to chase them off. 'We ought to be claiming the high ground,' he had said, satisfied with the blade's draw. 'Before they do.'

'Aye, we ought to,' Trencher had replied. 'But don't let it worry your pretty head. Lord Essex knows his business, Tom.' He had looked heavenward then. 'And the Good Lord is with us today.' He'd inhaled deeply, nostrils flaring as though filling with the Holy Spirit itself. 'Can't you feel it, lad?'

'If God is with us, Will, it's because He loves nothing better than to watch men slaughter each other,' Tom had said, at which Trencher had shaken his head wearily, Penn had glanced skyward as though expecting divine wrath, and Dobson had muttered that that being the case he was going to give God a show to remember.

Now, to make sure it was still in place, Tom touched the sprig of furze he had wedged between his helmet's visor and its skull. That morning, their hands cold and their breath clouding, every man in Parliament's army had picked broom or gorse, or else sent the younger lads in their troops to gather it, for the field sign was to be a green bough worn in their hats. To the amusement of the men Penn had braided three slender broom branches into a ring which he now wore on his pot like a laurel wreath or crown. Some of Haggett's troopers had taken to calling him *your majesty* and Penn played along, wafting his hands and affecting a haughty air.

'Try and finish the day in one piece this time, Tom,' Penn said now as Skippon's drummers began to beat the Battalia and the brigade began to march. 'No sleeping on the field to-night.'

Tom's guts twisted at the cold memory of lying all night with the dead and dying below the Edgehill escarpment. He could smell again the blood and faeces. The earth. That night he had seen men's ghosts climbing out of stiffening bodies. He had lain half dead himself, besieged by visions and the deepest terror he had ever known, as looters had sawn off his finger for the ring on it. Perhaps the bitter cold of that night *had* saved him, slowing the blood in his wounds. Or perhaps, as he had said, God had not wanted him for Heaven and Satan had not wanted him for Hell, so that he had lingered, his own thirst for revenge sustaining him. And yet, if he had died would he have been reunited with Martha? Had she been waiting for him only to be denied at the last? Had he failed her again?

'Remember the watchword, lads!' Corporal Mabb called above the drums and the officers' commands, the neighs of excited horses and the roar of cannon to the south of the field. 'Let's hear it, young Banks, if you please, lad.'

'Religion,' Trooper Banks said, his helmet's chin strap digging into his hairless face and whitening the flesh.

'Either my lugs are full of mud or else they're as old as the rest of me!' Mabb exclaimed, 'because for a moment there, Banks, you sounded like a little girl. I asked for the watchword.'

Banks frowned, embarrassed. 'Religion!' he yelled, his startled mount tossing its head.

Mabb nodded. 'That's better, lad. And don't forget it, neither,' he said to them all. 'And if your pal has lost his greenery be sure to tell him. You don't want some bugger putting a hole in you only to say how sorry he is when you find out you're both Parliament men.'

'Forward!' Colonel Haggett shouted, his raised hand signalling the advance. Out in front the vanguard, some five thousand men, were moving forward, their collective trepidation filling the grey dawn like the threat of a gathering storm. With them moved field artillery, oxen lowing as conductors urged them over the difficult ground, mud-slathered pioneers doing what they could with spades and levers to ease the passage, and all ensconced within companies of men armed with firelocks who provided close protection. Far off to their left in the Kennet valley Tom could just make out a small body of infantry and more field artillery on the move, the foremost of them already taking up a defensive position behind a great hedge separating the enclosures around Enbourne from a large force of Royalist horse. Tom supposed those musketeers and pikemen had been charged with preventing the Cavaliers from using the track to Hungerford to disrupt the Lord General's overall plan, whatever that happened to be. Much of the rest of the army, such as Essex's reserve of ten infantry regiments – another five thousand men – was hidden from view. And yet even what could be seen was enough to set the blood in men's limbs trembling like water coming to the boil.

'God be with you, lads,' Trencher said to the men around him. 'Send the devils to their graves. Every man you kill is one that can't kill you.'

Tom's loaded pistols were snug in his boots, their long barrels pressing against his flesh, their butts sticking out above the bucket tops but held close against the leg by garters cut from a scarf of Essex orange. His sword hung on its baldrick, the hilt in front of his left hip, the scabbarded blade beginning to whisper of its hunger for blood.

'I wish Weasel were here,' Penn said.

'Nayler, too,' Tom said, his memory conjuring their friend, bloodied sword in hand just feet from the ranks of the enemy, deep in the fray at Kineton Fight. Tom would have sworn he could hear Nayler now screaming at him to climb up behind him as hot lead shredded the smoke and the battle din filled the world as though the gates of Hell had been hauled open.

Get on, lad, we can't hang about here! Nayler had yelled, the words barely out before a musket ball had ripped open his throat.

'Hang on, what's going on here?' Trencher said, jerking Tom back to the present. The big man was lifting himself as much as he could, straining to see what was happening up ahead, and then Tom became aware that the drums were beating new orders and General Skippon's men had stopped.

'Hold!' Colonel Haggett raised a hand and the sixty-one

men at his back stopped too, some of them mumbling the usual curses of soldiers who, having steeled themselves for action, are brought to a halt knowing that their courage will dissipate like smoke on the breeze and they must summon it again before long.

Skippon's drums had fallen silent, but others beating on, towards Biggs Hill to their south and still more to the north towards the River Kennet, along with sporadic musket fire and the deeper cough of field artillery, announced that the battle was on.

'Seems we're to be held back,' Corporal Mabb said, not sounding unhappy at the prospect.

'We had better not be,' Tom gnarred, for he had not come to watch other men fight.

'Patience, lad,' Trencher said. 'We're the only horse hereabouts. Someone will find a job for us before long.'

'Well look who it is!' Ellis Lay, a trooper with a sharp beardless chin, announced, as the Lord General himself came over the rise to their left on a fine grey horse. Around him rode a retinue of cuirassiers, their armour dull in the dull day, and several harquebusiers armed to the teeth. And as the men in Skippon's vanguard saw their Lord General they cheered, the musketeers lifting their montero-caps to wave them in the air, and Essex acknowledged them with a stiff wave before disappearing from Tom's sight behind the massed ranks.

'Now we're safe,' someone called out. 'One glimpse o' the earl and Prince Rupert will take to 'is heels and be back in Germany before nightfall.' Men laughed and another trooper said he'd wager a half crown if he had one that Essex had come to order the general retreat on account of a hare having crossed his path, or having yellow speckles on his fingernails, or because his right cheek was burning which meant someone was talking ill of him. For Essex was known to be a superstitious man.

'Or because the enemy has taken the field and if we don't scarper he'll have to fight the buggers,' James Bowyer put in.

'Hold your damn tongues,' Corporal Mabb barked, as Colonel Haggett twisted in his saddle to shoot his men a reproachful look before turning back to greet an officer from the Lord General's party whom Tom had seen coming at a fair canter.

'I keep expecting to see the bastards coming over that spur,' Dobson said into his beard, eyes scouring the rising ground up towards Wash Common. 'The King's whole damned army and that devil prince.'

'Not seeing them is worse than seeing them,' Tom replied and Dobson agreed. For the shifting breeze was from the east again now, bringing the calls of the enemy's drums though the Cavaliers were still hidden from view.

'Listen up, lads,' Corporal Laney called as Colonel Haggett walked his horse towards them and the other officer cantered off, his horse's hooves flinging clods of dew-soaked earth.

'Men! Lord Essex will lead the vanguard! Sergeant-Major-General Skippon will remain with the reserve and assume command of Lieutenant-General Stapleton's horse. Our task is to ride up the escarpment and secure the highest point before the enemy does.'

'He doesn't look happy about it,' Trencher murmured.

'I'd imagine Essex chose him for the task because he did such a fine job of getting all that silver to Thame,' Penn put in, sharing a knowing look with Tom. But if that *was* true and Haggett's superiors thought him a brave and resourceful commander Tom did not mind in the least. Because they were to ride towards the enemy who waited unseen beyond the escarpment.

And his sword was hungry.

CHAPTER TWENTY-TWO

THEY RODE UP A SUNKEN LANE AT THE SITTING TROT, BODIES TENSE and shoulders hunched because they feared the sudden musket fire of King's men lining the hedges either side. The air here was still and heavy and Tom breathed deeply of it, savouring its damp earthiness, the meagre warmth of a low, corn-coloured sun now and then touching his left cheek through gaps in the hedgerow.

But the ambush never came and they continued round a bend, ascending the northern spur of the escarpment from the west-south-west knowing that they could not be seen by the enemy from their quarters in the Kennet valley. They kept an easy pace until midway up the escarpment where the gradient became more daunting for a stretch and here Tom and some of the others drew their pistols because they thought if an ambush was coming it would be at that place.

'If I were them I'd have killed us by now,' Trencher said a little later as the lane began to level out again. A cock pheasant clattered up from the hedge on their left, a streak of copper, metallic green and red, its *korr kok* carrying out across the fields. And men who had been startled had only just pulled their heads out of their shoulders when a ragged volley of musketry crackled to their right. A man ahead of Tom named Delbridge slumped forward and fell from his horse, so those behind were trying not to trample him even as they drew pistols and hauled carbines round. Somewhere else a horse was screaming.

'Up there!' Banks yelled, and through a break in the hedgerow Tom saw musketeers pouring black powder down muzzles and ramming balls and wadding home.

'Heya!' Tom gave his mare the spur and she responded, lurching forward into a canter, then scrambled up the muddy bank and through the breach in the hedge up onto the dew-slick grass. 'Go on, girl!' he cried, hauling his sword from its scabbard, not caring if any man had followed. But they had followed: Trencher and Penn, Dobson and Haggett's whole troop. And they all must have seen that the men who had fired on them were nothing more than a skirmishing party, thirty to forty musketeers in loose order who should never have shot at them if they'd had any sense.

A man lifted and shouldered his musket, the scouring stick still poking out from the muzzle, and fired and the stick flew past Tom's face as he swung his sword, striking the stock, the impact throwing the musketeer backwards into the grass. Then Tom hauled his mare round and spurred her forward and scythed his blade at another man, lopping off his left arm so that the musket fell with it and the man shrieked.

'King Jesus!' Trencher bellowed, riding a man down and hauling back on the reins so that his horse had no choice but to trample the flesh and bone beneath it.

Men were screaming like animals, dying badly, and Haggett's troopers were loosed to butchery. Tom wheeled right and saw Colonel Haggett fire his pistol and a man's face explode in a splash of blood and brain. A musketeer fired and flame roared from his matchlock's muzzle and Tom heard the thunk of it passing through Trooper Bayle's breastplate even as the young man rode off across the field – most likely dead though his horse didn't know it.

'Mercy!' a white-bearded musketeer called, falling to his

knees and hoisting his matchlock above his head. Corporal Mabb trotted past and leant over in his saddle, bringing his blade in a savage underarm arc that split the back of the musketeer's head open.

'No mercy for Cavalier devils!' Mabb called, spittle flying, eyes wide.

There was no order, no formation to the troop, just troopers riding men down across the field and musketeers having no time to reload and so reversing the matchlocks to use them like clubs, swinging them at their attackers, or brandishing their hangers clumsily, desperately, before being cut down.

'That one ain't dead!' Ellis Lay yelled, pointing at a musketeer who was lying face down in the grass by a clump of furze. 'I saw 'im move!'

Knowing the game was up the musketeer lifted his head and Tom saw the terror in his face as he clambered to his feet and began to run up the rise leaving his musket behind.

'The poor sod,' Penn muttered as he and Tom watched a handful of Haggett's men ride after the terrified musketeer; the rest of the skirmishers had been slaughtered.

'Aye, that's no way to go,' Dobson put in, walking his horse up to them, his big sword still in his hand. Some foul gobbet of dark meat was hanging from it, caught on a notch in the blade.

James Bowyer put his hands to his mouth. 'Run, you white-feathered merry-begotten bumfiddle!' he yelled; and men laughed as young Banks and four others, having caught up with the fugitive, surrounded him and drove him on, jeering and striking him with the flats of their swords.

'Can't we take him prisoner, sir?' Penn called to Colonel Haggett who was behind them leading Trooper Bayle's horse by the reins. Bayle's lifeless body was somehow still upright in the saddle though his head was slumped and jolting horribly.

The colonel shook his head. 'We must push on,' he called back. 'Corporal Laney, bring those men back and form battalia! Three deep. I'll not have us strung out like a damned rabble and tearing off like hounds after a fox!' Tom knew this was aimed at him, knew Colonel Haggett well enough to be sure that the man would be angry with him for leading the charge into the field without having awaited orders.

'And if we'd waited till the good colonel had us all formed up and sitting pretty those curs would have had the time to reload and give us another shower of lead. Maybe two,' Trencher said, detecting the same veiled reprimand in their commander's orders.

Tom paid no notice. He was watching the plight of the last musketeer still alive on the field. Struggling up the steepest part of the escarpment the man stumbled and fell, his tormentors heckling him to get to his feet and run, or else fight like a man.

'Where's your king now?' someone near Tom bellowed. The pursuers were a good two hundred paces away now, up near the summit of what must be the highest point for miles around, where green scrub bristled in the breeze against the charcoal grey of gathering rain clouds.

'Kill him and be done with it,' Tom murmured to himself, as one of the riders suddenly pulled up, his horse screeching, and the others did the same, Banks nearly falling as his mount fought against the bit.

A fusillade of pistol and carbine fire cracked at the summit and one of the troopers pitched forwards and fell from his horse.

'Oh Jesus!' Corporal Mabb exclaimed, pulling a pistol from its holster.

'Hold!' Tom roared. 'Hold!' Because Royalist cavalry were coming over the crest and Haggett's men were turning to flee.

Then Trencher was on his right and Penn on his left.

'Here we bloody go,' Dobson growled, coming up on Penn's left, drawing a pistol and pulling it to the full cock.

'Hold, damn you!' Tom bellowed at a knot of men who had turned their horses and were riding back down the hill. To his credit Colonel Haggett behind them was trying to stem the flow. Tom could hear him yelling at his men to turn back round and face the harquebusiers who were galloping down the hill, swords promising cold death. One of those Cavaliers caught up with Banks and hacked into his neck and the young man died in a crimson spray.

'Hold your fire!' Tom raised his own pistol, his other hand gripping the reins, trying to control his mount for she was terrified. 'Hold your fire! Wait until they're upon us!'

One hundred paces. 'Hold!' Fifty paces. 'Aim low!' The King's men came like a wave that threatened to sweep away all before it. There was no time to count them but there were enough. 'Fire!' Tom squeezed the trigger and a Cavalier flew back in his saddle as though knocked over by God's hand and at least thirty other men fired at the same time and all from close enough that Tom could see men's faces as they died, their killing wave shredded by lead. But the Royalists came on and Tom drew his second pistol and fired, hitting another man in the shoulder, and this time the salvo from those around him was ragged, but more Cavaliers fell.

'For God!' Trencher screamed, spurring his horse forward even as he drew his sword.

'Kill them!' Corporal Laney yelled, ramming his sword's point into a man's mouth.

Grunts and shrieks, the clang and clatter of blades on armour and the whinnies of beasts filled the world and yet above it all Tom could hear his own breathing loud inside his helmet and as rhythmic as the sea, as he let the battle-lust seize him body and soul. A blade bit through his buff-coat into the flesh of his left shoulder and he threw his sword arm across, slashing the broadsword into his attacker's raised left arm which was protected by a steel elbow gauntlet. Snarling like a beast the man hacked at him again but this time Tom caught the blow on his blade and for a long moment it was a battle of strength, each seeking to force the other's sword wide to make time for a killing blow. Tom felt his arm begin to tremble with the strain, muscles screaming. He was twisted awkwardly and his opponent was strong. Too strong.

'You're a dead man,' Tom spat, and with his left hand he grabbed the pistol from his left boot and brought it up against the Cavalier's blade, taking the strain, and in the same moment rammed his sword forward between the bars of the man's helmet and into his eye.

'Tom!' Penn yelled and Tom twisted round, saw another King's man aiming a wheellock at him and ducked just as the weapon exploded. Then Dobson spurred forward and brought his sword down, chopping off the Cavalier's hand which fell onto the grass still clutching the pistol. The wrist stump squirted into Tom's face and he tried to blink the gore away, unable to rub his eyes clear because of the bars of his pot, as the mutilated man shoved the spurting limb under his left arm and somehow brought his mount round then spurred off through the maelstrom. It seemed they were being overrun, that the fierce crashing wave of Royalist flesh and steel would obliterate them and they would die. But then came a surge the other way as the rest of Haggett's men ploughed into the fray, having found the courage to turn and fight.

'Told you the Lord was with us!' Trencher yelled to Tom, his grin revealing blood-smeared teeth as he lifted his arm to look at a gouge in his buff-coat torn by a pistol ball. But it was not over yet and he got his sword up just in time to parry a blow that might have cleaved open his face.

'God and Parliament!' someone cried and Tom caught a glimpse of Corporal Laney before he disappeared under a slaughter of blades.

'Go on, girl!' Tom urged his mare forward to add his weight to the momentum and slashed his sword at a man but missed, then another Cavalier was on him, had blind-sided him and plunged his poll-axe into Tom's mare's skull.

'Rebel scum!' the man barked, spitting at Tom as his horse stumbled and her legs buckled and she fell, but Tom pulled his feet from the stirrups and threw himself clear, hitting the ground, so that his bones clattered like dice in a cup. Having dropped his sword he made a grab for it now but could not get to it for a turmoil of legs and hooves that would have broken bones. So he scrambled clear and climbed to his feet, drawing his knife as all around him men fought for their lives. And yet there was no fear, only fury, a madness raging like fire in his chest as he ploughed through a gap between horseflesh, avoided gnashing teeth and the tossing head of another beast that would have hammered him into the ground like a nail, and came around the rump of the horse whose master was doomed.

He ran and grabbed a fistful of the baldrick criss-crossing the Cavalier's backplate and the man bellowed angrily, his horse plunging on so that Tom was hauled from his feet, yet he clung on. The rider flailed behind himself with his poll-axe, scoring a glancing blow across Tom's helmet, but Tom did not let go and his weight pulled the man back a little and that was all Tom needed. He wrenched the man further back and reached around, plunging the knife into his underarm right up to the hilt, and now the man shrieked. Tom let go of the belts and the knife and was pitched forward, for a moment flying, then smashed his helmet's face guard against the horse's rump, his head snapping back horribly as the ground rushed up to meet him and the wind was hammered from his lungs.

'Up you get, lad!' It was Corporal Mabb, his buff-coat black with blood, his horse's eyes rolling, spittle flying from its mouth. 'That were nicely done, Rivers,' the old man said, and for a heartbeat Tom was surprised to see that he was smiling but then realized why. The Royalists were withdrawing, extricating themselves from the mêlée. They had had enough.

'Back to your king with you, dogs!' a man shouted, as those harquebusiers not sporting green sprigs in their helmets turned their mounts and gave them the spur, hooves drumming against the earth, clods flying.

'God and Parliament!' James Bowyer bellowed, his dry, gruff voice buffeting its way through the animal shrieks of men yet gripped by blood-lust and the fierce joy of having survived murder.

'Are you alive, Tom?' Trencher called across the field, pouring black powder down his pistol's muzzle. At least seven men were not, by Tom's reckoning. Three more were wounded: blood-slathered and paling. He nodded to Trencher, the movement sending searing pain through his neck, and stood looking up the rise. The King's men were cresting the hill now, the first of them having already vanished beyond it, galloping headlong north-east back towards Newbury. But the roar of cannon to the south and the sporadic crackle of musketry and the beating of drums told him this battle was only just beginning.

Many of Haggett's men had dismounted and were even now searching the dead for plunder, spilling the contents of knapsacks onto the grass, yanking boots off dead limbs and thumbing tunic seams for coins secreted in the lining. But the only thing Tom wanted was his sword and was glad to feel it in his hand again – until he saw a fine pair of leather pistol holsters attached to the saddle on a dying horse. They would do nicely, he thought, wiping his sword through a fistful of grass before drying the blade on his breeches. But a whip-thin trooper named Crathorne had seen the holsters too.

'They're mine,' Tom said, thrusting his broadsword back into its scabbard. 'You can have all but the holsters.'

Crathorne nodded, clearly disappointed though not enough to argue. But then he stopped and thumbed his nose, blowing snot into the grass. 'Looks as though your pistols will have to live in your boots a while longer,' he said, turning to make his way back to his horse which was cropping the grass near by. For Colonel Haggett was bellowing at his men to mount and form up, in order to ride up to the summit over which the last of the Cavaliers had vanished.

'They might be preparing to come again,' Haggett called. 'I

351

want three ranks. Knee to knee. We'll come back for the dead and wounded once we've secured this hill.'

Tom ignored him and knelt by the dying horse to begin undoing the holsters' buckles and straps.

'That means you, too, Rivers!' the colonel yelled and Tom swore under his breath and stood, wincing at the hot pain in his neck, the bruises from his fall and where his back-and-breast had dug in, and the cut in his left shoulder. He noticed a dead Cavalier near by whose wheellock appeared to be unfired and so he went over, took the pistol from the cold hand and lowered the cock to the priming pan.

'Rivers!' the colonel shouted. 'Find yourself a horse, man!'

'Doubt you'll get far on that'n,' Crathorne said, mounting near by.

Tom put the wheellock's muzzle to the suffering horse's head and pulled the trigger, the sudden roar conspicuous now that the fight was over.

'Here, Tom, she's cut but she'll live,' Penn said, mounted and leading a stocky dun mare by the reins. Tom saw that his friend had also collected his blankets, knapsack and carbine from his dead horse, for which he was relieved because it meant he did not have to see the poor beast with its brains leaking from its skull.

He thrust the wheellock into his sword belt and took the mare's reins, putting his hand near her muzzle so that she might smell him and whispering soft greetings though his body still trembled with the battle fury. She had taken a cut on the forehead between the poll and the eyes, so that her fair forelock was stained red. Gently and with a shaking hand Tom parted the animal's mane to reveal an open bloody gouge that looked horribly painful though she was steady and uncomplaining.

'You'll be fine,' he said in a soft voice, 'we'll see to this soon, brave girl.' He looked up to Penn. 'Thank you,' he muttered, then adjusted the stirrups, loosened the saddle girth a touch and mounted. And that's when Trooper Dike, alone at the crest of the rise, began to shout.

'Pikes and muskets! Too many, sir, and coming with purpose!' Dike pulled his horse round and came down the slope, his single-bar pot doing nothing to hide the horror in his face.

Penn cursed. He was not alone, as men grabbed powder flasks, took spanners to wheellocks, put helmets back on or pulled face guards back down. Tom looked across at Colonel Haggett, expecting him to order the retreat.

'Form up!' Haggett yelled. 'For the love of God form up now!' And so they did, making three ranks of seventeen with the colonel out in front, and, leaving their dead and wounded behind, rode in good order up the furze-strewn slope. And when they got to the highest point, which Tom could now appreciate was the tip of the northern spur of the escarpment, there was a collective murmur from the men, cut with no few prayers. For an army was coming to take the hill.

Someone let out a soft whistle.

'God's fucking teeth,' another man growled.

'There's not less than five hundred men down there,' Bowyer said. Now the colonel did not look so sure and nor was Tom surprised given the sight before them. Three troops of foot were doggedly marching up the escarpment to the beat of their drums. A company of pikemen made the centre with a company of musketeers either side. On the enemy's right flank rode the remnants of their horse, those troopers with which Haggett's men had already mingled that morning.

'We cannot hope to hold this hill,' Colonel Haggett announced, scratching the new bristles on his sallow cheek, his eyes fixed on the advancing enemy. 'Not against that.'

Tom turned from the immediate threat and glanced westwards, down to where Parliament's regiments moved in cumbersome masses, some of their ensigns unfurled to greet the new day and whatever fate lay in store.

'We could give 'em a volley at least, sir,' Trencher suggested.

The colonel shook his head. 'On that ground we won't be moving fast enough,' he said, 'and any such volley would receive too vehement a reply. They would shred us.' Nervously, he rubbed his mare's poll. The animal snorted and nickered. 'No, we've done our best here but we cannot hold.'

'With respect, sir, we've got to damn well hold.' It was Corporal Mabb and he did not look any more eager for a fight than Haggett, and yet there he was pressing for one, a well-worn resignation engraved in lines on his old face. 'The bastards'll haul cannon up this hill in half a sparrow's fart once that lot are standing here where we are now. And if they get guns up here,' he said, thumbing to the west, 'our lads down there will take a rare drubbing.' He leant over, hawked and spat, then looked at his companions. 'I don't know why our betters never thought to take this hump before now, and God knows I wish it weren't us sitting atop of it this morning, but seeing as we are, it's up to us to keep it.' He sniffed, turning back to Colonel Haggett. 'Sir.'

Haggett grimaced and looked back towards the King's men coming up the slope. There was a man whose conscience was on the rack, Tom thought.

'I've seen that face before,' Will Trencher murmured beside Tom, 'in a painting of Abraham taking his only son for a walk up the mountain.'

'This hill's as good as an altar,' Penn said with a shrug. 'Besides, God saved Isaac at the last. The Lord will provide.'

'The Lord will watch us kill them,' Tom said, willing Haggett to stay and fight, for Corporal Mabb was right. If the enemy took that hill they would put their big guns on it and those guns would sing and the day might be lost. No battle, no fray. And Tom needed the fray. He fed upon it. Only in the fray might he wreak his vengeance against man and God. Only in the slaughter might his enemy, William, Lord Denton, be put before him and thus might Tom kill the father as he had killed the son.

'We must hold them off for as long as we can, sir,' Tom said.

'Don't presume to tell me my job, trooper,' Haggett snarled, 'and that goes for you, too, Corporal.'

'With respect, sir, it ain't just your job,' Corporal Mabb dared. 'We're here to fight. For God and Parliament. Ain't we, lads?'

One or two 'ayes' but nothing convincing, even given Mabb's popularity within the troop. Tom supposed most of them would rather ride away before the advancing infantry took ten more steps. Let the hill be someone else's problem.

Mabb lifted his face guard and put a leather flask to his lips. 'We can kill some of the buggers,' he said, taking a swig.

'Another word and I'll have you on a charge, Corporal,' Haggett blurted, his close-set eyes boring into the older man.

'Corporal Mabb is right. We can bleed them, sir,' Tom said. 'If we thin them they'll most likely retreat. Regroup to consider their options. That will buy us time to send to Lord Essex for reinforcements.'

'You'd have us ride against pike, Rivers? Are you mad?' Haggett glanced at his men but only for a heartbeat, his desire for their approval outweighed by the need to make the decision alone, to lead well men who needed leading.

Tom shook his head. 'I'd have us ride away from them, sir. Just over this brow. Let them think we've seen sense, that they've scared us off.'

'But?'

'But we'll be waiting. Just out of sight on the reverse slope. We'll lie flat until they're almost at the crest and then we'll tear them apart with a volley.'

'You'd let 'em practically stand on us?' Crathorne said.

'Like an adder in the grass,' Trencher put in with a savage grin.

'But we ain't bloody infantry,' Ellis Lay said, beardless chin jutting. His horse was savaging the bit in its mouth, eager to run. 'It ain't our job.'

Tom shrugged. 'They've got muskets. We can't match them at range.' He pulled the two pistols from his boots to make his point. 'But up close we'll give them reason to think again.'

'And if they keep coming?' Colonel Haggett asked.

'Then we mount and leave them the hill.'

'What if they send their horse before we have time to mount?'

'They won't,' Tom said.

They might, he thought. But the horse flanking the infantry coming up the hill towards them had already bled that morning, had already lost a score or more dead or wounded. And Tom thought that their commanding officer would rather see the foot do a share of the work before sending his men into another fight.

'Damn it but I have already lost too many. Including a fine young corporal.' Colonel Haggett was talking to himself, looking at the oncoming enemy, torn between duty to his cause and duty to his men, and for a moment Tom pitied him. He knew that deaths of the likes of Corporal Laney weighed heavy on Haggett and Tom was glad he was not an officer with an officer's responsibilities. Nevertheless . . .

'We must hold this hill,' Tom said, 'whatever the cost.'

Haggett made no sign of having heard, his eyes fixed upon the musketeers and pikemen below, his teeth worrying his thin bottom lip. But then he nodded.

Tom saw Trencher close his eyes and offer up a prayer, the spiritual communion no doubt petitioning the Lord's assistance in the coming butchery. Matthew Penn looked at Tom, one eyebrow lifting as he dipped his head, a gesture that said *good luck* and *kill well* all at once. Dobson mumbled a filthy curse into his unkempt beard.

'If I get killed up here I'll blame you, Rivers, you goddamned carbuncle.'

'No fear of that, Dobson. There's a length of rope waiting somewhere for you,' Tom said, at which the big man grinned savagely and cursed again.

'Fall back!' Colonel Haggett called, circling his arm above his head. 'Fall back!' For a moment Tom feared he had judged the colonel wrong, that Haggett really was going to leave the spur to the King's men. But then their eyes locked, just for an instant, and Tom saw, for the first time since he'd known the colonel, hard resolve. A purposefulness charged with the acceptance of grim violence and possible death. 'We will hold this hill for as long as we can,' he said loudly enough for those around to hear and those further away to get the idea of what he intended, as his troopers turned their mounts, showing the enemy – who were just about in musket range now – their backs as they moved off the crest.

'Keep coming, you swaggering bastards,' Tom growled down the slope, then hauled his mare round and joined the others, some of whom had already dismounted and were pulling pistols from saddle holsters.

Then the colonel told a man named Meshman, who had a slashed right arm from the earlier tangle with the King's Horse, to ride back to Lord Essex or Sergeant-Major-General Skippon, or else the first senior commander he came across.

'Tell them that Colonel Haggett would deny the enemy the advantage of this hill, which could prove of crucial importance in the coming battle, for as long as is humanly possible. Press upon them that we must place cannon on these heights before the King does.'

The man nodded, turned his horse and galloped off westward, back across the furze-covered escarpment towards Parliament's army.

'Lucky bastard,' someone murmured after him.

'No man shall say we did not do our duty this day,' Haggett said, as much to himself as to his men it seemed.

'Bloody duty? Not very inspiring, is he?' Dobson muttered, wincing as he pushed his hands into the small of his back, stiff from riding, and riding poorly at that, he'd be the first to admit. 'A drop of brandywine would put more fire in their bellies.'

'They'll stand,' Tom said, handing the reins of his horse to a young, pox-scarred trooper named Jeffes, one of eight men whom the colonel had tasked with holding six animals each steady until the order was given to retreat in the face of the enemy. This left just forty-three men crouching or lying on the dew-wet grass out of enemy sight over the crest of the round hill. Forty-three against not less than five hundred, Tom reflected. But those forty-three had borne hardships. Through battle or disease they had been halfway to Hell's gates and they had endured. Furthermore, whatever Tom thought of their commanding officer they were loyal to Haggett and respected the man. They would have followed his lead instead of Tom's that day in the woods with Parliament's silver had the colonel not been struck down with fever.

'If they don't it'll be a shambles,' Trencher said, grimacing as he lay awkwardly on his belly, the ridge of his breastplate digging into the ground.

They'll stand, Tom thought. And if they were lucky they would survive.

'We'll give them one good volley. Two if we can,' Colonel Haggett said, gripping his pistols in claw-like hands. 'The slope is steepest just below the ridge and that will slow them, giving us more time than it would seem.'

The enemy's drums were louder now, their monotonous beat seeming to swell and lift up and over the crest.

'If ye haven't already, now would be a good time to double shot those pistols,' Corporal Mabb said, stirring a flurry of activity as nervous hands fumbled at drawstrings and pulled out cold lead balls.

It was a good idea and so Tom went about double shotting his own firelocks. Given that every one of the forty-three troopers waiting in the wet grass had two pistols, that meant a volley of eighty-six bullets. Nearly half the men had carbines too, several taken from the dead – theirs and the enemy's – that very morning. If every man double shotted his weapons, which, given the slope and the proximity of the enemy when the order to fire came, was a good tactic, they would send a hail of around two hundred and twelve lead balls ripping into the densely packed ranks. Enough to get themselves noticed, Tom thought.

Then, in contrast to the flat beat of the drums, an insistent thin piping drew Tom's eyes heavenward. A pair of red kites high up against the iron-grey sky, soaring gracefully, oblivious of the carnage soon to be unleashed below. Or perhaps not oblivious at all. Perhaps waiting, Tom thought. Sent by some higher power to bear witness to man's folly.

'They'll feed on more than worms and sheep carcasses today,' Trencher said, following Tom's gaze as he wound his second wheellock. He passed his spanner to Tom who used it to wind the wheellock he had taken from a dead Cavalier earlier. Then he thrust the pistol into his baldrick where it sat snug against his breastplate.

'Well they're not getting me,' Penn said. 'Let them have the King. For his tyranny and his hubris.'

'And his damned taxes,' Dobson said. 'The haughty bastard.'

'No one is to give fire until I say,' Colonel Haggett called, looking left and right along the firing line. 'No one will show themselves until I give the command. It is imperative that we do not give ourselves away until the very last.' He caught Tom's eye then. 'Until they are almost upon us.' Tom gave an almost imperceptible nod, approving the instruction, for holding fire until face to face with the enemy was how Prince Rupert won every cavalry encounter he fought in. It took an iron nerve but it could be done.

Haggett looked about to give another command but thought better of it, for beyond the crest the enemy was close enough that their stink, of sweat and damp wool, stale pipe smoke and worse, filled Tom's nose. The drums were a dogged, incessant noise now, threatening to drown out a man's very thoughts. But that was good, Tom thought, because the Cavaliers would not hear the nickers, snorts and neighs of the twitchy horses being held less than twenty paces behind their position.

'God be with us,' Trencher murmured.

'I'd rather the Devil,' Tom said, the stump of his ring finger throbbing with the vague memory of Kineton Fight.

'Hold your tongues,' Corporal Mabb growled four or five places to Tom's right, though there was little chance of their being heard above the rattle of their foes' powder flasks and the roars of their officers, the crump of hundreds of trudging feet and even the laboured breathing of some two hundred armoured men, each hefting a sixteen-foot-long pike up the hill.

Tom tried to picture in his mind what he would see when the order was given to rise, for he did not want the shock of it to throw off his aim, his hands already trembling as they were with the beginnings of the battle thrill. Dew and last night's rain were soaking through his breeches and the leather of his boots. He clenched his feet, steeled the muscles in his thighs and arms. Readied them to explode into action. Yet held them in check.

'Come on, will you,' Trencher growled, though whether the man was willing the enemy onwards, or urging Colonel Haggett to give the command to rise, Tom did not know.

Not long now.

A stone's throw away, just over the gorse-lined brow, a sergeant was berating his front rank for their raggedness, bellowing at them to straighten up for they were Lord Wentworth's musketeers and not some rabble of wet-behind-the-ears London apprentices.

Tom inhaled, vaguely aware that it might be the last time he smelt wet grass and earth – and life – and held the breath in his lungs. Then he slowly let it seep out between his dry lips.

Two firelocks and a wheellock. *Three shots, three kills.*

Maybe more with them being double shotted.

Aim low.

'Oh ballocks!' someone exclaimed for there, no more than twenty paces away, stood a musketeer, a skirmisher no doubt, sent ahead of the advancing ranks, and his eyes were bulging like boiled eggs at the sight of what awaited them.

'Now!' Colonel Haggett yelled, and springing up and forward he raised a pistol and shot the musketeer dead before the man had even raised his matchlock, much less warned his comrades of the ambush. 'Now, men!' Haggett yelled, and Tom was up, the whole ambush line bursting forward like a breaking wave, men howling as they ran the twenty paces to the crest.

And there was the enemy, coming up the slope, a great mass of men and arms and self-righteousness.

'Fire!' Haggett screamed, his own remaining pistol aimed at the front rank of musketeers directly ahead, and Tom hardly needed to aim, his two pistols outstretched as though extensions of his arms. The weapons exploded, their roars lost amongst the furious thunder of others, and the front rank of Cavaliers crumpled, others further back falling too, struck in the face by the indignant hail. Then Tom bent to shove his pistols back into his boots and pulled the wheellock from his belt as others lifted carbines or spare pistols and another volley, this one desultory compared with the first, ripped into the King's men.

Who had raised their own muskets.

'Back! Fall back!' Colonel Haggett screamed, as below them officers barked at their men to fire, and, whilst the front rank of the nearest division was a bloody, reeling mess, that of the division to Tom's right was immaculate and untouched. Flame bloomed along its line and as Tom turned to run he saw Colonel Haggett fall to his knees, blood sheeting his narrow face, a musket ball having torn through his helmet.

'Run, you whoresons!' Corporal Mabb bawled as Trooper Dike pitched forward into the grass, a hole through his back-plate.

Tom's foot slipped out from under him and he fell to one

knee, expecting to die then, anticipating a massive, catastrophic blow as a musket ball punched through him.

'Don't tarry, lad,' Trencher snarled, grabbing a fistful of Tom's buff-coat sleeve and hauling him back from the hill crest. 'The stupid bastards shot high.'

'Load!' Dobson rumbled at Haggett's men as they scrambled away from the lead storm. 'Don't just run. Load, you damned grog-blossoms!'

Tom pulled a pistol from his boot and glanced around, seeing that he was over the brow and out of the enemy's sight.

'The colonel is dead!' someone yelled.

'Load, you bastards!' Dobson roared, his voice like a rock fall. The air was thick with smoke and men were down, some left behind at the crest, but others were hurriedly loading their pistols, grim-faced and diligent.

Powder charge and ball down the muzzle. Spanner onto the square section of the wheel shaft, rotating until the click. Prime the pan and pull the pan cover shut. Pull back the dog so that the pyrite in its jaws rests on the pan cover.

Tom loaded his firelocks unconsciously, as if in a dream, as though the brisk hands going about their business belonged to someone else, as he kept his eyes on the bluff's edge for the first wave of musketeers, or horse, to spill over it.

'You command now, Corporal!' someone yelled. 'Haggett's dead.'

'Just load that bloody carbine, Moundrell!' Mabb yelled back, down on one old knee, ramming his charge home.

Tom glanced behind him. The horses were still there, tossing their heads and pawing the ground, the eight men clutching the beasts' reins as though holding on to life itself, which they would be if the Cavaliers came over the rise. Yet not one of Haggett's men had mounted and ridden off. Not one had even retreated to within ten yards of the horses and Tom felt a fierce pride burn in his chest.

'We hold this hill like the colonel said!' Corporal Mabb

shouted, standing stiffly. 'Do you hear me, lads? We hold this bloody hill!'

'Aye, we'll hold it, won't we, lads?' Ellis Lay called, eyes on the crest, both wheellocks pointing straight ahead.

'God and Parliament!' a trooper cried.

'They've stopped,' Penn said, appearing at Tom's left shoulder. And sure enough the King's drummers were beating the Troop, which meant that Lord Wentworth's regiment had stopped advancing to draw in their order, ranks closing up in readiness for the next advance or to repel an attack. 'Why don't they finish it?'

Tom felt a grim smile twist his lips. 'They think we're luring them into a trap. That we've got a thousand men and a dozen cannon sitting here waiting for them.'

Penn grinned, realizing the truth of it. 'If only we had,' he said.

'They ain't coming, Corporal!' James Bowyer said, lifting his pot's face guard and spitting phlegm into a patch of furze. 'What shall we do?'

'Have no fear, lad, they'll come,' Mabb replied. 'They're just scrapin' the filth out their nails and puttin' on their Sunday best. Whoresons know how we like our guests well turned out for a feast.'

'Shouldn't we close up, sir?' a young trooper asked, 'present a decent formation to show we ain't scared?'

'And give their front rank a solid target the bastards can't miss?' Mabb said. He shook his head. 'No, cully, I think we'll give 'em plenty of holes to aim at if it's all the same to you.'

And that's when Tom heard it, felt it perhaps, like a great creature moving through the earth beneath their feet.

'Horse! Have a care!' Crathorne bawled. Tom looked to his right and his blood froze at the sight of some fifty Cavaliers cantering over the lip onto the plateau, swords in hand, jaws set. And then those harquebusiers saw the pitiful rabble arrayed against them, realized that there were no pikemen or musketeers waiting in ambush, no cannon ready to roar, and the lust for revenge ignited in them, so that they kicked their heels, savage grins spreading across their faces.

'Stand!' Corporal Mabb cried, because any man who turned to run was as good as dead, and Tom raised a pistol and picked his target, a Cavalier with a wide scarlet scarf from his right shoulder across his chest.

Come, then.

Around him Tom could feel men's nerve breaking, knew that some were running, thinking their only chance was to reach the horses. But for Tom time stood still. The world all but disappeared, reduced to a blur of colour and sound.

Keep coming.

The horse was a young stallion, grey as smoke and confident, as sure of who his enemy was as if his master had described Tom down to his bucket-top boots, his five-pound buff-coat with its pulled threads, and the wheellock in his baldrick. Thirty yards between them now and the rider lifted his sword for the killing stroke, sure that his enemy's bullet would miss, that his own sword would not.

'Not yet,' Tom said under his breath, his finger burning to squeeze the trigger. 'A little closer.'

The Cavalier's face was hate-filled and soured with fear. Tom could hear him yelling now, some incoherent babble. As he looked into the man's eyes.

And squeezed the trigger.

The Cavalier's head snapped back in a crimson spray but the stallion came on and Tom thought he would die then, but the beast swerved aside at the last and the Cavalier's wayward foot struck Tom's left shoulder, spinning him into the ground.

His breastplate had taken the impact but it felt like a hammer blow and for a moment he lay face down, tasting mud in his mouth, the right side bar of his pot's face guard bent in so that the cold steel pressed against his cheek.

Then suddenly the world came flooding back in, like the

ocean through a torn hull, and with it came the shrieks of the dying. He pushed himself up to find a scene of carnage, of mounted men slashing down at heads and shoulders with heavy swords and poll-axes, and of Haggett's men firing their pistols from devastating range, slaughtering men and beasts and even hauling some Cavaliers from their saddles to shoot them in the face.

'The horses!' James Bowyer yelled. 'Protect the horses!' But Trencher, Dobson and Penn were already there, standing in front of the horses, pistols raised because ten or more Cavaliers were circling like wolves, firing their pistols at the picket. One of the men left to hold the horses was dead but the animals had remained in a knot near the others and Tom ran towards them, leaping a corpse with a poll-axe buried in its face and hauling the weapon free. He saw Crathorne go down, shot through the cheek. Over on his right John Moundrell was staggering aimlessly, helmet gone, skull smashed, his face a bloody mask but for the whites of his eyes, but Tom did not stop. Blind-siding a rider he swung the poll-axe into a leg and the blade bit deep, to the bone, and the Cavalier wailed in shock, wide eyes gaping at the wound as Tom swung the poll-axe up taking him under the chin with a loud crack. Drenched in gore he pulled the blade out and the rider came with it, landing in a heap, the stench of his open bowels hitting Tom's nose.

'Back! Back!' a Cavalier officer was shouting. Tom spun and saw Trencher plunging a knife into a horse's neck, the beast gnashing its teeth and smashing its head down, trying to brain him. But Trencher had a fistful of bridle and a bull's strength and he held on, as Penn ran round and thrust his sword into the rider's underarm, between back- and breastplate, and yanked it free in an arc of bright blood.

'Disengage! Back!' the officer was still yelling, then he turned his mount and gave it the spur and raced off.

'Bloody cowards! Damned curs!' a man named Martindale shouted after the Cavaliers as they galloped off, their horses' hooves thundering upon the ground, but there was no heart in the tirade for in truth Martindale was glad to see their backs.

'Colonel Haggett's men to me!' Corporal Mabb called, limping over to the horses, not even bothering to take an inventory of casualties. His breeches were slick with blood and his old face was deathly white.

'We beat 'em off, Corporal,' young Jeffes said, holding the reins of six horses in one white-knuckled fist, a spent wheellock in the other.

'Aye, lad, we did well,' Mabb replied, catching Tom's eyes with a gesture that Tom understood. Tom knew the Cavaliers could have butchered them all one by one, for all that they would have suffered for the privilege, but why take the risk? They had ridden off, back over the crest to tell Lord Wentworth that the hill was as good as his. Let the infantry sweep away with one good volley any Parliament men foolish enough to linger. But young Jeffes did not need to know that. Not when a third of dead Colonel Haggett's troop lay butchered. Let the young fool think they had beaten the King's men back to their masters.

'Load up, lads, they'll be back sooner than you'd wish,' Corporal Mabb said, looking older than ever. The pain of his leg wound was there in his eyes though he was doing his best not to show it.

A breeze blew over the crest from the north bringing with it the flat beat of more drums and everyone knew that that meant another regiment was coming up the hill to kill them. Yet no one, it seemed, thought there was any point mentioning it.

'Wonder where I'd be if I hadn't met you, Rivers,' Dobson growled, thick powder-burnt fingers and thumb ramming the scouring stick down his wheellock's muzzle. 'Somewhere better than this, that's for bloody sure.'

'What could be better than killing Cavaliers?' Trencher asked him, handing his spanner to Tom again so that Tom could wind his spare pistol.

'I'd be in the Lord, half drowned in old Abiezer's best ale and up to my eyeballs in some pretty wench,' Penn said, a feral grin on his handsome face. 'What about you, Tom?'

'Where would I be if I hadn't met me?' Tom asked, loading his pistols, looking over the scene of slaughter before them. John Moundrell, whom Tom had last seen wandering bloody and benumbed, was lying dead, his head four feet from his body. Ruined creatures, man and beast, littered the ground. Men were moaning or screaming. Horses were shrieking or blowing, their great heads lifting now and then only to thump down again.

'I'd be here on this hill,' Tom said, then lifted his pistol, casually pointing it eastwards. 'Getting ready to kill the next man I see come over that ridge.'

'That's my boy,' Trencher said, nodding, licking the sweat that beaded over his top lip. 'That's my Black Tom.'

And then a massive salvo of musketry ripped the day apart.

CHAPTER TWENTY-THREE

THE CRACKLE OF DISTANT GUNFIRE WAS ALMOST CONTINUOUS NOW, cut with the occasional boom from a cannon or the guttural coughs of smaller field artillery. After a steadily escalating series of actions the King's army was now almost fully committed to battle with Essex. Perhaps because his army was short of rations or powder and shot, or else because he knew it would be vulnerable to attack in its marching formation, the earl's strategy, now that he had secured much of the high ground, was not to attack the King but rather to let His Majesty's army come at him. And Mun knew that meant there were many men in red sashes, many brave and loyal soldiers of the Crown, who would not be alive come nightfall, who were even now drawing their last breaths that damp September day.

'We should have 'ad a regiment and some cannon up there spittin' bloody fury before little cutty wren were singing the world awake,' Goffe said. His wind-flayed farmer's face was turned towards the escarpment up which Sir Nicholas Byron's brigade had marched and where it was now engaged on its left flank in a vicious firefight with musketeers from Major-General Skippon's brigade. A ragged troop of rebel harquebusiers had been first onto the high round hill and the King's officers had been kicking themselves ever since. For those doughty rebels had somehow held Lord Wentworth's regiment at bay, savaging his cavalry until Major-General Skippon had arrived with his three hundred musketeers. Now those harquebusiers and Skippon's men yet held the high ground, making a good show against Wentworth and Byron both, as Mun and his companions waited in formation amongst another Byron's regiment, this one led by Sir John who was Sir Nicholas's nephew.

'A bird of mixed omens the wren,' O'Brien said, stroking his mare's neck, his great shoulders low and loose. ''Twas a wren that led the Romans to our dear Christ in the Garden of Gethsemane.' He shrugged half-heartedly. 'And yet of course in folklore it is considered the King of the Birds.'

'The wren?' Mun shared a silent look with Jonathan, who raised his eyebrows and shrugged. 'I have never heard that. The wren is such a small bird.'

The Irishman's left hand flew to his breastplate, his mouth falling open with a gasp. 'Did you not have stories in your house, Edmund? Filling your wee head before your mamma tucked you in your bed?'

'My mother read us the plays,' Mun said, as the mare he was on snorted and pawed at the ground. The beast, a piebald mare which he had inherited from a dead man in Nehemiah Boone's troop, was sweating and kept turning its head towards its right flank, so that Mun was almost certain it had colic. He could do nothing about that now. 'Marlowe and Shakespeare,' he said, wishing he had not had to give Lady back to Godfrey, although at least he had returned the animal unharmed after the carnage of Bristol.

'And you, lad?' O'Brien asked Jonathan.

'My father is not a man for stories,' he said, clearly more interested in the exchange of musket fire towards the crest of the gorse-strewn escarpment.

O'Brien eyed them both and shook his head. 'Then I feel it is my charge to enlighten you while we wait.' The Irishman's teeth flashed white against his red beard.

'If you must,' Mun said flatly. In truth anything to distract them while they awaited orders – moreover, anything to take his mind off the prospect of riding an unfamiliar, colic-struck horse into a fight across ground unsuited to cavalry engagements – was welcome.

O'Brien nodded. 'Long ago the birds held a contest to see who could fly the highest. He that could would become the King of the Birds.' He lifted off his helmet and thrust a hand amongst his thick red hair, scratching vigorously. 'At first it looked as if the eagle would win, and you can't really blame them all for thinking it. But just as the eagle began to tire . . .' he raised his helmet, 'for he was so high that from the ground could be seen nothing but a speck, the wren, which had been hiding under the eagle's tail feathers do you see, crept out.' He fluttered meaty fingers into the air. 'That little cutty wren soared up and up, far above the tired old eagle, and shouted, "I'm the King!" And so he was. He proved that cleverness is better than strength.'

'What does that say about you, you great Irish gollumpus?' Mun asked, hoisting an eyebrow at Jonathan, who grinned.

'Why, that some of us are blessed with brain *and* brawn,' O'Brien said, 'whilst others must make do with nothing but good breeding and passable looks.'

But Mun did not bite as his friend clearly wanted him to. For he was thinking of the wren.

The relief he felt at having taken off his back- and breastplates was nullified by the vulnerability he felt without them. And yet he knew that removing all but the most essential of impedimenta, keeping only his helmet, buff-coat, pistols and a poll-axe instead of his sword, because of its comparative shortness, had been the right thing to do. For the ground on the north side of the ridge and tumuli if not muddy was boggy, the previous day's rain still lying in puddles here and there, so the leather of Mun's buff-coat was heavy with water. Crawling the three hundred paces they had so far managed had been hard enough without the added encumbrance of armour.

The waterlogged ground seething and hissing below him, Mun was reminded of crawling through the tunnel to blow the mine beneath Lichfield Cathedral. Only this time he had left O'Brien behind, convincing his friend that what he lacked so far as stealthiness was concerned, the big man made up for with his ability to inspire men.

'If something happens to me the troop is yours, Clancy,' Mun had told the Irishman after he had outlined the scheme by which he hoped to throw the rebels off the hill's summit, 'and you'll report to Prince Rupert directly, not that bastard Boone, and tell him you're taking the men home to Shear House.'

'If you go and get yourself killed, I'll tell your ma you left the estate to me and sell it for women and wine,' O'Brien had replied, then the two of them had gripped each other's forearms and wished each other luck.

Now, Mun, Jonathan, Tobias Fitch, Henry Jones and Walter Cade were crawling along a ditch that ran up the escarpment and along the northern edge of the round hill. On their right was the bank itself along whose summit ran a thick hedge of briar, hawthorn and field maple that was only broken here and there by elm, ash and oak. On their left was a margin of bramble and nettle beyond which the ground fell away, steeply in places, down to rough miry ground.

The ditch along which they crawled slowly but inexorably was dead ground, of no strategic value to infantry or horse. At least, that would be most men's thinking. Which was why Mun and his chosen men were on their hands and knees and sometimes their bellies – boots, breeches and buff-coats wicking water, wheellocks and firelocks thrust into boots or belts away from the damp. And yet Mun did not think so little of the enemy as to presume that they would not have eyes watching that dead ground from somewhere near the round hill's summit, where they staunchly held off two of His

Majesty's regiments. Of course it was entirely possible that the outnumbered rebels holding that hill had not even considered the dead ground or the possibility of a few men crawling up their hill like worms trying to get past the bird. Either way, nothing would change the fact that in half an hour by Sir John Byron's own timepiece, or else at the sound of pistol fire from the northern edge of the round hill, O'Brien would lead Mun's troop in single file up that ditch as quickly as he dared given the risk of the ground to horse and rider. By which time Mun and his handful of companions would be more than likely fighting for their lives.

Two fusillades of musketry ripped the morning and into the raw gashes poured the screams of ruined men and the urgent shrieks of officers seeking to impose order on stricken ranks.

'See anything?' Jonathan asked, coming up behind Mun who had stopped at a break in the hedge and crawled up the ridge to spy over the exposed roots of an old elm. He was almost level with Sir Nicholas Byron's musketeers who, incredibly, were being driven back, albeit the sergeants were doing their jobs, straightening ranks with their halberds, and the men were withdrawing in good order.

Mun edged back down the slick grass, the musket smoke from the nearby battle wafting over their heads in patchy grey clouds. 'We're losing,' he said.

'So what do we do?' Jonathan asked.

'We keep going.'

The young man nodded grimly and they continued along the ditch and after another forty yards Mun saw three rebel musketeers standing by a pale, lightning-scorched oak and another sitting astride a branch, his matchlock across his thighs. The men clearly had a good view of the fight, because all four were looking to their right, south across the plateau, more interested in their regiment's fate than in the narrow waterlogged strip of dead ground they were supposed to be watching.

Mun had gone still as a corpse. But for his heart. That was

racing, drumming against his breastbone like hooves galloping over hard ground.

'What now?' Jonathan hissed behind him.

Mun did not answer. His eyes were riveted to the rebels ahead and he had the notion that tearing his gaze away would alert them somehow, cause one or more to look down along the bank and ditch, and that would spell failure. Between himself, his men and their ten pistols and assorted bladed weapons Mun knew they could kill those four musketeers, would need to to give O'Brien and the others a chance to make their way up the ditch. But to kill them they would need to get close. Very close.

'What now, sir?' Jonathan asked, and Mun knew that the reckless young fool would spring up and run right at the enemy if he gave him the order to do so. Which was the only thing they could do, he realized then, his stomach feeling as empty as if he hadn't eaten for days. Half an hour must have passed. O'Brien and the others would be setting off up the hill, Sir John Byron – who had thought the idea too unsound to risk his own troopers though had had no problem letting Mun risk his – watching from his white Arab mare.

'If we go fast they will miss and have no chance to reload,' Mun said, and now he wrested his gaze from the enemy and slowly turned on his elbows to look at his men, for he needed to see their eyes, needed to know if they believed they could do what must be done. Henry Jones was blinking rapidly and Walter Cade was worrying his bottom lip with his teeth. Inside his helmet Tobias Fitch's face was slick with sweat, though that might have been from the effort of pulling his stonemason's brawn up the slope. Only Jonathan did not look afraid. For all that the pupils of his eyes were wide black holes, the young man seemed flushed with the thrill of it and eager to be unleashed.

'Might be my imagination, sir,' Cade said, keeping his head low, chin bending the grass, 'but I think I heard horses behind us.'

It was not Cade's imagination. Mun had heard it too: a whinny and hoof-beats on a swirl of breeze. 'We kill those sentries and buy O'Brien and the others time,' he said, holding each man's eye in turn as they nodded that they were with him. It would not be much time, for there was every chance that the rebel regiment would be alerted, either by their attack on the sentries or by the sentries themselves. But at least the Irishman and his riders would be much further up the hill before the enemy knew they were coming than they would have been if spotted by the men at the oak mere moments after starting out.

'Save a shot if you can. We'll need to take cover when it's done.' Mun's chest inside his buff-coat felt as if it were expanding. His senses were honed to a razor's edge in anticipation of action. 'Kill them all and do it quickly.' Four pairs of eyes bored into his and he knew he had picked the right men for the task. They would follow him into Hell. They had done as much before.

Slowly, carefully, Mun reached over his shoulder and gripped his poll-axe's haft, slipping it out of his baldrick. Then he pulled one of his long pistols from his boot and from the garter that kept its flared grip snug against his knee, and the others readied their own weapons, teeth gritted, lips tight, but for Cade's, which were working silently. A prayer perhaps, or more likely in Cade's case a recital of what he was going to do to the men at the oak.

Keeping low, the sweet vibrant scent of wet grass filling his nose, Mun turned back round, relieved to see that the sentries' attention was still fixed on the fight raging in the next field. Their only movements were to occasionally blow on their match to keep the tips glowing.

'After three,' Mun said, lifting his head, smelling the acrid tang of musket smoke that hung in the air like fog. Then another two great volleys of musketry boomed and Mun was up and running without having counted, hoping the battle's noise would drown out their own engagement. And then the rebel in the oak tree turned his face and saw them, his mouth open as he scrambled down from the branch, though Mun heard no shout above the ragged crackle of matchlocks beyond the bank and hedge. The rebels lined up beside the oak's blackened trunk, cocking their match and lifting the muskets to their shoulders, and then they fired and three of the weapons flashed and roared.

Too soon.

And they had missed as they surely must from such distance, and Mun did not break stride, boots squelching in the soft ground, waterlogged buff-coat feeling as heavy as cuirassiers' armour, heart threatening to explode. Then the last rebel's musket hang-fired and Walter Cade, now less than twenty paces from the foe, grunted and stumbled but Mun did not stop.

Three of the Parliament men turned their matchlocks round to use them as clubs and one dropped his, drawing a hanger which he gripped inexpertly in two hands, and this one Mun shot in the chest, even as he swung his poll-axe, the blade chopping into a musket stock and severing the fingers gripping it. The rebel shrieked, eyes wide, as Jonathan buried his own poll-axe into the rebel's face with a wet crack and Tobias Fitch stopped five feet away from another man and shot him in the face.

Henry Jones killed the last of them, all but thrusting his pistol into the musketeer's belly before pulling the trigger. Then, when the man was on his knees, guts leaking from the singed hole in his tunic, Jones hauled his head back by its long hair and sawed a long knife across his throat.

'They've seen us,' Jonathan warned, the words barely out when two musket balls smashed into the oak's trunk, spraying slivers of wood and causing them all to flinch or take cover. But Mun stepped out from the oak and looked across the hill's plateau and saw that the rearmost rank of Major-General Skippon's brigade had turned to face this new threat. They were firing independently, blooms of white smoke appearing sporadically before the percussion reached his ears, though for the moment they were not advancing back up the hill.

'It's those buggers over there that concern me, sir,' Henry Jones said, pointing his bloody knife across the sloping battlefield. There on the far side of Skippon's musketeers, firing pistols at Lord Wentworth's musketeers and looking as though they were forming up to charge, was a troop of horse. Or rather what was left of a troop.

'They're the stubborn bastards that were first up this hill and managed to kick our lot halfway back down it,' Fitch said, fishing a ball from his bullet bag and thrusting it down his wheellock's muzzle.

'And they know we're here,' Mun said, for he could see one of the harquebusiers pointing them out to a giant of a man whose face was all beard. 'But they're committed on that flank.' Another musket ball thwacked against the tree trunk and two more cracked amongst the brittle branches above their heads. 'They'll not trouble us yet.' He looked at Fitch. 'Cade?'

Fitch shook his head and pressed a hand against his own belly where the damp leather was a darker sand colour. 'A hole the size of a hand-basin,' he said. 'Right the way through.'

'Here they come,' Jonathan said and Mun cursed because that rear rank of musketeers, some fifty men, had disengaged from their battalia and were being hustled into a separate company three ranks deep.

'They know their business,' Jones said, turning the spanner on his wheellock until it clicked, and Mun agreed, feeling a grudging respect for these outnumbered rebels who seemed grimly determined to keep this hill.

'Come on, O'Brien, you sauntering Irish devil,' Mun heard himself growl as he looked back towards the ditch up which they had crawled for any sign of his troop.

'This what you wanted, lad?' Jones asked Jonathan, watching the oncoming musketeers who were holding their fire now, saving it for one volley that would obliterate them.

Jonathan did not reply. He simply stood facing the enemy, a pistol in each hand, the poll-axe tucked into his cross belts so that its blade sat against his chest.

'We've done what we came to do,' Mun said, then nodded towards the foe, 'but I'd have us draw those men further away from their colonel. I'd have them waste more shot too.'

The others nodded, understanding. For the further those fifty musketeers strayed from the relative safety of their battalia the more vulnerable they would be to O'Brien's men when they turned up. But it was more than that. Mun knew what a good volley from fifty well-trained musketeers could do to men and horses, and if there was a chance that he could diminish that firepower, leach out some of its ferocity, then he had to try.

'Jonathan, go back to the ditch. Tell me the moment you see them. Tell me again when they're fifty yards from the top. We'll make our stand here.' He stepped back against the tree.

'I'd rather stay here with you, sir,' Jonathan said.

'Do what I tell you,' Mun snapped, and the young man pressed his lips together and dropped his head, then ran back to the ditch. Then Mun nodded towards the rebels, who were now one hundred yards away. 'Fitch, haven't you got anything to say to those men?'

Fitch grinned and stepped clear of the oak. 'You merry-begotten, scab-faced jackanapeses!' he yelled, pistols held out wide, spittle flying. 'You couldn't hit the ground if you fell over! Come on, you squint-eyed, pox-ridden fartleberries! You stinking treacherous bumfiddles! I'll turn you inside out!'

A cannon roared to the south, the sound lingering and indignant like thunder. Beneath that fading rumble, thin as vapour in the air, came men's cheers, which made Mun think the cannon, whosever it was, had done more than simply frighten men. Its iron ball had killed.

'You think we're winning?' Jones asked, jerking his head towards the distant thrum of battle.

'I think I'd prefer to think that,' Mun said.

'I see them!' Jonathan called from behind them, but Mun kept his eyes on the musketeers coming towards them, on their sergeant with his halberd whose spear blade was pointed at the grey sky.

'Let's give them something to aim at,' Mun said and Fitch came to stand at his right shoulder whilst Jones drew level with his left. 'No point us shooting from this range but no harm in making them think we will.' The three of them raised six pistols towards the oncoming rebel company and held the weapons steady. 'Wait for it,' Mun growled.

'Sweet Jesus,' Jones mumbled. 'Think I shat myself.'

'Wait for it,' Mun growled, his pulse racing, the sound of his own heartbeat thrashing in his ears. Every muscle and sinew screamed at him to turn and run for the cover of the oak.

'Wait.'

The rebels were forty yards away now, the powder burns on fingers and cheeks visible, uncertainty or fear or efficient purpose readable in the eyes beneath their montero-caps. Ten more yards and they would halt and the first rank would fire.

'Fifty yards!' Jonathan called and Mun risked a glance behind him and saw Jonathan running to join them. It was too late to stop him now.

'Bloody fool,' Mun growled as the young man came to stand panting beside Fitch, his pistols raised like the rest of them.

Then Mun saw the rebel sergeant hoist his halberd, saw his mouth open and heard him give the command *present!* And saw the men move their matchlocks away from their bodies, muzzles pointing at the sky. Then the sergeant yelled, *give fire!* And those muskets' butts came up to shoulders, their barrels levelling out, muzzles promising flaming fury.

'Down!' Mun screamed, and they threw themselves down as gouts of flame flashed, hitting the ground and turning their heads – else their helmets' face guards would have kept them raised – and Mun heard the fierce hiss of musket balls tearing the air above his head. For two heartbeats he feared he had got it all wrong, but then he felt the ground tremble and vicious elation exploded in his blood. He wrenched his head round and there was O'Brien and the rest of his troop, blades in their hands, spurring onto the field and shrieking like fiends.

'Go on, lads!' Fitch was up on his knees, waving his fellows on with his pistols, his eyes wild. 'Get into 'em. Cut the bastards apart!'

'Fine day for it, Sir Edmund!' O'Brien bellowed as he galloped past, his poll-axe held wide, and Mun stood as the rebel second rank gave fire, plucking a trooper from his horse and sending a beast careening to crash to the ground, a musket ball embedded in its chest.

'Here, sir!' He turned to see John Cole and Farmer Goffe leading their horses and he considered taking Walter Cade's horse as Cade wouldn't be needing it now, but Mun's saddle was on the colic-struck piebald mare and so he mounted quickly with the others, turned, and spurred across the field to join in the slaughter.

Tom looked at Trencher and Trencher shrugged. The two of them ran forward to be greeted by a sight that neither man had dared hope to see: Major-General Skippon's brigade sweeping across from the left to pour a volley into Sir Nicholas Byron's regiment before the King's men had had the time to wheel fully to face the threat. Trooper Meshman had brought Skippon and the major-general had swept up the escarpment and into the enemy's flank just below the spur of the round hill.

'The good Lord has answered your prayers, lad,' Trencher said. Tom said nothing. Trencher knew very well that whatever prayers had been offered up from that cursed hill, none of them had come from Tom's lips. 'Still, it's going to take more than that,' the big man went on, squatting to wipe his knife on a dead Cavalier's breeches. 'Someone has still got to deal with those whoresons.' He pointed the knife at the other regiment, Colonel Wentworth's men, who had halted seventy paces short of the hill crest to await orders. The ranks of musketeers were blowing on their match, refilling the powder flasks hanging from their bandoliers, or else waiting patiently, matchlocks held across their chests. To their left a company of pikemen bristled in battle formation, ready to protect the musketeers against horse.

'We could retire now that a proper officer has come along, slip away over yonder slope and let someone else have a turn up here.' Trencher's eyes were on the musketeers who were only a stone's throw away, though they held their fire rather than waste a volley on just two men.

Behind Tom Haggett's men were stripping the dead of weapons, powder and shot, or else relieving them of armour if it was better than that which they themselves owned.

'But we're not going to slip away, are we?' Trencher said. A grey-bearded musketeer yelled an insult up the slope and Trencher returned a hand gesture that would have ruffled an innkeeper.

'No,' Tom said. 'Not until Lord Essex puts cannon and another thousand men up here.' The din of distant engagement, of cheers and screams, of artillery and musketry and cornets and drums, told Tom that battle had been joined as far north as the River Kennet and as far south as the River Enbourne. But none of that was his concern. He had told Colonel Haggett that they must hold that round hill, had convinced him that they must, even knowing that the cost would be high. And the colonel and many of his brave men had given their lives doing it. To ride away now would be to insult those dead men.

Trencher nodded towards the regiment facing them. 'So we keep those gooseberry-eyed gingamabobs busy until the good Lord sends us another miracle. Another regiment or two,' he said, 'and General Skippon will thank us for it. If we're still alive this afternoon.'

Corporal Mabb had appeared at Tom's shoulder and was taking in the scene.

'He'll do more than thank us,' Tom said. 'He can send us enough ale to drown in and ensure these men get their bread and their pound of flesh.'

'Aye and perhaps even some of the back pay we're owed.'

'Now that *would* be a miracle,' Tom said.

'Well? What now?' Corporal Mabb said, avoiding eye contact. Tom saw that the corporal had tied a scarf around the top of his bloody thigh. But all three of them knew Mabb didn't have long.

'Can you ride, Corporal?' Tom asked. The man's face and hands were bone white. Almost blue, actually. There could not have been an ale beaker's worth of blood left in his body and yet he was still standing.

'For a bit maybe,' Mabb said.

Tom nodded. 'Then get your men mounted, sir.' They turned to walk back towards the ragged knot of men who were still able to fight and Tom felt a hand grip his left arm just below the shoulder. Now Mabb held his eye, despite the rest of his features sagging and his head hanging low. He looked deeper into Tom's eyes than Tom would have liked, but Tom did not flinch.

'Don't waste these lads,' Corporal Mabb said. 'You're a fighter, Rivers, and God knows you've done well for us. But you've got a dark soul and I know you ain't afraid of death. If it's lost, if we can't hold this ground, promise me you'll get the lads away from this . . . damned place. They've done their best and neither God nor man could ask more.'

The hand on his arm clenched with a strength that surprised him.

'I'd have your word, Thomas Rivers,' Mabb said. There was a flintiness in the man's eyes then that Tom had never seen there before.

'You have my word,' Tom said and the corporal took his hand away. 'Now back in the saddle, sir, while you still can.'

Mabb nodded curtly and turned. 'Colonel Haggett's troop! Mount!' he yelled.

And Dobson shook his head and cursed. Because the fight had only just begun.

CHAPTER TWENTY-FOUR

'BACK!' TOM YELLED, TURNING HIS MOUNT AND THROWING HIMSELF flat against the mare's neck as another volley thundered, some of the musket balls thudding into flesh or thunking off armour or helmets. They spurred back up the rise, back onto the crown of the hill.

'Where's Corporal Mabb?' James Bowyer called, pressing his thumb into a new dent on his breastplate.

'There,' Penn replied, gesturing with his pistol back over the brow. Tom looked back to see Corporal Mabb still in the saddle, slumped over, his chin on his breastplate. He had been beside Mabb at the last advance and had not seen the man hit, and yet the corporal was clearly dead. Most likely his leg wound had quietly spilled his lifeblood down his mare's flank until death had come for him.

'Old sod did well to last as long as he did,' Dobson said.

'Who commands now?' Jeffes called, wheeling his horse round and round. The animal was bleeding from its neck and shrieking with fear. Near by, a young trooper was cursing God with his last breaths, lying on his back spitting blood and bile. 'Who commands?'

'I do,' Tom shouted. Trencher and Penn nodded their approval. Haggett's men had ridden to just outside effective musket range and were milling and keeping their horses moving, reloading pistols and carbines and steeling themselves to ride at the enemy again.

'Your orders, sir?' Dobson bellowed, his size and matching belligerence silencing any potential dissenters before they gave their objections voice.

'The same as Colonel Haggett's,' Tom replied, ramming a wad of cartridge paper pilfered from a dead musketeer down his pistol's muzzle. 'We hold this hill.'

'Thought you might say that,' Dobson rumbled, then lifted his face guard and drank from a flask.

On the far side of the field a company from Major-General Skippon's brigade had broken from the rear and was marching up the hill towards where the great hedge was broken by an old, skeletal oak. But from where he was Tom could see no enemy soldiers up there on what must surely yet be Parliament's side of the escarpment. Unless the enemy had somehow got up there unseen. His thoughts were hauled back to the very real and immediate threat from the east.

'Here they come!' Ellis Lay warned as the front rank of the enemy marched up over the ridge.

'They've even got a bloody fifer, the vainglorious tosspots,' James Bowyer said as the thin merry tune carried like smoke on the breeze.

'No wonder they look so damn pretty,' Trencher added, for fifers were rare because they were kept only at their commander's expense, which meant that Lord Wentworth was likely rich enough that his musketeers would not be running out of powder and shot any time soon. Furthermore, his pikemen were coming too, big strong men with their blade-tipped staves arrayed in a bristling hedge.

They mean to intimidate us, Tom thought. Fools think a show of force will break us. They have not managed it yet.

'Horse!' Penn called, and Tom muttered a dark curse because over on their left, at the rear of General Skippon's musketeers, a troop of harquebusiers had broken onto the field, appearing it seemed from nowhere.

'Where in God's name did they come from?' Trencher asked. 'I thought the ground beyond that hedge was impassable.'

'Maybe they're ours,' Ellis Lay suggested.

'They're not ours,' Tom said, and as if to prove it the troopers drew swords and poll-axes and galloped across the field towards Skippon's men, shrieking hellishly, their horses' hooves flinging mud.

And the rearmost rank of musketeers were still reloading.

'Should we help?' Penn asked Tom.

Tom shook his head. 'We've got our own fight.' He looked at Trencher, who was grimacing at the screams of Skippon's men who were being butchered with cold steel and lead. But Trencher nodded and turned his horse back round to face Lord Wentworth's oncoming musketeers.

'Sir! Sir!' someone was shouting and Dobson called to Tom and gestured to Trooper Logward who was threading his mount through the whirling mass of horseflesh and armed men to get to Tom.

'He means you, Tom,' Dobson said, and Tom felt a sudden coldness fill the marrow of his bones as it truly hit him that he was now commanding these men. That they had accepted him. For he could give them only death.

'Sir, drums, sir!' Logward twisted in his saddle and pointed west. 'From over there. Must be ours, sir! Must be.'

Tom could not hear the drums above the horses and the musketry and the yells and the screams, but the hope in Logward's eyes was good enough for him.

'About bloody time,' Dobson growled.

'Haggett's men! To me!' Tom roared. 'Are we going to let some unbloodied apprentices march up here and take all the glory?'

'Yes!' someone shouted. Tom ignored it.

He sat tall in the saddle and pointed his pistol towards

Wentworth's musketeers who had come into range now and had been given the order to halt and make ready to fire. 'We're going to slow those whoresons down. We're going to buy time for whoever Trooper Logward assures us is on their way.' He glared at Logward who was craning his neck, peering anxiously west as though hope itself was enough to summon Parliament soldiers.

'We're too few to charge them, sir,' Martindale said, hauling on his reins, struggling to control his horse. 'I'm no coward but charging them is suicide.'

'We're going to bleed their pike,' Tom called, scouring men's eyes with his own fierce glare. 'The musketeers will have to come to their aid. They will wheel and in doing so they will waste precious time.'

Martindale nodded.

'I like it, Tom,' Trencher said.

'I thought you might,' Tom said, feeling the murderous grin stretch his lips, for pikemen were only dangerous if you were within seventeen feet of them. Beyond that you could shoot at them all day long.

'Bloody fools,' Trencher murmured.

'Have a care!' someone yelled. Haggett's men bent over in their saddles and spurred back up the rise, giving ground.

'Give fire!' a Cavalier officer shouted and fifty or more burning matches kissed priming pans, and the manifold flashes preceded a resounding barrage and a wall of smoke.

'Now!' Tom called, kicking his mare into a canter that would take them obliquely across the second rank of musketeers who were stepping forward to fire their own weapons.

'God and Parliament!' Trencher cried and others took up the shout.

'God and Parliament!'

And the pike stand quivered, their sergeant roaring commands because they suddenly realized that the harquebusiers were coming for them.

Their horses' hooves thudded against the ground and men yelled their war-cries and the battle thrill boiled in Tom's veins as he led Haggett's men – his men now – across the rough, gorse-strewn hill. He pulled up twenty yards short of the wicked pike blades, far enough away to make those weapons impotent but close enough to see fear twist their bearers' faces beneath their pots.

'Kill them!' Tom raised his pistol and fired and a pikeman fell back, his stave clattering against other men's armour. All around Tom pistols and carbines spat flame and lead into the press of tightly packed enemy and they could not miss.

Some of the pistol balls clanked off breastplates or pots but even if they did not kill they caused mayhem and terror. The pike stand lumbered like a wounded beast and came on bravely, attacking because what else could it do? But Tom's men wheeled and rode away from their pikes only to turn and give fire again and by the time Lord Wentworth's musketeers had wheeled to their left to come to their comrades' aid the pike stand was a bloody, clamorous, chaotic mess.

And yet those musketeers *had* wheeled and they had done it as neatly and as quickly as Tom had ever seen, and he knew with sudden horror that he could not get his men away before the first volley.

'Withdraw!' he screamed. 'Back! Back, damn you!' He saw fear flash in men's eyes, saw the curses on their lips as they too realized they had lingered too long before the pike stand, drunk on the butchery.

'Everyone back!' Dobson bellowed.

'Fire!' a man screamed and in one glimpse Tom knew it was Lord Wentworth himself and he did not begrudge the man his furious joy as his musketeers gave fire.

James Bowyer's mare neighed and careened sidewards, horse and rider flayed, and Tom saw at least three other men slump or fall from their mounts, armour, flesh and bone crashing to the ground. The dead and dying hampered the escape of the living and four ragged breaths later the next rank fired and Penn, who had been hauling his mare around a mass of stricken flesh and flailing hooves, was hit in the back of the head, the ball passing through his helmet to lodge in his skull.

'Matt! Matt!' Trencher was screaming, heedless of the lead storm, as Penn tumbled from his horse, inanimate as only the killed can be.

Jeffes was down, his horse shot, and Martindale's horse made only twenty yards before it went down onto its knees, raw bloody flesh hanging from its rump.

'Back up the hill!' Tom screamed at those still mounted, then wheeled his horse and spurred over to Jeffes.

'Get on!' He held out an arm and Jeffes grasped it and then another volley thundered and Tom's horse shrieked and Jeffes's eyes bulged and he fell forward, two holes in his backplate. But Tom's horse was hit too and she fell sidewards, keening, eyes rolling, and Tom pulled his right foot from the stirrup before she hit the ground. He scrambled over the creature, putting its body between him and Wentworth's men. Another musket ball thumped into the mare's flesh and then came a huge cheer and Tom looked over the point of her hip to see that the pikemen had thrown down their pikes and drawn swords and knives and were charging up the field in a mad, vengeful horde. They butchered wounded men as they came, some of the pikemen stopping to loot but most coming on.

Martindale turned towards the onrushing tide and fired his pistol, then the wave swallowed him and Tom pulled his poll-axe free from his baldrick, the haft comforting in his hand even as he faced death.

'Come, then,' he spat, twirling the poll-axe once and looking for the pikeman who would die first. 'Come and kill me, you ugly shankers!' he bawled. Then he heard hoof-beats and yelling as the remains of Haggett's troop thundered past him, two firing pistols before all ploughed into the pikemen, their mounts knocking men to the ground, trampling them, their blades plunging and scything down onto heads and shoulders. Tom strode forward in their wake, into that cauldron of heinous murder, and swung his poll-axe into the neck of a man trying to rise, then had to put his boot on the pikeman's face to pull the axe free. A sword scraped off his backplate and he turned swinging, the poll-axe's spike ripping out a man's throat in a crimson gush.

But there were too many of them. They swarmed around Ellis Lay, plunging blades into his horse which was screaming, then as the beast went down they hauled Lay from his saddle and hacked him apart. For a moment Tom was shielded on either side by horses, the pikemen unable to get close, and he drew his sword, head snapping round, weapons raised. On his right Dobson was fighting like a bear, snarling as he hammered heads with his poll-axe, dropping men with almost every blow. On his left Trencher was wheeling his horse, scything his heavy sword at men who were, for the moment at least, backing off.

A pikeman slipped between two horses and swung a hanger which Tom caught on his own sword, in the same movement bringing the poll-axe across and chopping the man's sword arm off at the elbow, as Dobson roared in pain, the long spike of a sergeant's halberd driven through his left shoulder. Tom slammed his sword's hilt guard into the pikeman's face, dropping him, then saw the sergeant yank the spike back out and then ram it back into Dobson's arm and the giant could do nothing as another pikeman buried a ballock dagger into his thigh. But Dobson was frenzied and refused to die, swinging his poll-axe and bellowing, savaging men even as they pulled him from the saddle and he was lost from Tom's sight.

Every one of Haggett's troopers was down.

But for Trencher.

The big man's horse was blood-slathered, its eyes wide with terror as Trencher wrenched the reins and hauled it round and kicked his heels and screamed. Tom dropped his sword and the poll-axe and grasped the arm thrust towards him, his left hand somehow grabbing hold of Trencher's baldrick as he thundered past. He clung on, swords striking his buff-coat and backplate, his feet thumping against the ground as Trencher's brave mare carried them out of that murderous maelstrom, back up the rise past dead men and dead horses.

Towards the Red and Blue regiments of the London Trained Bands who had at last arrived to pour their musket fire into the Cavaliers and drive them from the hill.

His men had ploughed into the thin company, annihilating its cohesion, their horses' chests breaking arms and faces and crushing bones. Now Mun rode into that screaming chaos. Their pistols and carbines spat lead, punching holes in men. Their blades plunged and hacked and blood flew. O'Brien was slaying men who would have had more chance against the noose or fire or foul disease than they had against the Irishman. Some thrust up with the butts of their matchlocks, using the things like unwieldy clubs, but Mun's men had honed their skill through the last winter and become butchers.

A sword struck Mun's left thigh, not piercing his buff-coat, and he twisted in the saddle to bring his Irish hilt scything down, knocking the hanger from the musketeer's grasp then leaning out and ramming the point into the man's open mouth before drawing it back in a gout of blood.

Harley swept his sword down at a man who threw up his matchlock and caught the blade on its stock, but Godfrey came up behind him and struck down, taking off the man's ear, so that in a heartbeat his lace falling band bloomed bright red and he was mid scream when Godfrey finished the job with a better-aimed blow that cleaved his skull.

Milward shot a man who fell to his knees still gripping his musket, and John Cole urged his horse forward but the beast pulled up and refused to trample the musketeer and so Cole screamed a curse at the animal and clicked his tongue and kicked his heels. He had all but passed the rebel but then leant right over and drove his poll-axe's spike through broad-hat and skull and the rebel shook like a fox in a snare.

'Run, traitors! Run, you dogs!' Jones shouted as those rebels who were able dropped their matchlocks and ran, or limped, back to their fellow musketeers.

'Let them go,' Mun barked at those of his men who made to ride them down. For musketeers without muskets were next to useless on that escarpment, yet must still draw rations and encumber the enemy.

Besides which, Mun had more to worry about than chasing down unarmed men. The main body of Major-General Skippon's musketeers had discouraged Sir Nicholas Byron's brigade enough that Byron's men were no longer coming up the hill. Alarmingly they had the look of a regiment about to withdraw and Mun said as much. A few moments later their drummers confirmed his fear.

'We're too damn late,' O'Brien said, coming alongside Mun, blue eyes fixed on Skippon's men. Beads of blood glistened like rubies amongst the bristles of his beard, but the crimson spray up his breastplate told Mun that the blood was not the Irishman's own. 'You should have crawled faster.'

'You should have ridden faster,' Mun said.

'Whatever, we've buggered it up,' O'Brien said, which was true enough. If Skippon's musketeers had still been involved in a firefight with Sir Nicholas Byron's brigade Mun could have risked a charge to attack their rear. But Skippon had beaten Byron off, meaning that the rebels could turn their muskets, or at least a sufficient number of them, towards Mun's troop. To ride at so many loaded muskets would be reckless at best.

'And now we're on the wrong bloody side of the field,' O'Brien said.

'Well, we can't go that way round,' Goffe put in, pointing to the far side of the ridge where that troop of rebel harquebusiers were still fighting. They had ridden around Lord Wentworth's left flank and were now pouring pistol and carbine fire into his pike stand, the men of which were helpless, their panicked cries carrying over to where Mun's troop milled awaiting orders.

Mun wanted to lead his men across the crest to engage the rebel horse, for he did not think they would stand against him for all their bloody-minded tenacity. But he had heard drums coming from the west behind them and that could only mean another rebel regiment was coming up. The London Trained Bands probably. To ride across to the other side of the field now would be to risk becoming trapped between rebel foot and rebel horse.

'So let's take stock,' O'Brien said. 'Byron's retreating. Lord Wentworth's pike are being mauled and another regiment under Parliament's banner is coming up from the west.' He rubbed the back of his neck beneath the pot's neck guard. 'Have I missed anything?'

Mun swore under his breath. The tide had turned and they had all but lost the hill.

'If we stay close to the hedge we can slip past the bastards,' Fitch suggested, nodding towards the gap between the great hedge and the right flank of Skippon's musketeers.

O'Brien nodded agreement. 'With any luck they'll ignore us.'

Mun did not see that they had another choice. As for the dead or any too wounded to ride back with them, they would have to wait.

'I need to get my men off this hill,' he said by way of agreement with Fitch's suggestion.

'Shear House men! Form column!' His voice was raw and frayed and his throat felt as though it was closing up. His chest was as tight as a drum with the frustration of having failed. If only Byron had pushed on a little further Mun could have attacked the main body of Skippon's musketeers and they might have won the hill. Instead, whilst they had no doubt bloodied the rebels, they must now retreat. They must slink off like a fox before the farmer.

All eyes on him, Mun praised the Shear House men for their

valour and their honour but said that they must now give up the hill and return to their lines. They would do so by riding along the hedge and they would not engage with Skippon's musketeers.

'You've earned your beer today, lads,' O'Brien added. 'God knows you've brawled like bloody Spartans but it's time to save ourselves the trouble of getting killed.' He grinned. 'Last one to the bottom buys the falling down water.'

Mun was already moving, the others falling in behind in twos, so that it was in a neat if diminished column that they trotted over to the hedge in order to keep their distance from Parliament's musketeers. And they did not know that they were riding into a storm of black powder and lead.

The hedge seemed to come alive, roaring, spitting wrath, and Tobias Fitch beside Mun grunted and slumped forward and horses shrieked. Mun pulled up and wheeled his mount round in time to see Milward fall from his horse and Harley's mare stagger into the briar hedge, which spat more musket balls, ripping Harley's life from him.

'Go!' O'Brien bellowed, firing his pistol into the hedge, the other side of which bristled with rebel dragoons who had seized their chance to flay Mun's troop. 'Go, Sir Edmund!' But the Shear House men did not know whether to ride off or stay and fight, and others drew wheellocks or fired carbines into the hedge, their horses shrieking, eyes rolling.

'Ride!' Mun roared, knowing that to stay was to die, as the smoke rose from the hawthorn and rebel dragoons yelled insults and Mun's Shear House men reeled and died.

A pistol ball thunked off Mun's breastplate and then O'Brien was beside him, screaming at him to lead them out of that hell.

And so Mun dug in his heels and rode.

The musketeers of the London Trained Bands paid them no notice as Trencher rode towards them, Tom clinging on for his life. Then Trencher veered right and pulled up off their left flank and Tom at last let go of man and beast, falling to the ground in a heap. Trencher hauled his boots from the stirrups and stepped down, then stumbled and collapsed beside Tom, snatching his helmet from his head, his face a bloody mask of terror and fury. The two of them gasping for breath, they watched the Red and Blue regiments march down from the crest to engage the King's Cavaliers, though it seemed the Royalists had no intention of waiting and were in full retreat back down the hill.

'They're gone,' Tom said, pulling his own battered helmet off and raking sweat-soaked hair off his face. He ached in a hundred places and his body was shaking madly. 'They're all gone.'

'They're all gone,' Trencher confirmed, looking back down the hill towards where the remnants of Colonel Haggett's troop had made their last stand and been butchered. All of them slaughtered.

'They're dead because of me,' Tom said. His voice was a dry rasp, like the last confession of an ancient man.

'Maybe,' Trencher said, his chest working like a bellows, matched by that of his exhausted horse near by. 'But maybe it wasn't your doing. Those men should have died of fever weeks ago but they didn't. They stayed alive long enough to fight here today. To win this damned hill.'

Tom's mouth tasted sour. Bile was rising and he knew he would vomit.

'You think God saved them from the fever just so they could die here today? For Parliament?' He all but spat the words.

Trencher's face was all grimace. 'Who are you to say different?' he said.

Tom did not answer that.

He knew he was bleeding but he did not know where from. That could wait.

'We won this hill,' Trencher said. 'Perhaps no one will know it was us. Maybe they'll get the credit.' He nodded down at the musketeers. 'But we'll know.'

Tom did not care about the hill. He was thinking of Matthew Penn and Robert Dobson who were down there, still. Bloodied and broken in the grass. Defiled by steel and shot. Left behind.

'Why are we alive?' Tom said. 'How is it possible, Will?' Tom's stomach clenched and he gagged. But he had eaten nothing that day and so he spat the sourness into the grass.

'Come on, lad,' Trencher said, climbing to his feet and picking up his helmet. The next moment the big man's hand was grabbing Tom's breastplate above the arm hole. Tom was not sure his legs would work but somehow, and with Trencher's help, he clambered up. He was still shaking violently.

'Come on then, Tom Rivers,' Trencher said. 'We've got work to do.'

CHAPTER TWENTY-FIVE

NEITHER OF THEM HAD SPOKEN OVER DINNER AND NOW LORD Denton was filling his pipe whilst his fat servant cleared the table. The servant shook his head disapprovingly when he removed the untouched bowl of broth from in front of Bess but she affected not to notice. She ate most days but only enough that she would not starve, for she could not bring herself to enjoy the mouth-watering fare that was placed before them each day. Not with Joseph and Dane languishing down there in the dark.

Bess did not know for how long she had been Lord Denton's guest. Six weeks? Eight perhaps? Time had slowed to a crawl and she dreaded to think how the men were faring in the cellar bereft of light and comfort and subject to who knew what treatment at the hands of Denton and his men. She knew they were still alive, or rather she knew that one of them was – Dane if she had to guess, given Joseph's condition when she had last seen him – for Lord Denton would have the remains of dinner sent down along with wine and ale. But she knew no more than that and the worry ate away at her.

Fortunately Lord Denton was a busy man and she only had to bear his company when dinner was served and even then she would ignore his pretence at civility, not that this stopped him telling her of his day and of the fools with whom he must deal in his work at the Royal Mint. And yet she dared not antagonize him to the point of anger for all that she felt ashamed of her fear. Because there was something predacious about Lord Denton. That he sought revenge for his son Henry's death was clear, but there was a blade's glint in the man's eye that Bess believed would have any woman's virtue on edge. She knew poor Martha Green had aroused Lord Denton's base avidity and paid the price.

Now, Denton flicked a hand at his servant in a gesture that told the man to fill Bess's wine cup. At which Bess felt guilty for if she had denied herself food she had not denied herself wine. It numbed her.

She put the cup to her mouth and felt the wine on her lips and tongue. The white luminescence of a near-full moon spilled through the window to wash a third of the candle-lit room in its purer light. She had heard talk of a great battle at Newbury but she knew not the outcome nor which of the King's or Parliament's armies had clashed, though from Lord Denton's demeanour she guessed all had not gone well for the King. She had contemplated asking him about it but had decided against it lest he mistake curiosity for cordiality.

I must try to escape, she thought now, watching him, afraid even that he might somehow be able to read her mind. She realized then that she would gladly watch Dane kill Lord Denton. But Dane was helpless, a prisoner bound and gagged in the cellar below them, and she was alone.

'My brothers will come,' she said. 'When they find out I am a prisoner here, they will come.'

Lord Denton stopped thumbing tobacco into his pipe and looked up at her, his blue eyes glinting in the candlelight.

'Oh, Miss Rivers, but I'm counting on it,' he said.

ABOUT THE AUTHOR

Family history and his storytelling hero, Bernard Cornwell, inspired Giles Kristian to begin writing his action-packed Viking series. The first book, *Raven: Blood Eye*, was published to great acclaim and two further highly praised novels, *Sons of Thunder* and *Odin's Wolves*, complete the bestselling trilogy.

Giles's fascination with the English Civil War began at school, where he appreciated the cold efficiency of Cromwell's New Model Army but also revelled in the flamboyancy of the Cavaliers and the romance of the doomed Royalist cause. It is this complex and brutal conflict that provides the backcloth to his new historical series, *The Bleeding Land*.

He lives in Leicestershire. To find out more, visit www. gileskristian.com

As he's been working on *The Bleeding Land* series, Giles has been asked many questions about his writing, what inspires him and his choice of historical subject matter. The Q&A over the page lists just some of them.

A Q&A WITH GILES KRISTIAN

What first inspired you to think you might one day be a writer?
I don't know. Perhaps it was the poetry of Seamus Heaney. I remember reading 'Digging' from *Death of a Naturalist,* aged about seventeen, and feeling the words so keenly. The poem resonated with me utterly. It still does. I think that even back then, when I read it, I somehow knew that my path was to be a writer, too. I'm sitting here now remembering Seamus Heaney's poems, the likes of *Mid Term Break* about the death of his four-year-old brother, and I feel the power of his craft, the emotion of it balling hot in my chest. Since then I've wanted people to 'feel' my words as I 'felt' Heaney's.

Why do you think you are so drawn to history?
I live at once encumbered and yet quickened by a sense of history. It's an obsession really – not in terms of facts and figures, but rather I feel times and places in my blood. This is going to sound really weird, but it's as though part of my subconscious is there in the past and that my dreams are a gateway through which I catch glimpses and feelings. I write historical fiction because it is my way of going back. Until they invent time travel it's the best I can do.

Did you devour books as a child?
I was never much of a reader as a child. I know I should probably never admit that, but there it is. It wasn't until I was fourteen and off school with glandular fever that I read my first novel (by choice at least). That was *The Crystal Shard* by R. A. Salvatore and my mother had picked it up for me, no doubt thinking I'd be drawn in by the warriors and swords on the cover. She was right. I devoured the rest in the series and I think from then on I knew deep down that I wanted to write novels, to create worlds and tell tales.

Is there a sense of your legacy when you write your books?
I love the thought that long after I'm gone, my children and their children will be able to pick up my books and in some way connect

with me. Through my stories they will get a sense of who I was and what made me tick (they might find some of it quite alarming!). I may write fiction, but there's no doubt that a great deal of my heart and soul goes into my books. When I'm long gone my descendants might read my books and hear me whispering to them.

What inspired you to write about the English Civil War?
I felt it was time for a really gritty novel set during the period. I couldn't see one out there on the shelves and I thought this was strange given how extraordinary and important the Civil War was in the history of this land. I remember at school being captivated by illustrations of the Battle of Naseby in text books. Some years later I took up fencing and my favourite part of the lesson was the interval, when we would play Roundheads and Cavaliers. This invariably ended with a great melee of flashing foils in which you would sometimes be fencing against two or three opponents. For me there was nothing better.

Do you set yourself word-count targets each day or week?
If I write a thousand words in a day I am happy. Because so much of my day is spent on research it's not a question of simply sitting there and letting it pour out. But even then I suspect I'm on the slow side. I take my time over those thousand words and they change very little from the day they're first written. All authors work differently and I'm always fascinated by how others do it, but for myself I don't do draft after draft. My 'editing' process is perhaps unusual as it invariably involves adding words – the seasoning as I call it – not taking words away.

Does your own life and family work its way into your writing?
I think I always intended to tell the story from the point of view of three main characters, but what took me completely by surprise was how these people, Edmund, Tom and Bess Rivers were going to try to dominate the tale. And yet why shouldn't they? After all, it's through their eyes that we see the world. It's through them that I the writer and you the reader experience the time and place, find ourselves caught up in the maelstrom of bloody civil war. So what happened was that almost immediately the story became about the Rivers family and not the famous English Civil War battles, of which I had thought I was going to write. Of course, this is how it should be. Historical fiction – I suspect all fiction – only works if you empathize with the characters. And empathize I did, more than ever before in my writing. *The Bleeding Land* is close to home because it's a story about family. I found myself asking over and over again, what would I do if I had to face my own brother across the battlefield? How would my mother deal with it if one of her sons turned his back on the family in search of vengeance?

What would my sister do if she had to give birth amidst the horror of a siege? Putting my own family into the book helped me explore the tale at a deeper level, so that at times during the writing I found it all really quite emotional.

How do you convey the war scenes in such incredible detail?
Your readers say they can hear, smell and taste the scenes – that
they feel as though they are in the thick of the action.
I have always been intrigued by conflict and in some ways been drawn to it. I'm quite a physical person, having done karate, kickboxing, Krav Maga, rugby, fencing etc, all of which involve challenging and beating your opponent. Perhaps this physical competitiveness has given me some very small insight into what it must be like to face an enemy in battle. As well as that there is a whole weird spiritual side to me which is too complex to get into, but the short version being that I feel I have inherited memories and experiences from my ancestors. Told you it was weird!

The Bleeding Land series gives a sense of the futility of war. Is this deliberate?
Certainly there is a marked difference in the portrayal of violence between the *Raven* saga novels and *The Bleeding Land*. In the Viking books you expect the characters to get involved in some pretty gruesome activities, after all, they're Vikings! It's part of the job description. But with the Rivers family and the other characters in *The Bleeding Land* it's different. We think of the 17th century as a more civilized time than the Viking Age, so that when the violence does come it is much more shocking. Tom and Mun, Sir Francis and Lady Mary, are a family suddenly thrust into the horrors of war and each of them must commit terrible violence simply to stay alive. The fact that the family splits and they end up fighting on opposite sides just adds to the horror. So in a way the characters in my last novels gloried in violence whereas in *The Bleeding Land* they are utterly appalled by it.

Cavalier or Roundhead?
I'm sorry to say that I cannot answer this. Because the Rivers family is torn apart, with the brothers fighting on opposite sides, I would rather the reader decide whether I am for one side or the other if that is something that interests them. I don't want them to read the books with a prejudicial eye or suppose I wrote this or that scene because of some allegiance. Having said that, I do find it very interesting that even after all these years if you were to walk into a pub and ask this very question you would face a salvo of impassioned answers. It's intriguing that we still have some sense as to which side we would be on.